China Attacks

A Novel by
Chuck DeVore
and
Steven W. Mosher

Published in 2000

To the American fighting men and women who may be called upon to defend us from the coming storm…

To Lois & Peter,

Your tireless service to our Cause is an inspiration to all. Thanks & enjoy the book!

Chuck

ISBN 0-7414-0430-3

Published by:

Buy Books on the web.com
862 West Lancaster Avenue
Bryn Mawr, PA 19010-3222
Info@buybooksontheweb.com
www.buybooksontheweb.com
Toll-free (877) BUY BOOK
Local Phone (610) 519-0258

Printed in the United States of America
Printed on Recycled Paper
Published July-2000

PROLOGUE
Belgrade, May 7,1999

The American B-2 Spirit Stealth Bomber pilot suppressed a small wave of anxiety and concentrated on his radar imaging display. He *knew* he and his mission commander were as close to invulnerable as American science and engineering could make them—but he still had a tinge of fear. An Academy classmate of his was shot out of the sky in an F-117A Nighthawk Stealth Fighter only six weeks before. Thankfully, he was rescued. The incident made the tight-knit brotherhood of pilots based in Central Missouri's Whiteman Air Force Base somewhat circumspect during their nighttime bombing raids "downtown."

There—the headquarters building of the Yugoslavian Federal Directorate of Supply and Procurement came into view on his radar imager. Every building around the target checked out—this was the one, the building that housed the bureaucrats who worked to supply the Serbian genocide in Kosovo. Not that he needed to double-check the target manually, given the precise capabilities of his aircraft and weapons.

The two-man bomber crew had been in the air for 16 hours now. Three times they took manual control of the giant black flying wing: at take-off and during two mid-air refuelings. The rest of the time the bomber flew itself. The actual bombing run was no different. The GPS-Aided Targeting System perfectly pinpointed the aircraft's location as well as the target's. The system fed the data to the 2000-pound GPS guided glide bombs that were to be dropped on the target. The pilot simply validated the computer's work and toggled the switch to release the bombs.

Somehow, killing people seemed a little easier when a computer did it. The human in the loop was there only to veto an error in targeting. There were few errors. This system—highly trained pilots, B-2 Bomber, and GPS guided bomb—rarely missed. More accurate and reliable than the robotic cruise missile, or the older F-117A Stealth Fighter, the B-2 was used by NATO to reduce "collateral damage" (that euphemism of war referring to the undesired death and destruction caused when bombs fall astray or damage a wider area than intended). Less collateral damage would mean less opposition to the war back home and less international pressure to end it before forcing the Serbs to their

1

knees. Amazingly, the B-2s had inflicted no collateral damage at all. The heretofore unattainable ideal of a "surgical" air campaign had finally been realized.

Fu Zemin had never been in a war before. At first, he was terrified. The haughty Americans and their European NATO henchmen had been bombing targets in Belgrade for several weeks now. Almost every night Fu was held captive by the hammering explosions about the city. During the day, Fu tried to fight back, to even the score with the arrogant Americans by diligently exchanging intelligence with his Serbian counterparts.

Fu Zemin was a dedicated member of the Chinese Communist Party—so was everyone else in a position of power in his country. Of course, being a Communist did not necessarily mean that he believed in Communism. Communism was a dead ideology in China—as dead as Chairman Mao, as dead as Lenin. It was a convenient tool to justify control of the masses, no more. On the other hand, Zemin believed in the Party—or rather, the Party's power. The Party made his father important. The Party made it possible for his father to advance his career. It provided him perks and authority. He owed the Party everything. In return for his good fortune, he devoted his life to the Party. This was why he now found himself in the middle of a war zone, frightened for his life.

Fu was working late with a military attaché and three female Chinese intelligence agents (accredited to Belgrade as journalists and housed in the embassy's "press" offices). The quintet was finalizing an agreement to buy the crashed remains of an American Stealth Fighter from the Yugoslavians. They were almost ready to place the proposal's final terms and attached technical and political analysis in the next diplomatic pouch bound for Beijing when Fu stretched and said, "I've had so much tea that I'm ready to burst." The operatives tittered as Fu stood up to head to the restroom. Normally, a woman wouldn't dare laugh at Fu's comment—he was a man *and* a Party official. But, these women, spies all, were also part of China's elite. "We are all very tired. I want to review the final proposal and attachments one more time before it goes out under my signature. I'll be right back."

Fu walked down the nicely apportioned embassy hall and ducked into the restroom. He decided to take out a cigarette (he smoked casually, and then usually only very late at night to help himself stay awake). He sat down on the toilet and lit up.

Fu inhaled a buzz-inducing drag and simultaneously relieved himself. He began to think of how China might soon counter America's unchallenged global domination. He exhaled, slowly letting the smoke curl out of his nostrils. As if in a dream, the bathroom door blew off its hinges, the hallway flashed a bright white-orange, and the lights went out. Fu's cigarette burned a hole in the palm of his hand before he yelped from the corner of the bathroom where he cowered. A moment later another explosion ripped at the building, knocking the wind out of Fu's lungs and filling the air with a choking, hot dust.

Slowly getting to his feet, Fu heard muffled cries for help. They came from the direction of where his comrades were working. He saw flames swirling around the doorframe of the intelligence center and "press" room. He hesitated. Rescue operations were for military personnel and fire fighters and maybe bureaucrats—not up-and-coming Party officials. Fu turned his back on his countrymen and ran down the hallway illuminated only by emergency lighting and the spreading fire.

*   *   *

American B-2 Bomber pilots always hit their targets. The night of May 7th was no exception. The problem was not that the bombs missed, it was that the target moved. The Chinese Embassy in Belgrade had occupied the former offices of the Yugoslavian Federal Directorate of Supply and Procurement for more than a year. Unfortunately, no one in charge at the CIA or NATO headquarters knew this. And it was this point that really irked the Chinese—not that the Americans could have purposefully killed their spies and destroyed their intelligence center (the Chinese would have done the same thing in similar circumstances). The American explanation that the bombing was a "mistake" was deeply offensive to the Chinese—it showed the contempt that the West held for the Chinese—could anyone imagine the Americans "mistakenly" bombing the Russian or the British embassies? *Never.*

The American bombs that stained China's honor also stole Fu Zemin's honor (although his cowardice was known only to him). Fu returned to Beijing more committed than ever to restoring China's proper place in the world as its premier power—its hegemon. China's restoration would be Fu's and Fu wouldn't rest until both assumed their rightful places.

1
The People's Commando

Major Chu Dugen remained motionless in the predawn calm, the moon lay low in the west to his right. Small puffs of icy steam leaked out from his black ski mask, it was the only evidence of life coming from his carefully camouflaged position. He and three of his best men were high on a ridge overlooking a small, Muslim village in extreme western China near the borders of Afghanistan and Tajikistan.

The sniper next to Dugen shifted his weight and sighed slightly. The man had been in position for an hour now. The cold was beginning to bite into his muscles. Dugen put his hand on the soldier's shoulder. He said in a low, barely audible voice, "Huizi, relax. They won't move until the moon sets. Give your rifle to me and slowly stand up. Stretch. Just keep your movements slow and fluid." The commando officer knew there would be a period of total darkness for about 37 minutes before the dawn began to break.

The sniper soundlessly stood and began to limber up using Tai Chi. Dugen smiled under his mask. His men were completely at ease in his presence. He liked that. How different now than it was in 1989 when he led a platoon of conscripts in the assault on Tiananmen Square.

"Guangkai," Dugen addressed the compact sergeant perched above him on the rocky ledge, "You have been at the night scope long enough. Wannian take over. Guangkai prep the thermal scope, the moon is almost ready to leave us."

The men silently obeyed. Dugen kept his sniper from getting eye fatigue by having his other two men trade off observing the target house with a more powerful starlight scope set on a tripod. The starlight scope needed some illumination beyond that provided by its namesake, however, so Dugen was forced to use a thermal sight to cue his sniper once the moon set.

"Huizi, enough. Check your battery level." Dugen knew Huizi's American-made thermal scope ate through batteries at a fearful rate, especially in weather this cold.

Dugen shook his head almost imperceptibly—*those men down below were good.* Five more minutes and his starlight scope would be worthless at identifying the target. A thermal sight could pick out a man, but it wasn't at all good at identifying him, and for this mission, Dugen needed to strike the right target.

"Sir!" Wannian hissed, "The door is opening. I see two men. The target is not among them."

"Huizi?" Dugen asked.

"I see them," the sniper whispered.

A puff of wind blew across Dugen's mask, stealing the warmth off the end of his nose. "Wannian, look at the back of the house and up the slope." The house was one of five strung out along a dusty road. Their common backyard was a 1,000 meter high ridge.

"Three people and a donkey." Wannian's excitement was muted by his professionalism. "They're about 50 meters above and to the left of the house."

"The target will be riding the donkey," Dugen said. He knew he was stating the obvious. He had thoroughly briefed his men, they all knew what to do. In fact, everyone of them were qualified snipers as well—Huizi just happened to be the best.

Huizi adjusted his right elbow and became very still. Dugen knew he was melding with his rifle and his target.

Crack! The single rifle shot echoed through the canyon.

"Target's down!" Wannian said a little too loudly.

"Right. Pack up, let's go!" Dugen's men were already scrambling, pulling themselves up by the thin brown nylon rope they left in place to aid their ascent up the steep canyon wall. Dugen made sure his men were out of sight when he pulled a small pouch out of his field jacket and left it where Huizi only a moment before had fired his shot. For an instant Dugen wondered what was in the goatskin pouch, but he was forbidden to open it by Jia Battalion's political officer. It wasn't worth the risk to find out, he decided. A whiff of burnt gunpowder passed by his masked face and for a moment his mind filled with images of the bloody bodies of Tiananmen Square. He forced the unwelcome vision out of his head as he turned to pull himself up the rope.

2
Donna Klein, Spy

Donna Klein thought of herself as a spy. She always liked to use that term when thinking of her job, even when the most dangerous thing she faced was a paper cut. But, contrary to popular misconception, most of the CIA's employees were analysts such as herself, not field agents. Information, whether from the most highly placed spy or from an ultra-sophisticated reconnaissance satellite, was just useless data until she got to it, examined it, questioned it, massaged it, then molded it into intelligence in the form of a concise report or briefing that could be used to shape and execute policy.

Donna especially enjoyed the challenge of forecasting events. While earning her Masters in International Relations (magna cum laude) at Georgetown, she often felt compelled to examine the "what ifs?" in her papers, even if her professors didn't appreciate the extra effort. Working at the CIA gave her the opportunity to explore "what ifs?"—and actually get paid for it too!

Donna loved her job as a Chinese political specialist. Unfortunately, many of her pearls were being cast before pigs. She was coming to realize, after four short, intensive years, that much of her work was ignored, or, worse yet, misused by the political processes that made Washington tick. Unless one's work happened to be on the radar screen of official Washington it was often shunted aside in favor of the crisis du jour. Still, the challenge of producing great intelligence was a wonderful job, even if the final product was often under-appreciated.

Donna's left hand clicked her computer's mouse to minimize the window of the report she was working on—a brief update on Chinese military modernization progress. There were no rings on her left hand and her fingers were graceful, but the fingernails were carefully cut short and only had a coat of clear polish. The report vanished off of her modest 15" monitor (senior analysts had the big 17" screens). Her e-mail window, always open, always resting immediately beneath whatever she happened to be working on, flashed to life. She highlighted the second message out of eight unread messages—it was from her boss's boss, Mr. Scott:

> Donna,
>   Our office has been asked to participate in an interagency simulation involving China. I would normally go, but I'm tied up with Balkan issues. Please call the simulation coordinator,

LTC Gene Ramsey, at 697-3297 to make arrangements. The in-brief and start-up will be on Tuesday from 8 to 5. The simulation will run five hours each day from noon to 5, M-F, for 2 weeks. I'll expect you to complete all your normal work assignments during this period. I already spoke to Jack about this.
Thanks.
I think you'll enjoy this opportunity.
—S.

Donna smiled. A large mouth with generous lips—not too much lipstick—framed her straight white teeth. Yes, there'd be extra work. Yes, she'd catch even less sleep than normal. *Who needs six hours anyway?* But this was why she'd signed up for the job.

She wondered about the Balkan reference in the e-mail then realized that, while her boss was the head of the Office of Asian Pacific and Latin American Affairs within the Directorate of Intelligence, he was recently the section chief for China. His seniority and his long-time knowledge of China was being tapped to provide intelligence on Chinese intentions for the sections dealing with the latest Balkan debacle—especially important given the heightened Chinese sensitivity about the region after their embassy in Belgrade was bombed by the US in 1999.

She'd heard a few things about interagency simulations. Normally, some planners based in the Pentagon would round up representatives from State, DIA (Defense Intelligence Agency), CIA, the NSC (National Security Council), and sometimes Energy, or other appropriate Executive Branch agencies for the simulations. These representatives would role-play their respective agencies' advice or interests or be asked to participate in a red cell to act out hostile nations' actions. This provided military planners with potential reactions from allies, neutral nations, and potential aggressor states. They could then use that information to revise their military contingency plans.

This would be her first interagency war game. Donna smiled again, brushed back a strand of curly red hair, and tucked it behind her ear, revealing one small pearl earring. She picked up the phone to tell Lieutenant Colonel Ramsey at the Pentagon that she'd be there tomorrow.

After the call, she returned to her report. She wondered about including a passage on her idea about the military utility of motorized hang gliders in China's People's Liberation Army (PLA). Open source articles from the PLA itself discussed their military potential. She even saw a classified report detailing small-scale maneuvers. One of her male counterparts with military training (ten years in the Air Force) ridiculed the idea that motorized hang gliders could make any significant contribution to the modern battlefield—it was simply a low-tech stunt with toys, he snorted. Donna wasn't so sure—in her experience, the PLA wasn't much interested in toys. She decided to include a small passage about the hang gliders to illustrate how the Chinese often adapt common and inexpensive commercial technology for use in their military.

The remainder of the day at work passed routinely. Donna placed her working papers and research in her desk and locked it. She changed out of her black high-heeled shoes (with heels neither too tall nor too thin) and put on her running shoes. She signed the security checklist hanging inside her cubicle doorway, and headed down the hall, towards the doors of the SCIF (Special Compartmented Information Facility) she worked in. It was 7:47 PM and she was tired, having put in another 12-hour day.

The drive home along George Washington Parkway was uneventful. She decided there was one thing she didn't much like about working in the late fall and winter months—the lack of sunshine. When she arrived at work in the early morning, she could sometimes see the sun. In the evening, forget it. George Washington Parkway's scenery outside her windshield was about as close to a park as she got these days. Sadly, this time of year, her view time was cut in half by the early hour of darkness and her habitually late departure from work. That was the toughest part about moving to DC from San Diego. Of course, then there was the East's infamous summer humidity. . .

Donna was too tired to catch the news about the suicide bombing in East Timor.

3
The People's Prince

Fu Zemin propped his feet up on his expansive, darkly rich wooden desk. Other than a phone, a half-full ashtray (he started smoking more earnestly after the American bombs almost killed him in Belgrade) and a picture of his wife and only son, the desktop was clean. On a small table to the left of his desk sat a personal computer. A manila envelope lay across his lap. Fu's door was closed—the privacy a perk of his high-ranking Communist Party status. His star had risen high since his "heroic" brush with death—all the more so because it was the hated Americans who almost killed him *and* he accomplished his mission: the remains of the F-117A Stealth had been carefully dissected and studied for any secrets China did not already know. *Life was good.* He smiled at the photo on his desk, but the smile slowly turned to the frown of a driven man.

Fu lit up a prized Marlboro cigarette (he never saw the irony in his favored vice) and settled in with the classified report he asked one of his underlings to generate two days before. He knew the man stayed up late to produce the report. His lips curled up a little bit. He had done his time in the rice fields and now it was someone else's turn. If the report was particularly useful he would see to it that the man was recognized in due time. Fu read down the summary list of current American foreign military interventions:

1) Yugoslavia, provinces of Bosnia-Herzegovina, Kosovo, and Macedonia
2) Iraq, northern and southern no-fly zones
3) Kuwait
4) Republic of Korea
5) Western Europe/NATO
6) East Timor
7) Haiti
8) Sinai Peninsula
9) Counter-narcotics operations in South America

Fu's eyes narrowed with interest at the list—*there were vulnerabilities hidden away in these troop deployments.* An unwelcome rap at his door jerked him away from the report. "Comrade Fu?"

"Yes, what is it?" He did his best to sound impatient, Fu recognized the voice as an underling liaison with the internal security forces.

"Sir, I have some interesting news for you."

Fu flipped the report over, quickly combed his slicked hair, and said, "Enter."

"Sir, I have news about that special operation you recommended to the Party's Chief Representative to the General Political Department of the PLA."

Fu looked at the man with open contempt. "Shut the door and keep your voice down!" Fu brought his cigarette to his mouth and inhaled deeply. Exhaling, he lowered his voice and said, "You may tell me what you know. Leave out no detail, but be fast."

The man looked for a place to sit, then decided the safe course of action would be to remain standing. "A week ago a certain Muslim cleric was killed by a sniper about 10 kilometers from the Afghan border. Three days later an entire village of about 100 people, all Muslims, were killed in apparent retaliation. Yesterday, PLA commando forces intercepted a Muslim guerrilla force of 300 fighters preparing to exact revenge for the village massacre. The guerrilla force was destroyed."

Fu slowly sucked on his cigarette then suddenly crushed it out in the ashtray while letting smoke curl out of his nose. His face betrayed no emotion. "You have done well to tell me," Fu paused, trying to remember the man's name, "Comrade Chung. Cigarette?" Fu extended his pack of prized American smokes.

Chung's eyes lit up. Fu didn't think the man smoked, but that mattered little right now. Fu's small favor would keep the man reliably energized for at least a month.

The man bowed to Fu and turned to go. Once again alone, a toothy grin extended across Fu's face, revealing teeth stained by years of tea drinking.

4
East Timor

Colonel Mike Flint was a Marine's Marine. He relished command. He loved his Marines as much as he loved his wife and two children. He figured he wasn't likely to get promoted to general and sent to the Pentagon—he'd insulted too many people for that, even for a Marine. Freed of the need to pay homage to political correctness, he was a better combat commander and his Marines loved him for it.

Colonel Flint commanded the 31st Marine Expeditionary Unit (Special Operations Capable). Based on Okinawa in southernmost Japan, the 31st had a storied history, including the final evacuation of Saigon in 1975 and the Beirut barracks bombing in 1983. Colonel Flint was with the unit in that day of pain and peril. He was a captain. His most vivid military memories were of pulling the broken and tangled bodies of Marines from the shattered barracks. That was the only time he cried in uniform. He almost cried a second time, when he was a company commander and his unit was deactivated in 1985. The 31st Marine Amphibious Unit, as it was formerly known, was reborn as the 31st MEU in 1992. He was its third commander since reactivation.

The colonel wasn't surprised when the warning order for East Timor came. He saw this one coming a mile away, especially since the 3rd Marine Expeditionary Force (MEF) already had communications and reconnaissance assets in East Timor supporting the Australian-led peacekeeping force. It was only a matter of time before some crazy got lucky and killed a bunch of peacekeepers.

Last Friday Flint had ordered his staff to prepare a contingency plan and brief it to him the following Wednesday. Tuesday morning (Monday night in Washington, D.C.) he saw the President's speech on TV about East Timor explaining why the, "United States has a compelling interest to help the people of East Timor achieve peace and security." Since the 31st MEU was the closest, fastest reacting and most capable unit in the region, he figured they were going. The warning order's arrival was anticlimactic.

Of course, his staff was impressed at his foresight. Colonel Flint normally would have been mildly pleased at his staff's opinion of his brilliance, but now he was too worried to notice.

Every time he thought of the strife on Timor his memories of Beirut would burn through. He picked up his phone and jabbed the buttons with large, powerful fingers, "Colonel Burl, I need to see you."

Within a moment, Lieutenant Colonel Hank Burl was in his office, "Yes sir?" Burl's eyes traveled to a small plaque on the wall behind Colonel Flint's desk. It was below the large framed poster of John Wayne in a set of USMC dungarees with the inscription, *Life's tough, but it's tougher when you're stupid!* The plaque read, *Hair on a woman is her crowning glory. Hair on a Marine is an abomination.* Lieutenant Colonel Burl had advised Colonel Flint to remove the plaque. It might be construed as sexist and contributing to a hostile work environment for women. The Colonel had said at the time, "I'll take that under advisement." Which was mil-speak for go to hell. The plaque stayed.

"Have a seat Hank," Colonel Flint's voice was detached, his dark brown eyes fixed on a distant, unseen problem. "I need you to write up a request for Third MEF (III Marine Expeditionary Force) with a 'cc' to MARFORPAC (Marine Forces, Pacific) to clarify our rules of engagement for our little trip to Timor. I don't want to be sent in with beanbags and rubber bullets. Those bastards mean business down there."

The XO looked up, his blond eyebrows arching above his bright blue eyes. He wasn't a bad officer, Flint thought, he's just too pretty to be a Marine. He could see Burl as a naval aviator or a submariner, *but a Marine. . .* The officer was young for his rank and very mindful of perks, power and position. *Hell, he'll probably be Chairman of the JCS in ten years!*

Burl spoke, "We already received our rules of engagement from CINCPAC (Commander-in-Chief, Pacific Command)."

"Yes, and they suck! You know that. You want our Marines killed?"

"No sir."

"Then write the fricken letter and help me get these ROE changed! I began my career with a goat rope excuse of an ROE, but I'll be damned if I'm going to end it with one."

"Yes sir."

"Have the completed draft on my desk in two hours. Oh, and I already told Lieutenant General Hill of my intent, so I'm sure we have the support of our MEF commander across the street, we just

need to follow channels to make the request official. That is all."
Burl stood and wheeled out of Flint's office. Flint rubbed his left
hand against the back of his neck, feeling the prickly short nubs of
his meager allotment of light brown hair. *Time for another
haircut,* he thought, *my hair is almost visible again.*

Colonel Flint rarely locked up his officers in private, or in
public for that matter. Burl just had a way about him that grated
against Flint. *Old Marines versus the New Marines*, he guessed.
So much had changed in the last few years. Political correctness.
The loss of the fighting spirit. More sexual harassment and
sensitivity training, less combat training. Burl epitomized the new
Marine officer. *He'll go far*, Flint thought—*unless he gets fragged
by his men in combat*, he grunted to himself.

5

The Pentagon

Donna arose at 5 AM. She worked out lightly on her exercise bike while watching two cable news channels, clicking back and forth with her remote to catch as much international news as possible.

The news about the first American casualties among the handful of US military personnel in East Timor caught her attention. She was wondering what her counterparts in the Indonesian section would say when she saw the sound bite from the President's impromptu news conference the night before. She unconsciously frowned—*so now we're going to save East Timor.*

After working out, she showered and ate a light breakfast. She always ate in front of her PC, scrolling through various news sites, seeing what the open source world had to say. She was often amazed at how rapidly the full-time news networks reported world events. Of course, reporting *after* the fact was much different than anticipating events *before* they occur. Her morning routine was always the same. She liked to keep a familiar pattern, especially when things got crazy at work.

At 7 AM, she left her modest apartment and drove to the nearest Metro parking lot. Her stomach had a few small butterflies. She hoped the exercise would be enjoyable. She found a parking spot and walked to the Metro station. The air was brisk with a faint breeze. She could smell the damp, slowly decaying leaves of fall.

As an analyst, she didn't suspiciously survey her surroundings as a field agent might. As a woman in the DC area, however, she took the normal precautions. She saw no one but commuters, not even a panhandler (one advantage of living in Virginia, rather than in DC proper).

She fed a $5 bill into the Metro ticket vending machine. The machine took her money and spit out a business card-sized piece of paper with a magnetic strip down its length. She entered the station and waited six minutes for the train.

On the train she read both the *Washington Post* and the *Washington Times*. The stories that caught her eye were usually buried deeply behind the front page. *If it makes it to the front page without my knowing about it first*, she thought, *I've failed.* There was nothing in the papers that she already hadn't seen on the cable news or on the Internet earlier that morning. She wondered, as she always did after reading a paper, when newspapers were going to go the way of the buggy whip.

About 15 minutes later she got out of the train at Pentagon Station. It was the first time she actually left the train at the Pentagon Station. Most of the DC Metro's escalators are impressive, coming from deep within the earth to deposit their passengers, blinking in the light, upon the surface. The Pentagon Station was no exception. Its four banks of escalators must have had a vertical climb of at least 15 stories—*very impressive.*

She got to the top of the escalator and realized, amidst the pressing crowds, that the Pentagon was indeed a small city. Ahead were the metal detectors and guards, processing thousands of morning workers through this, the most popular Pentagon entrance. To her left was a gift shop and shoe shine stand, with three out of four seats occupied by an Air Force general, an Army sergeant, and one civilian in a gray suit.

She veered towards the visitor entrance desk and presented her ID. A young Army sergeant stood quietly behind the guards who took information from the visitors. He heard Donna's inquiry and passed her a badge on a silvery chain and said, "Good morning Ms. Klein, Here's your ID for the simulation. Please step through the metal detector and follow me to the simulation room for your in-briefing." Donna was already impressed with the Pentagon.

She went through the metal detector, looked to the right and noticed what must be the safest bank in the world: The Pentagon Federal Credit Union. The sergeant said in an urgent tone, "We're running a couple of minutes late, mind if we take the stairs instead of the elevator?"

"Not at all." Donna blushed a bit at the thought of being late. It was 7:50 am, she had 10 minutes to spare, but she supposed the sergeant was personally on the hook for her on-time arrival at wherever she was going. She followed the sergeant through the wide Pentagon halls to a stairwell. They briskly stepped down two flights of stairs to the basement. The sergeant led her to room B205 and dropped her off at the check-in desk where another sergeant, this one from the Air Force, welcomed her and examined her ID.

She walked into the room. It was dominated by one long table with about 20 chairs. Most chairs were occupied, about half by officers, the remainder by men in suits. On the table in front of each chair sat a briefing book and a nametag. Donna looked for her tag at an unoccupied chair. Other than an electronic white board and a TV at the left end of the room and a TV camera mounted on the right end of the room to the upper right corner of the ceiling, the room had no other adornments or visible equipment. Clearly this room was about as functional as they came in Washington.

She found her seat at the far end of the table, facing the door. To her right was a powerfully built Army Colonel with a massive West Point ring and wedding band on his sausage-like, hairy ring finger. To her left was a bored-looking middle-aged man from the State Department. His reading glasses hung on the end of his slender nose, his salt and pepper hair nicely groomed. Two more people made their way into the room, both men in their 40s wearing suits.

. Donna scanned the room—not a woman in the room save her, and all the men were at least in their early 40s and up. So, she was the youngest person and the only woman. That was fine. She liked a challenge.

Donna smiled as an Air Force general stood in front of the white board and cleared his throat. Their eyes briefly locked and Donna looked away, flushing slightly. "My name is Lieutenant General Tim Taylor. Thank you all for coming here today and taking time out from your busy schedules to participate in this important exercise. We'll conduct a brief orientation, review our goals and our schedule, and after a short break, we will provide you with the remainder of the day to review your role-playing packets, ask questions and make your initial decisions. Lunch will be delivered. I expect to get you all out of here today by 16, er, 4:30 PM."

Donna noticed the general's quick recovery from saying 1630 hours. His face had a kindly look to it, but there was sadness in the eyes. Donna took a breath—*the man's probably 20 years my senior, and married too, get a grip.*

The general continued, Donna saw the ring on his left hand, "As some of you know, this simulation will review Chinese options to reintegrate Taiwan into China. We are the red cell. Our goal is to overcome Taiwanese, American, and other nations' counters to our actions." The man from State sighed with disdain. Had Donna been looking at him, she would have also seen him roll his eyes briefly to the ceiling. The Army Colonel let out a barely perceptible grunt. Donna focused on the general's words. This could be one of the more interesting assignments she'd had since joining the CIA as a political analyst specializing in Chinese affairs.

The general drew a quick breath and focused his gaze on the civilians in the room, "We will have two opposition cells, a blue cell and a green cell. They will independently develop counters to your actions as a sort of American A and B team. There will also be separate cells for Taiwan, North and South Korea, and Japan. Each cell will have its own success criteria. After your first move, you will then have to generate two responses, one to counter each cell opposing you. The only requirement you have is that you must attempt to control Taiwan by the end of play."

The man from State muttered under his breath, "What a waste of time. . ."

"Five of you will be the controlling players in this simulation. The remaining 15 are support personnel representing Chinese political, military, diplomatic, and industrial leaders and analysts. We are using five players to provide our simulation with a leadership junta roughly similar to the collective authoritarian structure the PRC now uses. The five controlling players are as follows; please raise your hand when your name is called: Colonel Westly Lake will represent the People's Liberation Army," the Colonel to Donna's right raised his right hand. His face held the faintest of smiles; it almost looked predatory. "Mr. Amos Ye of Commerce will represent China's industrial interests and the Ministry of Economic Affairs," Donna looked around the room, leaning forward, she saw that Mr. Ye was seated just to the left of the bored looking man from State. "Dr. John Wendell from State will represent China's Foreign Ministry," Dr. Wendell reluctantly raised his hand, his elbow never leaving the table. "Donna Klein from the CIA will represent the Premier, the Head of Government," Donna raised her hand and held back a smile. She noticed a couple of arched eyebrows in the room full of men. "And, Cliff Dowling, on loan to the Pentagon from State serving as Deputy Assistant Secretary of Defense for the Asian and Pacific region, will represent the Chairman of the Communist Party who is also President, Head of State," The man to the right of Colonel Lake raised his hand and smiled. "Please take the next 30 minutes to review your packets with your specific instructions, then wait for further instructions from your group leader."

The Air Force general wrapped up by explaining where the bathrooms were and how to find a phone. He also apologized that pagers didn't work in this area due to extra electronic shielding put in place for security concerns. Donna was used to that. She only carried a pager outside of CIA headquarters. She glanced around the room and noticed that everyone was busy delving into their briefing books. She opened hers.

TOP SECRET, NOFORN
Scenario 1199 PRC/ROC
PRC Premier Briefing Packet

GOALS: You are the Chairman's right hand. You must control the government and bring all resources to bear as necessary to support the Chairman's policy of reunifying Taiwan with China through whatever means possible. You serve as the Chairman's crucial eyes and ears in determining support for his policies among the various government ministries and among the people.
ASSETS: All non-military, non-Communist Party advisors in this simulation work for you and will provide you with whatever information or advice you require.

The remainder of the packet provided additional background information and rules for the scenario. She even noticed a paragraph on the Premier's political modus operendi from a briefing she wrote a few months ago. *Good source material*, she grinned to herself.

Donna heard someone clear his throat. It was Cliff Dowling. "All right team, let's get this exercise moving. First, I want to reconfigure the seating arrangements. As President of China, I think I've the power to do that." Someone in the room chuckled and Dowling cracked a smile, "I'm going to sit at the end of the table, opposite the camera. Ms. Klein, I'd like you to sit on my right. I want Colonel Lake to my left. Dr. Wendell and Mr. Ye, please sit to Ms. Klein's right. The rest of you, if you're a military advisor or minor military role-player, please sit on Colonel Lake's side of the table. Everyone else, take any available seat. Take a ten minute break and then sit in your proper places." The room erupted with the noise of chairs scraping on linoleum tile floor and shuffling papers.

Dowling approached Donna with his outstretched hand. He was a bit on the tall side, about six foot to Donna's five foot four. He had thin brown hair, fairly closely cropped (*probably blends in better in the Pentagon*, Donna mused). His eyes were brown, the edges weathered, as if he'd been on one too many tough overseas assignments. "Thanks for coming, Donna, you come highly recommended. What do you think so far?"

"Well, sir, I'm looking forward to this, but frankly I'm a little concerned."

Dowling, now a little on guard, said, "Oh?"

"Yes sir. I mean, I've only been at the CIA four years and you have me playing the premier of China in a simulation? I hope it's not the only game in town—so to speak."

"I see. Well, as I'm sure you can appreciate, these simulations take quite a bit of time and money to prepare and run, not to mention the personnel diverted from their day-to-day tasks," Dowling was just the slightest bit stiff. Donna was momentarily regretful of her comment—just momentarily though—when she ran the show, things would be different. "In any event, you should take it as a career enhancing opportunity that you were chosen for this exercise. Now, if you'll excuse me." Dowling turned to go down the hall before his break time expired.

Donna looked for Colonel Lake. She found him talking with a captain from the Navy and another colonel. ". . . so this time I want to kick some serious ass, let's get imaginative, bend the rules till they break. I want to grab those bastards in the blue and green cells by the balls and. . ." the naval officer cleared his throat and looked over Colonel Lake's shoulder at Donna with a slight grin and a hint of embarrassment. Colonel Lake tried to recover, ". . . and show them how the game is played."

Donna smiled and addressed the Colonel, "You really shouldn't mix your metaphors in front of the Premier. It could get you demoted to the position of outpost commander in the Gobi Desert."

"Oh, hello. Ms. Klein, is it?" Colonel Lake thought his oldest daughter wasn't much younger than this CIA analyst. *Still, she's got something to contribute or she wouldn't be here*, he thought. He decided to try to make an ally of her. "I was just discussing with my comrades here how we are going to bring the capitalist pigs to their knees." Lake emphasized his southern accent on the word "comrade" so that it stood out like a relic from the Cold War. Clearly, this was an officer who took no prisoners.

"So, you've done this before?" Donna asked, feeling somewhat more secure in knowing there were some veteran simulation players around. *At least the Pentagon appeared to be trying to stay one step ahead of the latest crisis—which was more than could be said for the CIA lately.*

"Yes, twice now, but only with Pentagon personnel. Got my. . . fanny kicked twice by the US Navy both times just as my invasion of Taiwan got underway. This will be my first interagency war game. It should be interesting to get another perspective in here instead of just us professional warriors fighting it out."

Donna was beginning to like this officer. He enjoyed his work too. She winked, "You'll have to tell me about your failed efforts at bringing that renegade capitalist province back into line."

Colonel Lake grinned, "Why, Ms. Klein, I'd be happy to tell you about my glorious failures upon the field of battle."

Cliff Dowling strode back into the simulation room and buttonholed Mr. Ye. The others began searching for their seats.

Dowling set his face and sized up his audience, "Well, let's get going," he paused, eyes resting on Dr. Wendell for a moment, "I know some of you don't believe the People's Republic of China would ever try to conquer the Republic of China on Taiwan. If that's your opinion, that's fine. Keep it to yourself during this simulation. Our goal is to try our level best to achieve our aim, knowing what we know about the capabilities and weaknesses of the PRC. Ms. Klein, I want you to explore the possibilities of a federal reunification with Taiwan where they would maintain their local government and armed forces, but speak with one voice with the PRC on foreign affairs. Dr. Wendell, I want you to recommend ways to prevent US or Japanese interference should we decide to use the military option. I also want you to explore how we might more reliably integrate North Korea's capabilities into our plans. Mr. Ye, I want you to examine how our economy might be impacted by an economic embargo led by America. Also develop some timelines—tell me how long could we hold out, what would be our alternate sources of supply, etc. I also need a read on the unemployment picture, should our goods be boycotted by the West. Colonel Lake, I want you to draw up three options: first, using the PLA to intimidate Taiwan into agreeing to a federal union and not declaring their full independence; second, launching an all-out invasion to conquer Taiwan; and third, launching a full-scale invasion of Taiwan as a prelude to a sustained campaign to conquer Asia." Dowling's voice grew more authoritative with every sentence until, by the time he was giving instructions to his military chief, one could imagine him as the leader of a nation of 1.3 billion people.

"I want your recommendations briefed to me per the following schedule: Ms. Klein, from 3:30 to 3:35. Dr. Wendell, from 3:35 to 3:45. Mr. Ye, from 3:45 to 3:55. Colonel Lake, from 3:55 to 4:10, give me five minutes on each option. I expect that each briefing will stick to schedule. At the end of the briefings I will take a vote from my four key players on which option to take, then I will make my decision and set the proper preparations in motion for our blue and green team colleagues to react to tomorrow. If you have any questions, please see me."

Donna looked across the table to Colonel Lake. It was obvious that the Colonel wasn't much interested in option one. He wanted to flex his muscles.

Dr. Wendell spoke softly, leaning to his left so that his shoulder brushed up against Donna's "It looks like you've got the only realistic assignment. I can't believe the Chinese would throw away all the economic progress they've made in the last 20 years just to conquer a tiny island with no resources."

Donna didn't like the man from State's attitude. She replied tersely, "No one believed that Argentina would invade the Falkland Islands in 1982 either. Sometimes nations do things for reasons beyond their checkbook." Dr. Wendell snorted softly.

Donna went to work. She found a lieutenant colonel who was playing the role of a PRC Taiwan expert. He was recently back from a tour in Taipei as a defense attaché to what was in fact, if not in name, the American embassy in Taiwan. (It was called the American Institute in Taiwan to avoid offending Beijing.) Donna took the opportunity to gain some first-hand knowledge of the Taiwanese political scene from someone other than a CIA employee. What she found made her realize that her assigned task was virtually hopeless. The Taiwanese simply enjoyed their freedom too much to risk any sort of a political union with the Mainland that could take their freedom away. Further, the indigenous Taiwanese were becoming increasingly powerful; representing about 84% of the population, they had more pro-independence leanings than the Mainland Chinese and their descendants who came over with General Chiang Kai-shek in 1949. (Ironically, the Communists funded pro-independence movements in Taiwan through the 1960s and 70s when the Nationalist government in Taiwan still held designs of one day leading all of China.)

With the lieutenant colonel's assistance, Donna crafted a five minute briefing that concluded any political reunification with Taiwan could only come if the Communist Party loosened its grip on power, allowed dissent, and, completely unthinkable, allowed a multi-party republic with a strong, independent rule of law. In other words, reunification would only be possible through the death of the Communist Party as it now existed. Donna could only wonder at the fate of a Chinese Premier who made that recommendation to the President and Communist Party Chairman.

She read the briefing twice in her head, timing it to four minutes and forty-five seconds. *Perfect.* She looked up and noticed there was no clock on the wall. She glanced at her wristwatch, her one anomaly in her otherwise conservative dress, it was a old stainless steel and plastic Swatch watch with glow-in-the-dark hands and numbers, a collectable she paid over $150 for. *Noon. Lunch time.* Just as she thought it, two carts were wheeled in, one with chilled sodas and a few milks in a large iced bowl and one with sandwiches and fruit. *Not the Ritz, but timely and, by the looks of it, wholesome.* She grabbed a tuna fish sandwich and a Pepsi (she had a caffeine deficit to make-up, that was the room's one shortcoming—no coffeepot—she'd have to have a talk with the simulation coordinator).

She noticed that most of the military officers were eating standing up, talking earnestly with one another while most of the civilians were eating at the table, reading through their papers. *Interesting, why is that,* she wondered? She sat with her food and did what she did best: analyzed. *Hmmm. Well, most of the military personnel work at the Pentagon and many probably know each other. Talking together would make sense. Good networking. Common experiences, etc. Most of the civilians are probably from other agencies. Ye was from Commerce. The good doctor, from State with others, perhaps. No doubt there was the guy from Energy, a nuclear weapons analyst probably.* She saw a slightly familiar face in a suit across the table. The nametag on the table in front of the man was knocked down. *CIA?* She spoke up, "Donna Klein, CIA."

The forty-something man looked up. He was between mouthfuls. "O'Donnell, CIA." He returned to his sandwich. But just as he tucked his head down to take a large bite of pastrami, Donna could see his blue eyes smile at her from under his bushy red eyebrows.

"Does everyone from the CIA think they're super-spies or something? What are you doing here? Hal, is it?"

Hal O'Donnell took a large burning, fizzing drag of his Seven Up to down the huge bite of meat and bread he swallowed, "Why yes, Ms. Klein, how perceptive of you. I'm flattered you remembered my name. Do you remember what I do?" At the last comment he twice wriggled his eyebrows, making them look for all in the world like small rodents.

For some reason, the memory of Hal's specialty popped into Donna's head. Then she knew why; Hal taught a two-hour course to a group of freshmen analysts on the psychology of leaders. "You're a psychologist," she said firmly.

"Bingo, you win the cigar!" Hal exclaimed, revealing tobacco and coffee stained teeth. "I'm here to make sure all you warmongers don't choose a course of action that results in certain death for those who made the decision."

"I see," Donna retorted, "How do you figure in the Asian concept of face and dishonor?"

Hal looked mockingly serious, "*Veeery* carefully." His face then changed again to semi-serious, "Just think of me as the devil's advocate or the reality check—if you choose an everyone-dies, Armageddon scenario, it won't be easy with me around nagging you!"

Donna chuckled. "Nice to meet you again. Behave yourself or I'll have you executed so I can harvest your organs to finance my next junket to Paris!"

"Yes, Comrade Premier," Hal said impishly.

Colonel Lake walked up behind Hal just as he finished. "Comrade Premier, do you want me to fix this for you?" He said menacingly.

"No comrade people's general, you may let him keep his kidneys for another day," Donna turned serious in a heartbeat, "But Colonel Lake, I am very interested to hear more about your two previous simulations. Please take a seat and fill me in. By the way," she added as an afterthought, "Isn't it uncomfortable to eat standing up?"

The colonel grinned. His jaw was very square and she noticed that his nose was a bit askew. You couldn't tell from the profile but it was obvious this man had his nose broken at least once. "I guess you get used to eating standing up when all you have to sit on is sharp, hot rocks with scorpions lurking underneath. It's an Army thing." He walked around the end of the table and took Cliff Dowling's empty chair—Cliff had vanished as soon as lunch arrived. "What do you do for the Company?"

Donna thought briefly of using the old standby: if I told you I'd have to kill you—but thought better of it. It was time to get serious. "I work the China section as a political intelligence analyst in the Office of Asian Pacific and Latin American Affairs with the Directorate of Intelligence. And you?"

The colonel looked sadly contemplative, "I work for the Office of Secretary of Defense, Plans and Operations. I'm really a tanker who must have offended some god of war somewhere who decided to punish me by ending my career in the dreaded five sided building."

"So tell me about your last two failed attempts at attacking Taiwan."

"It was simple, really. I mobilized my forces. Crossed the straits. And was unceremoniously sunk by the US fleet. The few troops that made it across dry were rounded up by day two. I was humiliated." The Colonel gave a look of mock hurt.

"I see. How did it happen that the US fleet was there in force, did the PLA employ strategic deception?"

The Colonel nodded appreciatively, then said with quiet strength, "The game wasn't that sophisticated. It was mainly seen as a force-on-force exercise to see if the US Navy could still control the Taiwan Strait, protect Taiwan, and do so with acceptable casualties."

"And?"

"And they did so quite well. On the second scenario one of my Russian-built Kilo class attack subs actually got into position to torpedo a carrier but they declared EndEx before the skipper could pull the trigger."

"So they ended the exercise on you before you could exact some revenge? It sounds like the simulation was more tactical than this one."

"Yes. It was run in double real time. We squeezed in two days for every one day and ran it for five days. Didn't sleep much but I had a blast. Best time I've had, uh, since I was exiled to the Pentagon." (the Colonel was going to say, "Best time I've had with my clothes on since. . ." but his sexual harassment training kicked in and he squelched it.)

"Did you use NBC?" Donna used the military acronym for Nuclear, Biological and Chemical.

"Hell no, we weren't allowed to incorporate it into our game." Colonel Lake frowned, "I heard that the folks that wrote the scenario were overruled by some Sched Cs in the SECDEF's office. The little weasels thought the butchers of Tiananmen wouldn't slime their capitalist brothers across the straits—or that it wasn't politically correct to think so, anyway."

Donna picked up the reference to "Sched C", it stood for Schedule C employee, an employee exempted from civil service job protections by dint of the fact they were political appointees who worked in the government at the will of the President. They weren't high enough up the food chain to be confirmed by the Senate, but they formed the political backbone of any administration. Donna remembered that each administration could appoint about 1,100 Schedule Cs. They had a few at the CIA, not too many though—most political hacks from this administration couldn't get a CIA clearance. The reference to "slime" meant getting hit with chemical agents as she recalled from a CIA military analyst who had previously served in the Army before getting out and letting the GI Bill pay for his masters degree. "How would you do things differently Colonel?"

"I'd remove America from the way, either by deception or by intimidation. Then I'd use every asset at my disposal to make the invasion as swift and violent as possible. The quicker I could crush the opposition, the less chance for things to go wrong. Of course, there's one small problem. . ."

"What's that Colonel?"

"I'll need about $10 billion and a few years to prepare."

"Oh?"

"The Peoples' Liberation Army-Navy only has enough landing craft to lift about 20,000 combat troops into battle. Right now I could only take Quemoy or Matsu."

"I see. Why'd you even bother with the previous war games? Did they expect the ROC army to wait politely while you made 10 trips to get enough troops on shore?" Donna looked annoyed.

"Not exactly, the scenarios called for the securing of key beaches and port facilities using airborne troops and amphibious assault, then lifting the remaining forces using non-amphibious assets. A lift capacity of 20,000 isn't a large enough margin to do the job safely. Certainly not without many other factors playing in China's favor such as the neutralization of Taiwan's navy and air force and complete surprise."

"Well, how would you do it this time, if you were the Chinese?"

Cliff Dowling walked back into the room. Colonel Lake slid into his chair to the left of Dowling's and said in a stage whisper, "That you'll have to see at 1555 hours Comrade Premier!"

Dowling addressed the room, "Remain on schedule. I still expect the briefings to begin at 3:30."

6
An Idea

Fu Zemin sat up on a pillow watching TV and smoking. His son had gone to sleep early and he and his wife had uncharacteristically made love twice that night. His right arm was draped around his wife's snuggling form, his left hand cared for the cigarette.

State-run TV was blaring forth about casualties among the Australian and American troops in East Timor—*serves them right*, Fu thought. *How ironic that the Americans helped East Timor gain its independence.* A quarter century ago, China had provided some arms and training to the East Timorese independence movement, hoping to sting the Indonesian generals and their government that had so brutally destroyed Indonesia's Communist Party in the mid-60s, killing some 300,000 Communists and civilians alike. *What a delicious turn of events, the Americans helped complete what we failed to accomplish.*

One part of Fu, the nationalist part, didn't like the idea of America barging into another part of Asia and trying to peel away a troubled province from the mother country as they were doing to Yugoslavia with Kosovo. He thought of Tibet, even Taiwan. *No, the Americans were too full of themselves, too powerful. Something must be done to stop them.*

He wondered how American strength might be turned against them, just like in Vietnam where their self-assuredness and lack of historical awareness pulled them in, and power and face kept them there for far longer than any other nation would have stayed. He thought of the marshal arts where the weakest woman could best a strong but untrained man because she could use the man's strength and size against him. *Could the Americans be manipulated into another quagmire, this time in Asia, to accompany the ones they were mired in the Balkans and the Middle East? Could this be made to China's advantage?*

Fu yawned and snuffed out his cigarette. Tomorrow he would write up some recommendations for the Party to consider. *Perhaps it was time to be bold, really bold. Belgrade, the Stealth Fighter, the successful operation in Western China,* Fu counted up his chits and realized he had enough to spare. He could afford to make a gamble—*if this one pays off, I'll get noticed by the Chairman himself.* Fu smiled as he went to sleep.

7
War Games

Donna practiced her briefing two more times under her breath and consulted with more of the players in the room. There was a fair degree of experience and smarts in this room. She wondered why the CIA didn't take greater advantage of the expertise in the uniformed services. She vaguely remembered that someone decided back in the early 60s that two distinct pillars of intelligence, one military-based, the other, civilian, was supposed to prevent that dreaded Washington disease: groupthink—where all the analysts and decision-makers go along in a herd mentality, never daring to challenge the conventional wisdom.

Soon 3:30 PM rolled around and Donna gave her four minute and forty-five second briefing, summarizing how the PRC could achieve a peaceful reunification with Taiwan only by transforming themselves into a pluralistic democracy. As she said so, she thought about the idea of the Communist Party allowing a free and fair election with opposition party candidates. Stranger things have happened, but she wouldn't bet the farm on it. The Party leadership enjoyed too much power to simply give it all up to get Taiwan back. Other than a four year period from the end of Japanese occupation in 1945 until the Nationalists fled to the island in 1949, Taiwan hadn't been ruled from the Mainland since 1895 when Japan took possession of the island from a weakened Ch'ing Dynasty. One thing China was good at was waiting for the right moment—after more than 100 years, what's a few more years, give or take? She concluded by saying that a face-saving federation with China, especially in light of Hong Kong's treatment to date, might be acceptable to the Taiwanese if they perceived that America had completely abandoned them and that the military balance had swung irrevocably over to the Chinese side. Since Dowling wanted all questions held to after the briefings, Donna simply sat down when finished.

Dr. Wendell slowly got up. He perched his reading glasses on the end of his nose and held his yellow legal pad of hand-written notes about 18 inches from his face. He addressed his notes, not the exercise participants.

"I want to begin by saying that I don't believe the Chinese would ever risk military confrontation with the US over Taiwan," the doctor barely concealed his disdain for the process and those in the room. That being said, the man from State straightened, looking like something had been lifted off his chest.

Since he was a professional, he would humor the proceedings anyway and give them a dose of his wisdom. "China, in the unlikely event that it would seek to conquer Taiwan by force of arms, would probably seek to do so while the US was otherwise committed to a major engagement elsewhere in the world. For example, in the Middle East. Japanese interference should be negligible. While it is true that the Japanese fleet has technical and operational superiority over the Chinese, it is extremely unlikely that the Japanese would come to the aid of Taiwan." Dr. Wendell droned on, reading from his notes, listing more reasons why China should not expect to encounter interference unless it openly challenged US military power.

North Korea was another matter. Dr. Wendell paused to change the subject, flipping to a new sheet on his legal pad in the process, "North Korea's armed forces are in a state of complete disrepair. Their leadership is reclusive and simply trying to make it through another year. Should China actually want to enlist their assistance as an adjunct in a military campaign, presumably to threaten or tie down US forces, they could probably do so by massively increasing food and fuel shipments to Pyongyang. After a year or two of improved conditions, the nation and the military might be better prepared strike south. Of course, such assistance is in no way a guarantee of future cooperation from Pyongyang."

That was it. Instead of 10 minutes, Dr. Wendell blessed the room with four minutes of his "brilliance". A few faces expressed relief he was now quiet and had sat down. Dowling looked a little cheated.

Mr. Amos Ye, an international economist and trade advisor for the Commerce Department stood next. He wore an impeccable dark brown silk suit and a perfect poker face. He spoke like old money from the East Coast. Had Donna asked, she would have discovered that Ye's family had roots in San Francisco dating back to the mid-1800s. Holding a few three by five cards, Ye stood, smiled and began, "The United States imports and exports yearly an amount roughly equal to 20% of its GDP. For China, that number is 12%, but growing. China's main trading partners for exports are the US and Japan. China imports most of its goods from Japan, Taiwan and the US.

"While it true that trade is fungible, that is, easily shifted around narrow embargoes, it is uncertain if China could find a reliable market for the mass of consumer goods it ships to America. The Europeans, prone to protectionist sentiment behind the wall of the EU cannot be relied upon by China to pick up the slack from the United States." Mr. Ye continued, spicing his talk with detailed statistics and explanations. Clearly he liked conveying his knowledge—and he had the rapt attention of most in the room.

He concluded the economic impact portion of his talk, "The bottom line is that a truly effective US economic embargo, with Japanese participation, would result in about 25 million workers losing their jobs. This would increase unemployment by about three percent. But these job losses would be heavily concentrated in the cities where the export industries are located. Urban unemployment would actually increase by about 12 percent with rural unemployment being largely unaffected, at least initially. Lastly, due to the large trade surpluses China has run for several years, its foreign currency reserves are sufficient to fund imports of strategic materials and weapons from Russia for several years.

"As to the question of alternate supplies in the event of a wartime embargo or blockade, China is very vulnerable. China is the third largest importer of crude oil in the world. It needs about one million barrels per day and most of this supply comes via maritime routes as opposed to overland from Russia or the former Soviet Republics in Central Asia. China is the world's largest manufacturer of steel and it imports significant quantities of iron ore from abroad, although it does have sizable domestic production. China also imports large quantities of grain from Australia, the US, Canada and Argentina. Of note, China's merchant fleet is now the world's third largest, behind Japan and Greece. As to timelines, I do not know what the extent is of China's strategic mineral reserves, but as for food imports, China can make do with little to no maritime shipments. The Chinese can simply shift grain use away from feeding livestock directly to feeding people; this should be more than enough to make up any shortfall. The key commodity that China can't afford to be cut off from is oil. In this aspect, China is in a position very analogous to the position of Imperial Japan prior to World War Two when America led an effective oil boycott and later, once the US entered the war, a naval blockade. I currently see no way they can overcome a naval blockade of their sea lines of communication.

Unless agreements for reliable and sizable deliveries are made with overland neighbors such as Russia, China would grind to a halt in less than four months. Of course, that assumes an active naval blockade by the US fleet. A simple boycott of Chinese goods by America and Japan would not serve to cut China off from any needed items—other than some high tech equipment."

Mr. Ye offered a tight-lipped smile and took his seat. Donna noted he never glanced at the three by five cards he had prepared but held at his side during the briefing. It was now Colonel Lake's turn. The time was 3:54 PM; Ye had run over a few minutes, consuming Dr. Wendell's unused time. No one seemed to mind, Ye was good.

Colonel Lake looked across the table at Donna, drew a breath and stood up ramrod straight but looked at ease and relaxed. His light green long sleeve military shirt was adorned only with his nametag, the eagle epaulettes that signified his rank as a colonel, and the two-inch oval Office of the Secretary of Defense badge. His plain flat black tie was held to his pressed shirt with a simple silver tie clip that also was adorned by a miniature of the same rank-identifying eagle. The shirt had two sharp creases in it, each running straight down from the center of each pocket. Colonel Lake left his legal pad on the table and addressed the entire room as he spoke. Donna thought of the strange contradictions of the warrior class.

Colonel Lake began, all the familiarity of lunchtime gone from his voice, he was the epitome of a professional, "Good afternoon. I'm Colonel Lake and for this exercise I represent the Chief-of-Staff of the PLA." The colonel launched immediately into his briefing, highlighting the strengths and weaknesses of each course of action. He wrapped up with a summary of each.

"Option one, using the PLA's growing power to intimidate Taiwan has its attractions. First, it has worked before. In 1996, China fired missiles that detonated just off the coast of Taiwan in an attempt to dissuade a vote for the pro-independence presidential candidate. Whether such an approach could be used to force a union with Taiwan is a high-risk venture. If such a campaign of intimidation fails, China would lose face and its world standing would be diminished.

"Option two, launching a full-scale invasion to conquer Taiwan, offers the most rewards for the least risk. However, this option is not without danger. In the near-term, success could only be accomplished with three elements: surprise, the non-intervention of the US, and the use of chemical weapons to neutralize resistance at the invasion beaches. Using chemical weapons may cause a negative international response, but I might add, the Chinese may not be dissuaded, after all, Saddam Hussein killed his own people with nerve agent and barely raised a ripple. And, don't forget, the outrage in the world community caused by the PLA killing 5,000 unarmed students in Tiananmen Square in 1989 was short-lived. In the mid-term, a sustained three to five year naval construction program may provide the PLAN with enough amphibious capability to forego the use of NBC and simply invade Taiwan with overwhelming firepower.

"Option three, launching a full-scale invasion of Taiwan as a prelude to a sustained campaign to conquer Asia, is bold and imaginative, but hardly sustainable. Certainly, Chinese planners would have to contend with the possibility that America and Japan would not stand idly by while a major power consolidated its hold on Asia. This might be a viable option in 10 to 20 years, but not at the present time."

As the colonel wrapped up his presentation, he sat down in his chair and looked to Mr. Dowling. It was exactly 4:10 PM, right on schedule.

Cliff Dowling spoke up, "I've decided I want no discussions or questions to precede the vote. We all had plenty of time to interact with each other during the course of the day, and, most of us have our day jobs to attend to after we release for the day." Dowling continued, "So, let's get to the decision. I will ask the four primary players which one of Colonel Lake's options they prefer. With four votes, at least one option should receive two votes. At my discretion, I will ask for a second round of votes if the top vote getter only receives two votes in which case I'll leave off one of less preferred options.

"All those in favor of option one, intimidating Taiwan, please raise their hands." Dr. Wendell gave his characteristic half wave, his elbow still stuck to the table.

"All those in favor of option two, conquering Taiwan, please raise their hands." Donna and the colonel raised their hands opposite each other.

Dowling raised an eyebrow almost imperceptibly, "All those in favor of conquering Taiwan as a prelude to conquering Asia please raise his hand." Dowling had changed his sentence structure midway through as a slight gesture of humor. Mr. Ye raised his hand and shrugged, briefly cocking his head a bit to one side as he did so.

Dowling frowned, clearly he had not expected the economist to suggest a bold course of action. "I'd like to have a second round of voting, this time between options one and two only. All those in favor of option one?"

Ye and Wendell raised their hands. Donna thought about Ye's reasoning—all or nothing—certain amount of sense to that. She decided this man was worth some additional questioning and resolved to grill him at lunch tomorrow. Donna and the colonel raised their hands at Dowling's calling of the option two question.

Dowling smiled, "Well, it's a tie, and I get to cast the deciding vote. We'll game option two. I want to take Taiwan within 12 months. Colonel Lake, set in motion a heightened training and mobilization posture. Keep the preparations as secret as possible. Mr. Ye and Dr. Wendell, see to it that the Democratic People's Republic of Korea gets all the fuel and food it requires. Colonel Lake, provide our ally with a 'loan' of 300 of our oldest tanks, in good working order, of course, and begin to upgrade their air defense network. Make no effort to disguise these preparations, but don't telegraph them either. Ms. Klein, I want you to open up intense, government-to-government exchanges designed to engage the government on Taiwan at all levels. Make them feel that we truly want a political solution to reunification."

As Dowling spoke, each role player wrote down his orders. As soon as he finished, facilitators showed up at the side of each role player to understand the intent of their more detailed instructions. These actions would then be communicated to the Green and Blue cells and their auxiliary Japan, South Korea and Taiwan cells so that they could formulate a response for the Red cell by the next day at noon. Tomorrow, Donna's Red cell had to respond to two US alternative actions, by generating two reactions. It was a lot of work to pack into a day.

Donna finished fleshing out her response to the facilitator and headed quickly for the hall. About half of the game participants had already left. Today had been interesting and productive, but she had other things on her mind now. She toyed with the idea of going in to the office, but the chance to catch up on laundry and sleep proved more compelling.

Just before she reached the hallway she noticed General Taylor in the corner talking with a young-looking Air Force lieutenant colonel. In spite of herself, she hesitated. General Taylor clapped the man on the shoulder and slipped by him to address Donna. "Ms. Klein, I wanted to say thank you for your contribution. Has it been interesting for you so far?"

Donna thought the man was too friendly—*hasn't he learned with all the sexual scandal in the Pentagon?* "Thank you. Yes, I had an excellent time today. I hope all of our hard work will be put to good use."

Taylor smiled gently, "We're recording everything and we'll distill it down to lessons learned within a week. The National Security Council staff will even get an executive summary of this one."

Donna decided he reminded her of a younger, taller version of her father, Admiral Ben Klein, USN, retired. "Great. I hope the good guys win in the end."

"Don't we always?"

"We'll see. I'm on the bad guy side this week." Donna grinned slyly, turned on her heels, and walked out the door.

8
What to Do?

Fu Zemin, politico-military affairs advisor to the Chinese Communist Party, sat down at his PC and began to try to put to words his ambitious thoughts. After several false starts he lit up a cigarette. He sighed. He put the cigarette down and returned to the keyboard. His phone rang, making him flinch. Fu waited one more ring to calm himself before answering. Normally, his secretary screened his calls, direct calls only came from his wife or, rarely, higher ups who wanted something.

"Hello, Fu Zemin here."

"Comrade Fu, this is the office of the Chairman's Chief Central Military Commission Advisor. You are wanted for an informal meeting." It was a male voice.

Fu felt a shudder of anticipation from the surprise call—*the Central Military Commission, you can't get much higher than that.* "When?"

"Immediately, of course." The voice sounded impatient, "The discussion is already underway. Come to the CMC Chief Advisor's office."

"I'm on my way."

Fu rocked back in his leather bound chair, reached to the right top drawer, brought out his comb, and smoothed his hair—looking sloppy was a certain path to engendering a lack of confidence. Fortunately, the Chairman's working offices were just across the street from the Party headquarters. Since it was cold and rainy outside (he had a rare window office) he decided to take the tunnel connecting the two structures together under the wide thoroughfare.

He made it to the Central Military Commission's office in only seven minutes. Again a surprise, he was shown right in to Chief Advisor Soo's office. In addition to Soo, a thin man of about 50 who's sole vice was chain smoking, there were two PLA generals in the office, and a high-ranking man from the Foreign Ministry. Fu had socially met the other three men at various parties over the years. He remembered they all had wives, but he couldn't remember their names. He bowed and waited to be addressed.

"Comrade Fu, you write interesting memos," it was the man from the Foreign Ministry. He was in his 70s. He looked trim, fit, and alert, with a full head of closely cropped gray hair. The other men looked at him, waiting for a reaction. Soo sat behind his desk and a veil of cigarette smoke, the two generals seated to either side examining him as if he were a bug. Only the man from the Foreign Ministry had a look of kindness, almost grandfatherly, he was seated to Soo's right, facing the generals. It was apparent the four had been having a conference before he arrived.

"Yes Comrade Fong (he remembered the old man's name!), I try to do what I can for China." It was a safe answer, one couldn't be too careful, even nowadays, when dealing with power.

Soo began to look impatient, "Let me cut to the chase. Zemin, we have been watching you for some time. You are smart and ambitious. You even show signs of wisdom—for a man of only 36. We want to include you as part of our discussion group. Everything said here is in the strictest confidence, understand?"

"Yes, comrade."

"So, before you showed up for your first meeting late, Zemin," Soo cast a sly look to Fu, "We were discussing the issue of America's recent anti-missile tests. What is your opinion about the American missile defenses?" Four sets of eyes regarded the younger man.

Fu was beaming inwardly, outwardly, his face was impassive—he was advising men only one step removed from the Chairman himself! Fu began slowly, deliberately, "I believe this is a most unwelcome development for China. . ."

"We don't need you to tell us that! Eh?" One of the generals cracked. The other general laughed.

Soo cut them off with a curt wave, "What I really want to know is, what should we do about it?"

Fu swallowed, "We have three years, five at the most, before America develops theater defenses capable of making our ballistic missile force obsolete in Asia. Within six years, America might think herself invulnerable from nuclear attack. Our only course of action is to begin a build-up of long-range ballistic missiles—of course, that's what the Americans want us to do. . ."

"Eh?" It was the other general.

"The Americans want us to join them in an arms race. It weakened and eventually destroyed the Soviet Union and it could destroy us as well."

"So, what do we do?" Fong asked.

"Cigarette?" Soo offered.

"Why yes, thank you comrade." Fu gratefully accepted the proffered cigarette, a strong-tasting domestic. Fu began to reach for his lighter and Soo offered Fu his own—a heavy gold inlaid model. Fu felt the tension ease out of his muscles. The first puff brought him intensely into focus. "We must seize the initiative," one of the generals shifted forward in his chair, eyes intensely fixed on Fu, "No nation wins using only the defense. America today is a nation full of itself. America believes itself to be the world's only superpower. That is her greatest weakness. So long as the Americans believe that there is no real threat to their national interest, they will crusade around the globe, putting their noses into other people's business. I propose we use this to our advantage."

"Madness! If the Americans get any more active in the world how long will it be before they demand we hold a referendum on independence for Tibet or some other such nonsense?" It was the general who had made the sarcastic comment moments before.

Fu finally remembered the man's name while idly wondering if the lack of formal introductions was purposeful, "General Ching, the Americans have not yet intervened in a nation's internal business when that nation was capable of defending itself, now have they? Did America do anything when the Russians invaded Chechnya and crushed the rebels? Of course not. Likewise, *China* has nothing to fear from the Americans."

Fong spoke up, "Where first? Give us a concrete example of your idea so we may discuss its strengths and weaknesses."

"Indonesia."

"You mean East Timor?" Soo asked.

"No, Indonesia. All of it. It's a powder keg ready to explode with religious and ethnic strife. Because of its oil and its size, I believe the Americans will be compelled to intervene and stabilize the situation. . ."

Soo narrowed his eyes and said slowly, "Do you really believe it would be to China's advantage to have American troops stationed in another Asian country?" His question had a sharpness about it, even a hint of danger.

Fu was cautious. He decided the best course of action was to be firm, but careful. "Yes Comrade Soo, if the Americans come away from the deployment with a bad taste for Asian combat it would be good for us. Moreover, a larger American troop deployment will further reduce their strategic flexibility."

"What do you propose?" General Ching asked.

"Comrade General Ching, I propose we use whatever clandestine methods we have at our disposal to increase American casualties and frustrate their designs. An American failure in Asia, coming on the heels of the protracted stalemates in the Balkans and against Iraq would enhance our prestige and hand the Americans a serious loss of face." Fu swallowed, then continued, "Such a loss might make the Americans less likely to aid the province of Taiwan, should reunification be achieved with, ah, less than peaceful means in the near future." The generals chuckled softly, "And, let us not forget, the Americans are growing increasingly weary of their international commitments. Remember, their Congress recently voted to end registration for conscription. No nation has ever maintained world power status without the ability to draft soldiers."

Fong stroked his chin, then spoke, "What you propose is much easier said than done. Our infrastructure in Indonesia never recovered from the blow the fascist generals dealt it in the 1960s. If we aid the anti-independence militia in East Timor and get discovered, it could be unpleasant for us."

"I agree. That is why I said Indonesia should be our target, not just East Timor. Indonesia has thousands of islands. Our cargo ships visit many of them. There is also a large ethnic Chinese presence throughout the archipelago. Our agents could move with relative impunity throughout the region. Of course, Indonesia could be just the beginning, if the Americans show enough appetite for intervention, we could always destabilize the Philippines. . ."

"More than we do already?" Ching said with a grin.

"Yes. Think of this plan as what the Americans called the 'Reagan Doctrine', only in reverse. President Reagan funded and equipped counterrevolutionaries to challenge Soviet hegemony. We could do the same to challenge and reverse Pax Americana."

Fong furrowed his brow, "What if the Americans move to destabilize our government? We nearly lost control in 1989 and the Americans had nothing to do with it. The people have even less faith in the Party today than they did then, especially after the elections in Taiwan threw out the Nationalists. What makes you so sure we can drive the Americans from Asia with a few guerrilla wars? What is your end-state? So, we bloody America's nose and they still end up deploying missile defenses; how are we better off?"

Fu was shocked at Fong's candid admission of how close the Tiananmen Square uprising came to destroying the Communist Party's grip on power. Fu gathered his courage, "We can solve all our problems with the successful reunification of China—in victory, everyone's a patriot."

Fu's words hung like ripe fruit in the middle of the room. All the men could taste it, even while they knew it to be unreachable.

The general next to Ching spoke up, "Ha! Take Taiwan and everything will be fine! Easy for you to say! How many troops have you commanded in war?"

"None. . ."

"What do you expect us to do, swim across while we wait for the US Navy to pay us a visit?"

"No general. I expect a proud nation of 1.3 billion people can, with ingenuity and industriousness, figure out how to seize a small, rebellious island. As for the US fleet, I suspect there are ways to divert their attention until it is too late. If I may. . ."

"Please," Soo said, extending another cigarette, "We find your ideas most interesting. . ."

9
Good Intent

On the morning of December 26, the Island of Timor came into view. It was a dark green against a backdrop of brilliant blue skies and billowing cumulus clouds hovering over the island's mountainous spine. Even at sea it was beastly hot.

After almost a century of foreign interventions, most for the purpose of securing American lives and property, the 2nd Battalion, 4th Marines of the 31st Marine Expeditionary Unit prepared to go ashore on their latest mission. Colonel Flint gripped the railing on the deck of the USS *Belleau Wood* and looked at the tropical island that was his latest assignment.

*   *   *

The flare-up in East Timor combined with the decision to send in the Marines pulled Donna out of the Pentagon's China war game. "Tier Zero crisis coverage." Mr. Scott called it as he phoned Donna at home after the war game's first day. While Donna was a China expert, she was also known as a creative and flexible analyst. The Indonesia section was understaffed for the crisis, so Donna was brought in to augment their efforts.

Donna had been working on the East Timor crisis for a month when she stopped to consider its "Tier Zero" status. Presidential Decision Directive-35 sought to better prioritize intelligence requirements. "Tier Zero" was for crisis coverage, "Tier One" for countries that were enemies or potential enemies, and "Tier Two" for other countries of high priority. "Tier Zero" situations were first in line for resources. The PRC was "Tier Two". Donna had ceased struggling against this politically correct ranking—to even suggest China as a "Tier One" country was a sure route to being posted to Chad as Assistant to the Deputy CIA Station Chief.

Donna settled into her desk to review the morning traffic from China before getting caught up in her East Timor "day job". She absentmindedly untied her walking shoes and slipped on her modest high-heeled work shoes. She scanned and stored a wide range of facts from 21 pages of information: China now had 110 million unemployed; China was violently cracking down on Islamic unrest in its western provinces; China had taken delivery of another 50 front-line Russian Su-30 fighters; China's manned space program was slowing down due to a lack of resources; China's leadership was growing increasingly worried about religious "cells" in its major cities.

Donna looked at her watch and shook her head—*Time for the East Timor morning staff meeting.* She locked her stack of traffic up in her desk and knew there was intelligence to be made from that small pile of paper—*No time.*

10
Decisions

Communist Party Chairman Han Wudi stepped off the Boeing 737 into the welcome warmth of a Hainan afternoon. He paused at the top of the passenger ramp, letting the warmth envelop him like a blanket while his eyes feasted on the luxuriant green of this tropical island, China's southernmost province. What a relief to be out of the bitter cold of a Beijing January, with its parched landscape and incessant loess dust storms.

Welcome to China's Hawaii, Chairman Han said to himself without thinking. He immediately grimaced at his slip. *Never concede primacy to the US in anything*, he scolded himself. Lines from his recent secret speech to the CCP (Chinese Communist Party) Central Committee came unbidden into his mind: "The US is in decline, while China is rising. Someday soon China will replace the US as the world's hegemon. Our goal is to lead the world in the twenty-first century."

Han smiled. If things went as planned, the first concrete steps towards establishing—re-establishing, he corrected himself—Chinese hegemony over Asia would be taken at the upcoming expanded Politburo meeting. And that was only the beginning. Han's smile widened wickedly. *Someday American presidents will be riding in Chinese-made jets. And someday the world will refer to Hawaii as America's Hainan. That is, if we allow Hawaii to remain an American possession after what the Americans have done to Taiwan . . .*

Chairman Han was still smiling broadly as he descended the passenger ramp.   He was greeted effusively by the Hainan provincial party secretary, a longtime crony who had first served under him twenty years before when he was Minister of Electronics. He nodded politely as the underling gushed about the island's recent economic advances, listening with only half an ear. By now nearly all of the provincial party secretaries were his *habagou*, his lapdogs. After more than a decade in power he had managed to ease all of the possible contenders for his position into retirement, and to appoint dozens, no hundreds, of *habagou* to key posts in the party, military, and government.   They were all talented enough, but his first requirement had been loyalty. As a result, Chairman Han now reigned supreme and secure at the top of the party pyramid. As Chairman of the Military Affairs Committee he was also commander-in-chief of the largest military in the world. Having concentrated all power in his hands, it was time to expand his writ abroad.

His underling—the man's name escaped him—bowed low as Chairman Han got into the waiting Mercedes Benz. With the streets cleared by police escorts, he and they were out of the provincial capital of Haikou in minutes, speeding down a private and well-paved road towards the Thousand Palms Resort. *Mao Zedong Wansui*, he thought. *Hooray for Mao Zedong*. The late Chairman had projected the public image of a simple peasant, but had secretly nourished a taste for the good life. Every province had one or more palatial compounds that he had built exclusively for his own use. The one in Hainan was particularly luxurious, and had come in recent years to be used for meetings of senior leaders, particularly in the winter when everyone was eager to escape the biting cold and yellow grit of the North China plain.

Han stepped out of the Mercedes and addressed the assembled crowd of dignitaries, "Thank you all for coming to this expanded meeting of the Politburo," he began with a smile. "We have an important three days of work ahead of us. China must resume her rightful place in the world—and soon. Our decisions over the next three days will determine how and when that happens. We have spent the past half-century developing our economy, our technology and our military. China has the world's second largest economy, a rapidly expanding industrial base, and the world's largest military. A new century is dawning, and it belongs to China."

His eyes narrowed. "Yet we are still hemmed in by the American imperialists. They plot to destroy our Party and divide our country. They bomb our embassies. They prevent us from completing the liberation of the offshore islands and Taiwan. China must break out of this encirclement and assert its rightful place in the world!

"A half a century ago, upon the founding of the People's Republic of China, Chairman Mao proudly proclaimed that China has stood up. Now it is time—no, it is past time—for us to take bold steps, steps that will shake the world."

Premier Wang began clapping enthusiastically. The others joined in, including Chairman Han himself, for it was the Chinese custom to applaud oneself. Defense Minister Han's applause, along with that of one or two others, was distinctly perfunctory.

43

Fu Zemin was the first to arrive at the entrance to the assigned conference room—the Dragon Room, it was called—the following morning. His mind was racing as the guards meticulously searched his briefcase and person. He hadn't slept much the night before. Rather, gripped by an anxiety bordering on panic, he had spent the night making revisions to his speech, first taking a harder line, then a softer. Near dawn, exhausted, he had given up trying to guess the mood of the audience he was addressing and returned to his original draft.

The guards waved him through and he stepped through the moon-shaped entrance into the Dragon Room. His eyes widened in surprise—*So this was where the name came from.* The room was dominated by a large mural of a dragon, its serpentine body undulating in striking blue hues some 20 feet along the wall. How auspicious, thought Fu, that today's debate should take place in the presence of the ancient symbol of China's imperial glory. In this, the very Year of the Dragon.

Fu walked along the wall admiring the artist's handiwork. The dragon-serpent in Chinese mythology represented power without principle. It was the distilled essence of the male principle, the masculine Yang factor with all of the feminine Yin removed. The unknown artist had captured this perfectly. There was something menacingly male about the dragon's sinuous trunk, and his thick-muscled legs with their curving claws. The creature's glittering eyes were devoid of compassion, its massive jaws wide open and predatory. Fu shuddered delightfully.

For centuries untold his ancestors had worshipped the dragon-serpent. They had buried their dead on hillsides overlooking the ridges of distant hills, calling these the dragon's spine. They had centered the headstones of their grandfathers between twin pools of water, calling these the dragon's eyes. They even called themselves the descendants of the dragon, in some Olympian fantasy of dragon-man miscegenation. All this was done to summon the dragon-serpent so that he would confer power and prosperity on them and their descendants. Fu was not a superstitious man, but he caught himself invoking the power of this great creature to aid his speech today. Its eyes seemed to rest on him for a moment, then went lifeless again.

His weariness and anxieties seemed to have vanished. "I *will* convince them to move against Taiwan," he told the dragon under his breath. His fists clenched in anticipation of the debate.

Fu turned away from the mural to study the arrangement of the conference room. In the very center was a rectangular table, surrounded by ten chairs. On the table in front of each was a card containing the hand-brushed ideograph of its intended occupant. Chairman Han would be at the head of the table, of course, with Premier Wang occupying the opposite end. Two-dozen more chairs—each with its own card—were ranged along the walls. He made a quick circuit of the room, memorizing names, then staked out a position near the door. As the aides arrived he greeted them and made small talk, keeping an eye out for the key players, those who had a place at the rectangular table.

The members of the Military Affairs Commission were the first to arrive. Fu recognized General Li Zhongyang, the Vice Chairman of the MAC, a career military man who had in recent years equipped the PLA with the best hi-tech weapons Russia had to sell or the US had to steal from. He was followed by the Chief of Staff of the Army, General Lu Zhandui, the Chief of Staff of the Navy, Admiral Hai Zhanting, and the Chief of Staff of the Air Force, General Kung Huojian. General Kung was in animated conversation with his fellows, talking about a new smart bomb they had acquired from the United States. "It arrived in excellent condition from our friends in Belgrade last year," Fu heard General Kung say. "We were reverse engineering it—you know how difficult that is—when a complete computer profile of the same weapon and its controlling avionics fell into our hands from other sources. We will gear up for production by the end of the month!"

Another argument for accepting my plan, Fu thought smugly, as he turned to greet the next arrival: Vice Premier Mo Waijiao, who handled China's foreign relations. A sometime critic of Fu's more hard-line suggestions, Vice Premier Mo was nonetheless a courtly, diplomatic individual who responded to his greeting with a nod and a smile. "Have you met Defense Minister Han Fubai?" he asked, gesturing to the portly man in an immaculately tailored business suit by his side.

Fu Zemin bowed slightly.

"Is this the Secretary Fu with all the radical ideas?" Minister Han said to Vice Premier, ignoring Fu's bow.

"He's a genius," Vice Premier Mo chuckled, softening the blow, "but he's also relatively young and impetuous. For a hundred years the Chinese people have suffered the bitterness of being bullied by the foreign imperialist powers. He wants to settle these old scores overnight."

"Not overnight, Vice Premier," Fu countered, "but soon. If we wait . . . ."

"If we act *too* soon," the Defense Minister broke in, "we risk losing everything."

Party General Secretary Han Wudi arrived at that moment, bringing the exchange to an abrupt end. With him were Premier Wang Fuguo, Minister of the Interior Ren Baisha, Vice Premier for Economics and Trade Su Zhongqiang. Everyone found his seats as Chairman Han called the meeting to order.

The Vice Chairman of the Military Affairs Committee opened the first session. General Li Zhongyang was almost gloating as he listed the growing hi-tech capabilities of the People's Liberation Army. Modified Russian Su-27 Flankers, faster and lighter because of the use of American-made six-way milling machines, were rolling off the assembly lines at a rate of two dozen a month. Cruise missiles were being produced at a rate of one hundred a month. Smart bombs would soon be produced in quantity. Most importantly, a half-a-dozen lightweight nuclear weapons would soon be added to the Chinese arsenal—the fruits of two decades of no-holds-barred spying on the United States.

Fu was listening with only half an ear, concentrating on reading over the draft speech he held in his hand one last time. *As if I haven't rehearsed it a hundred times already,* he thought wryly.

It did not help that he was to speak at the outset, before he had a sense of where the others stood, of what consensus would emerge from the meeting. True, Chairman Han had spoken of liberating the offshore islands and Taiwan yesterday when he had arrived, but when he had talked to the members of the Military Affairs Committee later in the evening they had seemed cool to the idea. And Defense Minister Han this morning had seemed positively hostile. What if Chairman Han's remark had been merely a rhetorical flourish? Hadn't China's leaders blustered for 50 years about taking back Taiwan, and in the end done nothing?

Fu rubbed his bloodshot eyes wearily. This was the opportunity of a lifetime, he told himself for the thousandth time. If he favorably impressed Chairman Han and the others, there was no telling how high he might rise. *Yes, and if they reject your plan,* a voice within him ridiculed, *then you will sink back into obscurity. Or worse.* Yi luo qian jiang, he thought, recalling the ancient cry of the disgraced official, *A single misstep causes a fall of a thousand steps.* The General's mention of nuclear weapons brought him back to the present.

"As all of you know," General Li was saying, "in the mid-nineties we were able to secure exact data on all of America's most advanced nuclear weapons. We were able to acquire both the so-called 'legacy code', as well as the input data for individual weapons. (The legacy code was an enormous computer file—millions of lines of code—containing all the information US scientists had collected from over 40 years of nuclear tests.) From the legacy code, we learned how each and every type of US nuclear weapon will perform. From the input data, we learned the key inputs into each and every type of US nuclear weapon. By putting the two together we were able generate blueprints of all of America's nuclear weapons, from miniaturized nuclear bombs and neutron bombs, to electromagnetic pulse bombs and X-ray laser bombs."

Here General Li paused, permitting himself a triumphant smile. "Today I come before you to share some important news. All of the state-of-the-art nuclear weapons we care to have are now in production. China may now be considered a nuclear superpower. The day when the US can bully and humiliate us is over!"

The assembled officials burst into applause. Fu joined in vigorously. The story of China's incredible theft of America's entire nuclear arsenal know-how was a story he knew intimately. *How could the Americans have been so stupid as to let these weapons plans fall into our hands?* It was not the first time the thought had crossed his mind. *No matter.* He had already known that the first of these weapons was ready, and had incorporated their use into his plan. He was going to defeat the Americans, and their running dogs on Taiwan, with their own weapons. It was a classic adaptation of Sun Tzu's ancient strategic wisdom.

He heard his name called, and he walked slowly to the front of the room, trying to project a calm he did not feel. There was no applause. Chinese officials only applaud those senior in rank, and he was junior to the lot of them.

The title of his talk was simple, bold, and provocative: "The Liberation of Taiwan." He took a deep breath and began to speak, abandoning himself to the words he had so carefully crafted.

"The time has come to complete the unification of China," he began. "This renegade province, home to the remnants of Chiang Kai-Shek's bandits, has been too long outside of our control. The time has come for the People's Republic, under the brilliant leadership of Chairman Han, to complete the work that Chairman Mao began." Fu stole a glance at the Chairman, who seemed to be sitting up a little straighter in his chair.

"This will necessarily have to be accomplished by military force," Fu went on. "Given the strength of Taiwan's so-called 'independence movement', which is encouraged by the American imperialists, and the stubbornness of Chiang's Old Guard, Taiwan will never voluntarily rejoin the motherland. With only two percent of our land area, and less than two percent of our population, Taiwan will not be able to withstand a determined assault. I estimate that two-thirds of the PRC Air Force, the entire PLA Navy, and some 500,000 men will be necessary to bring this mission to a successful conclusion. . ."

A voice cut him off in mid-sentence. "And where will the American imperialist fleet be while you ferry a half million men across the Taiwan Straits?" the defense minister said sarcastically. "Carrying out humanitarian missions in Bangladesh?" There was muffled laughter in the room.

"The American imperialists . . . in Bangladesh?" Fu fumbled for a moment but finished strong. "No, Minister Han, the American fleet will not be in Bangladesh . . . It will be in the Persian Gulf, in the Adriatic and off the coast of Indonesia."

Fu's comeback elicited a scowl from the Defense Minister, but from others in the room came a murmur of interest. Premier Wang even nodded approvingly. Fu decided to let their curiosity build for a few minutes more before unveiling his strategy. "I'll get to the Indonesian diversion in a minute, but first let me give you a little more background. As you know, the American imperialists occupied Taiwan at the beginning of the Korean War. Eisenhower ordered the US Seventh Fleet to patrol the Taiwan Straits, violating our territorial waters, preventing—as the minister of defense has pointed out—our troops from reaching Taiwan. Later, the US opened an air base, for its Eighth Air Force, near the Taiwan city of Taichung, making an invasion that much more risky."

"Beginning the late 1970s the balance of forces in the Straits began to shift in our favor. Vice Premier Deng Xiaoping insisted that the last of the American occupying troops be withdrawn in 1978 as a condition of diplomatic recognition. The Seventh Fleet stopped patrolling the Taiwan Straits. The Mutual Security Treaty was abrogated. . ."

"Yes, but there is still the Taiwan Relations Act," interjected the Defense Minister. "It calls for the US to guarantee the security of Taiwan against invasion or blockade."

"Not exactly, Minister Han," Fu responded. "All the Taiwan Relations Act says is that"—here he quoted—"'. . .the US would consider any effort to determine the future of Taiwan by other than peaceful means . . . a threat to the peace and security of the Western Pacific area and of grave concern to the US.' It does not commit the US to defend Taiwan. That would be up to the US President."

Mention of the US leader, a weak man whose administration had been rocked by repeated scandals, many of them related to his out-of-control appetites, brought a round of ribald jokes.

"A bevy of our black-haired beauties could distract him while we take Taiwan," the Minister of Economics offered to general laughter.

"Beauties carrying bundles of unmarked bills would be a double distraction," riposted Premier Wang, "I understand he's already raising money for the next elections."

"And for his legal bills," the Minister of the Interior, Ren Baisha, added dryly. "So many women are suing him . . ."

"Maybe we could support him for UN Secretary General," the Minister of Economics, Su Zhongqiang, quipped. "As a foreign diplomat in the US, he would possess immunity from arrest."

The scornful joking continued for several more moments, with even Chairman Han joining in. Like most Party officials, Fu thought little of the American President, but he was still surprised by the depth of his own leaders' disdain. *So much the better,* he realized, *it will predispose them to accept my plan.*

As soon as things had quieted down, he began to hammer the point home. "We all agree that this American president is weak and indecisive," he said to a round of appreciative nods. "This is an argument for striking Taiwan hard now, before their next presidential elections remove him from office."

"The American military is weak now, too, particularly in Asia, weaker and more over extended than it has been at any time since the end of the Vietnam War. The Americans have been forced out of Vietnam, the Philippines and, of course, Taiwan. They have reduced their forces in Korea and Japan. What's left? A Marine division in Okinawa, 37,000 men in South Korea, and naval and air force elements in Japan."

"Is there some risk of US intervention?" Fu said dramatically. "Of course there is. But I'll tell you in a minute how we can minimize this risk. Let us first remember what is at stake here.

"Right now, Taiwan is a dagger pointed at the heart of China.

You've all read the reports. Our people are impressed by Taiwan's economic development; by per capita their incomes are ten times higher than ours. They are seduced by its so-called 'democratic' political system, the myth that the people themselves select their leaders. We in the Party know that moneybags democracy is a failure and a fraud. Only the Chinese Communist Party, the vanguard of the proletariat, can truly represent the interests of the Chinese people. Yet the people—some people— are taken in. By taking Taiwan we turn this dagger away from us and thrust it toward the United States.

"And think of the prize of Taiwan, with its first-world economy, its highly educated work force, and its cutting-edge technology. Gaining Hong Kong increased our GNP by about eight percent. Gaining Taiwan would increase our GNP by another ten percent overnight. Bringing Taiwan back into China will increase our military might, giving us ports from which our ships can steam farther, and airfields from which our planes can fly greater distances.

"But the prize here is larger than just Taiwan," Fu continued. "Taiwan is the key to control of the entire first island chain, from Japan and Korea in the north, down to the Philippines and Indonesia in the south. Once Taiwan has been absorbed, Japan and Korea will fall into our orbit. The Philippines and Southeast Asia will follow. Within a short time the countries of the first island chain will be in the hands of governments friendly to China, and hostile to the United States. China, not the United States, will be the regional hegemon."

The Chairman of the Chinese Communist Party spoke for the first time. "This is all very fine," Chairman Han said quietly. "But will the US stand idly by while we overrun their colony?"

"They will not be idle, Mr. Chairman," Fu said with a daring touch of smugness. "That's the beauty of my plan. The US Army will be tied down in Korea by troop mobilizations north of the border. Our friend Kim Jong-il will see to that. The US Navy will be responding to a crisis in the Middle East. Our friends in Iraq and Syria will see to that. And the US Marines," he paused here for effect, "will be fighting for their lives in East Timor and Indonesia. Before the US can bring in forces from Hawaii or the American West Coast, Taiwan will be ours."

As Fu expected, Defense Minister Han Fubai immediately spoke out against his plan.

"We all agree with the need to recapture Taiwan, by force if necessary," the Defense Minister grumbled. "But I say that we are not strong enough yet. Let us bide our time for a few more years. Our star is rising. That of the US is falling. In ten years we will have the world's largest economy, and the most powerful military. We have only to wait and Taiwan will have no choice but to kowtow.

"In ten more years we will have not just a handful but thousands of the new nuclear weapons that General Li has told us about. We will have not just 20 nuclear weapons pointed at the US but hundreds or maybe even thousands. These new compact weapons will be on hard-to-target mobile launchers, which we are only now developing, or clustered on our new ICBMs."

"China's economic health is very vulnerable," Vice Premier Su nodded in support of the Defense Minister. Vice Premier Su Zhongqiang had overall responsibility for economics and trade. "We are heavily reliant upon imported oil, gas, minerals, metals, chemicals and food. Cross-straits trade and investment means that Taiwan's manufacturing capability is already at our disposal, regardless of whose flag flies over the presidential palace."

"But we do need command of the sea lanes," the Admiral in charge of the PLA naval forces, Admiral Hai Zhanting, interjected. "Control over Taiwan and the South China Sea would put us in a much stronger position to guarantee the imports we need. We are very vulnerable to blockade. Does anyone here think that America will let us rise up to challenge their power? Were we in their position, would we let another nation grow more powerful than China? We *must* control our own destiny."

"That's the same argument that drove Imperial Japan and Nazi Germany to start World War Two," objected the Defense Minister. "Think of how dependent pre-war Japan and Germany were on foreign oil and ore. The Japanese went to war to capture Indonesian oil. The Germans went to war to capture Russian oil and to secure Swedish iron ore via Norway."

"Yes, and look what happened to them," added Vice Premier Su. "They were both defeated by America. It took their economies more than 20 years to recover."

Admiral Hai could barely contain his contempt for this line of reasoning, "The US *and* Russia defeated the Axis powers. Russia is on *our* side now. We could practically buy Russia tomorrow— we already own half their politicians. Besides, Japan only moved to capture Indonesian oil fields after America instituted an oil embargo on Japan. The Japanese reacted to an American

51

initiative. What would happen to us if we allowed the Americans to seize the initiative and cut off our oil?"

Defense Minister Han snorted, "This is madness! You're proposing war with America. We're not ready yet, I tell you!" Han glared at the room. His gaze assiduously avoided Chairman Han and Premier Wang.

There was a brief silence as the group absorbed this. "No one is proposing going to war against the US," Premier Wang said finally. "We are merely discussing Fu Zemin's proposal to recover our own sovereign territory, the renegade province of Taiwan."

Hearing his name mentioned by the Premier, Fu jumped back into the conversation.

"The time to act is now," he said, eyes flashing with confidence. "The United States is beginning to wake up to the 'China threat', even though our diplomatic establishment ridicules the idea every time it is aired. Our military buildup is too massive to hide from US spy satellites much longer. The next American President will remedy the deficiencies of the present one. Look at the Reagan military build-up following the Carter years. The next President will think about reinforcing the Pacific. We must preempt that. We can then offer peace to the new American President from a position of strength. He will be glad to accept peace in exchange for our hegemony over Asia."

The Vice Chairman of the Military Affairs Commission nodded vigorously. "We at the Military Affairs Commission are particularly concerned about America's successful anti-ballistic missile tests. There is already talk of putting up defensive shields over Japan, Korea, and Taiwan. How much leverage will our missiles give us over the reactionaries then? If we wait too long we may fritter away our advantages."

"And don't forget about the growing militarism in Japan," interjected General Lu Zhandui, commander of the PLA army forces. "The dwarf bandits have never apologized to us for their atrocities in World War II. They've started flying that son-of-a-turtle's-egg rising sun flag again, that hated symbol of Japanese imperialism. Mark my words, the day will come when Japan arms itself with nuclear weapons, and with 400 tons of plutonium on hand from their civilian nuclear industry they could build a lot of bombs."

At this, Admiral Hai spoke up again. "Worse yet, Japan's new defense treaty with the US invites the US Navy to patrol our shores."

"China is vulnerable to a hostile power possessing a more powerful navy," Defense Minister Han cautioned. "What if the US Navy blockades China in retaliation for invading Taiwan?"

Admiral Hai's voice cut through the air. "Give me Taiwan and the South China Sea and I will guarantee the safety of Chinese shipping down to Indonesia. Our new destroyers and cruisers are the equal of America's in almost every way."

"They should be," Vice Chairman Li said in mock whisper. "We stole the plans."

Admiral Hai permitted himself a brief smile at Li's remark before continuing, "The keels of many more warships are being laid as we speak. We already have the third largest merchant marine fleet in the world. The addition of Taiwan's fleet will put us in second place. Meanwhile, the US Navy continues to shrink."

"You speak bravely, Admiral Hai, but may I be permitted to inquire, how well can an unarmed keel fight?" the Defense Minister fixed his gaze on his jingoistic admiral.

"Even so," Premier Wang asserted, "An American blockade would be an act of war against China. Do any of you really think that America, under its current President, would dare to attack China? Unlike Iraq or Yugoslavia, *we* can hit back. America is brave when it can bully. Their bravery will turn to prudence against China."

The meeting broke up into small groups, some arguing in favor of, others against, Fu's proposal. Fu noted with some concern that Chairman Han did not express an opinion either way. He did his best. He advocated action and tried to break the more than half-century impasse with the Nationalists on Taiwan. His proposal and with it, his career, were now in the hands of the leadership. Fu found himself staring at the cold majesty of the dragon.

The meetings in the Dragon Room continued the second day, but the moon doors had been closed to Fu and the other aides. These sessions were for principals only. Fu spent his day on a nearby terrace, discussing with the aides who had gathered there the details of his plan. He was somewhat reassured by their reaction. Most approved of his plan and believed that the leaders would adopt it. But would they?

It was the morning of the third day. Fu was back in his seat alongside the other aides in the Dragon Room, eager to learn the outcome of the closed deliberations of the previous day. Chairman Han politely called the meeting to order.

"Our country's history is one of national greatness," he began quietly. "For most of our 5,000 years the Chinese Empire was second to none. It had the greatest land area, the largest population, the most productive economy, the most powerful army, and the most advanced technology of any power on earth. The West likes to brag about the Roman Empire, but our Han dynasty two millennia ago was twice as large, three times as populous, and had four times as many men under arms. And where are the Romans today? Gone. Swept away by history. Yet China lives on. Europe is broken up into petty states. What is 'great' about the country that calls itself Great Britain? It is smaller in size and population than many of our provinces. Calling it 'Little Britain' would be more appropriate." A wave of laughter went through the room. Chairman Han smiled. He continued, "Germany? The Third Reich was their last attempt at greatness. Hitler said it would last 1,000 years—it lasted less than 20 and at its greatest extent, it barely equaled for about one year our current landmass. France? A mere shadow of its former greatness."

Chairman Han has a nice smile, but he has iron teeth, Fu thought. Many Big Noses in the West continued to underestimate this man. They called him a transitional figure, until he outlasted their own leaders. They questioned his political astuteness, without realizing that he had survived political struggles far fiercer than their own. They were disarmed by his kindly demeanor, his horn-rimmed glasses that gave him an avuncular look, without realizing the iron will and ruthlessness that lay within. Few Chinese made the same mistake.

"Only 200 years ago, China dominated half the world. Half the world!" Han repeated, stretching out his arms for emphasis. "The Great Emperor Qian Long held sway over a vast territory. It stretched from the Russian Far East west across southern Siberia to Lake Baikal and into contemporary Kazakstan. It reached southeastward along the Himalayas to the Indian Ocean, and then eastward across Laos and northern Vietnam. Tribute came from Korea, Tibet, Nepal, Burma, Thailand, and Indochina. Japan did not dare to offend us. We were universally admired for our culture. We were everywhere feared for our military might. We

54

enjoyed hegemony.

"Then came the Big Noses." An unpleasant look crossed Chairman Han's face. "They imposed opium on our people, sapping their will. They took our best ports for themselves, and turned China into a semi-colony. In their treaty ports they treated us like dogs. No, *worse* than dogs. I'm from Shanghai. As a child my grandfather told me about a park in Shanghai's foreign concession which Chinese were forbidden to enter. A sign hung at its entrance. 'No dogs or Chinese allowed,' it read. Dogs were put ahead of Chinese! We were barred from our own soil!

"China's fall from greatness is a matter of shame for all living Chinese. This loss of face cannot be wiped away by merely allowing China to take its place among the so-called 'family of nations'. The rectification of China's historic grievances requires not merely diplomatic equality—we enjoy this already—but strategic dominance. The world needs a hegemon. Fate decreed that the hegemon of the nineteenth century would be 'Little Britain'. Fate decreed that the hegemon of the twentieth century would be the United States. And fate shall decree that the hegemon of the twenty-first century and beyond shall be China!

"We have built up our country out of the ruins of Western devastation. Economically, and yes, militarily. Thanks to the efforts of Premier Wang and Vice Premier Su, we have made it through the Asian economic crisis while maintaining near double digit growth. We have heard about our military advances, thanks to the excellent work of Vice Chairman Li and the PLA Chiefs-of-Staff."

Fu noted the absence of Defense Minister Han's name.

His voice began to swell in volume. "The Americans speak of Manifest Destiny. I am here to tell you that China has a manifest destiny of its own. It is destined to recover its traditional place in the world. We will be once again the Middle Kingdom, the kingdom at the center of the earth. We will once again be *tianxia*, the ruler of all under heaven!"

Chairman Han shouted the last sentence, and the group rewarded him with thunderous applause. Fu's chest swelled with pride—both nationalistic and personal.

"The lowering of the Union Jack in Hong Kong is a start," Chairman Han continued, his voice quieter now. "This has redeemed China's painful humiliation at the hands of the British in the Opium Wars. The Japanese were crushed in World War Two. The collapse of the Soviet Union has brought the Central Asian republics closer to us once again. All of this is good.

"But there is one country that has not been punished by history. One country which struts about the world stage. One country which bombs our embassies. Which sends its warships up and down our coasts. Which keeps China divided from its island province. Which keeps troops in our tributary states. This country's arrogance knows no bounds.

"I am sure that you all recall when I invited the American President to Beijing University for a joint press conference. But do you remember what he did? He *lectured* me about human rights. In my own country. In our national university. He lectured *me*, the Chairman of the Chinese Communist Party, the President of the People's Republic of China!

"At that moment, all China was insulted." Chairman Han's face went red with the remembrance. "I smiled at him through clenched teeth. Inwardly, I was furious. How dare he insult me in front of my people, I thought.

"Everywhere we look, we are hemmed in by the Americans. They have usurped the role of world hegemon, and threaten world peace. They promote a cold war mentality, now directed at us. They are expanding NATO eastward to check our ambitions in Central Asia. They are the principal prop of the Japanese. They are expanding the US-Japan alliance westward to check our rightful ambitions in the Pacific. They threaten and invade smaller countries, in order to bring them to heel. They use international economic organizations to control the flow of trade and investments in their favor.

"It is time for this to stop!" His voice rose once again to a crescendo. "It is time for the US to get out of Asia! It is time for the Seventh Fleet to leave our territorial waters. It is time for the American occupying troops to leave South Korea and allow the reunification of China's traditional ally under a pro-Beijing regime. It is time for Taiwan to rejoin the motherland!"

Once again the room exploded into applause. Fu found himself leaning forward in his seat in expectation, certain now that Chairman Han was going to announce that the invasion plan—*his* invasion plan—was going forward.

The Chairman looked at him, and seemed to smile. "This is the Year of the Dragon," he said quietly. "The leadership of the CCP, after extended debate, has unanimously decided to undertake Operation Dragon Strike. As a first step in the recovery of Taiwan, we will take Quemoy in a combined air, naval, and amphibious assault. The fall of Quemoy will force Taiwan into a political accommodation. Once Taiwan starts down that path, of course, it will eventually become ours."

The Chairman continued to speak, but Fu was no longer listening. He couldn't believe what he had just heard. The attack would be limited to Quemoy! Taiwan itself would be spared! Quemoy! A miserable little island only five miles long and three miles wide. The Chairman continued to speak but Fu was no longer listening.

"Half measures will never work," he blurted out. "You just buy time for the US to bring its great strength to bear." Fu was struggling—unsuccessfully—to keep the anger and disappointment out of his voice. "The shock of losing Quemoy will lead the US to arm Taiwan with the most modern weapons. A ballistic missile defense system will be deployed. US warships will again patrol the Taiwan Straits. Taiwan will be lost for a generation."

His voice trailed off as he realized what he had done. He had just interrupted, no, contradicted, the Chairman of the Chinese Communist Party in open session. What had he been thinking? He stood up quickly and bowed.

"Please forgive my impertinence, Chairman Han," he managed to mumble, then turned quickly and practically ran out of the room.

The secret conclave had ended that same afternoon. *And with it my career*, thought Fu Zemin morosely as he watched from the window of his *bieshu* as China's senior leaders departed one by one in their chauffeur-driven Mercedes Benzes.

He had just begun to pack his travel bags when a knock came at the door. He recognized his visitor as a member of Chairman Han's personal staff. "The Chairman would like to have dinner with you tonight," his visitor said, smiling.

Fu felt his heart leap within his breast. He could barely contain his excitement for the two hours' wait until dinner was to begin.

The Minister of the Interior, Ren Baisha, was alone with Chairman Han and Premier Wang. Ren looked grim, "If the Nationalist troops on Quemoy go on alert in the next few days, we will know that word of this meeting has reached them. It will confirm our conjecture that their spies have penetrated the upper echelons of the People's Government."

"Yes, but who?" Chairman Han said thoughtfully. "How much in the way of foreign investments does the Defense Minister have?"

"Our investigation turned up approximately 350 million. That's US dollars, not our own currency," the Interior Minister replied. "There may be more. The Swiss banks are particularly tight-lipped."

"Ahh . . ." murmured the premier, who had trouble conceiving of such a number. His own private investments, assembled from the hundreds of bribes that had come his way, totaled just a fraction of that.

"Why so much?" Chairman Han queried.

"When you forced the PLA to divest its holdings a couple of years ago Han Fubai made sure he was first in line to grab a small chunk of each spun off company," the Interior Minister replied. "Han sells everything from diesel generators to AK-47s overseas. His biggest market is the United States. The Defense Minister's annual income is something in the neighborhood of 30 million dollars. . . ."

The three of them silently contemplated that figure for a few minutes.

"The most interesting thing that we uncovered was a stake in several major Taiwan corporations," Ren continued. "Han Fubai is heavily invested on the island. There are frequent communications between his son, who is his business representative in Hong Kong, and certain individuals in Taiwan."

Chairman Han arched his eyebrows. "So you think . . ."

"The Minister of Defense *was* adamantly opposed to the invasion plan that Fu Zemin put forward," Ren reminded him. "This may be more than just a desire to protect his business empire. Han Fubai may be a defeatist, or he may be a . . ." Ren paused so his listeners could fill in the blank.

"What about Su Zhongqiang?" Chairman Han queried. "He also opposed our plans."

"Old Su is no traitor," Premier Wang answered. " 'War is bad for business, Fuguo,' he told me. 'After the Tiananmen incident, foreign investment dried up for a couple of years.' But then they came back, I pointed out, more eager than ever to build their factories here."

"I talked to him also," Minister Ren added. "I told him that our little action against Quemoy would be over in a matter of days. The capitalists need China's cheap labor and huge market too much to boycott us. He just shook his head and complained about the shock to the economy."

"We don't need a defeatist like him," Chairman Han said decisively. "Fuguo, I suggest you offer him an honorable retirement." Premier Wang nodded silently.

"Is there anyone else who's wavering?" Han asked already knowing the answer.

"Everyone else is with us," Ren assured his comrades.

Fu Zemin was escorted to the Chairman's quarters. The Chairman greeted him like an old friend, asking him to take the place of honor directly across from him at the table. "You know Minister Ren and Premier Wang, of course," the Chairman said, introducing the two others at the table.

The servers, young women selected for their grace and beauty, began to noiselessly bring delicacies to the table.

"Try some of this Dry Roasted Chicken," the Chairman suggested, delicately picking up one of the choicest pieces with his chopsticks and placing it on Fu's plate.

"You're too polite," Fu responded nervously, embarrassed by the Chairman's attentions. "I'll help myself." He popped the piece into his mouth immediately to show his appreciation. It felt like his mouth had been invaded by a torchlight procession. The Chairman, being from Shanghai, liked his food hot, Fu recalled too late. He could scarcely stop his eyes from watering.

"Little too hot, eh?" the Chairman chuckled. "You know my cook buys everything locally for me when we travel, everything except the hot peppers. Wherever we go he brings along a case of Hunan peppers, the hottest in China. Without them the food would be tasteless."

Minister Ren and Premier Wang smiled knowingly.

Now initiated into the inner circle, Fu just nodded dumbly, still unable to speak.

The other dishes proved as hot as the first, and Fu picked his way gingerly through the rest of the meal. The Chairman ate heartily, belched to show his appreciation of the cuisine, and then got down to business.

"You found my Hunan hot peppers a little too hot for your taste," he began with a smile. "Just so, some of my colleagues found your plan to invade Taiwan a little too hot for their taste."

"Please forgive my stupidity," Fu began apologizing. "I lack experience . . ."

The Chairman cut him off with a wave of his hand. "Don't apologize," he said. "Those of us seated at this table appreciate . . . no, we share . . . your breadth of vision. And although we can't adopt your plan to launch a full-scale attack on Taiwan itself at this time, we will incorporate important elements of it in Operation Dragon Strike, the assault on Quemoy. Your proposed diversions in Korea, the Mideast, and East Timor will all be used to thin the American ranks.

"To show our appreciation we are appointing you Special Emissary of the CCP Central Committee to the Fuzhou Military Region, which has overall responsibility for Dragon Strike. You will be the Party's eyes and ears in Fujian."

Fu opened his mouth but found he was unable to speak. A broad, sunlit path of advancement had opened before him, dazzling him with hope and promise. His grandest ambitions were about to be realized.

"And there is one more thing, Zemin," the Chairman said paternally, calling him by his given name for the first time. "In your capacity as Special Emissary you will report to me personally."

The path led to the very top. "Yes, Mr. Chairman," was all that Fu was finally able to say.

11
Only Son—Dusheng Dz

The road began to climb as soon as it left the suburbs of Amoy City. Chu Dugen, newly promoted to the rank of Lieutenant Colonel in the People's Liberation Army, bore down on the accelerator of the jeep he was driving. He zipped his parka up a little further against the February chill in the drafty four-by-four. Chu smiled in anticipation of the stir the jeep would cause in his native village. The vehicle leapt forward despite the grade, and he passed a slower-moving bus. Always before he had ridden such a bus back to the county seat, and then had to hitch a ride on a produce truck up the mountain to his village. Not this time. This time he would drive into the village in his own jeep, wearing the bright new stars of his new rank. "Dugen is now a Lieutenant Colonel!" the children would run about saying, "and he has his own jeep!"

Of course it wasn't *his* jeep. Lieutenant Colonels didn't have their own jeeps, at least not in PLA commando units. It was on loan from the commanding officer of his regiment, who had not wanted to give him leave just two days before his battalion was due to ship out. "Take my jeep, Dugen," Colonel Lin had said finally, handing over the keys this morning. "It'll save you time. But be back tomorrow night without fail. Jia Battalion's orders are top priority—and top secret. Even I don't know where you are going, or the special command to which you will be attached."

Neither did Chu, of course, but he had wanted to see his parents before he left—and to show off his new rank. It would give his father face, and his mother pleasure.

At 178 centimeters, Chu was tall for a southern Chinese. He had inherited his father's muscular frame and iron will. That, combined with his mother's piercing eyes and quiet intelligence, had placed him first in every classroom test and field competition since he had graduated from the PLA academy thirteen years before—and unexpectedly given him an extra star two years before his classmates. *This farmer's son has beaten the general's sons,* he thought to himself, still astonished at his good fortune. *Of course, a large part of your good fortune happens to be linked to Tiananmen Square and the fact that the platoon of southern farmers' sons you led willingly felled so many elitist college students that day.* Chu frowned as he usually did when thinking of the events in Tiananmen Square. . .

The road dipped into a familiar valley, the traffic began picking up again, and the outskirts of the Lipu City came into view. New two- and three-story shops closed in on both sides of the road, cutting off Chu's view of the surrounding rice paddies. He came up behind a truck loaded dangerously high with bags of fertilizer and was forced to slow to a crawl before finding an opening in the oncoming traffic to pass. As always, he was amazed at how this once-poor mountain town had grown in the years he had been gone. He had gone to the Lipu Number One High School when the town had a population of perhaps 20,000, and the largest building was the Lipu County Communist Party headquarters. Then the main road had been narrow and dirty, noisy from dawn till dusk with the sound of peasants hawking produce, and often so crowded with foot traffic that bicyclists had to dismount.

In the past 10 years the town had doubled in size. The main road had been widened and paved, and was lined with new construction. The hawkers had been relocated to an open-air farmer's market. Pedestrians no longer reigned supreme, having been forced to the sides of the road by an arrogant stream of cars, trucks and motorcycles. The largest building was now a Taiwanese-owned factory that produced extruded plastic toys for the American market. The Party headquarters, by comparison, looked small and dowdy, as if the economic reform had left it behind. *But that's not true*, Chu chided himself, remembering his political training. *The Party is responsible for all this progress.*

Chu accelerated again as he exited Lipu, anxious to make up for the time he had lost. The road left the valley and now began to climb in earnest. For a while rice terraces staggered up the hills after it, but then, as if exhausted by the climb, gave way to stands of broken corn stalks—harvest was long past—and the occasional orchard. Chu had the road largely to himself now. He enjoyed the challenge of following its twists and turns, accelerating as it dipped through narrow mountain valleys and then shifting down as it headed upward once more.

Chu's stomach growled, reminding him that he hadn't eaten since breakfast. No matter. His mother knew that he was returning home for a visit. He had called before leaving his army camp in Amoy. By now she would have started preparing a welcome home feast in honor of her only son and his promotion. There would be seven dishes, he estimated, mentally ticking them off—lean pork, fried fish, steamed prawns, broiled chicken, scrambled eggs with diced green onions, mixed vegetables with pork cubes and peanuts, and winter bokchoi, all stir-fried to his taste with just the right amount of peanut oil and pork drippings. Plus a large plate of Lipu's famous sweet oranges sliced into wedges for dessert. The thought of all this food brought another rumble from his stomach. Army food, even in the officers' mess, had nothing to compare with his mother's cooking.

And he had such good news for his parents! He had been selected for Lieutenant Colonel far ahead of his year group, and was being sent to a special command for intensive training.

The road became a series of switchbacks as it made the final climb to his village. This part of the road had been little more than a goat trail when Chu was growing up, but his father, the village head, had taken the lead in widening it two decades ago. "If we only have a real road," he had told his fellow villagers, "we can get our crops to market." Energized by his father's vision, driven by his iron will, twenty sandal-shod, black-jacketed men had worked tirelessly through the slack months of winter with adzes and shovels. By spring a road wide enough for a walking tractor and a narrow trailer had been carved out of the mountainside.

Buried in the mountains to the northwest of Lipu, possessing no rice paddy at all, Chu's village had been the poorest of a county of poor villages. But the road had transformed it, just as his father had promised it would. No longer limited to what a man could carry on his back, the villagers began sending trailerloads of produce to the Lipu market. His father and uncle, seeing that oranges grown at this altitude were sweet and without blemish, set about clearing additional land and planting trees. When the wisdom of their actions became apparent after a couple of years, the other villagers had joined them planting orchards of their own. The road had been widened further, until a 2-1/2-ton truck could make the journey.

The road crested into a small plateau, covered as far as the eye could see with orange groves. The village sat in the middle of this green opulence, several dozen new homes and a few older ones surrounding the old church. Of course it hadn't been a real church for decades. The Irish priest who had built it had been driven out by the Red Army, and the building itself had been "returned to the people." From the fifties through the seventies it had served as the headquarters of the agricultural collective, until the commune system was abandoned in turn and the land it controlled was returned to the villagers. It now served as the headquarters of the village council and all-around meeting hall, but it was still called, despite everything, "the old church." *The Irish priest had built well*, Chu reflected.

Chu pulled up in front of his father's house, surprised to see a white Toyota Landcruiser with government plates already parked there. Several young boys from the village ran up and, playing soldier, saluted smartly as he exited the jeep. Chu returned the salute.

"Are you a general yet, Uncle Dugen?" one of the boys asked hopefully.

Chu recognized the face of his cousin's son. "No, just a lowly Lieutenant Colonel," he laughed, pointing at the two bright stars that adorned his yellow epaulet. The boys were appropriately awed at this insignia of rank and called out to their fellows to come see.

From inside the house came the sound of raised voices. Chu frowned. "Who's come to visit?" he asked the boys, pointing at the government Toyota.

"Secretary Fu," came the reply.

For as long as Chu could remember, Fu Mingjie had been the head of the Lipu Party Committee. He was an arrogant little man, originally from Shantung province in the north, who was widely detested for both his manner and his accent. Thirty years in Lipu, and he had never bothered to learn the Fukienese dialect of these parts. Instead, he demanded that everyone speak to *him* in Mandarin. In the opinion of the people, he was a corrupt Party official. Not that the opinion of the people mattered. Fu was said to be very well connected in the Party hierarchy.

The voices grew louder, and the door of the house opened.

"I would rethink your position if I were you," he heard Secretary Fu say loudly in his tongue-twisting northern accent. "If you use our trucks, you won't have to pay the road tax."

"So now it's the road tax, is it?" his father shouted back in his own rough approximation of standard Chinese. "Don't forget who built the road in the first place!"

"All roads are the property of the people's government . . ." Fu broke off in mid-sentence as he saw a tall, uniformed officer of the PLA walking up to him.

"You remember my son, *Lieutenant Colonel* Chu Dugen," his father said, emphasizing Chu's new rank.

If Secretary Fu was impressed he didn't show it. "Since you have visitors, I'll be going," he said curtly, with the barest hint of a nod at Chu. "Think well on what I have said."

"*Bu song,*" Chu's father said, "I'll see you on your way." The traditional words of parting sounded distinctly unfriendly on his tongue.

Chu watched Fu drive away, then turned to his father with a quizzical glance. "What was all that about?"

"*Mafan,*" his father answered angrily. "Trouble. It's always trouble when he comes around." He fumbled a pack of cigarettes out of his pocket and lit one up.

Chu noticed that his father's hands were shaking badly. "What kind of trouble?" he pursued.

His father took a deep drag on his cigarette, holding the smoke in his lungs for a few seconds before exhaling. "It would be easier if he just came right out and asked for a bigger payoff," he said, calmer now. "Instead, he has set up what he calls a shipping company—using county government trucks, mind you—and wants us to pay him for shipping our oranges to Amoy City."

"What's wrong with that?"

"What's wrong with that!?!" his father sputtered. "What's wrong with that is that he wants to charge about five times the going rate for freight. We bought our own truck two years ago. We can ship our own fruit to market for the cost of diesel fuel and a driver."

"So do it," Chu said.

"I told him I intended to," his father replied. "That's when he imposed a new tax on shipments between villages. 'A road tax' he called it. Of course, if we use his trucks, we don't have to pay. So we're damned if we do and damned if we don't!" He threw the half-smoked cigarette down and ground it into the dirt. "He's a corrupt Party official, Dugen! A parasite on the working class!"

The conversation had veered onto dangerous ground, Chu thought. All Party bosses were corrupt to some degree. It went with the system. The Party had periodic campaigns to try and control corruption. Sometimes they kept it within manageable limits. More often not. "Surely it can't be as bad as all that," he said, trying to calm his father down. "You usually get along well with Secretary Fu."

"I have never gotten along with Secretary Fu!" his father snorted. "Twenty years ago your uncle and I started clearing wasteland and planting citrus groves. Fu encouraged us, telling us that we would be exempt from taxes. It was backbreaking work, and before the trees were firmly rooted we had to haul water with buckets and carrying poles. Each year we expanded, until we now have 160 mou under cultivation. Then when the crops started coming in, and we began to make money, he began showing up and demanding a cut."

This was news to Chu. "You mean taxes?"

"Taxes, dogshit!" his father burst out. "He wanted to line his own pocket. He demanded a payoff. If we didn't pay up, he told us that he would declare that we had planted the trees illegally on public land. We were afraid that the orchards would be confiscated, so we paid up. Every year since have given him about a third of our profits. He keeps track of how many truckloads of oranges we take to market, and comes over after the harvest to demand what he calls 'his share.' His share! The bloodsucker has never done an honest day's work in his life!" His voice took on a raw edge of anger. "He wants us to be his serfs again, just like under the commune system!"

"Father, Father, calm down," Chu said uneasily, taken aback by his father's unaccustomed vehemence. "Let's go see the orchards. I need to stretch my legs." *And get you off this dangerous subject*, he thought to himself.

A few strides took them into the nearest grove. This had been one of the earliest plantings, and the trees now towered twice as high as a man's head. They walked in silence for a few minutes. The luxuriant green foliage had a calming effect, and Chu sensed that his father's mood was beginning to shift.

His father began to talk, slowly at first, and then with increasing enthusiasm as they walked on. There was land to be cleared for another planting. There was next year's harvest to be estimated. The cooperative—voluntary, his father stressed—was to be expanded to include a couple of neighboring villages. They came to the edge of the orchard. "We've come this far," Chu's father urged. "Let's walk to the top of Turtle Knob. From there you can see the whole plateau. We're planting another ten mou on the slopes this winter."

Chu needed no convincing. From the time he was a little boy, he had always loved listening to his father describe his plans for the future. Each time his father had made his vision a reality. By strength of back and dint of will, his father had made a road, had planted an orchard, had prospered a village. His father was a man of his word, loved and trusted by all, and by no one more than his only son.

From the top of Turtle Knob, the orchards made an impressive sight, covering the entire plateau and running halfway up the gentle hills beyond. Someday, his father said, orange groves would run all the way to the top.

Chu had not the slightest doubt this would be the case. His father was a force of nature. He remembered a time when nothing but brush and scrub had covered these hills. He had spent hours walking their lower slopes, gathering grass, twigs, and anything that would burn for the cookstove in his mother's old kitchen lean-to. Now, thanks to the muscular, determined man standing beside him, those same slopes were covered with neat lines of orange trees. Now his mother cooked with propane in a bright, new tiled kitchen. And she cooked very well.

The entire village was at the Chu's that night. The men gathered around four circular tables that had been set up in the main room, the women retired to the kitchen to help with the last-minute preparations, while the children ran about, giggling and laughing, entertaining themselves.

As soon as the men were seated, Chu's father and uncle opened the several liters of rice liquor that Chu had brought from the base commissary. The liquor went directly from the bottles into the rice bowls that sat in front of each man. The rice would not be served until they had finished this bowl and more.

Chu's uncle then stood up, gestured for silence, and turned to face his nephew. *"Wo jing Zhongxiao Tongzhi yi bei!"* he said loudly, cupping his hands around his bowl in a posture of supplication, "I respectfully offer Comrade Lieutenant Colonel a toast." His mock formality caused great guffaws of laughter.

Chu leapt to his feet. *"Wo jing Bofu yi bei,"* he replied, "I respectfully offer my father's elder brother a toast."

Chu and his uncle both raised their bowls high in a sign of mutual respect before bringing them to their lips. While Chu's uncle downed a couple swallows of the fiery contents, Chu himself took only a small sip. He had been a guest of honor at a feast before. He knew what was coming. If he wanted to be on his feet at the end of the evening, he had to pace himself.

The room was boisterous with congratulations. Everyone insisted on toasting his promotion—one at a time. *"Ganbei,"* each of the men challenged him in their turn, holding his bowls high. "Bottoms up."

"Suiyi," he replied time and time again, "just a sip." He received several dozen toasts in quick and pungent succession. His uncle followed him around with the bottle, grinning, making sure his bowl stayed full.

Then he saw his father, who had been quiet up to that point, start to rise from his seat. "I respectfully offer my father a toast," Chu said quickly before his father could speak. "I owe you everything that I am." He lifted his bowl high with both hands, waited for his father to do the same, then took a sip.

His father slugged down the entire bowl of liquor in a single motion, eliciting "oohs" and "aahs" from his watching friends. Then he turned it upside down and shook it to show his son that not even a drop remained. *"Ganbei,"* he said firmly, with only a hint of a smile.

There was nothing Chu could do. Everyone's eyes were upon him. *"Ganbei,"* he said, shrugging helplessly, draining his own bowl in turn. His uncle was quick to refill it.

Then it was his turn to salute them. He raised his bowl to each in turn, careful to say *"Suiyi"* and take only a sip. Still, by the time he finished, there was a light, pleasant buzz in his head.

The first round of toasting came to an end with much laughing and joking. "I have more good news for you all," Chu couldn't resist saying. "I've been selected to head an elite battalion of commandos. Except for our political officer, it's an all-Fukienese-speaking unit."

Chu himself wasn't sure of the significance of this last fact. But it sounded mysterious and important to those present, who, like all Chinese, held their own province—in this case, Fukien—in high regard.

This announcement set off another round of toasting, though by this point in the evening the men scarcely needed an excuse. Chu's father rose, wobbly and unsmiling, to toast him again, and downed another great bowl of rice liquor.

The women had been listening from the kitchen, and before the men drank too much on empty stomachs began serving platter after platter of food. It turned out that Chu had underestimated his mother. In addition to the dishes on his imaginary menu she had added a broiled goose, a rare delicacy and his favorite. Steaming in its succulent juices, chopped into chopstick-sized pieces, she placed it in front of him with a smile. Chu reached out with his chopsticks and deftly snared a prime slice of goose. No one else would eat until the guest of honor had taken the first bite. He popped it in his mouth. It was delicious. "*Hao chi*," he pronounced. "Good to eat."

With that, everyone else tucked into the heaping platters of food with abandon. Everyone, that is, except Chu's father. He seemed more interested in the bottle of rice liquor sitting beside his bowl. Chu reached out with his chopsticks and attempted to put a slice of goose on his father's plate, but his father stopped him. "I'll serve myself," he said gruffly, and took a drink out of his bowl instead.

As the evening progressed, Chu noted that his father's mood seemed to darken further. He, who had always taken great pride in his son's accomplishments, didn't respond to his son's efforts to talk about his promotion or his new command. He took no notice of the talk and laughter that went swirling around him. Chu lost count of the number of times he refilled his bowl. If he doesn't stop, Chu thought, he's going to drink himself into a stupor.

His mother apparently shared his opinion, because she came over and attempted to fill up her husband's bowl with rice. He roughly pushed the rice scoop away. "Can't you see that it's already full, woman!" he slurred, pointing to the clear liquor in his bowl.

Chu regarded his father's red face with astonishment. He had never seen him drunk before.

Chu's father drained his bowl once again, refilled it, and then lurched to his feet. "A toast!" he shouted thickly, "I'd like to propose a toast." A dozen conversations died as everyone in the room turned to regard him. "I'd like to propose a toast to Secretary Fu Mingjie."

Secretary Fu was not a popular figure in Chu's village. The sound of his name was greeted by a muttered round of curses.

"I toast this corrupt, rapacious official," Chu's father said in a ominous tone. "We break our backs to make a living, and he drives around sucking our lifeblood. I toast this parasite! I toast this son of a bitch-dog." Chu's father lifted his bowl high, then flung it against the wall. It shattered into a dozen pieces with a loud crash.

He started to sway, and instantly Chu was at his side. "Why don't you go rest for awhile, Father," he said softly.

But his father grabbed onto the table and pulled himself up to his full height. "I swear before the tablets of my ancestors," he said slowly and distinctly. "If Secretary Fu harms my family again, I will kill him."

Chu half-carried, half-walked his drunken father out of the room. He was snoring as soon as he hit the bed.

Chu's uncle tried to make light of his younger brother's outburst, but the threat had cast a pall over the evening's festivities. The guests looked self-consciously at one another, and one by one excused themselves for the night. The room was soon empty.

When Chu came back into the central room, his mother was clearing the tables alone. "You go to bed, son," she said to him. "I'll clean up."

Chu didn't want to go to bed, at least not until he'd solved the mystery of his father. He carried a stack of rice bowls into the kitchen. "I always thought we got along well with Fu Mingjie," he said when he came back out.

His mother, who was wiping a table, stopped and looked at him. "We've always *pretended* to get along with him," she responded, "ever since he came to the village as an arrogant young official thirty years ago at the end of the Cultural Revolution." She started wiping the table again. "But your father has never forgiven him," she added in a low voice.

Chu was puzzled. "What do you mean, mother? Forgiven him for what? For demanding bribes?"

"The bribes came later," his mother responded. She moved to another table and continued to wipe. "A long time ago, when Fu was a junior official, he was in charge of the one-child policy in this part of the county. When population control first began." She took a deep breath and let out a sigh. "I was pregnant when the policy was announced. But since it was our first, your father and I thought we had nothing to worry about."

A look of inexpressible sadness came across her face. "Then we discovered that I was carrying twins."

Twins? Chu blinked in surprise. He had been a twin? He had always thought that he was an only child, the first of a generation of only children born under the one-child-per-couple rule. More than three-quarters of the men in his unit were *dusheng dz*, only sons. The military preferred them. They needed less training to kill on command.

"Fu told us we had to choose," his mother said, her eyes welling up with tears. "I couldn't choose. I wouldn't choose. But Fu said chose we must. 'We want the boy,' your father said, picking you up."

"And what happened to my . . . sister?" The word sounded strange on his tongue. He had had a twin *sister*.

His mother's shoulders slumped over and her chest began to heave. The sound of sobbing filled the air—and went on long enough for Chu to regret a dozen times over ever having asked the question. His mother only gradually regained her composure enough to speak.

"They did . . ." her voice broke. She made a visible effort to pull herself together, and started over. "They did what they always do with . . . with illegal children. They gave her a poison shot. She was killed at Fu Mingjie's orders."

"Why that son of a bitch-dog," Chu cursed. "That turtle's egg . . ."

"Don't talk like that, Dugen," his mother broke in. "You sound just like your father. What I just told you happened a long, long time ago. I am at peace about all of this. Your twin sister is with God, and I know that I will one day see her again. I have even forgiven Secretary Fu, though it took me many years to do so."

"I have told your father that he must forgive and forget, too," she went on, "but he will not listen to me. He is still filled with hate whenever he thinks about what happened to our daughter. Lately, he had even begun talking again about revenge. It doesn't help that Fu's demands for money have been escalating. When your father sees Fu he is filled with an almost uncontrollable rage. All I can do is pray for both of them."

Chu was a professional warrior. He knew that his father had been ready to kill tonight. And now his mother was telling him that she had seen him rage like this before. But it was her last word that he picked up on: "Pray?"

"Yes, pray," his mother answered firmly. "I never told you this before, but I am a Christian. I was baptized as a small girl by Father O'Reilly, the missionary priest."

"The imperialist spy, you mean!" Chu spat out with more vehemence than he intended, suddenly, irrationally angry over the loss of his sister.

"No, Dugen," she came back quietly yet sternly, in the same tone of voice she had used when correcting him as a small child. "Father O'Reilly was a kind man, who saved the entire village from dying of starvation when the Japanese occupied Amoy City. He went without food—he called it fasting—so that the rest of us could eat. Then when the Red Army came, they said he was a spy, and none of us dared say otherwise. But he was no spy."

Chu's head was spinning. This was too much to absorb in one night. His twin sister dead. His mother a secret Christian. The pillars of his world were collapsing one by one and he was left standing in the ruins.

His mother looked at him beseechingly. "Your father will not listen to me," she said. "But he will listen to you. Talk to your father tomorrow morning. Tell him that if he does anything to Fu it will ruin your career."

"Goodnight Mother." Stunned into deep thought, Chu brushed past his mother and made his way to bed.

Chu slept fitfully, then woke before daybreak and slipped out of his childhood home. He didn't talk to his father. He could not believe that, whatever had happened in the past, his father would strike out at the local party boss. To do so would be suicide. His parents were still asleep when he got in his jeep and drove back to base.

12

Quemoy and Quagmire

It was Fu's first visit back to Beijing since being assigned the previous month as Special Emissary of the CCP Central Committee to the Fuzhou Military District. In the City for only half a day, Fu was forbidden to see his wife and child—they thought he was in Baghdad on a secret diplomatic mission.

Fu waited only five minutes outside Chairman Han Wudi's office before a uniformed aide opened the door. Fu looked inside the Chairman's personal office for the first time. He fought back an urge to scan the room.

Chairman Han stood up. Chief Advisor Soo, already standing, the ever-present cigarette never far from his thin face, smiled. Chairman Han motioned him to one side of the office and led the other two men into a much smaller room equipped with four comfortable chairs, a small table, and a tea service. Soo snuffed out his cigarette and was the last to enter and close the door. It shut with a muffled sound. Fu noticed it was a very thick door.

The Chairman locked his eyes on Fu, "Well now, Zemin, you've been in Fujian long enough to get an opinion on our preparations, how are we doing?"

Fu was unprepared for the informality; his two days of preparation to give an official briefing were wasted, "Ah, Comrade Chairman. . ."

Chairman Han sat back in his chair, arms draped over the arm rests, "Relax, Zemin. I need your opinions, not a stiff presentation. Tea?"

Soo immediately poured tea into the three cups.

"Now, tell me about the invasion of Quemoy."

"Sir, all the military preparations are on track. We appear to be getting the priority we need for supplies and training. The Air Force has been a little slow to respond to our requests, but we have seen a marked improvement in their cooperation in the last week.

"I do have two major concerns, however," the Chairman and his Chief Military Advisor sat slightly forward in their chairs, "I worry that Admiral Wong has placed too much emphasis on rehearsals and I get little news as to our efforts to draw American attention to other areas."

Han spoke, "Wingji, I believe you can bring Zemin up to date."

Soo, looking a little uncomfortable without his cigarette, began, "We know about, and agree with Admiral Wong's plan to conduct several rehearsal amphibious assaults prior to the actual invasion. It is actually part of a long-standing contingency plan."

"To give away our strategic surprise?" Fu was incredulous.

If Soo was insulted, he didn't show it, "No. We believe it would be impossible to achieve strategic surprise over Taiwan anyway. Our plan is designed to achieve tactical surprise. Have you studied Egypt's attack across the Suez Canal in 1973 against Israel?"

"Yes. Yes!" Fu's eyes lit up, "The Egyptians practiced mock assaults for years. This did two things: they became well-practiced and their enemy became used to the motions. When the actual attack came, the Israelis thought it was another drill!"

"Precisely," Soo responded.

"But we don't have years. . ."

"True, but I bet that the Taiwanese will begin to relax after our third or fourth practice assault—after all, they have money to make. Sounding the alarm every time we move is bad for business, investors hate it. They'll get used to our moves in time. . ."

"Then we invade," Fu's eyes gleamed.

"Then we invade," Soo echoed.

Chairman Han watched this exchange with interest.

"What about the Americans?" Fu suddenly shifted gears.

Han's face darkened at the mention of the United States.

Soo pursed his lips and nodded his head, then glanced at Han. "The Americans are being wound so tight they won't know what to do when we strike. We have begun sending military supplies to the Democratic People's Republic of Korea and Iraq. We've also helped the Iranians install several new anti-ship missile batteries in the Straits of Hormuz. Most importantly, we have strengthened our network of agents in Indonesia. Anytime we wish we can cause that conglomeration of a 'nation' to fall apart."

"I have been unable to get detailed news of the Americans on East Timor, what about them?" Fu asked.

Soo smiled expansively and was about to begin when Chairman Han spoke up, "You'll be pleased to hear that the Marine division in Okinawa left two days ago for East Timor. It seems 'rouge' Indonesian Army elements have made life uncomfortable for the

UN peacekeepers there. The UN asked for reinforcements. Naturally, we supported the vote." Now Han smiled, "We are even contributing a battalion of police officers. I would say that East Timor, and perhaps even Indonesia, could become a long and costly commitment for the Americans."

"May I ask, when did we start our East Timor initiative?"

"Within a week of your recommendation last December. Even without the invasion of. . ." Han hesitated, ". . .Quemoy, the East Timor initiative had its own merits. As I said, we find your ideas interesting. . ."

The three men chuckled with Soo laughing a little too hard.

13
Spin Up

In India, northeast of the Indus River near the Kunlun Mountains and a patch of rugged territory in dispute between India and the People's Republic of China, a small, unmanned US monitoring station picked up some ground motion. This was not unusual. The station was located near the convergence of three tectonic plates. Earthquakes were quite common in the area. The monitoring station dutifully sent its data to an overhead commercial satellite that routed it around the globe to the regional US Geological Services office in Hawaii. Because the epicenter of this quake was within a certain zone of interest, the data was also routed automatically to a large, tree surrounded office complex in Northern Virginia named after the 41st President of the United States who was its one-time director. There, a few days later, the data were examined and compared with readings from a similar station in Kyrgyzstan as well as from the international civilian seismograph network.

*   *   *

Donna had been working with the East Timor crisis team for more than two months now. She tried to keep up with the steady flow of data from China, but it was growing increasingly difficult, especially now that US Marines were dying and evidence pointed to Chinese complicity in East Timor's continuing unrest.

The report on the computer monitor began to blur about six inches away from Donna's face. She wanted more coffee, but she was so tired she knew it would only make her shake. *Why are the Chinese sabotaging the peace in Timor? What do they have to gain? They don't even seem to be hiding it. . .*

". . .Ms. Klein, Ms. Klein?"

Donna looked up to see a middle-aged, vaguely familiar man in a white shirt, out of style blue polyester tie and a pocket protector. He was one of the few remaining seismologists the CIA had left after the end of the Cold War and the virtual halt to underground nuclear testing caused most of them to retire or return to academia.

"Ms. Klein. Can we talk?" The man stood hovering over Donna's work area.

Donna sighed. She wanted to go home and catch some sleep. It was almost 9 PM. "Sure. What do you have?"

"Well, we received an indication of some seismic activity in China."

"A quake?"

"Not exactly. Well, at least I don't think so. . ." the man looked very uneasy, almost sick.

Donna didn't have time for games at this time of the night after the fifth consecutive day of less than five hours of sleep. "What the hell do you mean, 'not exactly'?"

The analyst flinched at Donna's retort. He was afraid no one would welcome his hypothesis. "I'm sorry, I didn't mean to bother you, it's just that you have a reputation as someone who views China with a little more suspicion than most."

Donna was almost livid—*a 'reputation'?* "Tell me what you want to say and get it over with. I want to go home, it's late."

The man gulped, "I think the Chinese have conducted four nuclear tests. They were very small and timed in a way to make it look as if it was earthquake aftershock activity." The man blurted the last out as if he wanted to finish his report and run.

"Are you sure?" Donna stared at him with bloodshot eyes.

The man thought about his career. He was only a year away from a decent retirement. *The higher-ups wouldn't like this.* That's why he came to Donna Klein. He looked down at his shoes, "No. I'm fairly sure, but unless they test again in the same area, I can't for certain say they've resumed nuclear testing."

Donna began putting on her walking shoes. "Fine. Look, why don't you send me an e-mail. I'm going home."

It was snowing lightly for the drive home. Donna turned the news on and cranked the radio's volume. She also cracked her window an inch—the freezing air kept her awake. There was another casualty among the peacekeepers in East Timor, this time an Australian. She sighed and was about to switch to a music station when the anchor quickly transitioned. ". . .and in other military news, the White House announced the withdrawal of the nomination of General Smithton for Vice Chairman of the Joint Chiefs. General Smithton's nomination ran into trouble when it was rumored that he pressured a subordinate officer into having sex with him. In a surprise move, the White House nominated Air Force Lieutenant General Timothy Taylor for the post. If the Senate approves the move, the 51-year-old widower will be getting his fourth star and will be elevated to the nation's second highest military post."

Donna remembered Taylor from the war game—*so his interest, if more than professional, wasn't completely out of line.* She rolled her eyes—*the man was 24 years older and it was just a couple of lingering glances...*

*   *   *

Colonel Mike Flint took another sip of his strong, black coffee. Elements of the III Marine Expeditionary Force had landed three weeks ago. As their numbers built up to more than 12,000 Marines, Flint's 31st MEU gradually pulled back and re-supplied. One advantage of performing a real world mission was that his unit received supply priority. His MEU logistics officer could get parts delivered to the middle of nowhere in a week, instead of waiting four months for as was more often the case than not lately (he remembered it was last like this back in '78 when he was a newly minted second lieutenant).

Just as Flint was beginning to enjoy the morning, Lieutenant Colonel Burl, his XO, walked in. Redeemably, Major "Rez" Ramirez, his intelligence officer, was behind him.

"Hank, 'Rez', top of the morning to you! Coffee?" Colonel Flint smiled. The officially worried look on Burl's face was not a good sign.

"Sir, I've just come away from the daily UN staff briefing. It seems the commander of the Chinese police contingent is going to lodge a protest about your refusal to tell him about our operational plans." Burl's tone had a hint of self-justification. He'd warned Flint about the diplomatic minefield he was navigating.

"Who the hell is he going to tattle to? The Secretary General of the United Nations? Hell will freeze over and the President will join the Corps before I tell that sonofabitch when and where my Marines are going! We've already taken twenty-one needless casualties in this 'paradise' and I'll be damned if I'm going to get any more of my boys killed because some communist cop wants in on our plans."

Burl looked ill, "What should I say to the UN command, sir?"

"Don't say a damn thing."

"But. . ." Burl stammered.

"NOT A DAMN THING! Understood?"

Burl nodded silently.

Flint turned to Major Ramirez, "Rez and I have to talk.

78

Alone."

Burl stalked out the door of the white adobe command post.

Flint suddenly looked very old and very tired, "Rez, I just don't know if it's worth my staying on to see the bitter end for this. I can see it coming over the horizon. The bastards send us in to do their dirty work for them. Gradually, their Ivy League sensibilities get the best of them. Before you know it we'll be wearing blue helmets and we'll be left with pocketknives and a government-issued kazoo that we can hum 'Kum-ba-yah' with to all the locals so they can learn to get along with each other. This job isn't fun anymore. In fact, I really hate this job."

Ramirez's bemused look turned gradually to concern as Flint spoke. The colonel looked up and saw the effect his words were having and quickly turned things around, "Rez don't worry. I'm just having a dark moment. I'm sorry I let you see it. It was unprofessional of me. You're one of best officers I've ever had the pleasure of serving with. I take too much advantage of that." Flint smiled broadly and warmly, "As long as I can serve with Marines such as you I'll still love my job just enough to keep coming back for more.

"Say, you must have a reason for coming here. I know you don't pal around with Burl for shits and grins. What's up?" Flint was now completely transformed back to his old self. Ramirez marveled at his commander's resiliency.

Ramirez began slowly, reluctant to destroy his commander's newly reconstructed good mood, "Sir, I just came from the daily Third MEF intel brief. . ."

"And. . .?" Flint asked.

"And things are getting interesting."

"I don't like it when you intel types say 'things are getting interesting.'" Flint was mockingly petulant.

Ramirez chuckled, then in a flash was deadly serious, "Sir, three things. One, we've been told to expect greater activity from the extremist militia groups. Sources say they're being armed and equipped in base camps in Indonesia." Flint rolled his eyes—*this sounded too familiar—base camps, guerrillas. Who said things ever change?* "Rez" continued, "Two, we believe that Indonesian commandos are infiltrating into East Timor in platoon size units. They probably have up to a battalion in East Timor now. They're mainly in and around the Ramelau Mountain region." Ramelau Mountain was Timor's highest peak at 9,490 feet high. It was about 50 kilometers south, southwest of Dili. "Three, Iraq is building up armored forces on its border with Kuwait."

"So, why don't we just bomb them?" Flint demanded.

"Who?"

"Everyone. No, really. In Iraq, I thought we were supposed to be able to head off dangerous concentrations of armor."

"Not really, sir. Besides, Saudi Arabia and the other Gulf Cooperation Council states have really tightened the screws on our use of their airfields. They won't let us bomb Iraq from their bases anymore. We can only fly from Kuwait or from carriers."

Flint did not want to hear what was coming for his already over taxed Marines, "So, what impact does Iraq have on us?"

"Rumor has it that we will not be pulled out in two weeks to return to Okinawa as planned. In fact, the Third MEF may pull out and be sent to the Gulf. They're talking about putting a joint task force in place here and backfilling the Third MEF with Army units."

"That's fine. The Army likes to occupy anyway. Marines get restless after a few months in the same place. Any read on who?"

Ramirez shrugged, "Probably the 25th Infantry Division out of Hawaii. They're close and they're used to working under PACOM."

An urgent knock at the door interrupted the officers' discussion.

"Enter!" Flint's voice boomed authority.

"Colonel," the man nodded at Flint, "Major Ramirez, sorry to bother you here, but this is urgent." It was Gunnery Sergeant Hudson, one of Major Ramirez's intelligence NCOs.

"Go ahead sergeant." Ramirez said.

"Sir, we're getting a report that Ocussi is being overrun by militia. There's looting and burning. Our source on the ground says that a big massacre is in the works."

Ocussi was some 60 miles to the west of East Timor proper. Situated on the north coast, Ocussi was an East Timorese enclave about 40 kilometers wide by 20 kilometers deep completely surrounded by Indonesian territory. For the last three weeks it had been occupied by a company of Thai marines.

Flint jumped up, "Rez, call the Operations officer. I want a warning order to go out within 20 minutes. We may be asked to respond."

In less than 15 minutes the commanders of the Battalion Landing Team, the Aviation Combat Element, and the MEU Service Support Group 31 were all briefed on the potential for a new mission. They began planning the action with their staffs and commanders.

Half an hour later, the Third MEF commander called Colonel Flint, "Mike, this is General Hill."

"Yes sir."

"You hear about Ocussi? The Thai are having their asses handed to them. We need you to go in, guns blazing. If they take too many casualties, we may lose their participation. You have to ride to the rescue."

"Yes sir. I sent out a warning order 30 minutes ago. I can have two rifle companies there within an hour after your order."

Lieutenant General Hill pounced at the good news, "Excellent!"

"Sir, just one question. Can I use my tanks?"

"Negative." Hill clearly didn't even want to hear the question.

"Sir. Ocussi is very hot right now. I could use some tanks to calm things down." Flint's voice was level.

"Very well, if you can get them there in time to be useful, go ahead and try." Hill knew that Flint would have to bring in his LCACs, load the heavy tanks on, one per LCAC, then push 150 kilometers down the coast. It would probably take at least six hours before the M1s would arrive. By then, Colonel Flint's 31st MEU would have taken control of the situation and any controversial use of heavy armor could be avoided. "One more thing Mike. I don't want cluster bombs on your Harriers. Too much of a chance for collateral damage. There's a report of an American news crew in Ocussi. I don't want any footage of Marines slaughtering innocent civilians."

The last statement floored Flint. He opened his mouth before thinking, "General, was the decision about the cluster bombs your own, or did the Pentagon order that one?"

There was a pause as the general processed the comment, "At ease Marine. You'll do your job if all I give you to do it with is a stick! Out!"

And I'd take the stick and shove it up your. . . Flint's thought was interrupted by the crew chief for his Huey. "The bird's ready when you are sir. When're we going?"

"Be ready to fly in ten."

Flint had 12 "Frogs" and six Super Stallions in the air. He was in his Huey. Four Harriers, two Cobras and a Huey in a fire direction control role were already on station over Ocussi. The Thai unit was down to one platoon fighting for its life in a few downtown buildings. One by one the buildings the unit occupied were being set on fire, flushing the hard-pressed Thai troops out into the open and under the withering fire of machine gunners and snipers. The Huey reported seeing a civilian news crew amongst the militia. The Marine air units began to return fire with their cannons and miniguns. They concentrated on destroying any crew served weapons such as mortars or machine guns that might produce heavy casualties against the Marines.

Within sight of Dili the LCACs had embarked the M1s and were making their way to Ocussi at a fuel-gulping 40 knots, trailing a thick spray behind them. They'd arrive a little more than an hour-and-a-half after Golf and Foxtrot Companies had set down. The three ships in the ARG with the remainder of the 31st MEU were also steaming west and would be off shore in a little less than two hours.

Flint decided the area around the besieged Thais was too hot to land on top of. He ordered his BLT commander to land the two rifle companies 1,500 meters up wind of the firefight. One company with attachments from the Heavy Weapons Company would advance with the three LAVs brought by the CH-53s while the other company would remain in reserve by the three 155mm M198 artillery pieces slung in by the other three CH-53s.

Given the constrained and chaotic small urban area below, Flint uncharacteristically decided to stay in the air to orchestrate the fight. He'd let the commander of the 2nd Battalion, 4th Marines, Lieutenant Colonel "Skip" Bailey, do the honors on the ground.

Within minutes of landing, Bailey called in a report that chilled Flint's blood, "Bulldog One, this is Hammer One, over."

Flint heard something in Bailey's voice he had never heard before—something that scared him. "This is Bulldog One, go ahead, over."

"Bulldog One. . . Oh God, sir. . . Umm," Bailey was losing it, "Sir, I think we found some of the Thai troops. They were executed. Beheaded. Sir. . . Oh. . . Shit sir, you're not going to believe this. When we came up on the bodies we caught some of the militia drinking the blood of the Thai soldiers. These guys are friggen nuts sir. Ugghh! I'm going to be. . ." before he could say it, Bailey had wisely un-keyed the mike and barfed.

Flint had remembered reading about the barely suppressed warrior traditions of some of the Indonesian ethnic groups—some of whom still had living relatives who had been cannibals. He had read reports of the ritualistic drinking of the blood of the vanquished in the aftermath of ethnic battles within the year. He never dreamed any of his men would have to face something so barbaric.

"Hammer One, this is Bulldog One, did you capture the perpetrators, over?" Flint asked, not really wanting to hear that his Marines let the men live that did this.

"Bulldog One," Bailey had regained some of his composure, "We have two alive, they're wounded, but I think they'll live." He sounded disappointed.

"Roger. Have a squad stay with them until we can pick them up. I'll send a platoon from the reserve company to secure the EPWs as well as the atrocity site. This is a war crime and someone's going to pay. Out."

The helicopter lurched violently, then dove to the left, "What the hell?" Flint was wide-eyed.

A reddish-orange flash trailed by a thick medium gray smoke whooshed by the open right sliding door and exploded overhead. Flint heard the sharp "plings" and "thuds" of blast fragments on the top of the Huey. He waited for the aircraft to go down.

The pilot and copilot were busy avoiding ground fire, checking their instruments and looking for a place to land, just in case. The strong smell of aviation fuel filled the windy cabin. Hot hydraulic fluid squirted on Flint's back, *shit*, Flint keyed his helmet mike for intercom, "Hey! We're losing fluid." The pilot looked back and keying his intercom said, "I know sir, we've got to set down. Hold on for a rough one!"

The Huey's turbines began to whine at a different frequency. The helicopter started to shake. "Hammer One, we're hit and going down! I say again, we're hit and going down! I'm about one klick to your south. I see a school playground. It looks like we may try to set down there!" Flint called into the mike.

About 100 feet off the ground the Huey's tail rotor began to loose power. The aircraft began to spin, picking up speed as it dropped. They must have done a dozen 360s before they spun into the ground—the force of impact instantly stopped the spin on the skids, while the momentum on the top of the aircraft was still unabated. The Huey savagely twisted over, its rotor biting into the grass, then shattering into a thousand pieces. The helicopter was resting on its left side.

Colonel Flint's left arm felt broken. He unbuckled himself with his right hand and fell six inches (thankfully no more) to the muddy grass beneath him. Pain shot through his arm. He pushed his legs underneath him. The copilot's body looked lifeless and mangled. The pilot was trying to figure out how he could release himself and not fall into his copilot's body or get tangled in his controls.

One of the aircrew released himself and nearly fell on Flint's head. "Sorry sir! I didn't see you!"

"Stuff it and get everyone out of here before we catch fire!"

Just when Flint didn't think it could get worse he heard the rapid pop, pop, pop of small arms fire. Worse yet, he heard a few rounds plink home on the airframe of the downed Huey.

Amazingly, up on the open door frame of what used to the right side of the aircraft, a young Marine was returning fire with rifle. He yelled down into the now smoky shadows of the cabin, "I see about ten of them. There's an RPG! I'll cover! Get out of here, fast!"

Flint stood up. The pilot had just maneuvered out of his seat when a burst of heavy machine gun fire tore through the un-shattered half of the Plexiglas windshield and cut him down. The pilot's blood spattered Flint. He had to blink a few times to see again. Unseen hands lifted him from the chopper. He made it to the blistering daylight and wished he had the cover of darkness as the rounds swished angrily overhead. He rolled to the left onto the engine cowling and then shimmied forward of the turbine intake and fell hard on his left side onto the ground. The bolt of pain from his arm almost forced consciousness from him. A lesser man in a similar situation may have surrendered to the blissfully unaware state, but Colonel Flint had lives to save.

He rolled onto his belly and took in a 180 sweep of the land. About 40 meters away there was a small schoolhouse and a church building. Neither area showed any signs of activity. He forced his pain into submission and stood up. "Marine! Throw me your weapon, now!"

The lance corporal firing out of the right door at the top of the aircraft fired three more rounds, he screamed "I got the guy with the RPG!" He then quickly peaked over the lip what was the top of the doorframe to draw a bead on the colonel. The rifle sailed smoothly into Flint's right hand.

"A magazine, sir!" A 30-round magazine followed and hit the grass next to Flint's feet.

Flint stuck the rifle through the shattered cockpit Plexiglas and began firing one round every two to three seconds at the tree line some 80 meters away. He aimed to keep up this suppressive fire until everyone was out of the helicopter. He thought of the rocket propelled grenade launcher, now probably on the ground less than a football field away. He could see everything; he'd either have to expose himself to enemy fire by moving more to the left or he'd have to pick up stakes and move to the rear of the aircraft where he could fire over the tail boom, using it as the missing support for his useless left arm. He pulled the rifle out of the tangled cockpit and bent down to grab the clip. Good thing too, because he noticed the M-16's bolt was locked back—he was out of ammo. He was on his knees pushing the magazine release button when machine guns rounds smashed into the front of the aircraft just where he had been standing. *Damn! That was close.* It was easy to forget how young and disciplined you had to be to survive in combat. Move, move, always have to move—and in the right direction too. He slapped the new magazine home. While sitting on his butt with the rifle between his knees, he pulled the charging handle back and released it, hearing the satisfying "shlick!" of the bolt chambering a 5.56mm round into place.

He rolled over, got up and made his way to the tail. Behind him he heard a Marine hit the ground. He yelled over his shoulder, "Don't return fire from the front of the aircraft. They're aiming there. Try to make it to one of the buildings behind us and cover us from there. I'll cover your movement. Go!"

Flint looked under the tail boom to get a view of the right half of the firefight. He saw the new RPG gunner on his knees setting up to fire. One of his compatriots was behind him. There was a flash and a puff of smoke. The man behind the RPG was cut down by the backblast and was holding his face and rolling on the ground. The round sailed over the downed helicopter and exploded harmlessly in the grass just in front of the church.

I see we're dealing with amateurs here. Not that getting killed by an amateur made you any less dead than being killed by a professional. Flint put the rifle on the tail boom and fired once. He saw his round kick up a clod of dirt just in front of the RPG gunner who was struggling to put another grenade into the reusable launch tube. *Up and to the left ought to do it.* Flint squeezed the trigger. The M-16 kicked lightly and spit out a spent piece of brass. About 75 meters away the RPG gunner's chest spouted red as he spun into the ground.

Now to find the machine gun. His peripheral vision caught two more Marines dropping to the earth to his left. Three out of the aircraft. How many were left alive in there?

His left cheek felt it before his eyes processed it. Heat. Intense, burning heat. The Huey was finally catching on fire. Flint yelled, "Any one in there?"

"Yes sir!" It was the lance corporal who tossed him his rifle, "Lopez is in here! I'm getting him out of here!"

"Get out now Marine! You're on fire!"

"I can save him, sir!"

"Get out now!"

"I can't hear you sir!"

The Huey was burning brighter now. The engine cowling Flint had slid down on only moments before was fully engulfed. He saw the machine gunners behind a fallen log just inside the tree line. They presented Flint with a six-inch high target. *Bastards.* He drew a bead, breathed out, and squeezed one round. The front of the log chipped up to reveal a lightly colored wood. A man behind the log slumped. Flint squeezed again. Another man fell. And again. The last of the trio was hit.

A deep concussive sound came from inside the Huey. Smoke was pouring out of the crew compartment. A limp form came into view. Flint screamed, "Not that side, it's on fire!"

The unconscious form of Sergeant Lopez danced around to what used to be the bottom of the door. Flint fired two rounds down range, ducked under the tail boom and ran over to his dangling Marine, "Push him out, push him out!" He turned to fire three more rounds.

Sergeant Lopez fell. Flint broke his fall with his left shoulder, grimaced and began dragging Lopez by his equipment webbing behind his neck, while holding the M-16's black strap with the same hand. The Huey belched fire. Flint saw the lance corporal's hand vanish in smoke and flames.

Moments later he heard the welcome "whap, whap, whap" of a Cobra's rotor blades beating the air into submission. It hovered between Flint and the schoolhouse. Flint dropped Lopez to point his rifle in the direction of the enemy and fire several rounds. The Cobra rose about 20 feet and let loose with its 20mm Gatling gun. The entire wall of trees spit bark and wood. Great chunks of sod were thrown into the air. The Cobra took on more altitude and fired a barrage of 70mm rockets into the trees. Tree limbs were blown apart and a thick smoky dust began to rise from the area that probably once held 30 men.

Flint turned to drag Lopez to safety. He wondered how the rest of his unit was doing. He felt a blast of heat on the back of his neck and lost consciousness as his face was kicked into the grass by the explosion.

*   *   *

"Colonel Flint, Colonel Flint! Hey, Doc, the Colonel's awake!" It was a naval Corpsman. Flint was under a clean set of sheets and aboard the USS *Belleau Wood*.

"What happened? Ow, my head is killing me! What day is it?" Flint demanded, his voice picking up steam as he spoke.

The doctor, Lieutenant Colonel Myers walked over, "'What happened?' You got shot down. You broke your arm, cleanly and in one place. You got a concussion from the Huey as it exploded. I guess that also takes care of 'Ow, my head is killing me.' As for 'What day is it?' It's Tuesday, February the 14th."

The doctor's attempt at banter bounced off of the wounded Flint, "How many dead?"

The doctor's smile vanished, "12. Five in your aircraft and seven Marines from the BLT. The Thai weren't so lucky. They lost 86 men."

"How many. . ."

". . .wounded? 35 Marines. 34 should make it for sure. One is touch and go. We're also caring for 23 wounded or shell shocked Thai soldiers."

"When can I get out of here?" Flint fixed his eyes on the doctor.

"You can't. Not for a day anyway because of the concussion and the burns to the back of your neck. However, I have made provisions for you to visit with your wounded."

Flint choked up, "Thanks Doc."

*   *   *

Donna Klein saw the early morning report on the heavy Marine casualties on MSNBC. She sat atop her exercise bike and reviewed the likely fallout to US policy in East Timor and Indonesia at large. *Too much momentum now to stop it, too much at stake, just like in Vietnam.* She paused, ashamed at having thought first of policy implications rather than the tragic personal meaning of 12 Americans losing their lives in service to their nation. *Was this sacrifice necessary?* She asked herself, already knowing the answer in her heart.

14
Massacre

Indonesia was at a crossroads. The nation was an artificial construct built out of the ashes of the Dutch Empire following its collapse brought on by World War Two. For 55% of the Indonesian population, one overlord (the Javanese) simply replaced another (the Dutch). And that overlord, no longer constrained by the bounds of Western civilization, proceeded to throw away its moral mandate of leadership. As long as the price of oil kept the economic skids greased, the corrupt leadership of President Suharto could survive. In the midst of economic ruin the end came quickly, and with it, the last of the government's ability to keep a lid on the growing turmoil caused by an economic system that rewarded the families of those who already had it made. President Suharto was followed by a transitional figure, and, after an indecisive election in 1999, another figurehead with even less power.

This weak and tottering government could do little to stem religious and ethnic strife.

In the Indonesian town of Kupang on the western edge of Timor, not far from where the infamous Captain Bligh landed in 1789, a mosque full of worshippers was set on fire. The fire setters were not Christian, neither did they hold traditional beliefs. What mattered next was that a rumor was planted that wealthy Chinese businessman paid for this act of religious terrorism—a rumor intensified and spread by the virtually instantaneous passing out of handbills that reinforced the "fact". Within three hours, the town's business district was in flames as were all the town's churches. Dead littered the streets. The Indonesian police and military were nowhere to be seen.

In the city of Ambon on the island of the same name, some 300 miles to the north-northeast of Dili in East Timor, a similar outbreak of violence occurred. Only four hours later, almost 600 were dead.

In the province of Aceh, 1,090 miles northwest of Jakarta, on the northern tip of Sumatra, separatist rebels seized the provincial capital and began broadcasting from the local radio station. Civilian casualties were light, but the Indonesian military and police lost more than 200 men.

In Irian Jaya, the former Dutch colony in western half of New Guinea, pro-independence rebels attacked armories in Sorong and Manokwari, taking weapons and killing 54 security personnel.

Within a day, the government in Jakarta was reeling from strife, violence and military reverses across the length and breadth of its 13,600 islands. Under pressure from hard-liners, the military and police began to lash out.

Two days later, the nationwide death toll stood at more than 10,000 and rising. Churches were in flames and the Chinese minority, particularly hit hard, was on the move, fleeing out of the country any way they could.

Western news crews descended on the nation of islands in force (many of them coming from their East Timor assignments). It was only a matter of time before dramatic, live footage would make its way to America and move that nation closer to a large and forceful intervention. That footage arrived, as no other television news footage before, on Sunday, March 12, from the central Javanese city of Bandung.

A news crew had been filming a large demonstration of at least 30,000. The crowd had been enraged by the false rumor that a group of local Christian Chinese businessmen had made disparaging remarks about Islam. Further, they had supposedly paid a large sum to a crime boss to burn down the city's three most prominent Mosques.

The crowd advanced on one of the city's largest churches. Inside the church a Sunday service was being held for more than 800 frightened worshippers.

Someone in the mob noticed that the cameraman for the news crew was wearing a small cross. A stone was thrown. The news crew hastily retreated into the church.

The news crew's equipment was transmitting to their unmarked van parked less than half a mile away. From the van a satellite link fed the raw footage directly into the studios. Indonesia's propensity to produce dramatic stories caused the studio to shift to live coverage. It was 10 PM on Saturday night on the American East Coast.

The reporter, a veteran stringer from the Asia beat, seemed strangely detached. He let the cameraman pan the crowd in the church and kept his commentary to a minimum. The strained hymns and prayers in the church contrasted with the growing fury outside.

A brick crashed through a stained glass window. Then another.

A few seconds later a Molotov cocktail sailed through the broken glass and burst in the aisles. The fire spread up a curtain. As the church was modern and in a good part of the city it was equipped with fire sprinklers. They soon came on and doused the fire. The congregation cheered and praised God.

Someone in the mob discerned what was happening and worked his way around the building until he found the chained water shut off valve. Within five minutes he broke the chain and cut off the water.

The television news studio back in America was just about to cut off the live coverage when the fire sprinklers stopped and the church grew silent. A woman sobbed.

Another Molotov cocktail came in, followed by another. Four more. The congregates gave up trying to stomp out the flames and huddled closer and closer. The news crew stood on a pew to get above the spreading oily flames and get a better view of the ongoing action. The reporter began coughing and took out a handkerchief to cover his mouth.

Three men tried to pry open a door, but it was blocked shut.

The camera's last images were of writhing bodies in silhouette against the flames. Gut wrenching screams of pain and terror filled the air. The cameraman lost his grip and dropped the videocam. Its last images of inky smoke and its last sounds of crackling wood.

*   *   *

On Sunday in New York, the Chinese UN ambassador called for an emergency session of the Security Council to condemn, in the strongest words, the atrocities in Indonesia. He darkly warned of the reaction of the Chinese people to the word that thousands of their brothers had been murdered in a coordinated genocide. If the rest of the world refused to act, China might act alone. In America, he found an audience receptive to his message after the shock of seeing over 800 people martyred for their faith in Bandung on live television.

The Chinese resolution proposing a large UN intervention force (carefully drafted in secret more than a week before in Beijing) passed overwhelmingly. China's ambassador to America immediately went on a tour of major US cities to tout the importance of China and America agreeing jointly to intervene to bring peace and stability to Indonesia. The small protests against his visits by Tibetan, Christian, pro-democracy, and Taiwanese activists were ignored or treated with hostility by the American press.

Several large Chinese companies with close connections to the Communist Party placed media buys on American television. The ads were originally intended to soften American public opinion in the face of an expected campaign to intimidate Taiwan during the Taiwanese Presidential election in March. The ads were innocuous, mainly showcasing the famous hospitality of the Chinese to tourists. Some highlighted the growing market in China for American products. As a coordinated adjunct to the Chinese ads, several American high tech and aerospace companies with huge orders at stake in China also launched their own ad campaign. This effort was designed to ensure another year of normal trading relations with China since Congress was due to take the issue up again after its Easter recess.

The ads, combined with the ambassador's tour and the fawning afterglow of the major media outlets ("New Life for the UN?" "The US and China, the New Unstoppable Partnership?" "The New, New World Order" blazed the front covers of *Time, Newsweek, and US News and World Report*, respectively) had their desired effect. First, Americans felt optimistic that China's legions, if put in service for good with America, could bring a large measure of peace and stability to the world. Second, Americans' general attitude towards China turned around overnight. Those who publicly fretted about nuclear espionage or repression against Chinese Christians, cultists, Tibetans, or democracy activists were considered ill informed, out of date, or warmongers seeking a new Cold War. Finally, the propaganda offensive worked to divert American attention away from China's growing aggressiveness towards Taiwan. With the Balkans, Iraq, Indonesia and a couple of other hot spots to worry about, the US leadership considered China's offer for a substantial UN troop commitment to be a welcome lifeline to a dangerously over-committed US military.

In less than a week, military plans were approved (over Indonesian objections) to send 50,000 peace enforcers to Indonesia. The force mix would include 20,000 Chinese troops, 10,000 Pakistani, and an additional 8,000 American troops (including several thousand Army National Guard soldiers) on top of the 12,000 in East Timor who would be deployed outside the troubled former Portuguese colony.

*   *   *

Donna Klein reread the latest press accounts and shook her head. As she grew older she was becoming more and more aware at how fickle the American public could be. *In 1999 we were ready to hang the Chinese, now we can't thank them enough for saving us from having to battle the chaos of Indonesia alone.*

She read a classified commentary on the detailed negotiations behind the scenes at the UN—the gist of which would likely appear in the pages of the *New York Times* tomorrow. It seemed that the Chinese were more than willing to send 20,000 troops as long as the UN (read US) would pay for their transportation and cover 80% of their expenses while in Indonesia. She smiled incredulously when she read that the Administration was favorably disposed to this request.

She frowned. *Why the sudden turnabout for China? Why is it in their national interests to be in Indonesia? Certainly they hadn't suffered a sudden attack of good will.*

Something was up; she just couldn't put her finger on it yet. Her more immediate concern was to help assess the level of training of the troops China was to send to Indonesia as well as the reaction to those troops by the Indonesians. This would directly impact the safety of US troops. She couldn't remember the last time she thought about the long-term strategic implications of a policy or a trend. Management by crisis was becoming the norm.

15
The Price of Peace

As soon as the last of his Marines was aboard, Colonel Flint left the bridge and went down to sick bay four decks below. His arm was still itchy from the cast that had been removed a month before. He was greeted by the groans of freshly wounded men from a SAM ambush over Ocussi. Forty-one in all, bandaged and bloody. But still alive. One hundred and thirty-nine of their fellows had not been so fortunate in East Timor over the last few months. Colonel Flint flashed back to Lebanon. What a slaughter that had been. But then he hadn't been in command. This— carnage—was *his* responsibility.

He went from bunk to bunk, giving his wounded men—all but a handful were conscious—small words of encouragement. "A couple days on the beach in Satahip," he told them lightly, "and you'll be fine." The thought of Satahip brought a smile to most of the faces looking up at him. The Thai naval port for which they were bound was legendary for the quality of its resorts and the friendliness of its hostesses. Of course, the more seriously wounded would be immediately medevac'ed out of the nearby airport of Utapow to hospitals in the States, but he didn't tell them that.

The *Belleau Wood* shuddered slightly as it got underway. The 31st MEU had finally been relieved by the Army's 25th Infantry Division after weeks of going it alone in the wake of the 3rd MEF's redeployment to the Persian Gulf. In light of the 31st's casualities, the Army agreed it could live without the 31st as backup. It was now free to steam away and lick its wounds.

As he chatted with a gunnery sergeant—a likable young man who had received only a flesh wound—it occurred to Colonel Flint that his thirty-year career in the US Marine Corps was over. There would be no general's star for him. Instead he would be relieved of his command, and soon—probably as soon as the MEU returned to Okinawa. Some dispatcher was probably writing up orders for his replacement right now. He would be transferred to some dead-end desk job for a year or two before being put permanently out to pasture. He had disgraced his profession . . .

He shook his head in disgust at his own thoughts. This was not the time to mourn the end of his career. Not when so many of his men lay wounded or dead. He would not squander the little command time he had left on self-pity. He would not go out with a whimper.

He turned to his operations officer, "Assemble the command staff in the wardroom," he said grimly, "we have some planning to do."

The already sober visages of Colonel Flint's officers grew even grimmer as he began speaking. "We have failed in our mission, gentlemen. Our mission was to maintain law and order as part of the East Timorese transition to self-rule. We not only failed to carry out these orders, we blew it big time."

"The Chicken-in-Chief sent us into a death trap," Ramirez said in a whisper loud enough to be heard throughout the wardroom.

"Watch what you say," the XO cut in loudly. "The Commander-in-chief is above criticism, whatever you think about his personal life. The JCS has made very clear that we are not to speak ill of the elected officials that we serve."

"I serve the US Marine Corps," Ramirez smiled savagely, "not that draft-dodging, pot-smoking, womanizing SOB . . . "

"Cut the crap," Colonel Flint broke in. The room quieted instantly. "Maybe this mission *was* a mistake," he continued in a low voice. "Maybe it *was* ill-considered, ill-timed, politically motivated, and God knows what else. It *doesn't* matter, jarheads. We—I mean each and every one of us" he said, stabbing the air for emphasis, "failed to carry out our mission. Worse yet, we failed our junior officers and men. Two companies of Marines were cut to pieces."

There was a long silence, during which each man relived the recent tragedy.

"We should have anticipated the dangers," Colonel Flint said finally, in a voice so low his officers had to strain to hear it. "We should have developed contingency plans for different threats. Every snot-nosed second lieutenant knows that an assault is only as good as the planning that goes into it. We live or die by how well we practice the PERMA rule—planning, embarkation, rehearsal, movement, assault. This time good Marines died . . ."

The Colonel's head bowed, but only for a second. Then he stood up and squared his shoulders. His officers found their feet as one man. "Listen up, Marines. There will be no liberty in Satahip for the command staff. From this moment on this staff is in training. We will do map drills. We will plan assaults. Once we have embarked for Okinawa the entire MEU will run rehearsals. We will be in battle dress. We will do L-form, breaking out munitions from the ship's armories. We will board the boats, armored assault vehicles, and helos. By the time we get back to Okinawa, we will be ready for anything."

And I will be relieved of command, he thought to himself as his studied the faces of his officers. *But at least I will turn over the MEU in fighting trim.*

"Are there any questions?" he barked.

"No, sir," his officers said in unison.

"Then let's get busy planning an assault on Satahip and Utapow. Both the port and the airfield have fallen into enemy hands, and our Thai allies have requested help in retaking them. The warriors from the sea have been ordered into battle."

*　　*　　*

Donna carefully read and reread the reports on the disaster over Ocussi harbor. The SAMs used to down the American choppers were manufactured by a European defense contractor. Significantly, the Indonesian military was not known to possess this type of SAM. Donna ran down her mental list of who might have the money, access and motive to kill US Marines in Indonesia. *Indonesian nationalist groups? Too fractured and disorganized. Islamic terrorist groups? No previous interest shown in Indonesia. The Chinese? Too much to lose. . .*

Donna frowned. *Lose. Lose what? Would we actually accuse them of killing our soldiers? What would they gain?*

Donna knew she was on the verge of an epiphany but the months of double duty and little sleep were taking their toll. She had been pushed too far and too hard trying to provide support for America's appetite for intervention.

16
Rehearsing for War

Lieutenant Colonel Chu Dugen's Jia Battalion held 450 volunteer commandos. The best of the best in a nation of 1.3 billion people, Jia Battalion was the equal of any similar force around the world. For two months now the battalion had been practicing airfield assault and secure operations in a remote training post in the Gobi Desert. The training was too hard to be boring for the men, but the repetition was beginning to wear on the junior officers and senior NCOs. Even Dugen was beginning to wonder why he had been sent out to the middle of nowhere under a secret set of orders from the Ministry of the Interior.

Just when Dugen thought the training was getting monotonous, three new elements were introduced to liven things up. First, Jia Battalion began to fly into the airfield on an old Boeing 747 cargo aircraft that was converted into passenger configuration (it had very few passenger windows). Second, a special construction regiment which had arrived at the base in April had just completed building a mock set of 15 buildings out of cement block and plywood. The largest building was a huge terminal-like structure with two stories. It even had simulated luggage conveyer belts. Third, two battalions of the People's Armed Police (PAP) arrived to provide an opposition force for Dugen's men to work against. Dugen would have preferred PLA commandos or even Army regulars to the lightly armed paramilitary PAP, but he was thankful for the new fodder for his troops who took the new challenges with an intensity rarely seen by Dugen.

The training went in five-day cycles without a break.

Day one was spent at the north end of the runway in the old post buildings. The men cared for equipment and conducted physical training, including marshal arts workouts. The officers planned the next assault and briefed their chain-of-command.

Day two consisted of packing the 747 and rehearsals of actions on the objective, using an elaborately prepared sand table, replete with miniature renditions of the buildings to be assaulted at the south end of the runway.

On day three Jia Battalion boarded the 747, took off, and circled the runway for an hour and a half, then landed. Upon landing, the commandos burst out of the giant aircraft and began to take control of the airport from the PAP troops. Dugen and his men loved this part of the training—pyrotechnics erupted everywhere: smoke grenades, blank ammunition, grenade simulators and an occasional canister of CS gas riot control agent.

Day four usually held more of the same as Jia Battalion expanded its control to include the entire post. The hardest part of this portion of the training was capturing and detaining the larger force of PAP troops while aggressively taking and holding more buildings. Dugen was puzzled as to why his commandos weren't just ordered to "kill" the PAP defenders instead of taking the additional time and effort to "capture" them. Still, orders were orders.

Day five also held interesting training. Usually at midnight of Day four, Dugen was called into Lieutenant General Kung's office and given a follow-on mission. Often the assignment was a simple as "commandeering" some "civilian" vehicles and performing a route reconnaissance 30 kilometers to the nearest village. Of course, the route reconnaissance was never routine. Often PAP "guerrillas" planted "mines" along the road or tried to ambush Jia Battalion en-route.

After six five-day training cycles Jia Battalion was given a day off (not that Dugen's men could do anything personal with the time—they were not permitted to call or write home). Rather than allow his men to be idle and swap unhealthy rumors, Dugen arranged for a day of sports competition with the PAP men. Jia Battalion thoroughly enjoyed themselves. Other than a loss at the table tennis competition (one of the PAP battalions had an aspiring national champion in their ranks), Jia Battalion swept the games.

That evening, Dugen was called to General Kung's office.

"Colonel Chu," Kung looked at the young lieutenant colonel with a stone face as he always had, never betraying a hint of emotion and always keeping their contact painfully formal, "Jia Battalion has done well to date."

"Thank you General."

"My comment is a statement-of-fact, not a complement. Had your men not done well, you would have been removed from command weeks ago." Kung glared at Dugen.

"Yes General!" Dugen stood, ramrod straight, eyes fixed forward—the perfect model of a commando officer.

Kung sighed as if in the presence of mere mortals when he expected gods, "I am modifying your training regime. Beginning tomorrow you will do in three days what you have taking five to accomplish. On day one your men will rest while the officers conduct after action reports on the previous assault and plan the next one. On day two you will assault the airport and capture the PAP soldiers. One day three you will conduct your follow-on mission. I have another item for you to incorporate into your training as well: beginning with your second operation four days from now, your men will conduct their assault in chemical weapons protective gear. In addition, your assault will be conducted using live chemical agents."

Dugen's eyes narrowed. The bulky chemical weapons suits would make the assault very difficult, especially in the growing heat of the Gobi Desert spring. He would have to rigorously enforce hydration discipline to keep his men from becoming heat casualties. Still, with live chemical agents, the PAP would probably be worse off.

General Kung interrupted Dugen's calculations, "Do you have a problem with that, Colonel?"

"No, sir!"

"Do you have any questions Colonel Chu?"

"Yes General. May I ask, what chemical agents will be used?"

"We intend to use a variety of agents. We will begin with riot control agent. While effective against untrained mobs without protective masks, it has severe limitations against a force trained and equipped for chemical defense. Half of the PAP troops will be without protective masks, half will possess them—plan accordingly.

"Later we will introduce some classified agents. These agents are very hard to detect. Extremely small amounts can incapacitate the enemy. It is our belief that the correct agent, used in the proper fashion, can enable Jia Battalion to achieve their objectives with minimal casualties and in minimal time."

"Yes General!" *Now this training was getting very interesting.* As Dugen saluted and left the General's office he knew one of two things were happening. *Either Jia Battalion is being used as a testing ground for new commando tactics or Jia Battalion was going to be committed to a specific and very important combat operation in the very near future.*

*   *   *

Fu found himself growing to like Admiral Wong, the senior officer in charge of the Quemoy invasion preparations. The admiral was mostly jovial, although he was given to occasional dark moods. The first of these episodes took Fu aback. He had been in Admiral Wong's office listening to the Admiral's daily briefing when the Admiral stopped, looked at Fu and said, "I think we shall lose at least 100,000 men in the attack. Is it worth 100,000 lives to capture Quemoy?"

Fu, instantly on his guard, responded, "That is not up to you or me to determine. But, if you think it so, I will put it in my next report to the Party."

"Put in your report. I'm sure the leadership will not be deterred but I feel it my duty to honestly assess the costs of their actions."

Fu was troubled by such an attitude. His career was dependent on Admiral Wong's successful execution of the invasion of Quemoy. Admiral Wong's attitude was defeatist and dangerous. Still, the Admiral did display an exceptional amount of candor for an officer. Fu decided Wong's merits outweighed his frailties. To be safe, though, he still reported every nuance to Beijing.

In his constant touring of the Nanjing Military Region (this region included the Shanghai Garrison, Jiansu, Zhejiang, Fujian, Jiangxi and Anhui Military Districts of China's central East Coast) Fu was impressed by the thoroughness of the military preparations. Huge numbers of planes, rockets, and artillery were being mobilized. Much of the equipment was moved at night, then hidden in warehouses or caves.

Curiously, little of the equipment around Amoy under the direct command of Admiral Wong was hidden. Fu inquired about this and was assured that the PLA was making every effort to disguise the mobilization of the 85th Infantry Division and the eastward movement of the 71st and 73rd Infantry Divisions to staging areas around Amoy.

Even more difficult to conceal were the gathering naval forces of Admiral Wong's amphibious task force. Day by day more ships arrived until at last the Admiral had assembled 60 amphibious vessels capable of lifting almost 20,000 troops and 340 tanks into combat at once. In addition to these ships, People's Liberation Army-Navy (PLAN) had dispatched 11 destroyers, 19 frigates, 20 submarines and more than 100 patrol and missile craft. Amoy Bay was fairly bristling with armament.

Still, that was not enough. Other elements of the preparations surprised him. Hundreds of J-6 fighters had been flown in from other regions and packed into hangers, wingtip-to-wingtip. Dong Feng (East Wind) 11s and 15s, advanced, solid propellant, short-range ballistic missiles with ranges of 200 and 375 miles respectively, were being set up by the hundreds throughout the province. These road-mobile missiles, launched from a transporter-erector-launcher, were being set up under canopies and moved frequently in a shell game to keep foreign intelligence services from noticing too much. Fu knew they were equipped with new Global Positioning System (GPS) receivers to improve their accuracy—the army assured him that they could target and hit any major building in Taiwan now.

With such a massive amount of firepower concentrated on such a small space, Fu was sure that Quemoy's defenses would be quickly overwhelmed. *With a force like this it would be possible to assault Taiwan itself.* Fu dismissed the thought. *The leadership has made its decision and you have been charged with seeing it through. Perhaps the leadership is correct. Surely the Taiwanese will see that this force is unstoppable and we might reach a political accommodation—didn't Sun Tzu himself say that ". . .subduing the enemy without fighting was the acme of skill"?*

In early May, Fu had the opportunity to observe, first-hand, a practice naval operation. Having never been on the open ocean before, he was nervous. He hid his discomfort by being more officious than usual. In response, the naval officers around him were of no help, preferring instead to let him get seasick on the heaving deck of the flagship Luhu-class destroyer he was aboard.

Listening to the operations briefing in advance of the exercise, Fu was struck at how clinical and precise everything was. Admiral Wong's task force commander intended to move a screen of 35 warships in front of 20 amphibious assault ships to within one kilometer of Taiwan's territorial limits off Quemoy's main island. The operation had two main purposes: one, practice the coordination and timing needed for a successful attack; and two, analyze the Taiwanese Navy's reaction to the mock attack.

As Fu once more vomited into the brass pan offered to him (not out of sympathy, only out of a desire to keep the mess on the bridge to a minimum), he noted how wrong his initial academic impression was of this operation. All sailors manned their battle stations. The bridge was buzzing with activity. Orders were shouted. Eventually Fu's stomach was empty and, with weak knees, he noted the distinct smell of the salt air and the powerful vibrations of the ship's turbine engines. *Other than dealing with the ocean being in the navy wouldn't have been such a bad assignment,* Fu thought, not really caring that the idea was inherently foolish.

Suddenly the destroyer cut hard to starboard. Fu had to grasp his chair to keep from tumbling out of it. The horizon looked tilted at an impossible angle. Fu was certain the ship would capsize but all the officers on the bridge simply grabbed whatever handhold was nearest them and continued their work as if they were in an office on dry land.

Fu felt the destroyer slow down and a moment later he saw a French-made *Dauphin* helicopter take to the air, rapidly heading off the destroyer's port beam. Fu now felt strong enough to ask a question, "What's the helicopter doing?"

A junior officer replied, "Comrade Fu, we have launched an anti-submarine warfare helicopter. It will drop sonobuoys in an attempt to locate enemy submarines."

The officer never looked away from his radar screen. Fu knew he had been slighted. Fu also knew he hardly turned in an admirable performance on the flagship. He decided to let the young officer's insolence slide—this time.

"Where are we now?"

"118 degrees, 16 minutes, and 24 seconds east by 23 degrees, 46 minutes, and 37 seconds north," the officer was playing with him. Fu waited patiently for the answer he was really looking for and was not disappointed, "We are in Weitou Bay north of the Quemoy fishing village of Shamei—about one kilometer from enemy territorial waters."

The officer finally looked back at Special Emissary Fu Zemin with a thin smile, "Sir, if you please," he stepped aside and showed Fu his radar screen, gesturing for Fu to rise up and take a closer look.

Fu pushed himself to his unsteady feet and walked as quickly as he could to the radar station. The officer offered Fu his chair and Fu gratefully sat down.

"See these blips sir?" The officer showed Fu five pulsing dots to the center-left of the screen.

"Yes, of course." Fu said dismissively.

"These are Taiwanese naval vessels. And these. . ." the officer swept his right hand, palm outward with the back of his index finger touching the screen, to the right, ". . .are the ships of our task force."

A mass of radar returns filled the screen, dwarfing the enemy's fleet. *Too bad today was not the day—we could score a tremendous victory for China.*

"Has the enemy always reacted this way?" Fu inquired, knowing this was the third such exercise since April.

The officer, appreciating a good question from the political officer, responded with more respect, "Sir, the first time we sent 15 warships and 11 amphibious assault ships across Amoy Bay opposite the town of Chinmen. We elicited the reaction of the entire Quemoy naval flotilla—some nine vessels within an hour of our arrival at the territorial limits. Needless to say, we could have made it ashore before the enemy could have engaged us. Two weeks later we came at them with 12 warships and five assault ships from Amoy and another ten warships and nine assault ships that started down the coast from Fuzhou the day before. The Taiwanese bandits sent 15 ships out to meet our two-pronged 'attack'. The ships were waiting for us at their territorial limits. We also noticed a submarine operating with their flotilla. Today, we see five ships already on station. Intelligence tells us to expect another ten to 15 ships as well as a submarine. It seems the bandits are already becoming proficient at responding to our rehearsals."

Fu considered the information, *we are throwing away our ability to achieve strategic surprise in our assault on Quemoy. . .*

*   *   *

The ROC navy skipper of the Dutch-built Chien Lung-class submarine (one of two Taiwan possessed) looked at the tactical display. It showed a large PLAN flotilla charging towards Taiwan's territorial waters just north of Quemoy's main island. Even with his silent diesel-electric boat, the skipper knew he was vulnerable in the shallow waters. *Still, with the choppy seas and the confused currents, we should be able to sink a couple of destroyers, slip through their ASW screen and sink some amphibians too.* He tried to put out of his mind thought of the Western anti-submarine warfare equipment the Chinese had purchased. It was hard to be hunter and prey at the same time—to simultaneously think offensively and defensively.

"I want an accurate navigational reading, take us to periscope depth and get a GPS update for our inertial navigational system." he commanded. If he fired the first shot in a Taiwan-China skirmish, he wanted to be sure that he had a solid basis for doing so. *Just let the bastards cross the line—we'll shove some Taiwanese steel down their throats.*

"Sir!" it was the tactical officer, "the enemy has crossed into our territorial waters!"

"Calm yourself lieutenant," the skipper's rebuke was itself quietly assuring. "Weapons! Flood the forward torpedo tubes. Target the lead enemy destroyer on the plot." Hsaing then shouted, "Navigation, do we have our GPS update yet?"

A voice came from behind a control station, "We've just got our mast up, we should get a fix within five seconds. . . Got it! Feeding data into the inertials now sir!"

"Tactical?" the Captain looked at his young lieutenant.

"Sir, the plot's been refreshed. The Chinese ships are within 500 meters of boundary. They are not in our waters!"

The captain felt conflicting emotions. One part of him wanted to blast the Reds out of the ocean. The other part of him heaved a sigh of relief that his nation would not suffer today nor be threatened with loss of liberty. "Weapons, run solutions for both destroyers. Secure the torpedoes. It seems our 'friends' are just testing us again today."

Not today. The officer shuttered at how close he came to starting a war. *Discretion is the better part of valor. . .*

*   *   *

"Our agents in Taiwan report that orders have been given to transfer a division of ROC troops to Quemoy and reinforce the island with an additional Patriot air defense battery," Minister of the Interior Ren Baisha reported to Chairman Han Wudi.

"Any word on how Taiwan knew of our preparations?"

"Yes," the Interior Minister smiled grimly. "The traitor will be taken care of at the appropriate time."

"What of our Special Emissary?"

"Fu? He does well. He worries that our provocations are preparing the Taiwanese too well for the coming storm." Minister Ren gave his assessment as an approving uncle would of his nephew.

Chairman Han smiled from behind steepled hands, "Fu is a smart and ambitious young man. He will serve China well."

"Should we tell him about the state of the diversions we have prepared with Iraq and Korea?" Ren offered, "It might encourage him."

103

Han pursed his lips, "No. No need to tell him. The adversity will build his character."

*   *   *

What the hell were the Chinese doing? Donna Klein looked at the latest report of yet another Chinese naval maneuver off the coast of Quemoy. She did all she could to keep current on events in China, even though she was still assigned to the Indonesia task force. She grudgingly admitted that her assignment to the task force was becoming increasingly relevant, especially now that 20,000 PLA soldiers were in Indonesia—5,000 on Java, 8,000 on Sumatra, and 7,000 on Borneo.

She wanted some face time with Jack Benson, her China Section boss, to discuss the rapidly developing situation with China. While she was the unchallenged expert on China for the Indonesian crisis task force, she felt as if her knowledge on China proper was becoming dated. *Why were the Chinese cooperating with the UN deployment to Indonesia? What happened to their long-standing opposition to interfering in the "internal affairs" of other nations? Why pursue a policy of rapprochement with America on one hand while intimidating Taiwan on another?*

Donna signed for another classified report she had requested. She knew she'd pay for her extra reading with another late night— but she had to probe deeper into the mysteries of China's current policy shifts. Donna broke the seal on the manila envelope and began reading selected cables intercepted from Taiwan's Defense Ministry.

. . .Deploy the 8th Infantry Division to Quemoy. . .
. . .Reinforce Quemoy with one Patriot battery. . .
. . .Prepare to shift additional armor and artillery assets to Quemoy: up to a battalion of each. . .
. . .Reinforce Matsu with a battalion of infantry. . .
. . .Prepare to cancel military leaves and call up reserves on short notice. . .
. . .Additional PLA rocket artillery spotted within range of Quemoy. Estimated regiment of rocket artillery (122mm and 273mm) now deployed east of Amoy capable of reaching Hsiao Quemoy Island. . .
. . .Five Russian-made FROG-7 rockets with TELs spotted moving into position by Lianhe, capable of ranging most of Quemoy. . .

She skimmed through the cables, some of them still in the original Chinese. Clearly the Taiwanese were worried about the

Chinese build-up. Apparently *they* were convinced of the danger to the offshore islands of Quemoy and Matsu—situated perilously near the Mainland as close as six miles away. *Yet,* Donna shook her head, even the Taiwanese, those in the immediate path of danger, refused to take steps that could really get Beijing's attention. She noted with frustration that Taiwan considered scaling back economic ties with the Mainland, then refused to do so. *They're just like us. Worse even—it's their freedom at stake.*

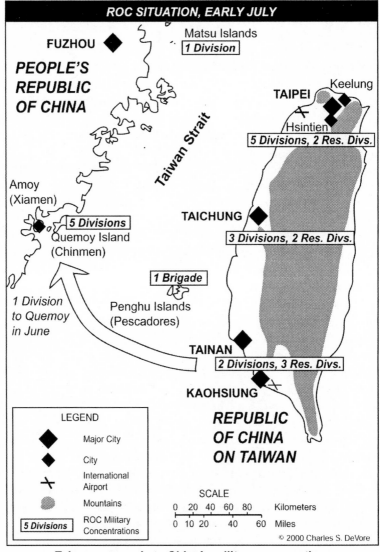

ROC SITUATION, EARLY JULY

FUZHOU

Matsu Islands
1 Division

PEOPLE'S REPUBLIC OF CHINA

Keelung

TAIPEI

Hsintien

5 Divisions, 2 Res. Divs.

Taiwan Strait

Amoy (Xiamen)

5 Divisions

Quemoy Island (Chinmen)

TAICHUNG

3 Divisions, 2 Res. Divs.

1 Brigade

1 Division to Quemoy in June

Penghu Islands (Pescadores)

TAINAN

2 Divisions, 3 Res. Divs.

KAOHSIUNG

LEGEND

◆ Major City

◆ City

✕ International Airport

▓ Mountains

5 Divisions ROC Military Concentrations

REPUBLIC OF CHINA ON TAIWAN

SCALE
0 20 40 60 80 Kilometers
0 10 20 40 60 Miles

© 2000 Charles S. DeVore

Taiwan responds to China's military provocations

Donna paused to massage her tired eyes. She kept meaning to get her eyes checked—she hoped she wouldn't need glasses but she wouldn't be surprised if she did.

"Sleeping on government time again, are we?" It was Jack Benson's voice.

Donna almost jumped, feeling a knee-jerk guilt even though she had already put in 42 hours this week and it was only Wednesday. "Jack, I'm glad you stopped by, I wanted to ask you a few questions and get your opinion on a few matters."

"Might these matters be about the People's Republic of China?" Benson asked with a theatric mock.

Donna was mildly annoyed at her boss's caviler attitude. She knew that he knew how much she resented the more or less permanent assignment to the "temporary" Indonesia task force. Making light of her desire to talk shop only intensified her longing for a return to the familiar.

"Jack, what's your read on China's build-up opposite Quemoy. Would they actually try to invade Quemoy?"

Jack began to get his serious face on, "What would they gain?"

Donna decided to throw the ball right back. "I don't know. Why are they building up then?"

"Political pressure. Taiwan had its second straight free transition of power from one president to another. Pro-independence parties and candidates won the largest share of the vote. It may be China's way of shaping the new administration in Taipei—showing them who's boss."

"Couldn't they have done the same thing just by firing a few missiles? That would have been cheaper." Donna was deep in thought, her gaze rested on Jack's chest, only glancing at his eyes as she finished her statement.

"China does a lot of things even us 'old China hands' don't understand. I don't know why they're building up, I just know they are—and I *still* don't believe they'd invade. They have too much to lose."

"Like what?" Donna was now looking directly at Jack with an intensity that always made the divorcee feel uncomfortable.

"Their standing in the world community. Investments from Taiwan, Japan, South Korea and the West. The growing riches of their emerging capitalist class. A return to the days of conquering by force can only set them back. *Hell*, Donna, if they just stay the course they'll have a larger economy than ours in less than two decades!"

"What if they thought they couldn't wait that long?" Donna knew she was pressing, it's just that it had become so rare recently that she actually had the pleasure of discussing strategic issues in a non-crisis atmosphere.

Jack was enjoying himself in spite of the fact that he thought Donna was too hard-line to be objective. *She was pretty after all.* "Why wouldn't they want to wait? The Chinese have a history thousands of years old. Only in the last couple of centuries have they fallen behind. Look at it this way: at their height in the early to mid-80s, the Soviet economy was about 55% of our own. They had about 110% of our population base. Their productivity was about half of ours. Today, China has about 55% of our GNP. They have about four-and-a-half times our population. Their productivity is about one-eighth of ours. China's economy is far less centrally managed today than was the Soviet economy of the mid-80s. In addition, the Chinese have a much stronger cultural affinity to business than do the Russians. I know you think as I do that it is overly conservative to project the Chinese eventually reaching half of our productivity. When they do, their economy will be two-and-a-half times larger than ours. Hell, I bet they could *buy* America by 2050!"

"Why buy the nation for real dollars when you can own the politicians for pennies?" Donna couldn't resist.

"Donna, Donna, Donna. You have to learn to control your wise-ass comments, even in front of friendly colleagues like myself. That attitude of yours is going to get you into trouble." Jack was moderately scolding.

Donna decided to shift arguments on Jack and try to keep him engaged on discussing China, "What about the accelerated pace of Chinese weapons purchases from Russia? If the Chinese are thinking long-term, why buy equipment that will rapidly be obsolete?"

"Why did Japan buy used British warships after World War One?" Jack struck back by answering a question with a question.

"Because they wanted to be a world power and they only had three percent of the steel production capacity of America. That doesn't really explain the Chinese situation Jack; they are now the world's largest producer of steel."

Jack responded with a smile, "I think it does explain the Chinese situation. Both nations could build military power more efficiently by relying on other nations for arms. In the case of the Japanese and the British, the Japanese were their allies in defeating Germany's Pacific possessions in World War One. The British economy was in tatters after the war and they saw a means of getting quick cash for old warships. This allowed Japan to concentrate on building its economy rather than shifting prematurely to a war footing. The same with China. They can upgrade their military with cheap Russian hardware while also buying production licenses for domestic manufacture. Eventually, they'll have the means to produce large amounts of armaments, if they chose. Now, however, I think they are satisfied with making large sums of money."

Donna had drifted into deep thought again. She mumbled under her breath, ". . .arsenal of despair."

"What was that, Donna?"

Donna fixed her eyes on Jack again. Jack knew Donna was smarter than he was. That intimidated him too.

"You know how Roosevelt referred to America as 'the Arsenal of Democracy' as World War Two was heating up?"

"Yes, yes, of course. He was referring to America being the reliable supplier of arms to the nations opposing Hitler."

Donna was preparing to smash a home run, she knew it and Jack could feel it, but he was helpless to stop it. "Well, Russia has become for China what we were then for Britain. They are 'the Arsenal of Despair.'"

"What are you suggesting?" Jack asked without really wanting to hear an answer that he knew would be well thought out and at odds with his own beliefs.

"I'm suggesting that China feels free to pursue a course of economic advancement *and* military strength. They don't need to concentrate on building a massive military-industrial complex— they already have the world's largest one at their disposal right next door! With international hard currency reserves in excess of $150 billion, I believe they can efficiently finance adequate purchases of hardware from the Russians." Donna paused to catch her breath. She stabbed her finger in the air and looked past Jack, in her own world again, "What's America's annual weapons procurement budget, about $60 billion or so? I'm sure Russia would be more than happy to supply the Chinese with at least $20 billion per year in missiles, ships, and aircraft. Heck, with Russia's debt problems, our banks would probably welcome the move with our own Treasury Department hailing the deal as good for the world economy!"

"Assuming China would really want to spend a fortune on a

military build-up in preparation for invading Quemoy, why would Russia be willing to sell large amounts of equipment to China—after all, the Russians view China as more of a 'Yellow Peril' than we do." Jack was still unconvinced.

"Cash. Cold, hard cash. It's also a way to tweak America's nose. Why did Russia sell Nazi Germany oil and war materials before the war? Between the world wars why did the Soviets allow the Germans to secretly practice the armored maneuvers on their soil that would eventually become known as 'blitzkrieg'? Russia has done quite a few unexpected things in the recent past. Why not agree to become China's arsenal? There's good money in it."

"Okay, granted." Jack was worn down on that point but was still skeptical of Donna's basic premise, "But you still have a long way to go to convince me or anyone else who matters that the Chinese are preparing to invade Quemoy—it just doesn't make any sense. They haven't even built, or bought, a large enough amphibious assault force yet. What are they going to do, row over to Quemoy?"

Donna smiled. She had at least scored a partial victory, "Well, we're back to the beginning of our discussion, aren't we? Why the build-up opposite Quemoy, boss? And, if they cared so much about the world community, why risk the resumption of underground nuclear testing a few months ago? Why does that make sense?"

"Oh, *come on* now Donna, we aren't even sure they resumed testing. . ." Jack was getting annoyed.

"That's right. Why bother? They stole all our nuclear designs and we gave them the nuclear testing software so they don't need to test anymore. But Jack, what if they did? Don't we owe it to the American people and the leaders we serve to find out?

"Oh, and one more thing, have you noticed that China's UN troop dispositions in Indonesia virtually mirror the crude oil production regions of that nation?"

Jack smiled, snorted and turned on his heels, dropping his left hand down and symbolically pushing Donna away as he retreated back into his comfortable conventional thinking.

17
The Boss Is Dead

Lipu County Party boss Fu Mingjie had almost collected enough money to provide his up-and-coming son with a handsome investment portfolio on the Shanghai Stock Exchange. *Zemin will never have to grub for bribes like I have—this will give him the untouchable reputation he needs to rise to the very top.* If he played it correctly, there would be enough left over that he could retire in modest style on the outskirts of Beijing, close to his grandson and close to his old home village.

Fu smiled as he urged his Landcruiser's big engine onward, up the steep incline to confront the troublemaker Chu. *Old Chu has resisted me one time too many.* He patted the old Makarov 9mm pistol in the holster buckled to his waist. *This ought to persuade Chu to see things my way—what will it be, the road tax or the county trucks?* He smiled again at the "choice" he would give Chu. *It was good to be the boss.*

Fu pulled his white Toyota 4X4 left up the narrow lane that led to the Chus' house. He looked in the mirror and smoothed his slicked back black hair—he had taken to dyeing it five years ago when he realized how old the gray made him look. He stepped down out of the truck. He looked around to see no one was watching, then straightened his large, tan cotton blouse shirt.

He permitted himself a twisted smile and walked deliberately to the door. He knocked.

No one home. Fu was annoyed that these *peasants* would spoil his entrance by not being home—they were probably working. He decided to go looking for Chu.

Fu rounded the house and started uphill to the citrus groves. In spite of himself he found their aroma delightful. *Ah, there was Chu's woman.* Fu kept his eyes fixed ahead, not acknowledging the presence of the strange woman who seemed both to lack hatred towards him and be unbowed by his power.

Chu Ling looked up from her work in the garden and gave Party Boss Fu a modest nod. As usual, Fu ignored her.

Fu saw Chu Pui pruning a leafy green orange tree. He was intent on his work, dusty, sweating, and, no doubt, smelly.

"Comrade Chu!" Fu called out loudly. Chu's head whipped around and his eyes narrowed in hatred at the Party boss.

"What brings *you* here to foul my orchard?"

"Come, come. At least you can be cordial when the People's

representative comes to visit."

"'People's representative'!" Chu spat out, "People's dogshit, maybe. Have you come here to try and rob me again?" Chu yelled more loudly than Fu yelled his false greeting.

Fu sharply drew in his breath and narrowed his eyes. He growled softly, "Chu, if you know what's good for you you'll pay the road tax or pay to use County trucks to bring your village's fruit to market. One or the other, your choice Chu." Fu stood with his hands on his hips, his right hand reassuringly resting on his pistol in its holster.

"Why you son of a turtle's egg." Chu then yelled again, "What are you going to do if I don't pay your bribe, bandit, shoot me?" He took a step towards Fu.

Fu suddenly realized that Chu was a powerfully built man, used to a life of hard work. Fu never did anything more demanding than shuffle papers or lift his chopsticks to his mouth. He felt his shaking hand lift the holster's leather flap. Fu took a step back. "Are you threatening a Party official?" Fu's voice cracked. "Look *Comrade* Chu, agree to pay today and your little outburst will be forgiven. If not, the road tax doubles tomorrow."

Fu caught movement out of his left eye. It was Chu's older brother and partner! He stepped back again. His foot landed on a large clod of dirt and painfully twisted as he lost his balance and fell.

Chu started towards him with a cruel gleam in his eye. Fu grabbed at his pistol and strained to remove it from its holster. Chu closed in, looking like a bear ready to attack. Just as Fu's violently shaking hand got the pistol free a piercing scream filled the air, "Pui! In God's name stop!"

As the scream began, Fu simultaneously started to pull the trigger and jerked his head around for a split second in reaction to the sound. Fu's pistol kicked back and a tarnished brass shell casing flicked out of the ejector port. A red blossom of blood erupted on Chu's thigh and Chu tumbled to the ground with a roar.

Chu yelled, "You've shot me!" It was a statement, not a cry.

Just out of sight Chu's wife screamed, "Stop!"

Chu lifted himself up on his hands, rocked back on one foot, and launched himself at Fu's pistol.

Fu fired again, this time the shot passed just to the left of Chu's heart, grazing the fleshy portion of the farmer's outstretched arm. If it hurt, Chu didn't show it.

Chu now had both hands on the pistol and was quickly

wrenching it around. Fu managed to pull the trigger once more. The action of the pistol's slide sliced open both of Chu's hands while his left hand received a nasty powder burn, but still the farmer pressed on.

The gun was now pointed at Fu's head. "Go ahead and pull the trigger now you bastard parasite." Chu triumphantly roared. Fu's gurgled cry was choked off when Chu's hands crushed down around Fu's right hand and squeezed the trigger. The bullet entered under Fu's jaw and came to a rest just under his cranium. The Party boss's body convulsed and went limp. Chu just lay there on top of Fu's lifeless form, not wanting to be pulled back into the world, back into facing the consequences of his action.

Chu looked up, blinking at the bright July sky. He saw his weeping wife. He saw his older brother, ashen-faced and frozen to the ground. There were four other villagers, good friends all, nearby.

Chu's wife spoke first. "We need to get you to a doctor. You are bleeding badly."

"No!" It was Chu Kwok, his brother. "We need to handle this ourselves. A doctor would only alert the Party. This is not good. Oh, my brother, what have you done?" Kwok voice betrayed little sympathy for his sibling.

"Something we all wanted to do years ago!" Chu fiercely said.

"Let's get you inside and stop the bleeding," his wife firmly said, "Help me!"

Two men from the village grabbed Chu around each arm and carried him down to the house. Chu carried Fu's pistol in his right hand like the head of a slain dragon.

Lee Bensui had been Lipu County's Deputy Party Administrator for 15 years now. Loyal to Fu Mingjie, he nonetheless resented the elder leader's authority, reach and complete control of all bribes. Fu treated him well enough by the standards in this province, giving him ten percent of all he collected. Lee's main gripe with Fu was that he allowed no other official corruption other than his own. *Everything* had to be channeled through him. A smaller man with less intelligence and drive than Fu, Lee made up for his shortcomings by developing a reputation for vicious retribution. Lee considered the local contingent of the People's Armed Police (PAP) to be his personal vanguard. Fu liked the arrangement as long as Lee kept in line—kind of a good cop, bad cop, *ying, yang* method that served Fu's leadership style wonderfully.

When the call came that Fu was killed, *murdered* by a local villager, Lee was ready to act immediately. If he reacted with enough force, two ends would be achieved: one, this dangerous rebellion would be quickly crushed, and two, his position as Party leader in Lipu County would be assured. With Fu's network of bribes already in place, Lee figured he ought to be a very wealthy man in no time at all!

Lee called out a company of the PAP and began the trip to bring Fu's killer to justice and teach those insolent hill people a lesson they'd never forget.

Lee anxiously drove his old brown GAZ-69 jeep in the middle of the convoy of ten trucks carrying a force of 121 men. They would reach the village just before nightfall.

The PAP convoy stopped 500 meters short of the edge of the plateau that held the village. The officers assembled their men and gave them final instructions in the failing light. A lone figure came out of the bushes near the road. He was stopped and frisked by the paramilitaries, then shown to Lee Bensui. The two men conversed for a moment. The man made hand signs and pointed up the road. Lee called the PAP's company commander over, then soon started up the hill.

A few minutes later, they were at Chu's house. The shadowed man was allowed to slip away. A platoon of 40 police armed with assault rifles surrounded the house. The captain walked carefully around the house with his pistol drawn, Lee following timidly behind him. The other 80 paramilitaries fanned out in groups of four to round up the rest of the small village.

The PAP captain heard a groan and carefully looked in a window. Inside, beside a kerosene lamp, was the prostrate and bandaged form of Chu Pui. At his bedside was Fu's Makarov.

"He's armed," the captain hissed.

Lee shuddered in the twilight, "Kill him."

The captain motioned for two of his men to come closer.

He whispered the situation to them and pushed them gently forward to the window. The captain stood right behind them, pistol drawn.

"Wait!" Lee rasped. "He's asleep. We shall capture him and give him a trial tomorrow. Then we shall execute him." *How* *could I forget? The going price for kidneys was now $2,000 each. Chu's other internal organs, if properly harvested, could bring another $5,000! I almost threw away a fortune!* Lee grinned mercilessly—*yes, it is good to be the boss.*

It was now almost midnight. Lee was tired, but elated. Except for one small hitch, the operation had gone smoothly. Fu's killer was in custody and the entire list of subversive religionists in this vile village were safely rounded up. 103 people in all. The only hitch came with trying to figure out what to do with the 42 children. After briefly conferring with the PAP captain, Lee decided to bring them all into town and place them in the Lipu orphanage while the Party decided what to do with their seditious parents.

The cries of the children were disconcerting, and Lee's anger only made it worse. He finally quieted the lot of them by firing a shot from his pistol into the air.

As the moon began to rise a lone man again stepped out the shadows to confer with Lee. Chu Ling strained her eyes from the back of the 2-1/2-ton truck. "Chu Kwok!" she yelled.

The shadowed man turned briefly.

A guard yelled at Chu Ling, then smashed her foot with the butt of his rifle. Chu Ling winced and yelled again, "God loves you Kwok. He can forgive you for what you have done!"

The guard cursed and swung the butt of his assault rifle at Ling's head. She felt a blinding pain and with a dull *thud*, fell into a heap in the bed of the truck.

*   *   *

Lieutenant Colonel Chu Dugen knew his men were ready; whatever for he didn't know, but he knew they were ready. It was nearing the end of the day, a Day One day in their endless cycle of airport attack training. He finished up two award recommendations. One for a young lieutenant who really excelled at teaching marshal arts techniques, the other for a very efficient Sergeant First Class of supply.

Chu heard the light knock at his door that could only mean one person—his political officer. "Come in comrade political officer!"

The young officer with a bad case of acne came in. In the beginning, this creature tried to lord it over Chu with his power—then Chu invited him along for a 40-kilometer speed march with his commandos. Every man had 40-kilograms of rucksack and equipment. Within an hour the poor specimen was weeping at Chu's feet. Ever since then, Chu had perfect control over the man. Their agreement was simple: Huang Enlai the political officer acted as Chu's intermediary to the Party, keeping him abreast of Party rumors while Chu kept the political officer out of trouble with his men. Chu knew it must be terribly lonely for the man, but that was Huang's problem.

"Colonel Chu," the political officer stammered, "I have some bad news for you."

"Come in, close the door," Chu's mind whipped wildly around behind a placid exterior. He suppressed an urge to ask, *Is it my father?*

"Colonel Chu, your father was arrested and executed for murdering the head of the Communist Party in Lipu County. Your mother and every adult in your village is being held on suspicion of sedition and on the unlawful practice of religion. Your uncle remains free. He is a true patriot. He turned in your father after your father murdered the Party official. Your uncle also vouched for you saying you had no foreknowledge of this heinous crime and that you are no Christian." The political officer looked down and waited for Chu to absorb this.

The full weight of the man's words were sinking into Chu's rapidly numbing mind. *First the Party kills my twin sister, then the Party steals the fruit of my father's labor, then the Party takes my father's life, and imprisons my mother and my entire village.*

"Colonel Chu," this was obviously a painful moment for the true-believer political officer, "The Party only asks one thing of you. One thing to be certain of your reliability: that you renounce this Christian religion. . ."

Chu looked up sharply and regarded the political officer as a bothersome insect.

He stammered on, ". . .that is, if you practice it. In return, if you perform well on your upcoming mission, the Party may see its way to showing clemency on your mother."

Chu dismissed the thought of his being a practitioner of an alien religion with the wave of his hand, "I'm no Christian, comrade, you can tell Chairman Han himself if you wish. It is also unfortunate about my mother. However, I am sure she had no part in this crime—she is no counterrevolutionary. My father was a hothead—what he did, he did on his own. Comrade, you mentioned a mission. . ." Chu wanted desperately to change the subject to something he could master. A military operation would focus his energies and could, as the political officer hinted, provide him with the means to save his mother.

At the Chu's mention of the word "mission" the young political officer's face went pale, "Oh my, you weren't supposed to be told . . . I mean. . ." The Party's military representative collapsed in a heap on a chair.

Chu's mind zeroed in on extracting the information he wanted out of this poor excuse for a man. "Huang Enlai, I already know we have an important mission; one that all China depends on for us to execute with valor and honor—*you*, you only need to provide the details my friend." Chu almost gagged at using the term "friend", but these were extraordinary times.

Huang looked around conspiratorially and lowered his voice to a whisper, "You must promise not to tell anyone that I told you."

Chu whispered back, "When were we to be told about the mission?"

"Tomorrow morning."

Chu suppressed a roll of his eyeballs, this man was worried about 12 hours. He resented the fact that this wretch stole half a day of prep time from his battalion of brave commandos. He pulled close to the contemptible creature and said, "Tell me now before I decide to assign you as lead man in the assault."

Huang's eyes bugged out and he began stammering again, "Jia. . . Jia Battalion is. . . is to fly to Hong Kong tomorrow evening. From there. . . once there. . . we will fly to Taiwan to seize Chaing Kai-Shek International Airport. We will be a diversion. . . China will attack Quemoy Island minutes after our assault. We will be heroes. . . Heroes of all China!"

And most assuredly dead heroes. No wonder why the dogs offered my mother mercy in exchange for my valor in this upcoming suicide mission. Once I'm dead, they can safely do what they wish to her without fear of embittering one of their most reliable assassins.

Chu smiled grimly at the pock-faced Huang, "Yes Enlai, we will be heroes."

*   *   *

Donna turned back to her memo. She was putting the finishing touches on a memo entitled, "Chinese Actions Towards Taiwan Signal a New, Dangerous Phase In Cross-Straits Relations." The memo cited several disturbing trends of recent Chinese behavior: increased naval maneuvers off the coast of Quemoy, an increased level of military preparedness in the Nanjing Military Region, additional PLA formations being moved into position opposite Quemoy and Matsu, a large build-up in short range ballistic missiles and artillery, and an unusual amount of military activity continuing after Taiwan's presidential elections last March.

She concluded her missive:

China's continued military build-up opposite Taiwan appears to be for political reasons, both domestic and international. Domestically, the build-up plays to the increasing nationalism China's leadership is fostering in the wake of continued economic turbulence. Internationally, China's actions are slowly building the case that China regards Taiwan as its own and will pursue whatever means required to recover the territory.

While a Chinese attack on Taiwan remains unlikely in the near future due to the lack of sufficient amphibious assault capacity and the vulnerability of an attack to Taiwan's air force and anti-ship missile capacity, an enumeration of China's relative advantages and disadvantages would be useful in viewing China's current actions:

China has the following advantages:
1) Any attack would likely achieve tactical surprise.
2) Hundreds of short-range ballistic missiles are now in place. These could be used to attack airfields and command, control and communications nodes to degrade Taiwan's defensive capabilities.
3) Much of China's fleet has been concentrated within one day's steaming time from Taiwan. China would have naval superiority, enabling China to effectively blockade Taiwan.

China has the following disadvantages:
1) Their amphibious capability is modest and not regarded as well-trained. At most, China could assault the offshore islands of Quemoy and Matsu with any real assurance of success.
2) China's build-up has placed Taiwan's armed forces on higher alert. Taiwan has moved to reinforce the offshore islands, making their successful capture more difficult.
3) China must continue to regard US intervention on behalf of Taiwan as a very real possibility. This complicates planning significantly for any invasion or blockade.

Donna reviewed her report. The conclusion was weak and didn't live up to the memo's heading. The memo also didn't come close to expressing her beliefs about China's likely aggression.

Time to think. She decided that a fresh cup of coffee was the proper medicine and pushed away from her desk.

Walking the 50 feet over to where her section kept the coffee pot was usually a therapeutic interlude for Donna. With the hours she kept, coffee was Donna's friend. Walking to get coffee was her excuse to think creatively. It wasn't much, but then, Donna didn't need much to spark her analytical capabilities.

What if China were to strike Taiwan? What would they gain by such an attack? How would they do it? Why the continuing military build-up and quickening operational tempo if not to attack? The Taiwanese are taking more precautions than normal—clearly they're worried. Yet, the Administration denies anything is amiss. Everyone at the top says China has too much to lose if they attack. . .

She rounded the corner and saw Mr. Scott talking to Jack Benson. "Slumming it today, Mr. Scott?"

"Donna! I was just talking with Jack about you. We've decided to release you from your Indonesia team commitments. Jack here has been complaining that you're not as effective at the China desk when you're working 70-hour weeks trying to do two jobs at once."

Donna blushed slightly at the attention, "Thank you sir, I like the extra work; it's a challenge and I appreciate your confidence in me." Donna didn't know whether to be thankful for the return to her "normal" work routine or to be upset that her boss may have recommended a career-limiting reduction in her responsibilities. She set her jaw, "Still, if it's all the same with you gentlemen, I'd rather continue working with the Indonesia team."

"No," Mr. Scott said firmly, "I think the worst is over. China is now a part of the UN peace enforcement mission. You provided great insight on their motivations and their troop quality and strength. If you have anything to contribute to the team, you know where to find them."

That was final, Donna thought, *no use fighting it.*

"Say, while I have the two of you here, what *is* going on with China these days?" Donna's question was upbeat. "I was looking at our quarterly estimates of Chinese military strength near Taiwan over a period of three years and I was surprised to see a large and steady increase over time with an almost doubling of combat power during the spring quarter."

Jack Benson jumped in immediately, "Oh Donna, what are they going to do? Invade? Kill the goose that laid the golden egg for

them? That Cold War paranoia thinking of yours has got to go—
you don't want us to be ridiculed again by overestimating our
potential foes, do you?"

Bradley Scott looked down at Benson, almost frowning,
"Jack. . ."

Benson looked back at Scott. The large, black, former Marine
made an imposing presence. Scott was a self-made leader and
analyst among an ivy-league dominated band of mostly privileged
white people. If Scott made him uncomfortable, he didn't know
what to think of Donna Klein—*a young, single female, beautiful,
Jewish, brash—very atypical for a Company analyst.* "Brad,
Donna and I had this conversation a week ago. I think her belief
that the Chinese might invade borders on an obsession. It's
clouding her ability to be objective. . ."

Donna was furious. She held her reply to a low growl, "Look,
Mr. Benson, just because one of your analysts doesn't go along
with the all the group think crap about China just wanting to get
rich doesn't mean her thinking is impaired. I thought *independent*
thought *was* supposed to be valued around here."

One of Donna's older male co-workers was heading for the
coffee pot. He heard Donna reply, quickly turned on his heel, and
retreated to his cubical.

*No matter what Mr. Scott claims to think now, that bastard
Benson just planted a seed of doubt.* For the first time since
joining the CIA, Donna was seriously considering resigning.

Mr. Scott began his soothing best, "Donna," he said stretching
out his hands, his right hand still clutching his coffee mug, "your
analysis is always appreciated around here. Just take it easy. Take
into account the prevailing wisdom in your reports—remember,
it's not enough for an analyst to be right, an analyst must also
convince his or her audience too. If you're correct and nobody
believes you, that's not much use to anyone, now is it?"

Donna first shot a piercing glance at Benson, then looked at
Mr. Scott, "No sir, it isn't."

18
Dragon Flight

The cruise ship was the pride of COSCO. It normally carried some 2,300 passengers in complete comfort from Amoy to Japan twice a week.

The ship's captain was shocked when six health inspectors from the Maritime Safety Administration of the Ministry of the Interior showed up on the 15th and inspected his potable water tanks. "You have harmful bacteria," they said. "For the health and safety of your passengers, you must cancel the trips leaving Amoy today for Japan and the return trip from Japan on the 17th as well as the trip back out to Japan on the evening of the 19th." The captain had no choice but to comply. "Don't worry, the state will refund your passengers and provide them with discount coupons for travel."

Their next order was even more curious. "You must immediately make for Fuzhou. There you will contact the harbor master and arrange to dock at Quay 103 by July 16th at 0300 hours. There, your ship's tanks will be thoroughly disinfected. Under no circumstances will you be late."

The captain knew the men meant what they said—they left one man behind to ensure total compliance.

The chief ferryboat captain was puzzled. On July 18, a team of five inspectors from something called the "Ministry of the Interior Maritime Safety Administration" had just given his boat a thorough going over. He suspected they wanted a bribe. He wouldn't give it to them, of course, his boat, like most others in the area, was half owned by the Guangdong Military District. He was even more perplexed when the leader of the five men congratulated him for having such a well-maintained vessel. The last mystery these strange men left were special instructions from the Ministry of the Interior regarding two men who would present themselves at his boat tomorrow. He and his crew were to do everything they ordered without question.

The master of the COSCO dry bulk carrier was proud of his modern vessel. Normally he carried tin ore from Thailand to be smelted and refined in Chinese factories and used eventually in his country's burgeoning electronics industry.

A few weeks ago, however, he received orders to go to Shantou Harbor to undergo minor modifications—modifications that appeared as if his ship was being outfitted to carry livestock.

Questions as to his ship's future went unanswered. When his paycheck arrived as usual, he just shrugged and figured COSCO knew what they were doing. *Perhaps the market for imported beef is improving and I will be sent to Australia more often—now that's a pleasant run!*

The pilot from the Mainland had worked for Cathay Pacific Airways for only a year. Since the re-absorption of Hong Kong back into China in 1997, Mainlanders were often placed in key positions within Hong Kong companies.

With his Mainland ties came also a strong and loyal connection to the Communist Party. When a special request from a well-placed source came into the chief scheduler, there was little concern. The pilot from the Mainland had been flying daily between Hong Kong and Chaing Kai-Shek International in Taiwan all this week anyway, so postponing his time off by a day would make little disruption to the schedule board. The unusual part of the request was that the pilot was to fly with a new copilot, also from China proper. The new man hadn't even had his entry paperwork completed yet, but the well-connected source insisted on his making the flight.

*   *   *

The PLA conscript almost looked forward to his time in the army. Everyone had to do it, at least for three years (well, the local Party boss'·son disappeared for a few years when he turned 18, somehow the private knew that son missed the draft). Anyway, joining the Army offered a chance to see a part of China other than his mud-paved village where there were to be seen more pigs and chickens in the street than bicycles and cars.

And now, rousted from his bunk in the middle of the night by the bellowing platoon sergeant, he was headed to the mysterious port city of Shantou. He'd only been there once before, completely amazed by its wealth: motorcycles, cars, nice clothing—even cellular phones.

The soldier's platoon-mates, each loaded down with 30

kilograms of gear, completely packed the bus. There were two men to a seat. Each with their rifle in between their knees, except for private Hufang who cradled a 18 kilogram AGS-17 30mm automatic grenade launcher and the four others, sight unseen, who had the unfortunate luck to be lugging the RPD 7.62mm squad light machine gun.

He noticed thick black cloth taped over all the windows save the driver's. Fortunately, since he was one of the last soldiers on the bus he got to sit near the front and the only view.

After 30 minutes of driving, the platoon sergeant stood up. He fiercely gritted his teeth and said in a low rumble, "Get quietly out of this bus and form up on me, not a sound from any of you."

The 19-year-old struggled to get up, get his pack, and get outside. He jumped off the bus and quickly trotted over to where his platoon sergeant was standing.

Behind the platoon sergeant was a smooth wall, perhaps about 20 meters away, somewhat reddish looking in the ambient city light. The soldier hazarded a glance over his shoulder and noticed a six-meter high wall of corrugated metal some 10 meters behind him.

As the platoon formed up, he looked straight ahead again, then followed the wall up and up until he noticed some unusual poles or booms jutting out from the wall. Sweeping his gaze swiftly to the right he realized that this was no wall at all in front of him, it was a gigantic ship of some sort. The immenseness of it held him in awe.

The platoon sergeant firmly but softly called the platoon to attention, ordered right face, then file to the left march. First squad stepped out single file, crisply turning left one at a time, following the platoon sergeant up a ramp and into the massive ship.

The first thing he sensed was the smell: oily, dusty, rusty. A few steps more and the private pushed through what must have been another hatch. This time noise assaulted him: the echoes of his own platoon were almost deafening. His feet crunched the floor underneath him. The floor was covered with rocks and dust. Someone ahead lost his footing and the young private fell over him in a tumble. Both men swore—but not too loudly, the platoon sergeant was easy to wrath.

After 15 minutes of standing in the dark, the private heard the sounds of another unit entering the ship. The platoon sergeant yelled to his men above the confusion, "See my red light?" The platoon sergeant held aloft his flashlight with a red lens on it. It glowed eerily in dusty hold. "Gather around it closely. Sit down. You may drink water. You may not smoke." The sergeant's voice grew uncharacteristically soft, "Try to sleep."

With that, the first year conscript from Manchuria sat down on a pile of rocks in the dark and tried to get some sleep.

*   *   *

Fu Zemin read the telegram and rocked back in his chair. His father Fu Mingjie had been shot to death in a small village in Lipu! The bandit that did the deed was already dead, captured and executed by the local authorities. In addition, more than 100 suspected accomplices were also rounded up and were being questioned at the Lipu County Jail.

Fu thought of his privileged childhood in rural Lipu County. He and the other children of high-ranking Party officials had a special school. Later, he was sent off to Beijing to study and only came home to see his father once a year (although, at times, his father came to see him when he had business in Beijing).

Fu couldn't fathom why anyone would harm his father. The county had grown and prospered under his stewardship. Oh, he knew there were some malcontents that somehow escaped the excesses of the Cultural Revolution of the 60s, but these reactionaries were few and discredited.

Fu began mourning—his father was dead. He would never live to see Fu's rise. Never share in his son's glory. He crumpled the telegram to his face and shed a tear.

It was July 19th. Evidently the Party knew about this crime for a few days. Given his current classified assignment and the routing of the telegram through Beijing, it probably took a while before the authorities could track him down.

He reflected on all his father had done for him. Providing him with the best education. Supplementing his modest income with generous gifts. Opening doors for him with the Party. His father *invested* in him, just like he invested in Lipu County. For his father, Fu was the future of China.

Fu pulled himself together. He had to be at Admiral Wong's morning situation briefing in five minutes. The invasion of Quemoy would commence in less than 24 hours. There would be last minute glitches, of course, but Fu was confident they would all be overcome.

He could not grieve for his father now—that would have to wait until after success. *And what better way to memorialize my father than to begin the process which will bring the wayward province back into the fold and make China whole again?*

Fu pushed back his chair and got up. The command bunker outside Amoy was spacious and well apportioned. Expanded over the years, the PLA knew the bunker would someday be used in actions to retake Taiwan. He looked at himself in the mirror he had installed on the back of his door and spent a few seconds grooming himself and admiring the view. His eyes were still a little red from crying moments ago, but his glasses obscured the view enough that no one would notice. *No one would dare look that closely at me anyway.*

The briefing room was just down the hall. Admiral Wong's chief-of-staff, a Lieutenant General in the PLA, was standing behind the podium, ready to begin the briefing. The general was always punctual—he never delayed a briefing for anyone—anyone with the exception of Admiral Wong.

Admiral Wong walked into the room and sat down. Fu sat to his right. The chief-of-staff began. "Let me begin by saying that all key preparations continue on schedule.

"The weather conditions should continue to be acceptable for amphibious operations. The heavy rain predicted for Taiwan next week may curtail some of the enemy's flights while the fairly clear and mild conditions over the offshore islands will work to our favor. Meteorological factors are especially favorable for our planned use of chemical agents.

"Now, then, the enemy situation. Taiwan shows no signs of moving additional forces to Quemoy. They currently have five full strength infantry divisions on the island. In addition, they have a battalion of light armor, an advanced rocket artillery battalion, and a Patriot air defense battalion. We estimate enemy strength at 43,000.

"Friendly forces continue their orderly build-up and logistics activities. The 71st, 73rd and 85th Infantry Divisions are now in place opposite Quemoy. The 101st Artillery Regiment of the 10th Artillery Division is now occupying concealed firing positions within range of Quemoy. The 3rd Mechanized Infantry Division and the 10th Tank Division, less one regiment, are in their assembly areas around Fuzhou. By tomorrow, additional amphibious assets with arrive in the area capable of lifting one of these heavy divisions into combat per day.

"Our deception plan continues on schedule as well. The 37th Infantry Division from the 12th Group Army has successfully positioned itself in Fuzhou. This division traveled during daylight and made no attempt to conceal its movement or its heavy equipment. We intend it to dilute the Taiwanese focus on Quemoy by making them think the 37th has been moved into position to reinforce an effort to take Matsu Island.

"Our operational plans continue unchanged. We expect to begin the assault with a bombardment of Quemoy Island and Hsiao Quemoy Island on the morning of July 20th at 0800 hours. We will use rocket-delivered chemical munitions as well as high explosive, delayed fuse HE, and dual-purpose improved conventional munitions in the bombardment. We expect to draw counterbattery fire at which point we will begin to eliminate the enemy's artillery in a counterbattery duel. The amphibious force of 7,500 troops of 73rd Infantry Division supported by the 103rd Tank Regiment of the 10th Tank Division will begin the invasion of Quemoy at 0810 hours.

"Supporting the operation will be 1,600 aircraft of the PLAAF. We will not directly engage the islands' air defenses, but rather will fly to the east of the islands and interdict any enemy aircraft that sortie from Taiwan. We can easily maintain air superiority in these waters at acceptable rates of exchange. Once our artillery knock out the air defenders on Quemoy, we will then move our air power into a direct support role.

"That summarizes the current situation. Should any of you commanders or senior staff have questions at this point, ask them now so that others may benefit. If the question truly only applies to your unit, we may choose to the answer the question later, after this briefing ends."

Fu looked past the chief-of-staff and sought the solace of his own world. In a day he would be a hero or a fool. *Perhaps it was better Father didn't live to see this day. . .*

19
Eagle Flight

Lieutenant Colonel Dan Alexander, California Army National Guard, reviewed the deployment schedule one more time. *So many things to do, so little time.* He cleared his head. *On the verge of spending more than seven months in-country and it comes down to a mad rush to pack.*

Alexander, XO of Task Force Grizzly, was activated for Indonesian peacekeeping duty along with more than 2,000 of his fellow Golden State Guardsmen some two months before. He would soon board the massive C-17 Globemaster with his M-1 tank *Traveller* and spend the better part of the next 24 hours flying to Bandung, Indonesia, scene of some of the most vicious ethnic and religious violence in that troubled nation.

After linking up with the Pakistani battalion at the airport, Alexander's advance party would send an "all clear" to Ft. Polk (where the Guardsmen trained up for six weeks) signaling the clearance to begin flying in the rest of Task Force Grizzly on giant C-5 Galaxies.

The flight to Indonesia would begin mid-day Thursday. The first leg would take the advance party non-stop to Elmendorf AFB in Alaska. One in-flight refueling would enable the four heavily laden Globemasters to make it to Alaska. On Friday morning at about 0400 hours, the four Globemasters would take off, graze the Aleutian Island chain, cross the international date line, refuel north of Japan, refuel again southwest of Okinawa, then land, 14 hours later, in Bandung Indonesia.

The jet lag for the last portion of the flight would be tough. In 14 hours of flight they'd lose a day but chase the sun the entire way, landing at 1000 hours on Saturday in Indonesia. As he always did on military aircraft, Dan planned to sleep as much as possible.

As he repacked his duffel bag (one of two), Dan reflected on his opinion of the deployment. In the intensity of training and preparing for the mission he hadn't the time or the luxury to think of why he was going—why he was leaving his wife and children behind and letting his private law practice die on the vine. Dan knew the mission had a noble intent. What he doubted was that there would be any lasting impact from his efforts. They'd keep a lid on the killing while they were deployed, but eventually, America would lose patience or be called elsewhere to execute a more pressing mission. In the end, Dan knew he would be risking life and limb and financial hardship for nothing. He thought about the people who ordered him on this mission, *I wonder if they know what they're doing to the military? The force that won the Cold War and defeated the fourth largest army in the world with an intense air campaign and 100 hours of fighting on the ground is slowly being ground to dust by the strain of constant deployments—Heaven help us if a real enemy emerges in the next few years.*

*   *   *

The final briefing before the planned invasion of Quemoy was on Friday evening. Fu could barely wait for it to begin. He knew that sleep would be very hard to come by that night. *Imagine how much worse it would be for the Taiwanese defenders to sleep tonight if they only knew of our plans!*

Fu walked into the briefing room in the command bunker. Admiral Wong himself stood behind the podium—*most unusual.* He looked ill at ease. Perhaps the same pre-invasion jitters everyone else has. Fu felt somehow comforted to know that even the hardened military officers were not immune to anxiety.

The admiral cleared his throat. "All preparations are in place. Everything is ready. There are two issues, however, that concern me and greatly complicate our planning."

Fu's blood began to run cold—*is this man going to wash his hands of a potential failure? Is he a defeatist?* Fu's antenna were up and he carefully gauged the room, looking for any facial clues that could support an understanding of what the admiral was going to say. Only the face of the intelligence officer revealed anything. He looked grimly determined.

Wong cleared his throat again, this time twice. *Was he afraid? Sick?* The pit of Fu's stomach churned. Only nine hours to H-Hour and the invasion's leader was in turmoil. Admiral Wong began slowly, "One of our signals intelligence vessels has been shadowing an American amphibious task force for the last 48 hours. The Americans came within 100 kilometers southeast of our bases on the Paracel Island group in the South China Sea."

We all know where the Paracels are—get to the point! Fu wanted to say.

"This task force contains four US Navy ships with more than 2,000 US Marines on board. Intelligence expects them to be

127

entering the Taiwan Strait just as we commence our operation. We believe the task force is carrying a US Marine unit back to its base in Okinawa after a tour in Indonesia. We are uncertain as to why it is going to enter the strait; perhaps it is due to the growing strength of the typhoon which is building to the east of Luzon Island—which brings me to the second issue of concern: weather."

Fu decided he could wait no more. This man was poisoning the atmosphere of victory with the thick mists of defeat. "Admiral Wong, surely you're not suggesting that we allow four American ships that will be what—100 or 200 kilometers away in international waters—prevent China's lawful actions to retake its own territory from rebellious reactionaries?" Fu arched his eyebrows expectantly at the end of his statement, inviting Admiral Wong to rise to the occasion.

The admiral paused. He knew the political officer was setting a trap for him—one does not rise to the rank of admiral in the PLAN without a deep understanding of political matters. The admiral swallowed and said in a strong, clear voice, "No comrade Fu, no one here has suggested that we call off the invasion—no one that is until you mentioned it."

Fu rocked imperceptibly back in his chair. The admiral directly challenged him in front of the more than 30 officers of the command and staff! And he was right! Perhaps it was Fu for whom the trap was set! Fu had to quickly think of a way out of this confrontation with dignity. It was essential that he keep the confidence of the senior leadership of the operation, "Then perhaps we should ask the Foreign Ministry to invite the Americans to send an observer from their task force to watch our operations!"

The room was silent for a split second, then, thankfully, a gruff divisional commander in the back of the room realized the political officer had just made a joke and started laughing. A fraction of a second later the bunker exploded with laughter. *A little too loud,* Fu thought, *but healthy.*

Admiral Wong looked at Fu with grudging admiration. The political officer escaped injury and like a man using the marshal arts, had managed to reverse a disadvantageous position and come out ahead. "Yes, comrade Fu, perhaps we could. In the event that they do not wish to watch our operation, however, I recommend that we obtain clarification from Beijing as to what our military options would be if the Americans decide to intervene. If we wait until we have to ask in battle, their answer will be too late to help us."

"You are correct, Admiral Wong. We will both ask the question—you through the PLA command channel and I through the Party. In any event, I suspect the leadership will direct us to ignore the Americans as irrelevant. I sincerely doubt the Americans have the stomach for confronting a major power over an issue of minor significance to them."

"Which brings us back to the weather," the Admiral said. "Our forecasters expect the weather to hold favorable for at least 48 hours. The typhoon's course at present is predicted to carry it over Hainan Island, well out of the zone of our operations."

Fu folded his hands and settled in for the rest of the briefing. *So, that was that. Everything is in place and the only unpredictable factor is what the Americans will do with their tiny flotilla—is four ships the best the once-mighty US Navy can do? I wonder if they know about our plans or if this is random chance?*

*   *   *

As Colonel Flint had promised, the drills continued after they left Thailand, this time involving the whole MEU. Several dozen newly minted Marines had joined the unit during its stopover in Satihip, providing an additional reason for some serious training. In addition, the unit took delivery of new helicopters to replace those lost in Indonesia.

Entering the South China Sea, the Colonel had them "take" Cam Ranh Bay and a nearby airfield in central Vietnam. The next day he turned their attention to Subic Bay and Clark Air Force base in the Philippines. The drills had gone smoothly. The MEU was near the top of its form. They would be back in Okinawa in two and a half more days, but Colonel Flint decided to get one more training exercise in.

"The Port of Kaohsiung and the Kaohsiung International Airport," he announced to his tired command staff. Everyone groaned. Two weeks of continuous drills had them all a little frayed around the edges. No one was more exhausted than the Colonel himself, who spent all his waking moments conducting the training exercises, and most of his rack time wondering what he could have done differently to save his Marines from dying needlessly in a far away land of no strategic import to America.

"But that's in Taiwan," his XO objected. "You know that the PRC is going to lodge a diplomatic protest if we approach their renegade province too closely, or launch Harriers and LCACs in their offshore waters."

"Renegade province, my ass," exploded Major Ramirez, who had developed a strong dislike for the politically correct XO. "The people of Taiwan have a democratic government and a free market economy. They're everything that Communist China is not. I say screw the PRC."

"That's why you'll never make colonel," said the XO starchly.

Ramirez rose from his chair.

"Sit down, Rez," Colonel Flint said mildly. "And XO, let me worry about the diplomatic niceties." Addressing the larger group, he continued, "The CATF (Captain of the Task Force) has agreed to put us about 15 miles offshore of Kaohsiung. You can all see from the map here that Kaohsiung is on Taiwan's southwest coast. This means that we'll be running the Straits all right, but there's a typhoon building to the southeast that will provide a convenient cover for our actions."

The XO looked as if he were about to speak. Colonel Flint fixed him with a glance, forcing Burl to begin studying his fingernails.

"This will probably be our last drill together, men," Colonel Flint continued after a moment, speaking in measured tones. "For this reason alone I'd like it to be picture perfect. But there's another reason I want you all to play this one for keeps. If China ever makes good on its threat to take Taiwan by force, they will try to take Kaohsiung early in the game. It's the island's best deepwater port, the key to bringing in enough PLA troops to take and hold the island. You Marines may one day have to go in with guns blazing."

Lieutenant Colonel Burl just slightly rolled his eyes. Only Major Ramirez saw it, increasing his contempt for the XO another notch, if that was possible.

20
Dragon Strike

Donna Klein sat staring at the photograph of the COSCO bulk freighter. It was three days old. Probably taken from a ship in Shantou harbor, although the source wasn't important. She looked at the note from the imagery analyst. It read, "Notice the top of the ship. There are piles of ore visible. Notice how the ship rides in the water, suggesting the ship is displacing less than 1/3 of its capacity."

Their sources in Shantou had reported unusual troop movements at night for the last few nights. Same with Amoy and Fuzhou. She wondered about Chinese intentions towards Taiwan. *What could they really do, anyway? They can only lift about 20,000 troops and 400 tanks into battle amphibiously. What's going on?*

Donna knew that senior leadership in Central Intelligence had been advised of an increased state of Chinese military readiness by their counterparts in Taiwan. Rumor had it that the Director himself was informed by his opposite number in Taipei that the Chinese might soon attack the offshore islands of Quemoy and Matsu. The Taiwanese were confident they could defend the islands without American assistance if the attack actually did occur.

She looked at the next photograph. This one was a black and white satellite image of an area of scattered trees. There were small white arrows pointing at six of the larger "trees." The imagery analyst had noted, "Camouflage netting probably concealing a new tactical ballistic missile battery. Judging by the vehicle tracks leading to the netting on the lower right, this is probably a new DF-11/M-11 battery."

Something was eating at her. Something in the conventional wisdom was wrong. She decided to call her father; this time, it would be business. She dialed, thinking intently while punching out the numbers. Rear Admiral Klein, USN (ret.), had to say, "Hello?" twice before Donna responded.

"Daddy, I have to ask you a question."

Klein, a 68-year-old widower, immediately recognized the voice of his youngest child. Admiral Klein always delighted in a call from Donna. "Sure, sweetie, what is it?" he asked.

"Tell me again about the Second Taiwan Straits crisis. You

commanded a destroyer, right? What was your chief concern, I mean, the Chinese didn't have much of a navy at the time, did they?"

"Well, the Chinese had a fair amount of artillery and they had a huge fleet of fishing boats. We were afraid they would massively bombard Quemoy then send a swarm of infantry over on fishing boats to capture the island. They tried doing that in 1949 with 29,000 troops, but were repulsed with heavy losses. But, you know all that, why the call?"

"Daddy, did you think they would invade?"

"Not with the US Navy around, I didn't."

Not with the US Navy around. Donna's blood ran cold. "Daddy, I have to go." She hung up.

Admiral Klein sat back in his chair and wondered what was eating at his daughter—the call had been so short and business-like.

*   *   *

Communist Party advisor Fu Zemin was shocked beyond belief. He was also scared. Five military policemen had just burst into Admiral Wong's command center and arrested the admiral, just two hours before the invasion of Quemoy was to proceed. Moments after Admiral Wong was removed from the underground bunker, the admiral's chief-of staff was handed a message by the senior military policeman. He bowed curtly, told his staff to continue operations and then walked over to Fu.

"Sir, you are wanted on the secure line. Please take the call in my office."

It happened all so fast. Fu's knees were almost knocking together. *Why had admiral Wong been arrested? Would he be next? What was wrong?* In a daze, he walked into the office. The chief-of-staff shut the door behind him leaving him alone in the room. The phone was blinking. Line one was on hold. He picked up the receiver, "This is Fu."

"You know who this is," Fu immediately recognized the voice of the President's Chief Military Council Advisor, Soo Wingji. "Open the pouch by the phone and read me the last line on the first page."

Fu tore open the mail pouch, noted the document was labeled

"TOP SECRET, EYES ONLY" and read the last line out loud, ". . .we are left with only one course of action."

"You have five minutes to read this document. When you are finished, destroy it by pouring water on it. Follow its directions to the letter. Do you understand?"

"Yes sir, I understand."

Fu's head was still spinning when he sat down to read the document. . .

*   *   *

Lieutenant Colonel Chu Dugen was finally airborne. The Boeing 747-400 had left Hong Kong an hour ago for the early Saturday morning business flight (Taiwan works a five-and-a-half day week) and was cruising flawlessly to its destination with 428 heavily armed and highly trained PLA commandos. He thought of the rich irony of what they were doing: flying into a center of capitalism in the most recognizable symbols of capitalist arrogance.

The Cathay Pacific 747-400 normally carried 416 passengers in three classes. The planners of Chu's mission entertained the notion of reconfiguring the seats to seat 460 commandos, but decided the additional manpower wasn't worth the risk of adding another intelligence warning and indicator to the suspicious Taiwanese or the curious Americans. So, 416 commandos sat in the passenger seats while an additional 12 commandos were accommodated by the unused flight attendant seats.

Each commando sat with his personal weapon, several hundred rounds of ammunition, six grenades (fragmentation, smoke, and CS riot gas). Unlike regular PLA soldiers, most of the commandos had the benefit of Kevlar body armor with ceramic trauma plates—they could take a small caliber rifle round in the chest and live to tell about it.

In the overhead luggage containers there were rocket-propelled grenade launchers and reloads, additional supplies of plastic explosives, man-portable surface-to-air missiles, and communications gear packed in plasticized aluminum foil. In the food preparation galleys there were large tanks of pressurized incapacitating agent.

The cargo hold in the belly of the Boeing carried additional supplies of ammunition, communications gear, and anti-aircraft artillery. The commandos did not expect to use this equipment, but the planners were loath to waste any space and carrying capacity—any extra military supplies would be useful to the follow-on airlanding forces (they assumed that this 747 would never take-off again following its high-risk mission).

Mentally, Dugen was ready. Everything he had trained for was now in focus. But, one thought kept invading his mental shield. Dugen tried to push the thought away, but it crept up on him and seized him. *His mother! How was she?* He knew now that his father was most certainly dead. Killed as the murderous traitor he was according to the Party. But his mother—she was so gentle and passive, she could never plot to kill another. *Certainly she did not deserve to die. Of course, the Party promised. . .*

"Colonel Chu, Colonel Chu, look, there's the coast. We are descending into CKS Airport. Soon we will reunite China!" It was his pimply-faced political officer. *Does this man ever give up?*

"Yes, Comrade Political Officer," Dugen still used the formal address as a means to keep this pest distant and to show his men that he was more of an Army man than a Party creature. "Please be still, I am finding my center." Dugen closed his right eye, the one on pimple-face's side, and winked at his XO and 1st Company commander seated to his left. The political officer gazed in awe at Colonel Chu, then fell silent and looked out the window.

The commercial aircraft banked right into its final approach with destiny. It was 7:45 AM.

*   *   *

The PLA private was hot, tired, and sore. For three days he existed in the hold of this terrible dark ship with his comrades. He just wanted a drink of water. Then he wanted to defecate in something other than the now overflowing and reeking portable toilet across from where his platoon was sprawled across the rocks and dust of tin ore. Still, a hopeful sign, the ship's engines had stopped two hours ago. With the stopping of the engines, however, what little circulation there was in the hold became even sparser. He thought he was going to pass out.

Some lights actually came on in the ship's hold. A string of incandescent bulbs protected by little plastic cages rose and fell, up and down every three meters, off into the dusty distance. Overhead about three-and-a-half meters, the private was surprised to see a metal ceiling. The metal must have been thin for he saw it warp and snap as whatever or whoever was up above moved about.

"Third Platoon!" the sound of the platoon sergeant's voice was actually welcome, "Gather round!" The sergeant had two large water containers at his side.

"Squad leaders, gather your men's canteens and fill them, all men must drink their entire canteens dry, then pass the canteens back to the squad leaders to be refilled. Do this silently and listen up!" The private noticed platoon-sized knots of other men also being gathered together. He was glad to be tall, occasionally he learned more about his surroundings than he would be if all he could see was the back of head of the person in front of him.

The private passed his canteen over to his squad leader.

"We are very honored to be on a very important patriotic mission. The Americans are threatening to seize the renegade province of Taiwan and use China's island as a launching pad of aggression against the Chinese people. We, of course, know their plans and are not helpless. We are going to frustrate the plans of America and reunite Taiwan under the rightful rule of China." The sergeant's voice easily carried above the sloshing water cans. The conscript thought of water, then realized that the sergeant was talking of war!

"Today we are in Taiwan in Tainan Harbor. Our mission is to secure the harbor from the American imperialists. Within 30 minutes we will leave this ship and occupy key harbor installations. We do not expect resistance from our Chinese brothers on Taiwan. Before we leave the ship we will put on our protective masks. To save the citizens of China from confusion and harm we will dispense incapacitating agent from this ship. This gas will render all who are not wearing protective masks incapable of resistance for about two hours. During this time we will be able to move about the harbor area freely and disarm and secure any police or military personnel we find."

The private's eyes shifted from the platoon sergeant to the clutch of canteens slowly being filled and passed out to the troops. A canteen reached him and he guzzled the water. He felt as if he would throw up, but he struggled to calm himself and settled his stomach. *Ahh water. War?*

"After putting on our masks and on my signal, our platoon will march down the ramp, turn left and proceed about 1,000 meters down the dockyard. There, we will occupy the Tainan Harbor Customs office building and await further instructions."

The private's brain was beginning to think of something other than water. *We're at war? We're saving Taiwan from the Americans?*

"One last thing, the Party has told the PLA that soldiers who distinguish themselves in this action will receive special dispensation from the government to have up to two children without penalty. In addition, all of us will receive a special 2,000 Yuan bonus (about $200) for having the honor of being here today!" There was a buzz of excitement in the hold. The men were coming to life and were looking forward to getting out of the inside of the ship—even if it meant fighting afterward.

The skipper of a ROC Navy Chien Lung-class submarine had seen this maneuver five times since last March: the PLAN amphibious assault ships would race up to the edge of Taiwan's territorial limits near Quemoy, then retreat. Each time the forces of the PLAN would be better organized, larger, and come closer than they had before. This time promised to be no different.

He just wished they'd come across the line, just once. He knew he and his crew of the quiet Dutch-built diesel submarine could sink more than a few ships with its six torpedo tubes and the new, made-in-Taiwan, Hsiung Feng II surface-to-surface missiles.

Sinking surface shipping wasn't his main concern—staying alive for more than ten minutes after firing his missiles and torpedoes was. In the last few years the PLAN had acquired some formidable anti-submarine warfare (ASW) systems; most worrisome were the three Russian-built Kilo class SSKs the PLAN were known to have operational with a fourth in trials. Those submarines, made with the benefit of ultra-quiet propeller blades built by computer-controlled nine-axis milling machines sold illegally by a Japanese company to the old Soviet Union some 15 years ago, were known by the nickname, "Pacific Black Hole." Completely covered with rubber insulation material, the Kilos were capable of moving undetected into attack position. The skipper probably wouldn't hear the enemy sub until it flooded its torpedo tubes in preparation to fire. Of course, then there were the

ASW helicopters armed with sonobuoys and A-244S Whitehead torpedoes. In any event, he hoped his colleagues on the surface would manage to keep the enemy helicopters off his back. Working as a team with surface combatants, the ROCN's Chien Lung-type sub was free to pursue enemy targets a bit more aggressively. He was absolutely confident that with the friendly naval task force overhead, his submarine could take a large toll of the enemy and live to fight again—assuming those Kilos weren't around.

He looked at the tactical display: this time it looked as if at least 30 vessels were closing in on Hsiao Quemoy Island (one of the islands of Quemoy) from the southwest across Amoy Bay—hardly a huge invasion force. He wondered what the picture was from Weituo Bay sector to the north. He knew that his friendly rival and commander of the other Dutch boat would be steaming well out of the way, probably around the Penghu Islands. He smiled—*poor bastard was missing out on all the action. If the PLAN decides to play today and I can sink a few of them,* he mused, *I'll be an admiral and he'll be serving me tea at naval headquarters.*

He ordered the crew to head for deeper waters to the east and to send a coded communication of his intent to the task force above. A month ago, fleet intelligence had hinted the Communists might try soon to take Quemoy as they last did in 1958 during the Second Taiwan Straits crisis. If today was going to result in a fight, he wanted some room to maneuver.

*   *   *

The pilot of the Russian built Ilyushin-76 aircraft was frantic. He was screaming for clearance to land at Sungshan.

Another hijacking. The senior air traffic controller at Taipei Sungshan Airport at the northeastern edge of Taipei proper had been through this before when he worked as a junior controller at CKS International Airport. He knew what to do, but what a rotten time for this to happen. Half of his crew was down with the flu. He was starting to feel under the weather today as well—a massive headache was coming on. And it was so early his tea hadn't time to fully take effect.

He never understood why the Mainlanders hijacked aircraft. The Taiwan authorities always arrested the hijackers and returned them to the Mainland where they most assuredly would be executed.

The pilot pleaded with the controllers. *Well, there were procedures to be followed.* The senior controller called airport security and informed them of the unfortunate situation. Next, he placed all inbound aircraft on indefinite delay, ordering them to circle overhead in a holding pattern.

The aircraft would be landing in a few minutes. He saw a few security police take up their stations. Everything was in order. He gave the hijacked Il-76 from Ganzhou clearance to land.

Now, to find something for that headache.

*   *   *

The Chinese J-6 jet fighter belonged in a museum. Still, it was the mainstay of the People's Liberation Army Air Force (PLAAF), accounting for over two-thirds of the more than 2,500 fighters in service. Highly maneuverable and fairly fast with a 1.45 Mach maximum speed, the J-6 boasted three 30mm cannons and two air-to-air missiles. Its wings began far forward and swept sharply back. The rudder and horizontal stabilizer was also swept back. The front of the aircraft featured a large air intake for its two Liming WP-6 afterburning turbojets. It looked almost exactly like the old Soviet-era MiG-19 from which it was a much-improved copy.

Unfortunately, the avionics were also antique; based on vacuum tubes and circuit breakers, they were slow to discover enemy aircraft and virtually blind when warning of hostile anti-air-missile launches. If flying against a primitive opponent, or with overwhelming numbers against a modern fleet, the J-6 might be able to inflict some losses; otherwise, it was a waste of pilot training and fuel on the cusp of the 21st Century.

Still, orders were orders and the pilot had a job to do. Normally assigned to the Mongolian border region at an air base on the edge of the Gobi Desert, the 1st Lieutenant was ordered to self-deploy with his squadron across thousands of kilometers of China to the southern coastal region. He hadn't been able to enjoy the local food or women, but when they eventually let him off base, he fully intended to take advantage of his luck. Of course, he first had to survive his mission.

He climbed into his cockpit and began his preflight check. He thought of the squadron commander's briefing 30 minutes before. The commander said this mission would be the most demanding, most exciting and most productive mission of their lives. He also said the PLA had some tricks up their sleeves and not to worry, everything was planned for. After all, if that wasn't the case, why would the commander be flying with them this day?

So, today he might see combat. His engines sped up and began spinning on their own power. He inhaled deeply and wondered why his radio transmitter was disabled by the ground crews. He supposed the generals figured tactical surprise outweighed the advantage of being able to communicate with his wing-mates in combat. The flagman on the grass beside the taxiway motioned for him to proceed to the runway to await the signal for takeoff.

Soon he was airborne and cruising at 50,000 feet. He noted the time. It was 0745 hours. Within 10 minutes they ought to be over the target and engaging the enemy. The sun in his eyes placed him at a tactical disadvantage, but the enemy's advanced radar really made it irrelevant who saw whom first. The ROCAF pilots would be able to launch three or four waves of long-range missiles before he would able to see and engage them. The PLAAF would have to rely on superior numbers and attrition to destroy their foes.

The squadron commander began to descend and turn slightly to the right. The 11 aircraft followed closely on their commander's tail. Soon they were back in the thin high altitude cloud layer— ice crystals, really. A few moments later they broke through the deck. What a beautiful sight. Far below the pilot saw the west coast of the island. There was a thin line of beach with dark green everywhere. Ahead and to the right he saw a range of mountains, almost black with vegetation and moisture and largely obscured by billowing thunderclouds. It was 0755 hours.

His radio crackled to life. It was the commander, "We'll be entering enemy airspace in 10 seconds. Be alert."

The pilot caught the inbound streaks of light out of the corner of his eye. An instant later Flight One's wingman exploded in an angry ball of molten metal and jet fuel. The commander began speaking when Flight One leader took a missile up the tailpipe and exploded. "Stay steady men. Keep the formation together," the colonel's voice was oddly calm, detached. This time, the explosion wasn't as catastrophic. As the wreckage of the damaged aircraft began to fall to the rear of the formation, the pilot could see that Flight One leader's canopy was intact. He hoped the officer would be able to parachute to safety on land. Suddenly, the last two aircraft from Flight One were engulfed in flames and spinning down to the ocean below. Four aircraft down in the space of five seconds and the enemy was nowhere to be seen!

Despite his discipline and his nationalistic feelings about Greater China, the pilot was beginning to panic. Once again, the colonel's voice came over his helmet radio receiver, "We're almost there men. . ."

A burst of rude static cut the colonel's voice off. The static was then replaced by a loud voice saying, "Pilot's of the People's Liberation Army Air Force, you are invading the airspace of the democratic peace-loving people's of the Republic of Taiwan. We are your brothers. . ."

The pilot was drawn to this unexpected statement for a moment, then training took over and he reached into his cockpit control panel and switched to the first alternate frequency. He heard the reassuring voice of the colonel, ". . .firm men, steady, we're. . ." Again static hammered the frequency. The pilot cursed the infernal interference from the renegade Taiwanese.

His missile warning light came on, and an audible signal buzzed malevolently in the cockpit. He instantly forgot about the jamming from one of Taiwan's C-130HE Sky Jam tactical command, control and communications countermeasures aircraft—he had more pressing concerns. He again cursed the unseen enemy and the enemy's superior equipment. *This was not much of a fight*, he thought; he wished he could at least see and engage his enemy once before he died.

*   *   *

The Communists had never defeated the Republic of China Air Force (ROCAF). The ROCAF had always maintained technical superiority and, most importantly, had always trained to a higher standard than the PLAAF. The ROC pilot, just promoted to captain last week, assured himself of this as he followed his wing commander's moves, still feeling very weak from the worst case of the flu he ever had. Still, he felt fortunate to be in the air. Fully half of the pilots in his squadron couldn't even make it to their aircraft when word came the PLAAF was coming across the Taiwan Strait on one of their largest practice sorties yet.

A few minutes before, they had scrambled out of the Hsinchu Air Base, some 55 kilometers west southwest of Taipei in their top-of-the-line French Mirage 2000-5s. The 2000-5 could take anything in the PLAAF inventory—except the new Russian-built Su-27s, called the J-11 by the Chinese. While lacking the speed, maneuverability, and offensive punch of the J-11/Su-27, the captain knew he had four advantages his PLAAF counterparts did not: better training, better missiles, better avionics and superior electronic counter measures (ECM). He hoped the Communist Chinese were unlikely to risk any of their 50 newly purchased Su-27s over the extremely hostile air environment that Taiwan projected.

Still, he was a little concerned when he received a report that at least 20 Su-27s were seen in the air near the Taiwanese-held Matsu Islands, just off the coast of Mainland China, headed towards Taipei. He became puzzled when HQ radioed that these aircraft had turned around and were headed back to the Mainland, leaving at least 800 of the old J-6s still inbound towards Taiwan. Of these, about half were headed for the northern part of the island, vectoring in on Taoyuan Air Base and Hsinchu Air Base. He ran the engagement math: 400 J-6s against the 18 Mirage 2000-5s from Hsinchu and about 30 F-5Es from Taoyuan. We should knock down a little over 130 aircraft on the first engagement, probably losing two or three Mirages and up to half of the F-5s. Then up to 75 F-5Es from Hualien (was that base hit by the flu too?) would get into the act. Arriving a few minutes later, they'd probably get another 100 aircraft, leaving a little over 160 for the air defenders to contend with. He knew he'd draw blood today, if the Mainlanders crossed the 12-mile mark and violated Taiwanese airspace. He just didn't know if he'd live to tell anyone about it.

Using data fed to them from the orbiting TW-3 airborne early warning aircraft (an E-2T Hawkeye, the same AEW aircraft the Americans used on their carriers), the ROCAF squadron was ordered to fly to 51,000 feet and come about to 110 degrees to intercept the enemy from above and behind. The captain's head's up display (HUD) showed the target squadron at 1 o'clock, below the cloud deck about 15 miles off. He could "see" four other squadrons as well on his HUD, further to the front and below this one, courtesy of his on-board radar and the enhanced radar returns from the TW-3.

The TW-3 was a key part of Taiwan's ability to repel a PLAAF attack. Taiwan's AWACS capability (one of only three Asian nations to have such capability along with Japan and Singapore) greatly enhanced warning time for the ROCAF. The TW-3 could detect targets hundreds of miles away and direct fighters to intercept hostile aircraft.

Their orders were simple, as soon as the lead enemy squadron passed into Taiwanese airspace they could engage at will. The new government in Taipei had been getting tired of Beijing's continuous provocations over the past half year. Especially irksome were Beijing's heavy-handed maneuvers during the last presidential election in March. This time, Beijing would be the one getting a message: Taiwan was not interested in reunifying with authoritarian bully under the barrel of a gun.

The captain's radio squawked to life, his flight commander ordered him to target the leftmost enemy flight of aircraft and fire when ready. The captain moved the weapons track to the left and highlighted four target aircraft. The Mirage's on board radar went into targeting mode and narrowed the beam to focus on the target area. He pushed the button that sent the targeting information to the four long-range French MATRA MICA radar guided missiles. He would save the two MATRA Magic II short-range infrared missiles for the close-in fight (if one called engaging up to eight nautical miles away close-in). His thumb flipped up the safety latch on top of the stick and pressed the launch button four times. With each press, he was rewarded with a smooth whoosh as the deadly accurate missile left its launch rail and streaked out towards its unseen target. He breathed a sigh of relief, maybe dogfighting with the flu wasn't so bad after all—in any event, a little virus wasn't about to stop him from being the first ROCAF pilot to become an ace in several decades.

*   *   *

Just outside the 12-mile territorial limits of Taiwan, a Chinese cruise ship was in trouble. One of five luxury passenger ships of the COSCO line based in Amoy across from Quemoy, the ship normally cruised twice weekly to Japan.

The Chinese captain had radioed a distress call. His engine room was on fire and his internal fire fighting equipment was malfunctioning. He had 2,300 passengers on board, three days out of Shanghai and was requesting immediate permission to enter

Taiwan's Keelung Harbor to receive fire fighting and humanitarian assistance.

Seeing an opportunity to score some propaganda points, the Maritime Police immediately agreed, sending two tug boats, a fireboat and a 32-meter Vosper patrol boat out to render assistance.

The captain of the cruise ship had already increased his speed to the limit of his ability. His ship was now making 15 knots and would be in the harbor inside 40 minutes.

There were five large military smoke generators aft producing a thick white smoke. This was augmented by a mound of burning tires on the deck to produce black smoke. The tires were concealed by a false deck of sheet metal to prevent easy observation by aircraft of the true nature of the fire. To cap off the deception, on board, there weren't 2,300 scared civilian passengers. Instead, 10,000 heavily armed troops of the PLA's 37th Infantry Division assigned to the 12th Group Army from the Nanjing Military Region were crammed inside.

*   *   *

The exercise to take the port and airport of Kaohsiung was going so well that Colonel Flint realized he hadn't thought about the fiasco on East Timor for at least a couple of hours. *A new record*, he thought sourly.

His Marines were just beginning their sixth L-Form in the last eight days. The helicopters were on the flight deck, engines warming up. The LCACs were roaring in the well decks of the *Belleau Wood* and the *Dubuque*. Ever since leaving Pattaya in Thailand he had run his men through L-Forms—intense training exercises for amphibious action. Because of the recent operations budget cutbacks they hadn't been able to afford too many L-Forms in the past few years. Now, however, his operations were still technically under the aegis of the UN's Timor peacekeeping funds. Any fuel and spare parts consumed now would come out of a separate pot of money and he decided to drain it dry if he could. With enough effort, he might recover half of the readiness and morale lost in Timor. L-forms were tough—doing them one day after another was a way to add the sharp steel edge back on his Marines as well as to exorcise the demons of Timor out of everyone's mind.

The ACE commander came up to bridge to report. "The CH-46s and CH-53s are all on deck and fueled. The Cobras are armed, and the lead planes in the Harrier Squadron are in the catapults."

He was followed by the Landing Craft-Air Cushion (LCAC), boats, and Assault Amphibian company commander, each of whom announced that his equipment was manned and ready. L-form was complete. His Marines were armed and ready to board their helos.

Colonel Flint had decided against a full-blown demonstration in favor of launching a few boats and a helo or Harrier or two. *Best not to be too provocative this close to the Dragon.* He was just about to give the order to launch when he noticed the Combat Information Officer running up to the ship's XO. *Running?*

He slipped out of his swivel chair and went below to the Combat Information Center (CIC). He presented his ID at the door as required and entered the dimly lit room filled with computer screens, radios and plotting screens. A knot of officers stood silently clustered around one large screen he recognized as the air situation plot.

On the screen of the air situation plot were two almost undifferentiated masses of radar returns to the west of the *Belleau Wood.* For a second he wondered if the ship's radar was malfunctioning, but as the masses shifted east in unison and resolved themselves into hundreds of separate blips he realized that he was witnessing a very unfriendly act. If each of those blips represent an aircraft, then close to a thousand planes were now flying towards Taiwan. The colonel whistled softly.

A junior naval officer heard the whistle and looked over his shoulder. "Oh, Colonel Flint, I didn't know you were here." The Lieutenant (junior grade) gestured at the screen. "The entire PLA air force seems to be headed our way."

By now Colonel Flint was completely absorbed in watching the slow-moving blips. "What's the situation?" he asked, his eyes never leaving the screen. He could now see several smaller masses of blips heading west from various points on Taiwan.

"Well, sir, I'm not the Combat Information Officer . . ." the lieutenant JG stammered.

"I asked you what the situation is, not whether or not you are qualified to give it to me." Colonel Flint started out hard, but finished soft. "Besides, I'm just a dumb ol' jarhead, not a fancy-pants naval officer like yourself. I'm sure that you'll bring me up to speed better than I could on my own just squinting at your screen there."

The young officer relaxed. "We estimate that there are at least 900 PLA aircraft, six hundred in this mass here," he pointed at the mass of blips in the north, "and three hundred in this mass here," he pointed at the mass of blips in the south, which were rapidly approaching their own position off Kaohsiung. "The ROC air force is preparing a welcoming party," pointing at the smaller masses of blips heading west."

"And Sir, there's more. Ten minutes ago, just before we made radar contact, we received a navigational warning from the PRC that the Taiwan Strait was closed to all north and southbound traffic south of the line 21 degrees north latitude and 25 degrees north latitude. We're well north of 21 degrees right now, so we're caught right in the middle of this, whatever this is."

"What do you mean, son?"

"Well, you remember in 1996 during the Taiwanese presidential elections they fired short-range missiles into the ocean just north and south of Taiwan. This could be a similar effort to intimidate Taiwan or it could be . . ."

". . .that we're going to find ourselves in a real shooting war," Colonel Flint completed his sentence for him. He picked up the nearest phone and punched in the numbers for the MEU command post. His XO answered the phone. "Hank, we've got about a thousand Red Chinese fighters heading our way. I want all our Marines on board their helos, engines running. And get Ramirez down here to CIC on the double. I need his brains."

"Sir," a third class petty officer warbled, "we're getting a message on open channel."

"Put it on the overhead speaker," the lieutenant JG ordered.

After a crackle of static, a heavy Chinese accent intoned. "Warning to all international shipping. Warning to all international flights. You are hereby ordered to clear the Taiwan Straits at once. There is a military exercise underway. Repeat, there is a military exercise underway. The People's Republic of China Air Force and Navy are engaged in military exercises around the province of Taiwan. Clear the Straits at once. Clear the air space over Taiwan at once. Those who disobey this order will bear full responsibility for their actions." The message began repeating.

"Well, Colonel Flint, what do you think we ought to do?"

The Colonel turned and saw that the ARG captain had entered the CIC, closely followed by his CIC-OIC. "You Navy guys are the ones with the brains," he responded. "We grunts just supply the brawn. What does Washington say about this?"

"They know that the Chinese have demanded that the Taiwan Straits be cleared, although they are mystified that the Chinese have given us so little notice this time around. This business with the aircraft we're sending live via MILSTAR to CINCPAC in Hawaii. So far no comments, just 'ohhs' and 'ahhs' and 'be careful, guys.'"

The hair on the back of Colonel Flint's neck stood up, just like it had in 'Nam 30 years before. He had been a 19-year-old Lance Corporal leading a squad of torn-up and scared Marines back to base after a brutal firefight. The trail had divided and he had taken the left fork—the more direct route—without thinking. That's when his instincts began screaming danger at him. He had stopped inches in front of the tripwire that would have carved his name on the Vietnam Veteran's Memorial in the D.C. Mall for all time. He carefully backed up, took the right fork, and from that time forward vowed to trust his instincts whenever he got in a tight spot. And at this moment his instincts were on overload, screaming danger.

"Captain Bright, I've got a feeling that the Chinese aren't bluffing this time around. We're about to be in the middle of a war we weren't invited to."

"What do you suggest we do, Colonel?"

"Get me a little closer to land, captain," Colonel Flint replied with a tight smile. "My Marines don't swim too well."

Captain Bright increased speed to flank and headed for the 12-mile limit.

*   *   *

Lieutenant Colonel Dan Alexander of the California Army National Guard was trying to get some sleep. The flight from Ft. Polk in the C-17 began a day ago, technically two days ago since they passed the international date line, first an overnight stop in Alaska at Elmendorf AFB, then a mid-air refueling southwest of Shemya at the end of the Aleutian Island chain. They were now about to begin their second mid-air refueling west of Okinawa—nine hours into a 14-hour flight. Task Force Grizzly left Alaska at about five in the morning in the ever-light summer of the near Arctic and let the sun chase them west. By the time they reached Bandung, Indonesia, it would be about 1100 hours—11:00 AM National Guard time.

The bench of nylon netting that passed for seating on this aircraft was starting to cut into his butt. He unstrapped himself, looked enviously at his young snoring troops and went forward to chat with the Globemaster's aircrew. The loadmaster was studying a math text—*was that calculus?* He brushed past the loadmaster and announced himself to the flight commander, Lieutenant Colonel Giannini, "Colonel, I need to whine, my ass hurts too much to sleep, I'm bored, your service is lousy, and the flight attendant is ugly!"

The loadmaster, hearing the last, put down his textbook and yelled above the dull roar, "Hey, sir, I resemble that remark!"

"Seriously, what's up colonel, tell me where we are."

Lieutenant Colonel Joe Giannini turned in his seat with a grin and said, "Pull up a jump seat and tell us why you're going to Indonesia again." He pulled off his headset and laid it on his lap.

Alexander gratefully sat down on something resembling a real seat, "Well, you see it's like this: people hate each other, people kill each other, journalists broadcast the carnage, Americans feel bad, the President feels the pain, and we get sent in to tell everyone to get along or else we'll kill all of 'em regardless of their religion or ethnicity!"

The Air Force colonel fixed Alexander with a pilot's gaze and said, "Don't think the mission is worth your time?"

Alexander sighed, "Joe, I was in the LA Riots in '92. I was a company commander in the Cal Guard. As soon as we got on the scene, the rioting stopped. People would yell to us from their porches, 'Thank God you're here, God bless you.' After Cold War ended and my life got busier, I wanted to quit. Every time I thought about quitting, I'd think of LA.

"You know the difference between Los Angeles, California and Bandung, Indonesia? You know why LA didn't tear itself apart again as soon as we left town? Two words: 'freedom,' 'justice.' We may have problems in America but we have a system to fix them. It's not perfect, but it beats the hell out of all the other systems.

"The thing that frustrates me to no end with this deployment is the futility of it all. We're simply going to Indonesia to stop the bloodshed. As soon as we leave, it'll be back to bloodshed."

"Well," said Joe, "I've almost quit a few times myself for the same reasons. I only stay for the high pay and the pretty flight attendants!" Joe yelled the last comment.

The loadmaster looked up and made a kissy-face to his commander.

Joe grinned, "I won't ask!"

"And, I won't tell, sir!" The loadmaster went back to his book.

"Why don't you quit, Joe?"

"Look, I stay in for the same reasons you do, 'To support and defend the Constitution. . .', professional pride, occasional job satisfaction. I know I could triple my salary working for the airlines, but then I'd just be doing a job." Joe smiled warmly, his crow's feet showing at the edges of his brown eyes.

The copilot pointed out the cockpit at 10 o'clock. Joe's face lit-up, "Hey, have you ever seen a mid-air refueling from the cockpit?"

Dan was interested, "No. I usually catch up on my sleep on military aircraft."

"Look over there. That's a KC-135 tanker out of Okinawa. He's going to refuel the lead C-17 first. After he's done, we'll move up a take a long drink from the straw. It will give us enough fuel to make it the rest of the way down to Java."

Joe's copilot motioned for him to put on his headset. Joe excused himself and turned to the cockpit. Within a few seconds Dan could see him toggle the intercom switch on the headset. The loadmaster stirred to life and brought Dan a headset, plugging it in as he did so. Curious, Dan listened in.

"Tango Five-Niner, this is Okinawa Control. We have a situation in the Taiwan Strait. Amphibious Squadron 11 has reported intense military air activity in the Strait. Suggest you exercise caution. Please come about to heading one-seven-zero degrees until you clear 22 degrees north latitude. PACOM has decided we don't need any more US military assets in the area at present. Please acknowledge."

Joe responded, "This is Tango Five-Niner, that's a wilco. Coming about to one-seven-zero degrees." Joe pursed his lips and looked back at Dan, then he wrinkled his forehead in concentration.

"Okinawa Control, this is Tango Five-Niner. What freq is the Amphibious Squadron 11 on? I'd like to give them a call."

Okinawa Control responded with an unencrypted voice frequency.

"Amphibious Squadron 11, this is Tango Five-Niner, a United States Aircraft en-route to Indonesia, over."

"Last calling station, this is Amphibious Squadron 11, please say again last transmission, over." The response was loud and clear.

"Amphibious Squadron 11, this is Tango Five-Niner, a United States Aircraft en-route to Indonesia, over."

"United States Aircraft, please identify, over."

"I'm a flight of C-17s headed south out of Elmendorf, over."

"What are you doing on this frequency, over?"

"We got your freq from Okinawa Control. We heard there's some action in the neighborhood. I like to know what's going on in the world around me, so I decided to give the Navy a call, over."

An older voice got on the radio, "United States C-17s, this is the USS *Belleau Wood*. We are picking up hundreds of aircraft flying east out of Mainland China towards Taiwan. We don't know their intent yet, but you may wish to put some distance between Taiwan and yourself right now, over."

"Roger. We'll keep our eyes peeled. If we can do anything for you, let us know. We'll monitor this freq. Tango Five-Niner, out."

*   *   *

For the last three days the missile sat erect on its mobile launcher, a large, eight-wheeled vehicle that looked vaguely like a fire truck, underneath a huge spreading canopy of camouflage netting held aloft by 20 meter high poles. From the air, the missile site would look like the canopy of a giant, leafy tree. It blended in quite well with the surrounding terrain near the rocky Chinese coast.

The political officer marched into the missile launch site, as he always did, with an air of overbearing smugness. The missile technicians followed him, as they always did, looking calm and self-assured. The troops who manned the missile launcher wondered why all the fuss and attention for their unit. Rumors were rife, of course. Some suspected that theirs was a new missile type, others that a special warhead was being tested. Of course, no one told them anything.

This day, however, things were different. One of the missile technicians mounted a lift basket, the kind the soldiers from the big cities often saw being used to lift utility workers up to telephone poles and traffic lights. He then carefully maneuvered himself next to the nose cone of the erect CSS-7/M-11 short-range ballistic missile. He opened an access panel and took out an electronic box from which he connected a few wires into the unknown payload. He called down to his co-workers, working through a checklist with acronyms the soldiers didn't understand nor dared to inquire about.

When the technician was finished, he removed the box and closed the panel, but didn't screw it shut. He lowered himself, then handed the box over to the political officer who quickly climbed into the basket. He was almost grinning.

The political officer then repeated the missile technician's routine. When he was done, he removed the box and shut the access panel, screwing in all five screws.

As the political officer reached the ground he called for the missile battery commander. A few words were exchanged. The commander turned to his troops and commanded them to open the camouflage netting that covered the missile and its six wheeled transporter-erector-launcher. Within moments, the netting parted down the middle, allowing the missile to face the high overcast sky.

Off to the south some of the sharper-eyed soldiers could see dozens of jet aircraft flying west towards the Mainland. They were dropping rapidly, as if in an attack profile or in a hurry to land. Since the jets were not threatening them and since they had received no warning of hostile aircraft, they ignored the aircraft returned to their work.

Soon the commander yelled for everyone to man their launch stations. The battery sergeants called off the troop roster to ensure all were accounted for. The commander, the political officer and four of the technicians climbed into the launch control van, parked just behind a small rise from the missile and its launcher. It too was covered with camouflage netting.

It was 7:59 AM on Saturday morning. For some reason the

political officer had affixed a loud speaker outside the launch van. His voice counted down. . . "Five, four, three, two, one, fire!"

The solid rocket motor ignited immediately and the missile roared into flight, heading straight up, leaving a trail of choking white smoke. Within a few seconds the missile began to slowly tilt towards the east, looking like a small orange sun peering through the high white clouds. About 15 seconds later it disappeared behind the high cloud layer.

Inside the launch van the political officer had tuned a short wave radio to a Taiwanese radio station. This, of course, was exceptionally illegal for anyone to do. But, no one would dare challenge a political officer, so not a thing was said.

At one minute and ten seconds into the missile's flight, the eastern sky faintly flashed. The radio made a sound like it had picked up a distant lightning strike, then the station went dead. The political officer looked at his watch, the time was 8:03:12. He picked up the radio and slowly spun the dial through the short-wave band—he picked up Beijing Radio's broadcast. The radio receiver still worked. He was told this was probably a good sign.

His role in the patriotic effort to bring Taiwan back into the Middle Kingdom's orbit was complete. In the Year of the Dragon, July 22, the dragon had finally returned. Chinese hegemony was at last at hand.

*   *   *

Brigadier General Mao had a most unfortunate name for a general in the ROC Army. Still, it was a measure of the society he grew up in that his name earned him an occasional jibe, but nothing more.

General Mao was close to the pinnacle of his military career. In charge of an infantry brigade on the heavily fortified island of Hsaio Quemoy, General Mao was pleased with the precautions that had been taken to meet the coming invaders.

Since the Communist Chinese began their latest series of provocations a few months ago, Taipei had seen fit to send another division of infantry to add to the four that were regularly stationed on the Quemoy Island group. In addition, military intelligence now had it from a reliable source that the PLA might actually try to invade within the next 48 hours!

General Mao was absolutely confident that his troops could beat back any invader. He had the most extensive series of bunkers and fortifications with interlocking fields of fire that 50 years of preparation could imagine. He had ammunition, food and water enough to last six months. And he had right on his side. He knew he was fighting for freedom.

He surveyed the situation map. Across the bay at Amoy he saw the 85th Infantry Division, still in the position it had traditionally occupied for the last several years. In addition, intelligence had picked up indicators that elements of two divisions from the 11th Group Army, the 71st and 73rd, had moved from their stations inland and were now in the vicinity of Amoy. These forces, combined with the Chinese forces around Fuzhou to the north, could achieve local superiority against Quemoy—assuming they were supported by the PLAAF and a massive amount of accurate artillery.

A phone rang in the command bunker, the signalman made a note in the staff journal and handed the phone to General Mao.

"General Mao speaking."

"General Mao, this is Admiral Tin, we have indications that a sizable PLAN amphibious task force is headed your way. They were heading southeast just outside our territorial waters and are now swinging to the northeast. We estimate that they'll violate our waters in two to three minutes. We have a task force observing them but we cannot guarantee that we will sink every last ship if it comes to a fight."

"Is that all?"

"No general, the force is estimated to be capable of carrying approximately 7,000 troops and 150 tanks. We are also seeing a large massing of fishing boats to your west in Amoy Bay."

"Thank you for the information, we'll be ready. Tell the sailors to leave some of the Communists dry so we can have our turn too." General Mao revealed a toothy, tea-stained grin. So, this was probably the culmination of months of Communist bluster and rehearsal. They had already practiced invading his five mile long island four times since last February. Each time, the amphibious force got larger and closer to his beach defenses. Each time, they turned back. Now, with the report from intelligence, it looked like this might be the time.

The general turned to his Operations Officer. "We may finally have some unpleasant company. Order the men to increase their chemical weapons protective posture to level four (this put all men not in bunkers with overpressure filtration systems into their chemical suits with gloves and masks on). Alert all personnel, I want 100% manning at all posts." Thankfully, the mysterious flu from Taiwan hadn't hit Quemoy, probably because an infected person hadn't flown to the islands yet.

The speaker box attached to tactical landline network squawked to life, "This is Counterbattery Station Four, we're picking up inbound artillery and rocket fire. Estimated impact time: 15 seconds. Impact area: island-wide. This is huge! They must be firing ten battalions on us!"

Already, the counterbattery radars had sent their data to the computers that calculated the estimated point of impact as well as the estimated location of the firing battery. If any firing battery was within range, General Mao had given standing orders to shoot back. Unfortunately, all the attacking rocket artillery was out of range. There were some tube artillery within range, though, and General Mao felt the satisfying vibrations of outgoing artillery just seconds before the incoming rounds burst on his little island.

The artillery fell so fast and hard it sounded like the roar of a storm and an earthquake even though the bunker was buried 30 feet down. "Give me Taipei before our comm links get cut!"

Within seconds, the signal corpsman handed him a phone. He had raised Army Command in Taipei. "This is Brigadier General Mao on Hsiao Quemoy. We are under heavy bombardment. We are returning counterbattery fire. We are preparing to receive an enemy amphibious assault."

"Understood, stand-by, General Ming wants to. . ." In a loud crack of static, the line went dead.

General Mao was now left alone to face what he was sure was the first Chinese landing attempt on Nationalist soil since 1949.

21
War

Two Chinese M-11 missiles roared skyward from two launch sites in coastal China. One flew in the direction of northern Taiwan, the other, the southern half of the island.

Taiwan's missile defense network picked up the incoming missiles three minutes after launch and a few seconds later they determined the launch points and the aim points. Taiwan's air defense officers were pleased to see that the missiles would impact into the Pacific Ocean well to the east of Taiwan. Clearly, these missiles were intended to intimidate, not damage, just like the Chinese missiles fired into the sea in March 1996. The officers ordered the Patriot surface-to-air missile batteries to a state of alert and passed word of the Chinese launch up the chain of command to the civilian authorities.

In the space of two milliseconds, the People's Republic of China had tied the previous record for the use of atomic weaponry in combat set by the United States in 1945. Then, as now, the nuclear bombs were used against nations that held no countervailing deterrent.

Unlike the crude bombs used over Japan, however, these bombs were not designed to kill people, vaporize military equipment or crush buildings. These bombs, painstakingly built from plans stolen from America ten years before, were specifically designed to minimize the three traditional destructive components of atomic weapons: thermal energy, blast, and radiation. Instead, these weapons produced a highly concentrated and extremely brief pulse of electro-magnetic energy. This electro-magnetic pulse (EMP) effect didn't even interest the original users of the A-bomb in 1945. But, in 21st Century, the effects of an EMP burst would prove devastating to a modern society, its military machine, and, most importantly, its national command authority.

Using the highly accurate time signal from the US Global Positioning System (GPS) satellites, the warheads were set to go off within milliseconds of each other at an altitude of 100 miles to deliver a crippling blow to the electronics below for a diameter of 200 miles.

The bombs were extremely specialized, but not especially complex nuclear ordnance. Their nuclear efficiency wasn't very high—when detonating, they left a fair amount of nuclear fuel unburned. The bombs worked on a simple principle: convert the energy of a nuclear explosion into a highly focused unidirectional cone of electromagnetic energy.

A standard nuclear bomb is composed of a sphere of conventional explosives encircling the nuclear material. The explosives are carefully designed to rapidly compress the fissionable material into a dense critical mass to trigger a self-sustaining and explosive nuclear chain reaction.

The nuclear-driven E-bomb was different; it had an atypical arrangement of explosive lenses encircling its fissionable material—much like an upside-down fluted glass. The explosive part of the bomb was itself surrounded by two coils of an alloy of platinum and depleted uranium. Each coil was embedded within a non-conductive composite ceramic and Kevlar epoxy case, itself within a tube of super hardened steel.

The bomb's detonation cycle began with a sudden electrical current surging through the coils from a capacitor. At the peak of electrical discharge and concurrent magnetic energy generated by the coils, the bomb began its detonation. Explosives at the closed end of the upside-down glass started to compress the Uranium 235, beginning a chain reaction. Within nanoseconds, the explosive ring fired downward, sending a shock wave of compression into the fissionable material just ahead of the spreading nuclear reaction. The material was held in place long enough (a few nanoseconds) by the plate at the bottom, so that it did not fly apart until it had accomplished its purpose.

This carefully timed directional nuclear blast multiplied the electrical and magnetic forces in the surrounding coils 10,000 times over, creating what engineers call an explosively pumped flux compression generator. Each coil was tuned to produce a desired frequency to maximize destruction of the intended target systems. The resulting electromagnetic shock wave raced downward in a focused cone, destroying most things electrical in its path.

The damage inflicted by the nuclear driven E-bombs was similar to the damage from a nearby lightning strike. Commercial computers, aircraft avionics, the civilian electrical grid and especially anything connected to an antenna were damaged. Interestingly, many transmitters, especially radars, continued to operate; however, without a functional radar receiver or computer to display the information, the transmitter was useless.

To protect their own systems, the Chinese had taken simple precautions. They were highly confident the E-bombs would perform as the engineers and scientists said they would, only producing a cone of electronic destruction aimed at Taiwan. Just in case, however, military electronics were turned off just before the detonation. Batteries were disconnected from devices. Antennas were disconnected. Radios and computers were wrapped in aluminum foil. Submarines stayed submerged.

Ironically, old, vacuum tube-based electronics were relatively immune from the effects of EMP. Thus, many of the older Chinese systems were hardened to EMP by virtue of their obsolete design.

To minimize any potential damage to the civilian infrastructure, the power grid for southeast China was blacked out five minutes before the detonations. The energy from the blasts was tightly focused. There was no collateral damage on Mainland China.

A few civil aircraft, both Chinese and foreign, inadvertently fell victim as well. These were counted as regrettable and unavoidable losses of war. To be safe, key officials were kept out of aircraft near the danger zone.

Chinese policy planners had pondered long and hard about engaging in what some thought amounted to nuclear war. They decided that the United States would not respond for three reasons—first, the E-bombs would produce no direct civilian casualties; second, Chinese ICBMs and its one nuclear missile submarine could threaten American cities; and third, there would probably be no damage to US military forces, especially its space assets. Regarding the latter, the Chinese knew that most US military satellites were carefully hardened against EMP. If the E-bombs focused their energy downward, with any luck, the US would lose no major systems and would therefore have no grounds for complaint or immediate concern.

Japan and South Korea would, of course, view the use of nuclear weapons with alarm, but, Chinese planners had taken this into account as well. If the US could be shown to be powerless to stop a Chinese takeover of Taiwan, the strategists were confident that, within a year, East Asia would be under the protective umbrella of Chinese military might. There was simply nothing any other nation could do to stop it.

*　　*　　*

As suddenly as it began, the Mainlander onslaught passed. Brigadier General Mao was puzzled. He ordered the signalman to do a radio net call and assess his troops' condition. All radios were silent; not even static. He noticed the bunker's emergency lights were on. Not surprising, the barrage probably cut the power lines. He ordered the landlines used—he had assumed the intense barrage would have severed some of the lines. To his surprise, all of the stations reported, save one.

The brigade intelligence officer had been working on the situation simultaneously and walked up to his commanding officer to brief him on what he knew, "Sir, I have some information."

"Please, major, proceed." The general was heartened that they had absorbed the enemy's first blow and were still functioning with military efficiency.

"Sir, the bombardment of our positions lasted only five minutes, although, I must admit, it was a robust bombardment. Initial estimates are that 10 battalions of rocket and tube artillery participated in the attack. We were able to contact Quemoy via our underwater cable link. They are fine. No bombardment. They have lost contact with our naval elements in the vicinity, however. Sir, one more thing: Quemoy HQ can't raise Taipei on the radio. In fact, they can't hear anything on their radios."

One of the signalmen, looking very nervous, interrupted, "Sirs, I believe all of our radio receiver circuits have been burned out."

"What?" Both the general and the major asked in unison.

Looking more comfortable, the signalman continued, "Sirs, it's as if all our topside antennas got hit by lightning."

The major's stomach went more queasy then it did in the middle of the barrage, "General, sir, I believe I know what happened. The Communists have exploded a nuclear bomb somewhere nearby. The bomb's electro-magnetic pulse has destroyed all non-protected electronic equipment. We have been sheltered because we are buried, but our radios have a direct electrical link with the outside world through their antennas. The land lines work because they're buried."

"Send out a nuclear and chemical reconnaissance team. I want to know what happened." Turning to his operations officer, the general said, "Colonel, keep the men on full alert for at least the next four hours, then begin a 16 hours on, eight hours off schedule for everyone. We may be here for a while."

*   *   *

Fu Zemin could hardly believe the orders he had just read and was

157

busy destroying with a bottle of mineral water. *Taiwan itself was being invaded! Not the insignificant island of Quemoy! My recommendation was accepted*! He only had seconds to wonder why he was sent here to watch over Admiral Wong and the Quemoy invasion preparations. Fu was being ordered to fly to Taiwan with elements of the 85th Infantry Division and be the Party's official representative on the island until relieved! He could hardly believe his luck!

He wished he could tell someone, then he thought of how he was getting to Taiwan—with elements of the 85th Infantry Division. *The military. War. Danger.* He remembered how he hated personal privations. How he avoided military service through his father's Party connections. Still, how dangerous could it be if the Party chieftains were willing to send him, a highly placed and very knowledgeable Party foreign affairs advisor, to Taiwan?

He speculated on whether the Party had accepted the rest of his memo—his recommendation to follow-up the reunification of Taiwan with a campaign to conquer East Asia before an anti-China grouping of states could contain China's rightful ambitions.

He smiled. He was a hero of China. He himself might even rule Asia some day.

*   *   *

The 747-400 had just touched down at Chaing Kai-Shek International Airport—just another Chinese flight from Hong Kong as far as anyone outside of the aircraft was concerned— routine business travel.

The aircraft was taxiing towards the terminal when all its electrical systems went dead. The aircraft's engines flamed out and it slowly came to a halt just shy of the terminal. Normally this would have greatly concerned the tower, but they had larger troubles to worry about. Just a few minutes before the understaffed tower (40% of the air traffic controllers were on sick call) received a report about a large force of Mainland jet aircraft approaching Taiwan. They were to clear the skies of civil aviation, vectoring them away from the potential areas of confrontation. As they were redirecting aircraft all of their radio equipment popped and began smoking, the terminal and approach radars went down, and the power went out. The emergency systems failed to kick in. The tower was dead.

The controllers were flabbergasted. For a space of five seconds—an eternity in air traffic control—the tower was completely silent. The chief controller finally spoke, "Did we get a lightning strike? I didn't hear any thunder. You there, Ju, go down the tower and check for external damage, maybe we were hit by something. Lin, call Taipei control and tell them we're out of business. What the? Flight 557 from Hong Kong, the 747, it looks like its in trouble!"

The senior controller pointed down to the 747 at the far end of the terminal. Steam seemed to be billowing out of its now open passenger exits.

*   *   *

Lieutenant Colonel Chu Dugen looked at his watch through his protective mask. He always hated wearing the bulky things, but they worked, and, if one trained in them enough, they weren't much of a hindrance. The commandos used Israeli protective masks. The wide lenses offered much more peripheral vision than the old goggle-eyed Soviet-era protective masks the PLA used.

In two more minutes, the 747 would have finished disgorging its supply of the incapacitating agent, a phenothiazine-type compound that affected its victims in a non-lethal fashion, rendering them, in most cases, unable to act upon the information their brains processed. Another two minutes after that and the first missile-delivered incapacitating agent would burst over the airport. If all went according to plan, every armed defender within five kilometers would be rendered passive for half a day or longer, giving the commandos precious time to secure CKS International for the follow-on forces.

Another minute went by. Dugen hazarded a look out of the passenger window. He saw three airport workers pointing and laughing at the 'steaming' 747. Dugen smiled. The agent was taking effect. A fourth worker was simply staring into space, a large fire extinguisher at his side.

The Chinese attackers had been ingenious in their attack planning. Rather than using only one type of incapacitating agent, the high command decided on three, each with its own advantages.

The first type, used in areas where direct military contact was expected, such as CKS International Airport, was a compound based on phenothiazine. This drug, easy to deliver in militarily significant doses via air burst bombs or missiles, acted as a depressant on the central nervous system. The people so affected would not have their higher reasoning powers seriously impaired; they would understand their surroundings—they just wouldn't care about what they saw. They would completely lack any motivation to resist or follow orders. This drug had another advantage: it was easily counteracted with amphetamines. This was key because, if the drug remained in the air in aerosol form or was somehow absorbed into the skin, the attackers would also be subject to its effects within a few hours. Thus, by wearing a protective mask, the attackers could remain immune from the more immediate effects of inhalation and, because the agent's effects could be reversed, the wearing of a bulky and constraining protective suit could be avoided.

The second compound used on the assault was BZ. Experimented with by the Americans in their war in Southeast Asia, BZ was quickly discarded as militarily useless by the US Army. The Chinese tested it and thought otherwise. BZ acts on acetylcholine in the nerve endings. It disrupts the high integrative functions of memory, problem solving, attention, and comprehension. At high doses, it produces delirium, destroying a soldier's ability to perform any military task. It also is more difficult to treat, requiring sustained medical attention with a drip IV or several shots over a period of hours. Because of this, the Chinese planned to use BZ in large doses on the invasion beaches and in areas where reserve forces were known to be.

The last agent used in quantity during the assault was d-lysergic acid diethylamide or LSD. Extremely effective at very small doses, absorbed through both inhalation and on contact with the skin, this agent was a stimulant of the central nervous system. LSD causes excessive nervous system activity. It floods the cortex and other higher regulatory centers with too much information. This flooding makes concentration difficult and causes indecisiveness and an inability to act in a sustained, purposeful manner. For this reason, and because there was no known way to counteract the agent (other than time) LSD was chosen as the agent for the assault on Taipei. While the EMP attack was probably more than enough to take away the eyes, ears and voice of the leadership in Taipei, the LSD follow-on assault also took away the mind, destroying the enemy's ability to think rationally.

Overall, the Chinese were very pleased with their unconventional warfare planning efforts. They estimated that the actual civilian fatalities caused by a combined EMP/incapacitating agent assault would be less than 2,000. The EMP attack would decapitate a modern, information-age society. It would also make it very difficult for the Taiwanese to wire large sums of money out of their nation's banks to overseas locations. The use of incapacitating agents could easily be spun by Beijing's propagandists as simply a variation on tear gas and other routine civil disturbance control measures. Non-lethal in principle, these agents would preserve as much of the Taiwanese people and economic engine as possible while simultaneously adding to Beijing's "internal matter" cover story. They also hoped the minimal amount of deaths would lower the response from Washington, Tokyo, and Seoul.

Dugen heard some faint "pops" overhead. He knew these would be the chemical warheads exploding over the airport. Delivered by the solid fueled M-9 rocket, each warhead was filled with 800 pounds of phenothiazine compound packaged into hundreds of small aerosol cans. As the warhead reached the target area, it split open and dispersed the cans, which immediately began spraying the agent as they fell to earth on streamers. If inhaled, the compound would begin to work in minutes.

The M-9 missile, known as the Dong Feng (East Wind)-15 employed a Western manufactured GPS-based terminal guidance system. This commercially based system improved the missile's accuracy by greater than a factor of three, giving it a circular error probable of less than 300 feet (CEP is defined as a 50% likelihood of a missile or bomb landing within a given circular or oval area).

With an intact Taiwanese early warning defense system, the follow-on attack by the M-9 missiles might have faced some opposition. But the E-bomb strike destroyed Taiwan's missile early warning radar that was to give the defenders a 90 second reaction time. Unfortunately, even with a 90 second warning, the American-supplied Patriot PAC-2+ would only achieve a four in ten chance of intercepting the missile's warhead—and by then, the missile would be close enough to the target that its load of chemical agent would still disperse over much of the target area.

Dugen looked at his watch again. By now the entire airport area should have been blanketed by the incapacitating agent. He went on the 747's intercom system, his voice muffled and tinny from the voice meter of the protective mask, "Attention men of Jia Battalion, we are about to begin the reintegration of the renegade province of Taiwan into China. You know your assignments. You have trained and rehearsed very hard. You are the best soldiers China has ever produced." Dugen's enthusiasm was buoyed by his finding out, only an hour before, that his mission was not to be a diversion, but the lead assault in a massive air landing effort.

Dugen paused, took a large gulp of filtered air and exhorted, "On my signal now, ten seconds, nine, eight, seven, six, five, four, three, two, one, go, go, go!"

At each emergency exit, Dugen's troops pulled open the hatches and triggered the automatic inflatable slides. Because sharp-edged military equipment would quickly snag and deflate the slides, the soldiers were equipped with thin plastic sleds to protect the slides.

The visual image of tough, heavily armed commandos sledding down plastic ramps as if they were at a water park was too much for the intoxicated ramp workers. The one with the fire extinguisher stumbled away, sensing danger and feebly reacting to it. The other three pointed at the soldiers and giggled uncontrollably.

Dugen's soldiers hit the ground running. Dugen had devised a special tactic for the initial phase of his operation. He had 19 commando teams of ten men each in the first wave of the assault. Each team had a specific objective. Some teams also had one or more follow-on missions. The other 19 teams each trailed a lead team, having the same mission as the first if the first was unable to complete its mission. As a secondary role, the follow-on teams used plastic zip lock tabs to bind the arms and feet of any military, police, security or official personnel they encountered. Dugen held four teams in reserve to meet unforeseen challenges. The remaining eight soldiers were part of Lieutenant Colonel Chu Dugen's command group.

By the time Dugen hit the tarmac, about half of his soldiers were already in operation. Because wearing a protective mask hides one's identity and distorts the voice, Dugen had every commando wear a coded number on the mask's front and on the back of the rubberized hood. Dugen's number was 0001. His Executive officer was 0002. The squad leader of commando team two was 0201, etc. In this fashion, his entire team knew exactly who was in charge on the scene—and who everyone was—key hurdles when fighting in a chemical weapons environment.

Not one shot had been fired yet. Dugen was encouraged. They might even run ahead of schedule.

Dugen looked out from underneath the jumbo jet's massive cluster of center landing gear at the runway. He immediately saw a huge problem, rather, five huge problems that dozens of rehearsals hadn't taken into account: scattered about on CKS International's runways were five commercial jets. These aircraft, if not moved, would effectively deny the army the use of the airfield he had worked so hard to get. Dugen had to think quickly.

He decided to commit his reserve early. He called for his reserve leaders—men instructed not to leave earshot until assigned a mission, "Reserve squad leaders!" Four men ran to Dugen's position under the aircraft. Dugen suddenly felt very vulnerable, having a tactical conference under the belly of a fuel and ammunition-laden 747 in the middle of an invasion. *Another oversight from the rehearsals.*

"I need you to tow those aircraft off the runways. Cluster them near the terminal. The tow vehicles ought to work (Dugen remembered the short technical briefing on the effects of the E-bomb they gave him just before takeoff). If you need technical help, grab some of the airport workers. They should still be able to talk. Treat them nicely. Tell them you're from the army and you're here to help. Any questions? Go!"

For some reason, Dugen was more at ease. He had encountered a problem and believed he had the means to solve it. A challenge-free operation meant he was missing something. He set to work clearing the airport for the Chinese army forces that were due to fly in within the hour.

*   *   *

The inside of the dry bulk container ship in Kaohsiung Harbor held more than 4,000 Chinese infantry—an entire regiment and some divisional support elements of the 97th Infantry Division, 14th Group Army. Every weapon they had was man-portable. Vehicles and larger crew-served weapons such as medium and heavy artillery would have to wait for the follow-on forces.

The noise in the ship was an echoing madness. The private was ready to throw up the water he had consumed so quickly a few minutes before. Three days in this hell hole had left him fatigued.

Now, adding insult, the platoon sergeant ordered the platoon to don their protective masks.

The air inside the mask was thankfully free of the odor of the overflowing toilets, but the mask offered little else in the way of consolation.

The private and his fellow soldiers were crammed into a ship that normally carried ore. To increase its human cargo capacity, the PLAN secretly and hurriedly added an inexpensive network of metal shelving within the ship's hold. As an afterthought (and for general hygienic reasons) portable toilets had been brought into the hold as well. To complete the deception, a layer of shelving was added to the top of the ship upon which a thin layer of ore was placed. From the air, the ship looked loaded. To facilitate easy ingress and egress, several hatches were carefully cut into the side of the ship, allowing the troops the leave rapidly from the hull, rather then climbing up through the top and back down the sides again.

Due to the pursuit of normalized relations and lucrative trade and investment opportunities, there had been direct cargo connections between the Mainland and Taiwan for a few years now. It was this routine activity the Chinese sought to exploit for military gain. A cargo vessel is not the most ideal platform for launching a seaborne invasion. However, with total surprise, somewhat akin to the Trojan Horse, a ship could get into a harbor and might successfully get its troops into battle as was done by the Germans in 1940 in Norway.

The Chinese plan called for the use of three such outfitted cargo ships, docking, from north to south, at: Taichung Harbor, Tainan and Kaohsiung. Each ship carried about 4,000 men. In addition, the Chinese pressed one of COSCO's luxury cruise ships into service to take the port of Keelung in the far north, only 20 miles northeast of Taipei. This ship carried an entire infantry division, less its heavy equipment. Thus, without a shot being fired, the Chinese landed 22,000 troops—the better part of two divisions—on Taiwan. (China possessed a traditional amphibious assault force capability of only 20,000.)

In the meantime, the soldiers in Kaohsiung had the element of surprise and the force multiplying effects of the E-bomb and the incapacitating agent. The former had just detonated when the cargo ship began to spew the latter out of its smoke stacks.

164

The wind was stiffening to the west, carrying much of the agent harmlessly out to sea. Some of it did affect the dockworkers and Customs agents down the length of Penglai Road astride the main dockyards, the rest intoxicated the upscale residents of Chichin Island. The city center was untouched until six M-9 missiles rained down their canisters of aerosol phenothiazine agent.

A feeling of claustrophobia was about to overtake the private when a brilliant shaft of light shown through into the dusty chamber. The platoon sergeant roared a muffled command through his mask. All he could say that his troops could understand was, "Go! Go! Go!" The sergeant kicked, shoved and pushed his men towards the open hatch.

The private stumbled out into the sunlight with wobbly legs. The gangplank to the dock was only a meter wide and about eight meters long. He almost lost his balance and fell ten meters into the oily harbor waters below. He was surprised to see that he was the first soldier on the narrow, bouncing ramp. Obviously allies had positioned the walkway there, but they were nowhere to be seen.

A mass of soldiers began piling up behind the private and pushed him forward. He stumbled down the ramp and came face-to-face with a uniformed Customs officer of the Republic of China. He held out his hand to stop the Mainlander private, "Stop. Who are you? Where are your papers?" He yelled. Accustomed to obeying authority in uniform, the private skidded to a halt, forcing two soldiers to jump off the ramp and onto the quay, while a third lost his balance and fell into the water below, his mask stifling the cry on the way down.

The Customs officer began to laugh. The private was confused. His tremendous fatigue and dehydration were compounded by the protective mask's confinement. He heard yelling behind him. It sounded like the platoon sergeant. He was yelling, "Shoot him! Shoot! Shoot him!"

The private brought his assault rifle to his hip and pulled back the charging handle to chamber a round. The Customs officer, stood there, giggling uncontrollably, "Ha! You're going to shoot me?" In a brief moment, mirth turned to fear, but the officer didn't move.

The private fired once into the officer's stomach. The officer doubled over as if punched in the midsection. He staggered back, tripped and landed on his back, pain slowly clouding his eyes. He reached for his pistol. At that instant, the other two conscripts on the dock saw the danger and fired on full automatic at the Customs officer. The officer was killed by the second round—a shot to the head—but the excited and marginally trained young soldiers wasted another 25 rounds on the corpse.

The private was pushed aside by a rush of soldiers trying to get to the dock, then make their way down Penglai Road to the port's main Customs office. The platoon sergeant stomped by and grabbed him roughly by the wrist, "Come on, 'Hero of all China,' let's move it!"

*   *   *

The ROC submarine captain was making his way to one of his pre-arranged attack positions in deeper water. The Dutch submarine was designed to function quite well in the shallow waters off a river's delta—but, when given a choice, it was always better to have more room to maneuver and hide. Of course, the Taiwanese surface fleet knew where he might be lurking and would avoid attacking that area (no sense in being sunk by your friends).

The tactical display showed the six ROC Navy vessels due north about two nautical miles. They formed an air defense cluster just inside the territorial waters surrounding Quemoy Island. To the east-northeast, about five enemy vessels had broken away from the main group of 25 remaining ships and were pressing in towards the defenders.

With careful maneuvering, he knew he could get into position to attack the southernmost part of what was probably the main amphibious invasion force. He thought of the satisfaction of sinking a landing ship filled with troops and tanks from the Communist Mainland. "Tactical officer!" the statement was an exclamation, the volume, however, was tightly measured—like controlled thunder. "Give me a read on the ship types in the enemy flotilla as soon as possible."

"Yes sir, already working the problem," the tactical officer was supervising the chief sonar technician who was running a comparative analysis of the propeller and engine sounds from the Mainlander fleet.

"Sir, so far we see none of the 'A' list ships. There are two Jiangwei-type frigates here and here," the tactical officer said,

166

pointing at the sonar scope. He knew his captain loved to see the data live right off the screen, rather than looking pretty on the tactical display. "We see only one amphibious ship, a Shan-Class LST (Landing Ship Tank). Other than one Haiqing ASW patrol craft, the other 25 ships are small patrol and fast attack craft."

The skipper was visibly disappointed. The Shan-class displaced 4,080 tons and could only carry 150 troops and 16 tanks—and it was the largest ship in the enemy flotilla out there this morning. Clearly, this was not the vanguard of an invasion fleet. Still. . . If the enemy crossed the line today, he had orders to make them pay a price.

Suddenly, the chief sonar operator jumped in his seat and placed both hands on his earphones. The tactical officer, who was holding an earphone over one ear said, "Sir, someone's been hit by a missile or torpedo! Wait, there's three more. Oh shit! Multiple detonations! Sir, the war has started!"

"Steady now, Lieutenant," the captain was calm and reassuring. "Target the Shan with two torpedoes. Target the Jiangweis with one each. Target the Haiqing with one. Let's keep one ready in case we get unexpected company. Prepare to fire."

The boat's torpedo tubes flooded with water in preparation for launch.

"Sir, I'm picking up more explosions. Sir, this isn't good, two of our ships are no longer under way, we've lost contact." When using passive sonar, the submarine relied on the noise produced by a vessel to make an identification of the ship's type and location. While not perfect, especially in shallow coastal waters with the layers of salt and fresh, warm and cold water, modern tracking and processing equipment made the job much easier and more reliable.

"Transient to our rear! 1,500 yards!" The tactical officer was almost beside himself.

"Retarget four torpedoes on the new target area and fire when ready, then fire on the Shan after the first four torps are gone!" Hsaing directly addressed the enlisted weapons technician. Now the boat's captain was excited. He wasn't thinking of death, only of doing the job he was trained for as quickly and expertly as possible. "Go active at 750 meters and cut the wires!"

The boat softly trembled with the launching of the torpedoes. "Set the torpedoes for the Shan wake home at 2,500 yards. As soon as all torpedoes clear, launch three decoys and come about to 100 degrees, then slow to two knots and let's find bottom."

The boat shuddered twice more with the last two torpedoes.

"Sir, there's two torpedoes in the water heading our way. Both from the same vicinity. I still hear nothing else. Pinging! One of the torpedoes is pinging for us! Pinging. We have two pinging for us!" The tactical officer was pressing the earphone so hard into his ear it looked as if he was going to crush the side of his head.

He resisted the urge to run. To order flank speed and make the noise that would make the enemy's task of finding him and killing him that much easier. "Helm, all stop! Cut the power and drift to the bottom. We'll hide in the mud."

The tactical officer spoke, this time more calmly, "Sir, the torpedoes appear to be heading towards the decoys. Our torpedoes should start pinging soon."

"Any read on what fired those torpedoes?" He almost wished it was one of the Kilos.

"No sir. We can hear nothing out there." The tactical officer sounded sorry. "Our torpedoes are searching! I hear the pings."

Maybe they'd get away this time. Six shots off. Maybe they landed the first blows to connect with the enemy in this latest confrontation in the seven decades-long struggle between the Chinese on Taiwan and the Communists on the Mainland.

"One of the inbounds has gone to continuous ping. It's at 300 meters and closing!" The tactical officer was pleading with his captain, his eyes betraying fear.

"What's the status of our torpedoes?" The captain wanted his quarry.

"Still in search mode."

"Drop four decoys! Hard right rudder, all ahead flank! Get to periscope depth. Come on, move it!" His only hope lay in rising rapidly to the layer of warmer and fresher surface water. Perhaps then the torpedo's sonar return would be deflected or distorted enough that they could break its lock.

"It's closing. 100 meters, sir." The tactical officer was pale and quiet now, resigned to his fate.

Well, that was a quick war. The enemy torpedo struck aft. Its explosion shattered the boat's hull. The pressure of 150 feet of water did the rest. There were no survivors.

*   *   *

The hijacked Il-76 combi jet (passenger and cargo) had touched down at 8:00 AM. The senior controller ordered the aircraft to proceed to the end of the runway (where the hijackers would either give up or be killed by the special security police).

The senior controller's headache wasn't any better. This flu was bad. Might as well be at work; he felt too sick to enjoy the nice day. There was only a high cloud cover and it wasn't supposed to rain for at least a day—or until that typhoon east of the Philippines started to affect the weather. The high was forecast at 88 degrees. Nice day. The pain in his skull brought him back to focus on work.

He radioed the hijacked aircraft. No reply. He had five flights stacked up waiting for approval to land. *Better send them to CKS, this may take awhile.* He had no need to tell security; they were already monitoring his communications with the aircraft.

The senior controller folded his hands behind his head and arched his back, looking out the top of the control tower window at the northern sky. He saw a flash. Simultaneously the control tower erupted in a bang as every radio spit sparks and the acrid smoke of burning wire insulation filled the air. "What the. . .? Get the fire extinguishers!"

The tower personnel were too busy to observe the Il-76. The aircraft rippled with small puffs of smoke. Fifty to one hundred yards away, small canisters began spewing smoke. A dozen grenade launchers had been attached to the aircraft. These devices, usually bolted to armored vehicles to quickly dispense smoke grenades in combat, were being employed instead to conduct a preemptive strike on the surrounding security forces. Some canisters held tear gas, others, the same agent used at almost the same instant some 20 miles to the west at CKS International Airport.

The leader of this commando team, a major, wanted to use non-persistent nerve agent in his assault. His request was vetoed by Beijing. First, Beijing wanted moral high ground of claiming (truthfully) that no lethal nuclear or chemical agents were used in its attack. Second, tear gas worked instantly, nerve agent took a few minutes. The commandos intended to be gone before anyone could react—they certainly didn't have the time to be waiting around in chemical protective gear until the last policeman finished convulsing and died.

The cargo ramp at the rear of the Il-76 rapidly lowered. The surprised security police were scrambling to get their protective masks on. Some weren't equipped and were already choking on their own mucus, violently retching and trying to get air. The ones lucky enough to get their masks on quickly had to blink back tears and could barely see to fire on the three armored cars that came racing out of the Il-76.

One security officer had only just arrived on the scene riding his motorcycle, an old, but reliable Yamaha. He stayed upwind from the spraying canisters and was soon shocked to see three Taiwanese LAV-150 Commando armored vehicles rolling down the aircraft's ramp. *What were these ROC Army vehicles doing in this "hijacked" aircraft?* He tried to call base with the news. He didn't know that the circuit boards in his state-of-the-art hand-held radio were destroyed by the high-altitude E-bomb attack.

Inside the second armored car, the major was quietly confident that all would go as planned. He was sure he could complete his mission. All he had to do was lead his team from Sungshan Airport downtown only 7.8 kilometers to the Presidential Building where they would arrest the so-called President of the Republic of China on Taiwan—or kill him while trying.

The mission would be made all the easier by the E-bomb attack, which the planners told him, would destroy the enemy's ability to communicate. Finally, conducting the raid using Taiwanese-type vehicles (quietly purchased from the Sudan, then refurbished) would only add to the surprise and confusion. No one at all would know 39 soldiers of the PLA, dressed in ROC Army uniforms, were coming.

The major followed the lead car just after it rammed down the airport's cyclone fence. The nimble four-wheeled 9.8-ton armored car had a 202 hp V-8 diesel with a top speed of 55 mph—perfect for city driving. The small convoy turned onto Pingchaing Road in the light industrial district just north of the airport. It was 8:10 AM. There was only one moving car on this street. There were two other cars stalled in the middle of the street with their hoods open and their owners fretting over the engines. The major was glad most workers were already at their Saturday morning jobs.

Free from the area of chemical attack, the commandos removed their protective masks, greatly improving their ability to see and communicate. This would also lessen public suspicion.

The convoy turned south and ground to a halt. Traffic at the intersection was completely tangled. The light was out and there was a fender-bender between two old cars and a rusty truck. The commando team leader ordered his vehicles to push ahead on the sidewalk. Several cars were edged aside in the process. The cross street, Mintsu East Road was bumper-to-bumper. *This was not in the plan!*

The lead armored car nosed its way through the stalled traffic, clearing a way. The major curiously noticed that almost every car's driver was out and most cars had their hoods up.

The front bumper of a new Mercedes was snagged by the armored car and torn off. The wealthy businessman who owned the car was trying to get a dial tone on a nearby public phone (his cell phone ceased working) when he saw his car being wrecked by the military. *That a lowly member of the Army had the gall to damage his car!* The owner bolted out of the phone booth and ran over to his car as the second armored vehicle was ready to squeeze through. The businessman was dissuaded from further complaint when the commando major pointed the roof-mounted 20mm machine gun at the Mercedes owner's chest.

The team edged on through the city, making far slower progress than originally anticipated. The commander knew he had only 15 minutes remaining before they'd have to put their masks back on and button-up or be themselves incapacitated by a massive chemical attack.

Back at the airport, the junior security officer grasped the significance of the vehicles that roared out of the Il-76, breached the airport fence and disappeared into the city. He yelled at three of his colleagues who were upwind from the chemical attack. "You men! Come with me!" In the confusion, the men were relieved to follow someone who had a plan. He rapidly told them of the impending danger.

"We need to warn the authorities as fast as possible. With three vehicles they can attack at least three facilities. Certainly, the President will be one of their targets. Who else?"

One of the security officers reflected, "Certainly not the police station. They're too heavily armed. What about City Hall?"

"Yes, excellent! The President and City Hall, who else?"

"The National Assembly?" asked another.

The lieutenant grew impatient, "No, they're not in session and besides, there's too many of them to kill them all. Look, we're wasting time now. We're agreed that City Hall and the President's house are the two prime targets. I'll get on my motorcycle and drive to warn the President." He then pointed rapidly at each of the three men, "You get to City Hall. You get up to the Army barracks at Neihu and tell them the capital is under assault. You, find a different vehicle and get to the President's house too.

Between the both of us, one of us might make it before that assassination squad does! Let's go!"

The lieutenant ran to his bike and kick started the engine to life. He noticed that the other three security officers were having problems getting any vehicles to start. He shouted encouragement at them as rumbled by, "Keep trying, some of them have to work!"

The E-bomb's powerful wave of energy acted in two general ways: first, it produced a high voltage spike which directly damaged most commercial computer devices by breaking down their delicate Metal Oxide Semiconductor components; second, the energy wave was picked up by any receiver, whether an antenna or a simple power line, and transmitted directly to any attached device. This second mode of electronic attack was similar to sending a huge bolt of lightning down every antenna and wire in the city. Not only was the power grid destroyed, but most every computer chip was fried as well. The effect on any vehicle built in the 1980s or later was devastating. Most simply quit running at the instant of the attack.

The PLA major was getting frustrated. The streets were clogged with disabled cars, he was only halfway to his objective, and he was running out of time. It was 8:15 AM. He now had ten minutes remaining before his life was about to get much more complicated. The commandos turned south on Chengteh Road. The road was completely blocked and the sidewalks were too cluttered with vendor's stands and people to move through. *Only four kilometers to go.*

He decided to go on foot. He left a driver and vehicle commander/ machine-gunner in each LAV-150 and set out with 32 of his remaining team. At a jog they could cover at least two kilometers before the missiles rained down on key parts of the city. After that, with their masks on, he hoped they could make it to their objective before the chemical agent started to penetrate their unprotected skin.

The major gave the sign to abandon the vehicles. He knew the crews he left behind would do everything they could to catch up to his team at the Presidential Building. On each vehicle three crew hatches opened, one on each side and one in the rear. From each armored car 11 men quietly assembled on the sidewalk,

172

purposefully not taking up defensive positions nor looking threatening. Within 15 seconds they set off to the south at a fast jog, leaving the vehicle crews to figure out how to maneuver through the worst traffic jam in Taipei's history.

The lieutenant was almost to the Presidential Building. From the airport he decided to take the Chienkuo flyover south to the Jenai Road exit. He weaved expertly between the masses of broken down cars. This was a very puzzling situation and it most certainly did not bode well for the young democracy he owed allegiance to.

The young officer pulled up to the Presidential complex and was almost shot by the ring of anxious presidential guards stationed outside the main building. "I'm a special airport security officer!" he yelled, hopping off his motorcycle and letting it tip over on the sidewalk, "The President is in danger! An assassination team from China is heading this way in armored vehicles!"

By the time he finished his sentence, three presidential guards had tackled him, taken his pistol and pinned him painfully to the ground with their knees on his back and neck. "Please," he rasped, "I must speak with the officer in charge!" He felt his wallet being taken from his back pocket, "Yes, check my identification. I must speak to someone in charge."

He was handcuffed and four guards bodily carried him into a side entrance, down a hall and into a small command post. A colonel glared at him, "Speak immediately! I don't have time for this!"

The lieutenant took a deep breath and tried to tell his story as quickly and convincingly as possible.

"When did the armored vehicles leave the airport?" the colonel demanded.

"About 10 to 15 minutes ago, I guess." the lieutenant glanced at his digital watch. "I'm not sure, my watch seems to be broken, perhaps by the fall I took outside when your guards tackled me."

"A reasonable precaution when dealing with an armed madman near the President's office, don't you think?" The colonel glared.

The lieutenant blushed, "Yes sir. One of my fellow security officers should be arriving shortly, please don't shoot him. Is the President safe?"

The colonel softened, "As soon as the power failed and the

phones went down we moved the President to a safe location."

A chilling thought hit the young security officer, "Sir, the men at the airport used tear gas on us. The cars stranded all over town suggest a full-scale attack of some kind is on. Do you think the Mainlanders could have detonated a nuclear bomb nearby? Maybe at Keelung to aid an amphibious assault? Sir, does the Presidential Building have protection against chemical attack?"

"That is classified information Lieutenant." The colonel's reply was defensive.

The commando major glanced at his wind-up watch. "Platoon, halt! Get your protective masks on! Put your gloves on too!" His men had leather gloves, not rubber ones, and no suits. When the chemical strike came he figured they'd have at most an hour of functionality before being overcome. *They could do a lot of damage in an hour.* With the mask over his sweating face his lungs labored to get enough oxygen to function. Each inhalation was a struggle. They trained and trained for this, even running three times a week for five kilometers in their protective masks. It still didn't make it easy or enjoyable.

The commandos began jogging down the street again, this time slower and to the fear and amazement of the residents of Taipei. A police officer even gestured for them to stop, but the major simply gave him a friendly wave and ran on, leaving the lawman to wonder who that masked man was.

Two minutes after masking up, he heard something that sounded like a giant piece of fabric ripping in the sky. Moments later he saw a few canisters fall to earth trailing streamers. Each canister sprayed a fine mist. As long as his men didn't come into direct contact with that spray, their masks should be able to protect them—or so the mission planners maintained.

Each canister held about 225 grams of militarized d-lysergic acid diethylamide (LSD). Each rocket warhead held 1,500 canisters. One rocket filled with the tremendously potent drug could theoretically incapacitate the entire city for at least 12 hours—the Chinese fired a dozen.

The major's team made it to the serene beauty of New Park in the city center only four blocks from Chieh Shou Hall, the Presidential Building. Several canisters were visible in the park. Fearing the worst, pedestrians naturally tried to escape the spreading fumes. The PLA officer decided to make the assault without the support of the armored vehicles and without waiting for the effects of the agent to take hold.

He and his men had drilled non-stop for two months on the plans of the Presidential Building. They knew exactly where the President's command bunker was. They also felt fairly confident that he'd be inside. Once they captured the President they planned to take him to the roof of the building where a helicopter would whisk them away to either the harbor at Keelung or to the expanding air head at CKS International Airport, whichever was the most secure location. From there, the former leader of Taiwan would be taken to China for a show trial to convict him of treason.

The major led his men at a greatly reduced pace. He wanted them to catch their breaths as best they could with the masks on. They each downed a half-liter of water as well by hooking up the small flexible drinking tube on their masks to a canteen so they were able to refresh themselves without risking contamination. He also wanted to begin to exercise caution as he approached the heavily protected Presidential Building. Normally, the building was protected by about 25 uniformed police and 100 military members of the Presidential Guard. He estimated that no more than 20 would be covering the external entrance of any given side, and these would, by requirement, be outside of the building. An additional 20-30 might be inside the building. He expected that at no time would he have less than one-to-one odds on the defenders. Add to that surprise, superior equipment (including the latest British body armor) and training, and the PLA commandos had a high degree of confidence they'd accomplish their mission.

With his men now rejuvenated and ready to go, he moved out of the relatively open killing zone of the park and west onto Chiehshou Road. He sent his first squad across the car-strewn and now abandoned street and was about to send a second when a withering crossfire from the east and west cut down five of his men. Tossing smoke grenades left and right, his commandos created a curtain of concealment and weaved in and out of cars to avoid the hidden scythe of the machine guns. The smoke did little to conceal the snipers on the roofs above, however, and soon half his men were down. The remainder the men with no or only minor injuries pressed the attack across the street (the seriously wounded men were trained to die in place, keeping up as much supporting fire as possible).

The team broke into the building just north of the Presidential building, spraying the guards at the entrance with automatic weapons fire. The major knew he needed every advantage he could muster at this critical phase of his operation. He tossed a CS (riot) gas grenade into the foyer and motioned his men to go down the hall. This entrance was the primary entrance they trained on. At this point, based on his previous practice runs, he only expected to have 13 men remaining. The fact that he had 16 and the defenders probably had no functioning radios or surveillance equipment to direct their defense, or track his movements, meant that he still had an advantage.

The lieutenant and the Presidential Guard colonel felt rather than heard the dull thuds of gunfire through the building. "It sounds like you were right, lieutenant, the nation owes you a debt of gratitude." The colonel turned around and unlocked a weapons cabinet. "I trust you know how to use one of these?" He handed the young lieutenant an M-16 assault rifle and two 30 round clips.

"Yes, sir." As the lieutenant spoke he was already slapping a magazine into place and pulling the charging handle to chamber a round, "Locked and loaded, sir!"

"Follow me." The colonel bounded down the hall to a stairwell and started down, two steps at a time. The lieutenant was surprised at the colonel's dexterity. They went down four flights of stairs until four guards in front of a heavy steel blast door stopped them. The colonel briefed them about the enemy commando force topside and reaffirmed their standing orders to protect the entrance to the President's command bunker with their lives.

The colonel turned to the lieutenant. "Until relieved by a superior officer, I'm placing you in command of this guard post. Let no one pass. I'm going back to lead the defense of this building."

The colonel's lips seemed to move slowly. The young officer was concerned the colonel was showing his age. "Yes, sir. Are you all right sir?"

The colonel seemed annoyed. "Of course I am. Good luck, I'll see you soon!"

With that the colonel turned to go. The lieutenant was puzzled by the colonel's actions. There was danger everywhere and he was moving so slowly! The colonel seemed to bounce languidly up the stairs. The lieutenant turned to face the four guards. Instead of the human guards he thought he was leading, each guard had the head of a gargoyle. The lieutenant tried to suppress his surprise. His whole body shuddered. One of the gargoyles began talking. The words radiated from the Gargoyle's mouth like the waves of a pebble in a pond. The lieutenant looked down at his rifle. It was a long, deadly serpent. A serpent that spit fire and destroyed his enemies. Thunderous blasts of yellow and red filled his eyes. The gargoyles were shattered. The smell of their death was overpowering. He put his gas mask on to guard against the spirits of the dead gargoyles.

The major was down to five men. They had exhausted their supply of hand grenades and most of their ammunition to get this far and now only had the explosives needed to penetrate the President's bunker and a few CS grenades. He heard the sound of automatic weapons fire from the stairwell leading to the bunker. *Curious.*

The lieutenant smelled the steps of the advancing enemy. He filled his serpent with more venom and turned to face his new tormentors. A small package hit the ground in front of him and began hissing smoke. The smoke billowed and spoke to him, although he divined no meaning. Through the smoke came a gargoyle. The serpent reached out and killed it. Another slowly advanced. It was killed. The junior officer smelled perfume through the mask. Or was it the smell of tea? A three-headed monster edged through the mists and his deadly serpent struck them all down. His shoulder was vibrating warmth. He looked at it. A large red spider sat there, feeding off him, growing stronger off his blood. The spider began singing the Taiwanese national anthem.

The lieutenant tore his mask off and charged up the stairs, blindly firing the last of his 15 rounds. The lieutenant's last round caught the PLA major in the leg as the commando shot his ROC counterpart in the head.

The major's wound was too serious for him to continue his mission. *To fail at the very doorstep of success!* In the uniform of the ROC Army, the commando knew his fate if captured. He quickly turned his weapon on himself and ended it.

*   *   *

At 35,000 feet, 15 miles to the west of Taiwan's northern shore, the ROC fighter pilot was elated. He had engaged the PLA fighters at maximum range and destroyed four of them just as they passed over Taiwan's shores. His colleagues were similarly blessed with success. Together, their flight of four Mirage 2000-5s destroyed an entire squadron of 11 enemy aircraft and had downed another three aircraft in a second squadron.

His flight commander ordered them to go to afterburner and descend, closing the distance between them and the still advancing aircraft below. With their long-range radar guided missiles gone, they'd have to get within at least seven nautical miles to launch their infrared missiles. After that, they'd assess their odds and consider fighting the enemy tooth and tong with the two 30mm cannons their French jets mounted.

The captain began to throttle up to afterburner when he caught a flash in the sky. The headset in his helmet cracked painfully loud. His HUD (heads up display) went blank. Every digital instrument in his cockpit went dead. And, his fly-by-wire control stick was completely unresponsive.

Ten miles to the east, the seven remaining J-6 fighters of PLA 1st lieutenant's squadron also felt the effects of the E-bomb. The radio receivers burned out and the newly acquired commercial GPS devices were also destroyed. The missile-warning indicator also failed. Fortunately, the advanced radar guided missile that had locked onto his jet was now an unguided missile. It simply went ballistic and flared by his canopy window, disappearing into the distance.

The pilot did not understand what happened. All he knew was that he was alive and that his aircraft had somehow sustained damage, but was still flying. An indicator light told him his air-to-air missiles were not functioning. Well, he still had his three 30mm cannon and, if he ever got behind the enemy, he certainly knew how to use those.

The squadron commander began a long banking turn to the right. He followed. They were now heading west, back to China! About 20 seconds later, he could see specks in the sky. These had to be their tormentors. The fact that he hadn't been shot down yet must mean that the enemy ran out of missiles. He would now have his chance to even the score.

The ROC pilot was madly trying to reset his electrical circuit breakers. His engine had flamed out. His controls were completely unresponsive. His Mirage was nosing down and about to go into an uncontrollable spin. It pained him greatly to bail out of his beautiful aircraft, but he saw no choice.

The PLA pilot could hardly believe his eyes: three Mirage 2000s were spinning out of the sky. Above the fighter jets, ejection seats were visible, stabilized by small drogue chutes.

The ROC captain bailed out cleanly. The freezing air bit at his exposed skin. In less than two minutes he'd fall from 30,000 feet to 10,000 feet where his ejection seat would automatically deploy his parachute. If he could deploy his survival raft and get in, he'd live. Then he saw unwelcome visitors.

The 1st lieutenant's commander saw the ejecting pilots and began a slow descent circling after them. The pilot understood his commander did not have a humanitarian interest in seeing these enemy pilots to safety. Once the first pilot's parachute opened, his squadron commander swooped in, 30mm cannons blazing. The colonel missed. The 1st lieutenant's flight leader followed his commander's example and missed as well. Next came the lieutenant's turn. He squeezed the firing trigger for his 30mm cannons.

The ROC captain couldn't believe they were shooting at him. It wasn't simply the blatant violation of the Geneva Convention that surprised him—it was that death was so personal and close. He had always assumed that if he died in aerial combat it would be by an unseen enemy using a long-range missile. The cannon rounds ripped the air around him. He closed his eyes. He never felt the round that killed him.

*   *   *

The commander of the PLA's 37th Infantry Division, 12th Group Army knew about his mission for the last month. He told his staff about the mission 12 days ago, sequestering them to cut off all contact with their friends and family. Security to maintain surprise was paramount. Seven days ago he told his regimental commanders about the mission and confined them to base. Five days ago he canceled all leaves and imposed total isolation on his troops. Three days ago, they all boarded the cruise ship bound for Keelung.

It ranked as one of the biggest military gambles in history— sailing an unarmed cruise ship right into the enemy's second busiest harbor. *No*, the general had to correct himself, *not a gamble, rather, a calculated risk.* An avid student of military history, the general was well versed in everything from Sun Tzu to Erwin Rommel. *And, wasn't it Field Marshal Rommel who said that he never gambled but took calculated risks?* On the face of it, the cost to benefit calculation was very favorable. The cruise ship itself only cost COSCO some $25 million to purchase. Of the embarked soldiers of the 37th Infantry Division, about 1,000 were professionals, the rest were conscripts. Further, without their vehicles and little artillery, the force committed was fairly cheap. *If we achieved success it would rank as almost equaling the Trojan Horse gambit.* (For security reasons, the general had no knowledge of the freighters being drafted into troopship service in Tainan, Kaohsiung and Taichung, nor of the commando raids at CKS Airport or in Taipei itself.) *If we failed, less PLA troops would die than in 1949 when we tried to take Quemoy.*

The general knew Keelung as an important city that had an interesting and violent past featuring both Asian and European conquerors. An excellent natural port, Keelung was ringed by historical fortifications that dotted the steep hills that tightly penned the city against the sea.

Taking the port and using it were two different problems. The city itself had no depth. There were only a few hundred meters of dense concrete buildings before the city gave way to heavily vegetated bluffs. The division commander could take the city in

180

half an hour. To keep it, he'd have to secure the high ground on three sides. Finally, to keep the port open, both the east and west side of the harbor's five kilometer long entrance would have to be cleared of the enemy's heavy weapons. Then there was the historic fortress island of Peace, sitting squarely astride the Keelung Inlet, just like a cork in a very expensive bottle of brandy.

For years Peace Island and the hills surrounding Keelung Islet were strictly controlled by the ROC military. Now, as commercial interests grew and the iron discipline faded, those restrictions had been partially lifted. This allowed Mainlander spies the opportunity to carefully map many bunkers and emplacements in the strategic region. The general intended to make the Islanders pay dearly for their softness.

Still smoking mightily, the cruise ship entered the harbor. The fireboat tried to maneuver into place to begin to put water on the flame but the cruise ship pressed on, making 12 knots for the port. The captain of the ROC patrol boat on the scene was about to radio for back up when the E-bomb detonated, cutting off all communications between ship and shore.

Virtually helpless to stop such a giant vessel with his 30-meter patrol boat, the ROC captain decided to race ahead to warn the port authorities about the mad dog skipper. The patrol boat revved up and began pulling ahead of the cruise ship. The general resisted the temptation to destroy the vessel with the crew-served weapons he had attached to the deck and concealed by canvas coverings. Opening up on the pesky patrol craft would only offer a warning to the ROC Marines he knew were stationed in the hills. If he could get dockside with nothing more than some police to contend with (larger, missile-carrying patrol boats had been likely rendered incapable of firing their missiles due to the E-bomb), then Keelung would be his. He ran the timing in his head: the patrol craft could make it to port in a little under five minutes, while he could make it in about 14 minutes (assuming he slowed down a bit just before plowing into the docks). With a nine minute warning the Taiwanese could really do nothing more than offer small arms fire to stop him. He decided to let the boat go—he'd catch up to it later.

By now the general's division staff and his commanders from the regimental level down to selected company commanders, 112 officers in all, were performing a mini leaders' reconnaissance. Situated behind the cruise ship's ample picture windows so as not to be seen from the shore, the officers took in the view of the terrain they were about to master. The general knew that even this cursory look would greatly enhance his leaders' confidence and ability to prevail in battle.

Five minutes passed. The patrol boat ought to be reaching Keelung now. What would the captain say? Even with the tension of imminent combat, the general had to smile. That poor patrol boat captain would have a rough time explaining the situation—especially after the incapacitating agent burst overhead.

A few seconds later, over the bluffs on either side of the cruise ship, the general saw what looked like wisps of steam in the air as the incoming warheads burst open and spilled their canisters onto the ground.

Ten minutes passed. Keelung's hills loomed above them on three sides. The port looked like it was hard at work, loading and unloading dozens of cargo ships. On closer inspection, however, the first glance was deceitful. On every loading dock and ship a few workers stood around, pointing at the steaming canisters.

The cruise ship captain began to slow the vessel and aim for an open quay.

From the ship's port side, three patrol boats raced in on a course to intercept. On the ship's bow, a fireboat and a tugboat closed in, one behind the other.

The general gave the order to prepare to land. The company commanders had already gone below to be with their men. All along the upper decks of the ship, canvas was pulled back to reveal crew-served weapons. The general thought this his best adaptation yet of the lessons of history—borrowing the idea from the famous commerce raiders of Germany and the American Confederacy. While the cruise ship had no protective armor, it fairly bristled with armament. The cruise ship was about 225 meters long. Its eight decks above the waterline and hundreds of cabin windows provided more than enough firing ports for 12.7mm Type-77 heavy machine guns and AGS-17 30mm grenade launchers. Reserving the upper decks for the heavier equipment, the general stationed an entire battalion of 18 37mm Type-74 anti-aircraft guns topside as well as an anti-tank battalion with Red Arrow 8 anti-tank guided missiles (the latter's fiery backblast made it impractical to launch from within an enclosed space). His greatest idea was figuring out a way to secure and conceal three 122mm Type-83 towed artillery pieces to the small bow section. He knew his ersatz gunship couldn't take punishment well, but it could sure dish it out.

One of the patrol boats fired its heavy machine gun across the cruise ship's bow. Seconds later, hundreds of cabin windows popped out of the cruise ship and a massive volume of fire from no less than 50 machine guns and grenade launchers cut the patrol boat to pieces. While the other two patrol boats hadn't responded, they too received the same treatment.

The fireboat and tugboat were a different matter. They came straight on where none of the ship's heavy weapons could target them (the weapons on the upper decks couldn't depress enough to hit the charging boats). The skipper of the fireboat had already been affected by the phenothiazine agent. He calmly aimed to ram the oncoming ship—unconcerned about the consequences that might bring on him and his beloved fireboat. The tugboat captain followed, also impaired by the chemical. He was simply following the fireboat, although he was having difficulty remembering why.

Between the bow wave a large ship makes as it moves through the water, and the narrowness of the bow itself, it's hard to hit a ship head on in the water. Even if one tried, a glancing blow would be the more likely result. Recognizing this, the fireboat captain turned hard to starboard a few seconds before impact. The cruise ship's forward momentum was slightly checked as it sliced the 35-meter long fireboat in two, sustaining minor damage to its bow in the process.

Seeing this calamity occur only 50 meters in front of him, the tugboat captain snapped out of his stupor long enough to steer his boat to safety. Unfortunately, this brought him within the view of the cruise ship's gun crews who immediately destroyed his boat.

The general noticed three small ROC patrol craft tied alongside their naval wharf, just like intelligence said they'd be. There was no sign of activity on the boats. He told his operations officer to call ceasefire over the ship's intercom. No point in wasting ammunition and causing more damage than necessary.

The cruise ship's propellers were straining on full reverse as the ship ponderously scraped alongside the empty cargo pier, then smashed bow-first into the boardwalk at three knots. Combined with the damage from ramming the fireboat, this impact was enough to render the ship unseaworthy. This was of little importance now to the division commander—the ship had gotten his men safely to Keelung. If it sank in the shallow pier side waters it was no matter. The ship would still be useful as an artillery and anti-aircraft platform regardless.

If all went according to plan, the northern pathway to the heart of the enemy would be his in less than three hours.

*   *   *

In the American C-17 Globemaster, Lieutenant Colonel Alexander thought about the conversation he just overheard. US Marines in the Taiwan Strait were observing a war brewing between Taiwan and China. And just as he was going to Indonesia as part of a UN mandate to bring peace and stability to that riotous land. Interestingly enough—as part of a UN mandate with full Chinese approval and cooperation. He wondered if more than a coincidence was at work here. Dan took off his headset to scratch his scalp. He heard a crackling sound. The hand holding his headset jerked as if it had been jolted by electricity. The cabin lights went out. Fortunately there was plenty of sunshine coming through the cockpit window. Just before he looked to see how Joe was doing, Dan noticed his arm hair was standing straight up. *Curious.*

Joe was slumped over the control yoke. The smell of burnt wires and singed hair filled the cockpit. Dan was shocked to see smoke. Fire, in a new state-of-art-aircraft—with him onboard, what rotten luck. The aircraft nosed gently down and to the right. The copilot was frantically reading his instrument panel and pushing buttons.

Dan unstrapped himself from the jump seat and squeezed Joe's shoulder. No response. Dan worked his way around to Joe's seat and hit the release on his seat belt and shoulder harness. The copilot noticed Dan's effort and yelled, "We've been struck by lightning! Somehow it arced into the aircraft's intercom system. I think Colonel Giannini's been electrocuted!" The copilot rapidly flipped switches, never breaking stride while he yelled.

"Oh shit!" The copilot had looked up and momentarily froze. Dan reflexively looked up too, not really sure he wanted to see what caused the copilot's discomfort. In the distance, about a half a mile ahead, the lead C-17 and the KC-135 tanker aircraft were in trouble. The aircraft must have somehow collided during refueling. The C-17 was pitching up steeply. The KC-135 was missing its refueling boom and its tail section looked severely damaged. They rapidly closed on the stalling C-17. Dan saw a gaping hole just behind the cockpit. The wounded cargo jet began to keel over to the left. The copilot banked sharply to the right.

184

Trailing bits of debris, the C-17 was going down.

"Atlas One, Atlas One, this is Warrior Two, over." The copilot used the flight's fixed call signs to try and raise the first aircraft.

His voice got more desperate, "Atlas, One, Atlas One, Atlas One, this is Warrior Two, do you copy, over."

A warning indicator on the copilot's instrument panel began flashing red. All thought of the other aircraft vanished and the copilot went back to contending with his stricken aircraft.

Dan grabbed Joe from under his arms, lifting and dragging him from the cockpit. He laid him out on the deck and felt for a pulse. None. Dan checked for breathing. None.

"Oh dear God," Dan said quietly. He wondered why the loadmaster wasn't helping, looked up and saw him limp and unconscious in his seat, his headset still on.

Dan had to try to save these men, but he'd need help to do so. He sprang up and ran out into the cargo hold, yelling for help. He had 15 troops with him in the aircraft. All but two were fast asleep. Those two immediately responded, unstrapped themselves and ran to their Commander, steadying themselves with whatever hand holds they could find along the way. "Perez, Green, the loadmaster has probably been hit by lightning. Check his vitals and begin CPR if needed." The slight young Private Perez and the well-muscled and much older Sergeant First Class Green knew what to do without explanation.

Training took over for Dan. He put one hand on Joe's forehead and the other on his chin, tilting the head back to open a better breathing passage. He quickly pulled opened Joe's mouth, looking to see if Joe had swallowed his tongue. *Everything okay.* He placed one hand on top of the other on the unconscious man's chest and began heart massage. One. Two. Three. Four. Five. He pressed 15 times. Then down, pinching Joe's nose shut with one hand while placing his mouth fully over Joe's. *Blow out, then let him exhale. Blow out, then let him exhale. Blow out, then let him exhale.* Dan was going to quickly check for a pulse when he saw Joe's body shudder underneath him. Joe's chest heaved and he took a gulp of air on his own. "Thanks God," Dan said under his breath. Dan saw his men working to revive the loadmaster.

Dan carefully watched the pilot's breathing. It was now shallow, but steady. He looked at Perez and Green. Perez was doing the mouth-to-mouth. Green the heart massage. He slid over to the loadmaster and tried to find a pulse. Nothing. "Keep on it guys!" Dan looked around for something to keep the pilot warm and to elevate his feet to get more blood to the brain. He made his way back to his still sleeping 13 men and raided a couple of soft, warm camouflage poncho liners from Jones and Gutierrez who began to protest then fell into a confused silence when they saw it was their battalion commander who was taking their warmth from them.

While he was back among his men Dan barked, "Everyone, get up! Get up! We have an in-flight emergency. The crew thinks we've been hit by lightning. I want everyone alert!"

Dan went back to attend to Joe, checking for a pulse on the loadmaster on his way. Still nothing. He covered the pilot and made him as comfortable as possible. It had been about two minutes since the lightning strike. "Come on guys, keep trying!" Colonel Alexander exhorted his men.

Dan searched his memory. He seemed to remember one of his men was a private pilot. He bolted back to the cargo and passenger hold. "Blackwell! Don't you have a pilot's license?"

Staff Sergeant Blackwell spoke up, "Yes sir. Multi-engine instrument rating, sir!"

"Get up to the cockpit and see if our copilot could use any help. And Blackwell, let me know what's going on when you can."

"On the way sir!"

Dan thought about the situation. They were cruising at 28,000 feet. There were some high clouds above them. Joe discussed a typhoon far to the south, but certainly they weren't upon that weather system yet. He had heard stories about clear sky lightning, but how did that explain the other C-17 apparently spinning out of control? He glanced at his watch. He had a inexpensive but reliable battery-driven Timex with both analog and digital function. The digital LED readout was blank. The watch's second hand was motionless. He thought of the transmission from the *Belleau Wood* and Okinawa Control. A deep chill gripped his neck and arms—*could they really have done it? Did the Chinese attack Taiwan using nuclear weapons? Certainly it could explain the electrical damage in the aircraft as well as the other C-17s misfortune. If so, where were the flash and the shock?* Dan thought of his family back in California and hoped that he'd see them again. The idea of dying of radiation sickness wasn't especially appealing—literally retching your guts out. Still, he felt okay.

He walked past Joe's gently breathing chest. Green and Perez were still working on the lifeless loadmaster. Speculation turned suddenly to military certainty. They were in the middle of a war whether they wanted to be or not.

He tapped the copilot's left shoulder. Not turning, the Air Force major said, "Yes?"

"If you want it, I found some help for you. Sergeant Blackwell here is a pilot with an instrument rating. He could at least keep an eye out for you."

"Right."

"Major, I know what happened to us. Somewhere, someone, probably the Chinese, exploded a nuclear device. We were hit by EMP."

"Colonel, we lost an engine, we have no nav systems, all our comms are down. Go away." The copilot began to fray at the edges.

Dan paused. Now was not the time to confront an overloaded pilot. "What are you going to do, Major?"

"I'm going to set this bird down at the nearest airport I can see." As he said this, he pointed down and to the right at about two o'clock, "Right there!"

Sergeant Blackwell began climbing into the pilot's seat and strapping in. The copilot grabbed his chart book and handed it without looking to Blackwell. "Here, find me the closest airport in northern Taiwan. We need to land—right now!"

Blackwell, never before behind the controls of a C-17, was, nevertheless, immediately at home with the familiar navigational chart book, "You got it, sir!"

Having provided the copilot with some relief, Dan decided he could risk one more interaction with the stressed-out flyer, "Major, do you have any idea if the other two aircraft are still with us?"

"No, sir. But if I know Collins and Shaw, they'll be right behind me, at least making sure I'm okay."

The Major addressed Sergeant Blackwell, "What's the nearest airport?"

"Taipei Sungshan Airport. It's Taipei's domestic airport on the northeast side of the city. Its runways are 9 Left and 27 Right. They're 7,000-foot runways. The tower frequency is 87.5. Taipei control is 127.3. The runway is about 20 miles to the west of the coast."

Following standard procedure, the Major tried to reach Taipei Control, Taipei Tower, and Okinawa Control. He had no idea if his calls could be heard by anyone. It was possible that he was transmitting and not receiving, or that Taipei had already been knocked off the air and couldn't hear him or respond.

The Major swung the military cargo aircraft around to the right and began his approach into Taipei Sungshan Airport. "I hope they know we're not bad guys."

Dan looked back at Sergeant Green and Private Perez, his eyes trying to adjust to the relatively dark interior of the unlit cabin. They were beside the limp body of the loadmaster. Green looked back at his battalion commander, the whites of his eyes burning brightly behind his dark black face. Green just sadly shook his head. "How's the Colonel?"

"I think he'll make it, sir," Green responded.

Dan slapped his hand to his forehead and said, "Damn! Everyone get to MOPP-4, right now!" He ran back to the cargo hold and began taking the cargo netting off of their stowed personnel gear. He found his rucksack and began tearing into it, breaking out the new charcoal-lined chemical suit from its plastic container.

He pulled on the jacket, then thought twice and took it off. He reached for his Kevlar vest and donned it. Dan told his four tankers to leave their flak vests off. Then he put on the chemical jacket and the pants. Another soldier automatically helped him button the three snaps in the back that completed the seal. He pulled on the rubber booties over his combat boots and laced them up, pulling the pant legs down over them to prevent chemicals from getting inside his boots. He and his men would now be protected from many of the most unsavory aspects of modern warfare—*when in doubt. . .*

Dan made his way back to the cockpit. He was surprised to see the runway only a few miles off. An aircraft sat dead center in the middle of the runway. Sergeant Blackwell looked back and was startled by Colonel Alexander's chemical suit and mask. Dan yelled through the voice meter, "Get yours on as soon as we're down. I'll have someone break it out for you."

"Thanks, sir. You better strap in. The runway looks short today."

"Right."

"Sir, what the hell are we getting ourselves into?"

"Sergeant," came the muffled reply out of the mask, "I'll let you know when it's over."

Lieutenant Colonel Dan Alexander saw it at the end of the runway: a Soviet-era four-engine cargo aircraft with its ramp down. A few uniformed men milled about the Iluyshin-76. His old Cold War paranoia activated. He thought of the last hectic 15 minutes. *One C-17 and a KC-135 missing and presumed down. A complete loss of communications. Almost total electronic and electrical failure, including the surge of electricity into LTC Giannini's headset resulting in his near death. Now a suspicious-looking Il-76.*

Images from the Soviet invasion of Afghanistan in 1979 popped into his head. He had just completed his basic training at Ft. Jackson, South Carolina—a brand new private in the dismal days of American military retreat. He vividly remembered the TV shots of the Soviet transport aircraft in Kabul—the Soviets had seized control of the airport and simply flew their troops in to the heart of the country. President Carter declared a grain embargo and boycotted the Moscow summer Olympics in protest. Private Alexander went off to his Advanced Individual Training, Armor School at Ft. Knox, Kentucky. From there he went to West Germany where he served in a cavalry unit in the Fulda Gap. He cut his military teeth expecting to face the Soviet military in the World War Three that never happened. Seeing Soviet-built military hardware caused an unavoidable, reflexive hostility in him. His rational being knew it wasn't fair. He just hadn't been deprogrammed yet.

The C-17 touched down. The brakes thankfully slowed the crippled aircraft to a crawl just short of the two-engine commuter aircraft that blocked the runway. The copilot swerved the C-17 into the grass to give the aircraft behind him more room to stop. The C-17, designed for short and unimproved runways just roared on, plowing over the grass. He gunned the engines and pulled back onto the runway.

They taxied to the west end the of the runway about 100 meters to the left of the Il-76. Dan noticed most of the military personnel around the Il-76 were wearing protective masks. A few of the personnel milled about aimlessly. Others appeared to be gesturing wildly at the wandering soldiers.

Dan shuffled over to his troops, the large rubber chemical suit booties making maneuver in the cramped aircraft tough, "Peña, Jones, Hernandez! Get in the tank. Perez, take my place in the TC's position. Button-up. Power-up. Take your masks off. Prepare for combat. We have unidentified troops out on the tarmac. Watch me through the periscope." The men immediately climbed into the tank.

"Sergeant Noreiga, get the rest of the men to cut the tank free, right now! When you're done, get your personal weapons and take up positions covering the ramp area. There are troops out there and I don't know if they're friendly!" Dan took a big draught of air. Yelling with a protective mask on was exhausting.

Dan made his way back to the cockpit.

Just before the C-17 came to a full halt, the copilot turned the aircraft to the left 90 degrees. He excitedly pointed to his left, back up the runway. "They made it! I see two Globemasters! Hot damn!" His smile was so wide Dan thought he'd crack his face.

They were stopped, on the ground and in one piece. Lieutenant Colonel Giannini stirred, mumbling. Dan took a deep breath and spoke loudly through his protective mask, "Thanks for the safe landing. Joe's in bad shape. I've got to get off the aircraft. I don't like the welcoming committee. You stay here." He turned toward the door. "The loadmaster is dead. Can you lower the ramp from here?"

The copilot turned in his seat and began unstrapping, "No. Power to the ramp hydraulics is out. I'll have to climb in the back and let it down manually."

Dan followed the copilot to the back of the aircraft. His men had just finished unhooking the tank. The copilot released a safety latch and turned a few hydraulic valves. The cargo ramp slowly descended. The light from outside the aircraft fairly blinded them. They heard the whine of the other jets coming down the runway. Two seconds later, they saw more than a dozen masked soldiers surrounding the aircraft with submachine guns and light anti-tank weapons (LAWs) leveled on them. "Whoa! Don't shoot! Americans! We're Americans!" the copilot shouted as they both raised their hands skyward.

Dan looked up at the tank. He hoped his men grasped the delicateness of the situation. The copilot was wrung dry. His ability to think and react, especially with an unexpected ground situation, was limited. Dan had to do something fast to avoid bloodshed. Perhaps the fact that they hadn't been immediately attacked meant that these soldiers were not the enemy. Dan remembered they had all sewn the American flag high on their right sleeves. Unfortunately, the chemical suit covered it up. The troops outside shifted nervously. Only five seconds had passed since the ramp lowered. His hands held high, Dan walked down the ramp and into the sunlight. He slowly reached one hand down to his mask and removed it. He hoped his blue eyes and closely cropped blonde hair would show these men he was an American. "American. We are Americans!"

A soldier advanced, pointing his pistol at Dan's head. Dan slowly unbuttoned and unzipped the front of his chemical suit and peeled it back to reveal the American flag patch on his BDUs.

The soldier spoke to him in near-perfect English from behind his protective mask, "Put your mask on. There has been a chemical attack." He turned to the other soldiers and spoke in Chinese. Dan heard the sound of muffled cheers through 20 protective masks. The soldier turned back to Dan, "You have arrived quicker than we hoped. Thank you for coming to help us defend our freedoms."

*   *   *

Colonel Flint watched the air situation display as the east and west moving masses of blips moved relentlessly towards one another. Just as the two masses appeared poised to merge, blips began to disappear from the leading edge of the east-moving masses. Colonel Flint watched with satisfaction as the mainly US-equipped ROC air force tore into its larger but antiquated counterpart. *At this kill rate*, he smiled to himself, *the air war will soon be over.*

His equanimity froze into anxiety as he noticed a very rapidly moving radar return well to the south of the ongoing dogfight. "Is that what I think it is?" he asked, pointing at the flashing symbol.

"Sir," came the voice of young radar operator. "That's a ballistic missile. I'm running a trajectory on it. It should clear Taiwan more than 150 miles up and land near Philippine territorial waters about 50 miles north of Luzon."

"That ought to win friends and influence enemies," Colonel Flint observed dryly.

Major Ramirez showed up at his left elbow. "What's up, sir?"

"You tell me, Rez," Colonel Flint half-whispered in his intelligence officer's ear. "Those are Chinese aircraft," he said, gesturing at the air situation display. "Those are Taiwanese aircraft. And that blinking SOB is a ballistic missile that the Chinese are lobbing over Taiwan. But it won't even come close. It will splash down north of Luzon Island. Are Chinese missiles that inaccurate?"

"Sir," Lieutenant Colonel Ramirez' mind was racing. "You wanted the birds warmed up, right?"

"Yes . . ."

191

"We've got to shut them down—right now!" Ramirez was sure of himself: bet your rank on it sure. "That missile is carrying a nuke. The Chinese are going to explode it over Taiwan. Shut down everything we have and disconnect the antennas."

Colonel Flint was on the hook to his aviation combat element before his intelligence officer had finished speaking. "Shut down immediately and secure for nuclear attack!"

"What about the ships, sir?" Ramirez knew the difficulty of that question. A Marine convincing a naval officer to turn off his vital electronics within 60 seconds was a stretch, but he knew his colonel would have to give it a try.

Colonel Flint spoke in a machine gun staccato. "Rez, you speak to the CIC OIC. I'll call the Captain." His finger was already punching the Captain's number. Precious seconds ticked away as he waited for someone to find the Captain.

"Colonel Flint here. We are about to receive a nuclear attack. We have to secure all ship's electronics. . ."

At that instant the missile reached its apogee high in the sky over southern Taiwan. The Captain's answer was drowned in a large crack of static, and the phone receiver in Flint's hand went dead. The radar screen briefly flashed white and then went black. The ship's lights wavered and went out, replaced by ghostly glow of emergency lighting. The radiomen tore off their headphones, cursing loudly and holding their ears in pain. "What in the h-e-l-l was that?" someone exclaimed.

Colonel Flint didn't exactly know, but he had a very bad feeling. A standard nuclear weapon would have produced a noise and a shock wave, but the only sound in the Combat Information Center had been a loud electrical pop. And the ship had not been hit by a concussion, at least one he could feel. "Rez?" he said questioningly.

"It was a nuke all right," his intelligence officer said quietly. "but, judging by where it detonated, one designed to channel all its energy into a giant electro-magnetic pulse. I'm betting that every radar and radio receiver on board has been blown out, at least those that were on."

So the Chinese had actually used a nuke in combat. The thought made his blood run cold. The Cold War, with its bluff and bluster and brinksmanship, suddenly seemed like child's play in comparison. *Get a grip, Flint*, he told himself.

"Rez, get to the Captain, tell him what happened, and that the MEU is preparing to disembark. Then assemble the A Command team and meet me on the deck. Let's wing out of here before the Chinese draw a bead on one of these deaf, dumb, and blind sitting ducks."

Colonel Flint was not far off the mark in his assessment. The four ships of the flotilla were blind and deaf, if not completely dumb. Every radar and radio receiver was blown by the massive electro-magnetic shock wave. Most of their computer systems, hardened at great cost to withstand just such an attack, survived. A fair amount of electrical wiring was burned through, however, and anything attached to an antenna was toast.

"Jeff, how did the birds come through the attack?" Colonel Flint was addressing his ACE commander, Lieutenant Colonel Jefferson.

Lieutenant Colonel Jefferson looked grave. "Sir, every radio receiver we've checked is burned out. Navigational gear is mostly gone too, except for the inertial systems and the compasses. The engines are functional. We had just enough time to shut down and switch off before the pulse hit us."

"So the Harriers and the helos will fly?"

"Yes, Colonel. We have wings, but I wouldn't want to fly at night or for long distances over water."

"We're only 12 miles from friendly territory, Jeff. The ROC forces know that we're here doing exercises, and won't fire upon us, I hope."

"Yes, Colonel," Lieutenant Colonel Jefferson nodded. "But what about those other guys?" He gestured west.

"I don't intend to be here when they come back," Colonel Flint said evenly. "Make sure at least one Harrier has a functioning radio, then launch her on a recon flight. I want the pilot to check on our pre-selected landing sites around the port and airport and report back." He turned to go, then said over his shoulder. "And, Jeff, grab enough stores to repair the other receivers and weapons systems of the Cobras and Harriers once we get ashore."

"Already started, sir!"

"I knew there was a reason you were the only rotor-head I loved!"

Lieutenant Colonel Jefferson flashed a broad, toothy grin and turned, yelling orders. A few seconds later the catapult whooshed, and a Harrier leapt into the sky.

Colonel Flint heard Rez's familiar voice clearing behind him.

"Sir, we're in a pickle. All the radar and ship self-defense systems have been knocked off line. The Curtis Wilbur has some spare components for its CIWS and is trying to get one back to on line, but the amphibians are hurting. Hell, the *Dubuque* was down to one CIWS for lack of spare parts prior to the attack. Sir, we're like newborn puppies out here."

"Blind and defenseless," Colonel Flint said under his breath. He looked at the horizon, then up at the sky. There was nothing in view except a handful of cumulus clouds, but his instincts were screaming danger again, louder than before. Gathering himself up, he turned to his command team. "Prepare to disembark the MEU. We will remain on station until the recon pilot reports back, then select our landing sites."

"Sir," his XO piped up, "wouldn't that be committing US ground troops for the defense of Taiwan?"

"Those are my orders," Colonel Flint said firmly, projecting the command presence that his Marines would follow into the Gates of Hell itself. "Carry them out—now." His subordinates leaped into action.

All but one. The XO quailed under Colonel Flint's fierce gaze, but stood his ground.

"Alright, XO," Colonel Flint said easily. "You want an explanation. I'll give you an explanation. We have been attacked by the Chinese in international waters. That is a de facto declaration of war."

"But all that happened was that some radios, computers and wiring got fried," the XO protested. "No one was killed."

"Just because no one got killed doesn't mean that we're not under attack," Colonel Flint replied. "Look, XO, it is not my intent to drag America into a conflict the Commander-in-Chief hasn't yet authorized, but it's my responsibility to ensure the safety of the Marines in my charge. I am going to take them out of harm's way. You know as well as I do that we are completely defenseless out here. Anything could take us out."

"You're right, sir," the XO admitted grudgingly. "It's just that . . ." The first of the CH-53s lifted off, drowning out the rest of his sentence.

"I don't have time for this right now." The Colonel's voice began to escalate. "Have you become ball-less like the rest of them? Like the Joint Chiefs, like the Commander-in-Chief? Look, it's easy to start a war when the bastards can't shoot back very well, or when they don't have nukes. But these guys are playing for keeps. XO, if they win, they get all the marbles—you can kiss the US of A goodbye in the 21st century. Damn it, I'm not going down quietly with the ship. I'm taking my Marines and making a stand on Taiwan."

The XO sighed and looked at his feet. Behind him another helicopter rose into the sky, then another. The catapult whooshed and yet another Harrier took flight. The LCACs were emerging from the flooded bay of the USS Germantown. "My heart tells me you're right," he said finally. "My head tells me that helping to start World War Three would not be a good career move."

"I'm glad you're with me, XO," Colonel Flint said dryly. "Now go take up your post as the head of B Command."

"Yes, sir," the XO said, not bothering to salute.

Colonel Flint watched his Marines running for their helos. Within two minutes six CH-46 Sea Knights were orbiting the USS *Dubuque* while the USS *Belleau Wood* had five CH-53 Super Stallions and eight Sea Knights airborne. The bay doors of the USS *Germantown* opened, and the LCAC floated out, then cranked up their fan rotors to put some distance between themselves and the ship. The slower Assault Amphibians then emerged, looking like awkward sea turtles bobbing up and down in the waves. These were his problem, he realized, for they could only travel five knots in calm seas. By the time these men got ashore they would be puking their guts out.

The commodore of Amphibious Squadron Eleven, Captain Bright, watched the helos head for shore, followed by the swift boats and LCAC, and the slow, clumsy, turtle-like Assault Amphibians. He heaved a sigh of relief.

*   *   *

American intelligence knew about the Chinese C-301, also known as the HY-3, long-range supersonic anti-ship missile. They thought it was not yet deployed and in service with the People's Liberation Army-Navy. Unfortunately, this was not so. The Chinese tested the missile in 1997. They decided it had so much potential that they ordered 1,000 be built within 18 months with 1,000 per year built thereafter through 2004. The missile could be launched from ship or from land. It had four solid rocket boosters and two kerosene-fueled ramjet engines which together, boosted the missile to a speed of Mach 2.0 (covering the distance of a mile in about 2.5 seconds). It had a range of 150 miles and used commercially obtained GPS receivers to achieve 10-meter accuracy to a waypoint. It would cruise at about 500 feet, then dive to 100 feet just before the active-radar terminal phase began. Its 800-pound warhead was very destructive, especially to modern warships, most of which lacked armor.

Prior to launching the first wave of 300 C-301s, the Chinese computed all known locations of ROC naval shipping and input the coordinates into the missiles. With the coordinates, the missiles would fly out to a pre-set location, then begin searching for targets in the target "box". Once a target was identified, the missile would dive in for the kill.

Normally, the fast, large and unmaneuverable missile was easy prey for CIWS (Close-In Weapon System) such as the US Phalanx. In a fair fight, the Chinese planned to use saturation tactics, launching as many as 50 of the powerful missiles at a single capital ship. Of course, one of the central objects in war is not to engage in a fair fight. The E-bomb attack was expected to neutralize the ROC fleet's advantage in advanced electronics and defensive systems. This in turn would ensure a field day for the C-301s.

At Central China Coastal Defense Headquarters in Quanzhou, about 130 miles across the Strait from Taichung, Taiwan, the PLAN admiral in charge of sweeping the seas of the enemy faced a dilemma. His targeting efforts bore much fruit. He estimated his missile strike, timed to launch only ten minutes after the E-bomb attack (giving the missile crews time to re-connect crucial electrical systems in case the E-bombs were a little more powerful or less focused than expected) would sink or seriously damage 50% of the ROC fleet. The remainder of the enemy ships were in port or underway out of range. This was exceptional. The PLAN would rapidly and easily achieve naval superiority in the Straits. Combined with the PLAAF strike on ROCAF air assets, the rebellious island would be stripped bare of its defenses and ripe for the taking.

No, the admiral's dilemma was not due to a lack of success, it was due to too much success. His targeting efforts had also revealed the location and speed of the USS *Belleau Wood* task force. These four United States vessels together possessed an impressive array of defensive and offensive firepower, as well as the training and the record to prove it. The admiral hated to admit it, but he admired American naval and military prowess.

He knew there was a very strong likelihood that the American ships would at least be temporarily blinded by the E-bomb attack as they were only 20 kilometers off the coast of Taiwan—well within the projected envelop of electronic destruction. The question was whether or not to purposefully attack the Americans.

He noted the presence of a small, but important ROC naval group only five kilometers away from the Americans. If he targeted these ROC vessels, surely a stray missile or two would attack the American fleet. An accidental attack in these situations might be viewed by the Americans as an attack on purpose. This would certainly propel the Americans into the war on the side of the Taiwanese as surely as the Japanese attack on Pearl Harbor sealed the destruction of the Axis powers.

Or would it? The admiral thought of the USS *Stark*, an American frigate "accidentally" hit by an Iraqi French-made Exocet missile in 1986 during the Iran-Iraq war. Or the USS *Liberty*, an American spy ship attacked by Israel in the 1967 war. In both cases, the US did not respond militarily.

The thought of taking down four modern American ships was too much to resist. *But, what would Beijing say?* The American ships were in the Strait against the express warning of the Government of the PRC. *They can't say we didn't warn them, can they?*

The admiral gave the go ahead for a full-scale attack. They would target every naval and ROC commercial vessel in the Strait as planned. He was careful not to specify that by "naval" he meant the American naval forces too. He knew his staff well and they knew him well. He didn't have to leave a paper trail—they understood his intent.

The Admiral smiled to himself. It would be a fine thing to give the Americans a taste of their own medicine after the brazen American attack on the Chinese Embassy in Belgrade in 1999.

He mentally tallied up his targets. His list began with Americans:

USS *Belleau Wood*, LHA 3, displacement: 39,400 tons

USS *Dubuque*, LPD 8, displacement: 17,000 tons

USS *Germantown*, LSD 42, displacement: 15,939 tons

USS *Curtis Wilbur*, DDG 54, displacement: 8,300 tons

·

It was 0817 hours local time. On the Chinese coast, 150 miles to the west four minutes and fifteen seconds before, the first wave of C-301 missiles were launched. The missiles leapt off their launch rails and accelerated rapidly to Mach 1.8. As the four solid rocket motors fell away, two ramjets kicked in and took the speed to Mach 2.0. The ROC ships in and around Quemoy Island were already on fire or sinking. The same fate attended to those ships near Matsu Island. The PLAN admiral had designated 30 missiles for the box containing the American ships. He ordered another 12 sent beyond the Americans to attack the three ROC Navy ships further to the east. *It would all look so perfectly accidental. What could the Americans claim?* If they said that the Chinese targeted them on purpose, it would mean a war that the Americans were neither materially, nor mentally prepared to wage. If the Americans backed down, the loss of face would cause their immediate expulsion from Asia—or at least their complete irrelevance.

On board the *Curtis Wilbur*, DDG-54, the crews were struggling mightily to get the Aegis phased array radar system back on line. The shock wave of electro-magnetic energy had overwhelmed the super sensitive radar system. It was designed to be electronically hard, but there was only so much hardening possible. Fortunately, the surface-to-air Standard Missiles had been protected within their launch canisters, but, without radar to provide warning and guidance and without a computer to calculate and control, the missiles were next to worthless. One of the Phalanx close-in weapon systems held some hope of being repaired. The little white protective system, shaped like half of a medicine capsule, had a radar under the domed part and a 20mm Gatling gun at the bottom. The aft CIWS was partially shielded from the worst effects of the pulse by the ship's superstructure. It sustained minimal damage. Repair crews were frantically performing diagnostics on it while stringing a new power line up to it to replace the burnt-out internal wiring.

The commodore of Amphibious Squadron 11, Captain Bright, reluctantly gave his approval to Colonel Flint's plan. He didn't like the idea of the Marines preparing to jump ship, but he really couldn't blame them.

On the well deck of the *Germantown* four LCACs screamed to life, their jet turbines lifting them off the water of the flooded well deck and into the open ocean. Each LCAC carried one M1A1 Abrams tank. On the *Belleau Wood*'s smaller well deck a single LCAC roared to life. It held four LAVs and 24 Marines.

While none of the ships had a functioning radio, they all still had Morse signal-lamps. With this primitive, but reliable communications method, Captain Bright marshaled his crippled fleet. If his signal-lamps failed, he could send his commands with semaphores or flying pennants. He thanked God the Navy had 225-year-old traditions unencumbered by progress. He ordered the four ships to draw closer together (thankfully, they all still had full power to their shafts) to enhance any protection the single CIWS on the *Curtis Wilbur* might provide as soon as it got back on line.

The first missiles came like a sudden thunderstorm out of the west. Piercing sonic booms raked the US ships as five missiles headed overhead to strike unseen targets to the east.

Two seconds later a seaman performing lookout duties on board the USS *Germantown* picked himself off the deck and looked into the distance with his binoculars. He saw four orange dots low on the horizon. They suddenly dipped and for a moment the orange dots looked like small candle flames. He screamed over the hurriedly repaired intercom, "Missiles inbound! Four missiles inbound!"

Half a second later a cloud of aluminum chaff strips ejected from the rear of the ship, attempting to decoy the missiles off. Normally, with a radar giving plenty of warning, the chaff would be fired much sooner. With only visual detection, the Mk 36 Super Rapid-Blooming Off Board Chaff System (SRBOC) was fired when the missiles were only a mile off.

One missile was decoyed, flying 50 feet off the stern before exploding in the sea. The other three dove into the ship, their 800 lb. semi-armor piercing warheads used a delayed impact fuse. One missile hit at the waterline and penetrated two decks below. The fuse failed on impact and the warhead simply lodged in the ship. The other two missiles punched their way in aft and exploded in the well deck in open air, just above where the four LCACs were resting only seconds before. The well deck's flooding mechanism and stern door were a shambles but otherwise, the *Germantown* was still in good condition.

700 yards away to the north the crew of the *USS Dubuque* heard the sonic booms and fired a round of chaff. This was fortunate as six missiles were homing in on the ship. The extra 2.5 seconds of reaction time added another 88 feet of distance between the chaff cloud and the ship. The Mk 36 chaff system claimed two missiles. Within three seconds the other four missiles dove into the ship from 100 feet up, each impacting just 10 to 20 feet above the water line, then detonating deep within the ship. The blasts tore through the hull. Water poured into the wounded port side. The ship was listing 35 degrees within a half-minute.

The *Dubuque* was mortally wounded. Her captain, Commander Peggy Brown, lay dying in her CIC—the first American female ship captain to die in combat. Her last, desperate thoughts were of her two sons who would now grow up without their mother.

The USS *Belleau Wood* presented the largest and most lucrative target for the missiles. Eight missiles streaked towards the 820-foot ship. They dove to just under 100 feet above the ocean and began their active radar sweep. The Mk 36 chaff system's wiring had been burnt through and wasn't repaired yet. Both Phalanx systems were still off line.

Some 600 yards to the north of the *Belleau Wood*, the USS *Curtis Wilbur's* crew had helplessly watched as one of ships it was to protect was struck, then two. The repair crew on the aft CIWS replaced the last burnt out black box and restored power. On automatic search mode, the CIWS scanned the skies for the fast Doppler shift of an incoming missile. It found its first target— brrrapp, brrrapp—hundreds of 20mm rounds cracked down range to intercept the missiles. The CIWS is an excellent defense of last resort for a ship under attack, especially if the missile is coming directly at the ship. However, for an oblique defense, the system is less than optimal. The CIWS downed two of the eight missiles heading for the *Belleau Wood*, then the system picked up two missiles bound for the *Curtis Wilbur* itself and turned to face the new threats.

Six C-301s began their final dive on the *Belleau Wood* from

100 feet. The first two struck center mass amidships, burrowing their way through 20 feet of hull and decking before exploding. Colonel Flint was on the flight deck preparing to board his UH-1N flying command post. The concussions of the twin explosions knocked him off his feet.

The third missile struck the bridge, instantly killing the PHIBRON 11 Commodore, Captain Bright and the captain in command of the *Belleau Wood*.

The fourth missile found the gaping hole created by the first two and traveled 30 feet within the ship before striking enough metal to trigger the penetrating warhead's timer. The warhead traveled another 20 feet before detonating against the keel. Water began rushing in through a 15-foot hole in the bottom of the ship.

The fifth missile tore through the flight deck aft and wrecked the well deck's water barrier.

Colonel Flint picked himself up and boarded his Huey chopper. Several staff officers were also on board. He saw another UH-1N airborne too. He hoped Rez and the XO made it. The skids of the helicopter lifted off the flight deck.

The last missile doomed the crippled ship. Flying through the same hole traveled and enlarged by three previous missiles, it reached two-thirds of the way through the beam of the ship before exploding, breaking the ship's back. The front half of the ship lifted up and away from the still underway stern. Thousands of tons of water slammed against the exposed leading edge of the stern at 20 miles per hour, crushing bulkheads and flinging aside watertight hatches. The sudden deceleration swept a Harrier off the flight deck and into the sea. Within ten seconds only 20 feet of the now stopped stern was visible above the waves, its twin propellers pointing uselessly at the gray sky. More than 100 male and female sailors were dead or soon destined to be.

The last two of the first wave of 30 missiles descended on the *USS Curtis Wilbur* (DDG-54). The CIWS' wall of super-dense tungsten bolts downed one. The other pushed on, decoyed slightly to the stern by the chaff. The missile struck aft, destroying the engine room and killing 26 sailors and wounding another 10.

In less than 90 seconds, the four ships of PHIBRON 11 were badly hit. The flagship was torn in two and sinking, the USS *Dubuque* would soon capsize, the USS *Germantown* sustained serious damage but still had power, and the USS *Curtis Wilbur* was on fire and dead in the water. The human cost was dramatic by modern American standards: 580 dead or missing, and 322 wounded. It could have been worse.

Due to Colonel Flint's foresight and aggressive actions all but three of 31st MEU's aircraft were in flight while every operational LCAC and assault amphibian was in the water. In all, he had 18 Sea Knights, nine Super Stallions, four Super Cobras, two Hueys, and five Harriers carrying 781 Marines, including crew, safe in the air—for the moment. In addition, he had another 65 Marines and seamen aboard five LCACs and 264 Marines inside 11 Assault Amphibians. Colonel Flint had half of his 2,200 Marines on the move, one step ahead of disaster. With hard work and Providence, he'd make landfall quickly and return to rescue as many Marines and sailors as possible.

*   *   *

Donna Klein was burning to speak with Jack Benson all day. He was either avoiding her or engaged in meetings. She couldn't stand it anymore—she had time critical information and analysis to discuss.

She decided to risk a call to her old boss Mr. Scott—her boss' boss. "No, Ms. Klein," Mr. Scott's secretary droned, "Mr. Scott is not available, he is in a meeting right now." And, so it went for the remainder of the afternoon—*What a Friday.*

Finally, at 7:10 PM, she decided to personally visit Mr. Scott. Donna again called Mr. Scott's office. Surprisingly, the secretary was still at her post. Donna had no patience for this. "Is Mr. Scott in his office?" she inquired, barely keeping a diplomatic tone.

"Yes, Ms. Klein. . ." Donna hung up and raced upstairs to the Office of the Director of Asian Pacific and Latin American Affairs.

The secretary looked alarmed to see her and moved to stop her. Donna swerved to avoid the woman's intercept, knocked twice and threw open the door without waiting for an invitation. She was surprised to see her boss, Jack Benson, the China section chief.

"Donna. . ." Mr. Scott began.

"Look, I'm sorry to do this, but I'm certain. . ." Mr. Scott's secretary was on the phone behind the open door.

Mr. Scott spoke, "Ms. Kesler, it's okay," he said to his secretary. "Donna, please close the door behind you."

"Sir, I have to talk to you about China. I'm convinced they are preparing to invade Taiwan, probably within the next day or two!" Donna was flushed and still short of breath from her bolt up the stairs.

Benson broke in, sounding calm and reassured, "That's why I'm here, I was just telling my boss that I believe China will try to take Quemoy in an attempt to force the issue of reunification, focus domestic attention away from the growing list of problems there, and challenge the US to back away from its vague defense commitments to Taiwan. You know the Chinese just announced a temporary naval exclusion zone to block international traffic through the Taiwan Strait. We even have indications that they have shipped large quantities of fuel, food and equipment to North Korea, probably to distract us from their true objective."

"No! That's not it at all!" Donna paused, gathered her herself and fixed her gaze solidly at Mr. Scott, "The PRC is going to invade Taiwan proper. They're going to do it within 48 hours, and they're going to do it with enough force to crush resistance within days. They intend to present us with a fait accompli—there'll be no way we can intervene in time. We'll be faced with the choice of accepting Chinese aggression or mounting a costly assault on a prepared defense on a small island against a nation with four times as many people and the world's second largest economy! This isn't Serbia or Indonesia we're talking about here. China can defeat us if she sets her mind to do so!"

Jack Benson looked angry and embarrassed. Donna had committed the ultimate sin: she went over his head to his boss with a harebrained, lunatic fringe story and tried to pass it off as real intelligence, "I'm sorry for this outburst Mr. Scott. You know the pressure Donna's been under recently. Donna, see me in my office immediately!" Benson started to get up.

Mr. Scott said firmly, "Donna, stay right here. Jack, remember what it was like during the Cold War? Remember when the Chinese invaded Vietnam in 1979 and you were the only analyst to call it? Remember how everyone ignored you until it was already underway? Well, damn it Jack, let your analyst have her day. Donna may be politically incorrect in her suspicions of Chinese motives, but has she yet been wrong on anything important?"

Scott's STU-IX secure phone rang. He picked it up, "Scott

here." His whole countenance dropped as he fell back into his chair. "Yes, I understand. . . Benson's here right now. . . Klein? Of course she's available. . . Yes, I understand."

Mr. Scott hung up and buried his face in his hands. He inhaled deeply, gathered his strength and faced Donna, all but forgetting Jack Benson. "Donna, that was our desk at NORAD, the PRC just detonated at least one nuclear device over Taiwan. A DPS bird (Defense Program Satellite—designed to detect missile launches) was dazzled, probably temporarily. We're also getting indications that a couple of civilian satellites in LEO (Low Earth Orbit) over the Asia-Pacific region have been impacted too. Probably a low Earth orbit EMP attack. By the way, the Pentagon wants you down at the 'Nimic' (the National Military Command Center - NMCC) ASAP. The Joint Chiefs' office asked for you by name. They want someone with a solid handle on the Chinese to provide immediate on-the-spot crisis management assistance."

Donna looked devastated, "I'm sorry I failed sir. I didn't provide enough warning. I. . ."

Mr. Scott put up his hand and said, "Donna, Donna! Don't beat yourself up! You're the only one in the building who called it. You can't help it we were so blinded by the official policy of engagement, appeasement, whatever, that we didn't want to see it coming." He looked at Benson. His tone shifted to gentle encouragement, "Besides, you've got a job to do and you're obviously better suited for it than anyone else around here. I'll call for a car. Donna looked up, she had started to cry but was recovering quickly. She had a job to do and the future of her nation was in the balance.

22
Blocking the Eagle

The Panama Canal had been a key part of American defense plans for an entire century. All US fighting ships were designed to be just thin enough to transit the canal. Aside from its obvious economic benefits, the canal provided the US Navy with crucial strategic mobility. Without the canal, shifting naval power from the Atlantic to the Pacific and vice versa would take two added weeks as the ships had to head south to transit the Drake Passage.

It had been many years since the Canal Zone was American territory. Now, it was no longer home to American troops either. In fact, a Hong Kong-based Chinese company had purchased key commercial concessions in the former Canal Zone—in effect, China now ran the canal that the United States had dug almost 100 years before.

Regardless of the canal's status, it was very vulnerable to sabotage. On Friday evening, only an hour after China's attack on Taiwan, a large, but aging ship from China's COSCO line weighed anchor and entered the Miraflores Locks just outside of Panama City.

A Panamanian official inspected the ship. But a $2,000 cash bribe kept him from being too curious.

The freighter was carrying ammonium nitrate. Tens of thousands of gallons of diesel fuel from the ship's fuel bunkers had been sprayed into the cargo hold two days before. A PLA special operations demolition team placed thousands of pounds of explosives on top of the now 25,000-ton fertilizer bomb. They then covered the explosives with drums of sand to direct the blast downward.

Once in the locks the demolition team set the timers on the explosives. The first device to detonate was an incendiary bomb in the engine room. Its flames quickly engulfed the compartment, trapping three crewmembers. This "accident" was to provide the barest of cover to throw the Americans off and conceal the enormous magnitude of the coordination involved in the Chinese attack.

With the fire out of control, the demolition team spread panic and warned the crew to abandon ship. Climbing down ropes, 29 merchant crewmen and demolition team members escaped from the doomed ship. The sailors stayed on the concrete casing of the lock, close to their vessel. The ten-member demolition team ran hundreds of meters away to the top of a small tree-covered hill. Panamanian security thought it odd but simply marked it up to fear—the smoking ship gave them bigger and more immediate concerns to deal with.

The explosives detonated with perfect timing. The shock wave heated and compressed the mixture of fertilizer and diesel. This action allowed the rapid release of the stored chemical energy in the mixture. In less than a second, almost 10,000 tons of explosive fuel had released its fury, unharnessing the equivalent of a two-kiloton nuclear bomb.

The lock the ship rested in was the first casualty. The lock's towering but hollow steel doors, with their internal piping and valves, blew out like pieces of aluminum foil. This itself would not have presented a huge problem as the Canal Authority had spare lock doors as well as a second lock channel for opposing traffic just 60 feet away. Unfortunately, the massive fertilizer bomb had a more ambitious purpose than simply cutting the Panama Canal's traffic in half for a few days. The true target of the assault was the lock's concrete casing. The explosion shattered the casing, rupturing the water lines that power the canal's hydraulics. It also destroyed the rails upon which the diesel train engines worked as tugs to pull the ships along the lock system. The huge shock wave continued to propagate through the concrete and earth, seeking voids and weak spots. When the wave reached the empty lock for Pacific-bound traffic it collapsed the concrete wall into the lock. The Panama Canal would be shut down for many, many months.

With the exception of the demolition team members, every witness to the "accident" died in the explosion. The demolition team, deaf and bleeding at the nose and ears from the concussive overpressure, straggled into the outskirts of Panama City. They soon found their safehouse. They cleaned up and changed their clothes. Within an hour they transferred to another safehouse. They were prepared to remain out of sight for a very long time.

23
Build-up

Fu Zemin loved irony. Here he was, a Communist Party official, flying in as a conqueror to an airport named after a man who dedicated his career to fighting Communists. Chaing Kai-Shek International Airport was an hour away from Zhangzhou by way of the twin turboprop Y-7 he was aboard. Fu knew the ROC air force had to be substantially destroyed before someone of his stature would be allowed to make the flight over, but that still didn't make him feel entirely comfortable flying in a small, slow airplane.

Just prior to leaving, a liaison from PLA Military Intelligence boarded the aircraft. The officer presented his papers to Fu. "Comrade Fu, I am Major General Wei. My job is to keep you current on the strategic and operational situation. The Party leadership believes your assessments will be of greater utility to them if you are kept informed."

Fu felt the surge of pride and power well up within him. He had his own general of intelligence to brief *him*—now that was prestige. "Please, General Wei, be seated and tell me what you know about our efforts."

"Sir, my information is only," the general glanced at his watch, "15 minutes old." It was 10:30 AM. "Sir, I understand you read the briefing packet that gave you a detailed understanding of the strategic situation?"

"Yes."

"So then, I will concentrate on the recent operational details." The general was obviously used to briefing VIPs. He was completely at ease.

"Comrade Fu, first, the enemy overview. Prior to our electro-magnetic attack, the ROC ground forces were estimated to be at 50 percent effective manning levels due to the genetically engineered flu virus we introduced on the island 11 days ago. The electro-magnetic attack should result in a further erosion of their military effectiveness through degraded command, control and communications ability. We destroyed 40 to 60% of the ROC Air Force. And we estimate ROC Navy losses to be in excess of 60%."

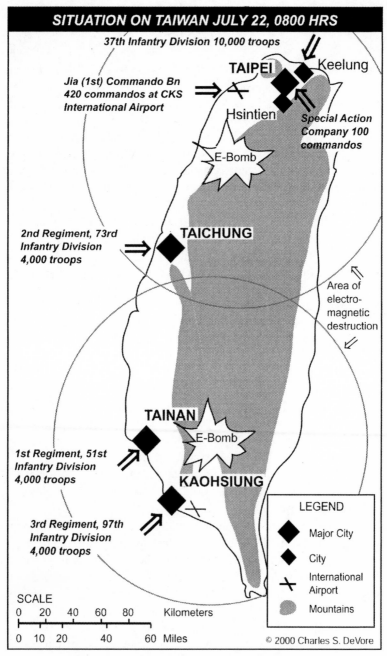

SITUATION ON TAIWAN JULY 22, 0800 HRS

37th Infantry Division 10,000 troops

TAIPEI Keelung

Jia (1st) Commando Bn
420 commandos at CKS
International Airport

Hsintien

Special Action
Company 100
commandos

E-Bomb

2nd Regiment, 73rd
Infantry Division
4,000 troops

TAICHUNG

Area of
electro-
magnetic
destruction

TAINAN

E-Bomb

1st Regiment, 51st
Infantry Division
4,000 troops

KAOHSIUNG

3rd Regiment, 97th
Infantry Division
4,000 troops

LEGEND

Major City

City

International
Airport

Mountains

SCALE
0   20   40   60   80   Kilometers

0   10   20   40   60   Miles

© 2000 Charles S. DeVore

China's surprise assault enjoys success

"What about the American flotilla at the south end of the Straits?" Fu demanded.

"We have no word on them. We warned them not to enter the Taiwan Strait. We currently have no specific information on them, their location or their condition."

"The moment you hear anything about the Americans, I want to know."

"Yes sir. Now, if you please, I will brief you on the friendly situation. Using deceptive measures we have landed strong forces on Taiwan by unconventional means. Friendly casualties have been remarkably light. We have 10,000 soldiers of the 37th Infantry Division Keelung only 15 miles northeast of Taipei. We have reinforced regiments of about 4,000 men each in all three of the major west coast ports: Taichung, Tainan, and Kaohsiung. We have air dropped a regiment of the 2nd Airborne Division on Shalu to help secure Taichung's harbor for follow-on forces. We have also air dropped the remainder of the 2nd Airborne Division on Highway 1, nine kilometers southeast of CKS Airport. Lastly, we have airlanded a battalion of commandos at CKS and secured the airport. Other airborne and airlanding operations are in progress.

"Beginning one hour after we captured the airport we have been landing aircraft every five minutes at CKS. By now we ought to have an entire regiment of the 87th Infantry Division in place with one regiment arriving every hour. Using commercial shipping and civilian ferries, reinforcements will arrive by sea in less than eight hours at every port facility we have seized. We have pressed into service every ocean-capable ferry in China from Guangzhou to Shanghai as well as most of our nearby merchant fleet. Our conventional amphibious forces will concentrate on landing troops and armor at Keelung and on the beaches near CKS.

"At the moment, the ROC forces in the field in Taiwan equal the equivalent of nine infantry divisions and two tank divisions with two-thirds of an artillery division. Our forces on the ground equal approximately three infantry divisions without heavy equipment." General Wei looked satisfied at his briefing.

Fu Zemin had a drawn look on his face, "You mean we are outnumbered by almost three to one?"

The general smiled reassuringly, "Comrade Fu, remember the damage we inflicted on the renegade province before our attack. Their military has been hard hit by our virus. They can only fight at about 50 percent manning—about six divisions. You see, they only outnumber us two to one." The general smiled thinly.

"Oh, I feel better already," Fu let his sarcasm get the best of him. The general's eyebrows arched.

"Sir, I don't want to sound overconfident, but the enemy divisions are without communications. Without the ability to communicate, they cannot react to our moves. Further, when a military unit has half of its people sick in bed it is at less than half effectiveness. In fact most major militaries of the world consider a unit with only 50 percent of its personnel to be completely combat ineffective."

Still looking worried, Fu changed the subject, "General Wei, you said we destroyed 40-60% of the ROC Air Force. I expected a better result. Why did we not destroy more?"

"Sir, since our airborne surveillance aircraft and reconnaissance ships would affected by the E-bomb we did not have them out collecting at the moment of detonation. As best as we could determine prior to the electronic attack, the ROCAF had only sortied about half of its fighters in response to our attack. This was a smaller response than we anticipated." The general showed an air of disappointment.

Fu became angry. He wanted to rule Asia someday, but he didn't want to get shot out of the sky in the process of trying to do so, "Did you military geniuses ever stop to think that a few pilots might be grounded because of the flu?"

General Wei, stared at the seatback in front of him, not really focusing on anything. This man was obviously an intelligence professional, more concerned with data than with saving face. The general turned to Fu, "Of course!" His face lit up, "That's got to explain it. I congratulate you Comrade Fu. I will relay this to the invasion headquarters immediately."

General Wei removed an odd-looking cellular phone from his equipment belt and dialed a number, "Raven here. . . Something to consider. . . Maybe too many pilots had the flu. . . Right. I recommend you recalculate the attrition rate and plan accordingly. Oh, I also need any information on the status of the American ships. . . Right, I'll wait."

"General Wei, isn't that a commercial satellite phone?" Fu was incredulous at the thought of a military intelligence officer using a regular commercial phone.

Wei hit the mute button on the phone. "Why yes sir, it is. It's an Iridium satellite system digital phone—good anywhere on Earth. Highly resistant to jamming. And, actually fairly hard for the Americans to intercept. Because it's digital and the system handles so many calls world-wide, we calculated it to be more secure than our normal scrambled voice communications. We have equipped every commander down to the regimental level with one." The general was glowing with pride.

Fu was shocked that the PLA would place so much reliance on an American commercial communications system, "What if the Americans turn it off?"

"Well, first of all, we don't expect to be fighting that long. Secondly, we own part of Iridium. It's technically not even an American company—it's based in Bermuda and we even have two members on its board of directors. If the American government eventually shuts down our calling privileges we'll be no worse off than we were before. We will simply shift to using traditional modes. . ." Fu could hear someone on the other end of the phone. ". . .of communication. Pardon me. Yes. . . Yes. Excellent! No, that is all. Raven out." The general turned to Fu with a broad grin, "We found the American naval task force. Our reconnaissance aircraft report seeing one capsized ship. A destroyer is on fire. Another ship appears to be damaged. And. . ." Wei's smile became still larger, "we have sighted the sinking stern section of their flagship, the USS *Belleau Wood*. Fortune smiles upon us."

"We attacked the *Americans*?" Fu was shocked at the implications. "Who ordered *that*?"

Wei looked not least bit concerned, "I'm sure it was a 'mistake', sir. After all, the American ships were in a war zone. We warned them, didn't we?"

Fu fell silent. In the last few hours, China began a war of conquest and attacked the US Navy. Everything had moved so quickly since the sudden arrest of Admiral Wong in his bunker. There had been no time to think. Only time to follow orders and react. It seemed like days ago, but it only happened less than four hours ago. Fu turned around in his seat and noticed the first passengers (all PLA officers) were four rows back. There was no one in the two rows of seats between them and the cockpit. He had his suspicions, but he had to know for sure. "General Wei," Fu gathered himself to project his best aura of leadership and confidence, "Just how knowledgeable are you on the planning of this operation?"

"I have been working on the contingency plans for the invasion of Taiwan for the last eight years," the general's statement was matter-of-fact. No pride—simple truth. "We have actually been making and revising invasion contingency plans since 1949. We have an entire secret staff section of the PLA dedicated to doing nothing but that."

"When did you learn of the actual approval for the operation?" Fu's question was cool, but he was dying to know the answer for it would be an indicator of just how trusted an aid he was to the Party.

"I was notified in January, six months ago."

Fu was crestfallen. With effort he kept his face impassive. This lowly PLA general knew about the operation shortly after the extraordinary planning session—the session in which Fu advocated a swift campaign to capture all of Taiwan and follow it up with a bold move to eject America from Asia—only his plan was rejected! Instead, the leadership approved a strategy of meek half-measures that he, Fu, was mandated to oversee.

The true extent of the leadership's brilliance was becoming clear. He was simply used as a pawn in a game much larger and more complex then he ever imagined. Now he knew for sure, "So, the planned invasion of Quemoy was simply a ruse? Was the arrest of Admiral Wong a ruse too?"

General Wei looked at Fu with admiration. "For a politician, you are a quick study in the art of war. Yes, the preparations for the invasion of Quemoy were part of our deception plan. Unfortunately, the arrest of Admiral Wong was not. The man is a traitor. After we extract as much useful information out of him as we can, he will be dealt with in the customary fashion."

Fu was quickly forgetting about the slight the Party showed him by not revealing their true battle plans—after all, he was now the Party's liaison on the province of Taiwan. That was reward enough to prove that he was not out of favor. "General, we have only 15 minutes before we land. Provide me as much detail as you can on our deception efforts. I believe a thorough understanding of this operation's foundation is essential for my efforts on behalf of the Party."

"Certainly, Comrade Fu. As you know, Sun Tzu said, 'All warfare is based on deception.' Our plan was simple: lead the Taiwanese into believing that we wanted to invade Quemoy and Matsu then, under cover of this invasion plan, prepare for the invasion of the Taiwanese main island. The reactionaries on Taiwan would believe what they wanted to believe and our preparations could continue without giving away our true plans.

"The leadership decided in January to accept your

recommendations. You are to be lauded for that. I have read some of your memos and have heard about your briefings to the Party. However, it was the statement you made during the extraordinary session that was the clearest argument to date for acting now, rather than waiting. But, because of security concerns, the leadership announced that our military objectives would be limited. As was expected, this decision was communicated to our enemies on Taiwan. In fact. . ." the general's face brightened as he had a revelation, ". . .yes, of course, that is why Admiral Wong was put in charge of the Quemoy operation! He was a traitor and we knew it all along! All of our preparations for the larger invasion of Taiwan itself were then masked by Admiral Wong's invasion preparations for Quemoy and the communications he no doubt had with the enemy. The stage was then set for the enemy to believe what he wanted to believe—that we would only invade Quemoy and perhaps the other offshore islands.

"Once the enemy received word of our plans, later confirmed by the indicators of our offensive preparation, he reacted as we wanted him to. Only six weeks ago, Taiwan landed another division of infantry, a battalion of tanks and a battalion of artillery on Quemoy. This removed another five percent of the enemy's active force from the decisive theater of operations!

"With half of Taiwan's infantry divisions packed on to a few tiny, unimportant islands, we are now in the position of being able to do what the Americans did to Japan more than 50 years ago. We are simply hopping over Quemoy and Matsu to strike at the heart of the enemy. Once Taiwan surrenders, Quemoy and Matsu will fall to us like overripe fruit."

Fu was awed at the magnitude of the deception and its success. Still, he was concerned about the fact that they were flying on to an island where the enemy outnumbered them and would do so for days. The course of action he recommended was to pummel the rebellious province into submission with missiles tipped with chemical and high explosive warheads. Obviously, they weren't doing that. "So, now that we have the enemy where we want them, how do we achieve victory while outnumbered?"

"Very simple. We follow Sun Tzu's advice; we follow the principles of Offensive Strategy against our enemy. We'll take his state intact, capture his army, attack his strategy, and disrupt his alliances."

"Alliances. What about the Americans?"

"Taiwan's alliance with America is weak, at best. You'll recall in 1996, when last we conducted large scale exercises to intimidate Taiwan—why do you suppose the US fleet never ventured closer than 200 kilometers off the coast of Taiwan?" Before Fu could reply, the now animated general said, "One of our generals threatened the destruction of Los Angeles if the Americans intervened to save Taiwan! That's why! The Americans were paralyzed, we called their bluff; they did nothing. They didn't even demand the removal of the general or an apology. This shows the almost complete abandonment of Taiwan by her so-called ally. And, if that isn't enough, Iraqi military demonstrations in the past couple of months have drawn off two divisions of US troops—including the Marine division usually stationed at Okinawa while North Korea is conducting very impressive maneuvers within a few kilometers of the DMZ. I'd say the Americans have their hands very full right now."

"Very impressive, general. But the Taiwanese have Sun Tzu too. Can we not expect them to develop plans of their own?"

"Of course, but we will shape the enemy and the battlefield. We will force the enemy to do what we want him to. Our plan is simple: degrade and slow the enemy by non-lethal biological, chemical and electronic attack. Land our forces along the length of the Taiwan to engage the enemy and tie him down. Quickly build combat power in the north. Cut off Taipei from the rest of the nation. Then defeat the inevitable counterattack to relieve the city. After that, the enemy is ours. Taipei is the enemy's center of gravity. Destroying the enemy's ability to relieve Taipei is the defeat mechanism. We will win this war because we have already won."

Fu wasn't entirely convinced. "General you know your Sun Tzu well, as should be expected by a professional military man. I too know some Sun Tzu and I believe you forget one thing, 'The army destined to defeat fights in the hope of winning.' I am confident, but I do not think it will be easy."

The intercom broke their conversation. It was the pilot announcing that they would land at CKS International Airport within a few minutes. Fu Zemin was about to embark on his most important assignment yet for the Party.

*   *   *

The five LCACs noisily roared east at 35 knots. They could have gone faster, but Colonel Flint wanted to conserve enough fuel to make as many return trips as possible to the *Germantown* and pick up more Marines, equipment and survivors. Overwatching the LCACs were two Harrier jets. Just above the horizon about 10 miles to the east of the LCACs the 31st MEU's helicopters could be seen. Far behind the 11 Assault Amphibians struggled through the heaving southeasterly swell.

Colonel Flint's Huey had just one working radio. The EMP attack destroyed most of his unit's radio gear. The lack of radio traffic presented an odd dichotomy. On one hand, no traffic was a sign of no contact with the enemy. In addition, a well-disciplined force doesn't need to crowd the airwaves with jabber. On the other hand, a destroyed force doesn't talk much either. Flint decided he'd go with the former definition. No news was good news.

He sent three of his Harriers ahead to scout out Kaohsiung's port and the international airport five kilometers to the southeast of the city. They reported back a city almost devoid of any activity.

As the Harriers returned from their reconnaissance and flew over Chichin Island (which forms the seabreak for Kaohsiung Harbor), they were fired upon. A shoulder-fired missile streaked out from the deck of a large dry bulk cargo ship. The Harriers dropped infrared decoy flares and dove for the water, ducking low over the east side of island about 30 feet above Chichin Beach. The missile veered onto a flare and exploded harmlessly in the air, looking like a small skyrocket.

The flight leader, Captain Hill, radioed Colonel Flint, "Bulldog One, Bulldog One, this is Dragon One One, over."

Flint keyed his mike, "Dragon One One, this is Bulldog One, go ahead over."

"Bulldog One, we got some fire in here. Looked like an SA-7 launched from a cargo ship in the harbor."

Colonel Flint knew if anyone was hit Hill would have said so, "Did you get a look at the ship, over?"

"Wait one." Captain Hill had expected this question. He had brought his jet to a hover and slowly increased his altitude until he could just see the ship over the nice houses on Chichin Island. The ship made no secret of its identity—a red flag with one large yellow star in the upper right corner cradled by a crescent of four yellow stars proudly snapped in the northwesterly wind. "Bulldog One. Got a positive ID on the ship. People's Republic of China. I say again, the People's Republic of China, over."

Flint processed this new information. He called for his intelligence officer in other UH-1N, "Red Two Two, Red Two Two, this is Bulldog One, over."

"Bulldog One, this is Red Two Two, over." Major Ramirez responded quickly.

Colonel Flint smiled, he imagined Major "Rez" Ramirez holding the mike, not letting the XO touch it. "Did you copy last transmission, over?"

Ramirez paused and thought, but only for a moment, "Roger. Looks like the enemy sent a ship or two in to seize the harbor. Probably more to follow. Surprised the airport's clear, over."

"Recommendations, over?" Flint already had a good idea of what he wanted to do, but Rez's advice would confirm his thoughts.

"Bad guys probably have no clue we're here. We can secure the airport. Place LP/OPs at the north and south end of Chichin. When their reinforcements arrive we can send the Harriers out from the airport and bomb the ships as they're entering the Harbor, over." Rez was in top form as usual.

"What about our M1s or AT weapons, over?"

"Like a popgun against a 20,000 ton ship. Use them to secure the airport and leave the ship-busting to the Harriers, over."

"I agree. Mercury Three, Mercury Three, Bulldog One, over." Flint was calling his LCACs.

"This is Mercury Three, over."

"Mercury Three, I want you to land just north of Kaohsiung Talinpu. There should be beach there. You probably can't find a place to land in the harbor, plus there's a boat-load of bad guys in there, over."

"Wilco."

Flint loved the reply "wilco"—it was the ultimate in military efficiency, meaning, "I understand and will comply." Flint's plan was deceptively simple. He figured he had more than 1,000 Marines and a little more than 100 pilots, aircrew and sailors. He would establish a beachhead southeast of Kaohsiung, then rapidly push north to secure the international airport. He'd take the airport with two rifle companies, two platoons of the weapons company and the tank platoon. He'd leave the remainder of his battalion to guard the beachhead and establish a rest, refit, and refuel spot for his aircrews. These Marines would also keep an eye on the southern approach into the harbor. He planned on sending his reconnaissance platoon and the four LAVs he managed to save to the north of Chichin Island where they could watch the northern approach into the harbor as well as observe Kaohsiung itself. With luck, they'd establish an LP/OP on top of the hill at Shoushan Park overlooking the city and the harbor.

"Red Three Three, Red Three Three, this is Bulldog One, over." Flint was calling his S-3 (Operations Officer), Lieutenant Colonel Cook.

"Bulldog One, this is Red Three Three, over."

"Red Three Three, we need a frago (fragmentary order) to seize the docks at Kaohsiung and destroy the enemy force there. After we secure the airport and the beach I want to be prepared to go into Kaohsiung Harbor and prevent the enemy from bringing in further reinforcements."

"Roger Bulldog One, we already prepared the branch plan onboard ship. We're ready to go, and Hammer One has already been briefed. "

"Roger, Bulldog One, out." Flint didn't have time to be pleased with his staff. If they lived to tell about it, that would be reward enough for most of them.

For almost being wiped out in America's worst naval defeat since Pearl Harbor Flint felt remarkably at ease. He and most of the combat elements of the 31st MEU were alive and capable of fighting. Sustaining any action beyond a couple of days would be a challenge without the Combat Service Support Element, but he'd deal with that problem in a day or two. In spite of the situation, Colonel Flint smiled—he had a *real* war to fight now.

"Dragon One One, Bulldog One, over."

"Dragon One One here." The Harrier pilot replied.

"Dragon One One, sink the bastards and get over to the airport ASAP, over."

"Wilco!"

Flint could hear the excitement in the Captain Hill's voice—he was about to run the sort of mission he was trained for with no one from Washington looking over his shoulder and telling him not to use all the tools in his kit.

The PLA commander in charge of the 3rd Infantry Regiment, 97th Infantry Division radioed his status back to headquarters on the Mainland. Both of the busy men only had time for a brief situation update. The senior colonel said, "Sir, we've gotten one battalion of infantry off the ship. We're trying to eliminate some sniper fire before we bring the other battalions and the support elements off. We just fired on some enemy aircraft. We saw three of them. Our recon element has just reported the airport is not yet defended." The colonel was reluctant to mention his main real problem: dehydration and heat prostration. While more the fault of the men who planned the mission using a cargo ship hastily converted into a troop carrier, admitting a problem was to admit poor preparation—or worse yet, be thought of accusing his commander of a mistake. Either path was a sure way to be relieved of command.

The major general responded, "You are getting behind on your timetable. I do not care about snipers. Get your men off that ship immediately! We must have the docks and the landing beaches secured within three hours. I'm not holding up the rest of the division for you!"

*　　*　　*

General Wei's SATCOM phone chirped. Fu eyed him carefully, looking for indications. "I see. . . Certainly an unexpected development. . . Let me know the soonest you hear anything more." Wei looked at Fu and flipped the phone shut. "Comrade Fu, it seems there has been a complication introduced into our operation. The American Marines have landed on Taiwan. . ."

"What?" Fu felt years of planning beginning to crumble.

"Sir, I'm sure it's only the remnants of the force we attacked off Kaohsiung. I recall from the American order of battle that there could be no more than 2,100 Marines in the force we attacked. A little more than 2,000 dazed American Marines could hardly be considered a threat, eh?" Wei sounded his reassuring best.

*　　*　　*

Captain Mike "Mole" Hill (his nickname earned by his constant telling of mountainous tales involving his favorite subject: Captain Hill) keyed the radio to speak with his wingmen. "Snake, Dingo, I'm going to position for an attack run on that freighter. I'm going to come in from the southeast and drop my iron. Suppress the bastards for me, over."

First Lieutenant "Snake" Gilbert responded, "Roger, Mole, we'll keep their heads down. Hey, I've got 16 500 pounders, I want to play too!"

"Shut up and cover me!" Hill grinned behind his oxygen mask then banked his aircraft to the right and streaked off just over the wave tops, leaving the other two Harriers in a hover over the beach. About three miles away Hill pulled up and looped to the left. With his wingmen able to suppress the ship's shoulder-fired SAM teams with rapid fire from their six-barreled 25mm guns as well as 2.75 inch rocket fire, Hill figured he could run a classic dive bomb attack on the freighter and damage it or even sink it with the six Mk 83 1,000 pound general purpose bombs he carried.

At 10,000 feet Hill lined up for his attack run. To his left about two miles away, he could see the angry white spray of the LCACs making their way to the beach. Above them he saw the ACE's helicopters. The freighter looked innocent, still and harmless off in the crowded harbor. Fortunately, it was one of the larger ships and appeared to be a bulk carrier as opposed to a container ship as most of the other ships were. It was easy to pick out in the harbor.

Hill keyed his mike, "I'm going in. You may fire when ready Gridley."

Hill armed the bombs and waited until the ship was obscured by the nose of his aircraft. He nosed the Harrier down to a 45 degree angle, quickly found his target, and sped up to almost 600 mph. To the left, just behind the row of buildings on Chichin Island about a mile away from the freighter, Hill saw his two wingmen rise up and begin firing their cannons at the ship. Tracers arced across the bay into the ship's superstructure. Hill had about seven seconds to dive, line up, and release his iron bombs about 5,000 feet above the target with the aid of his AN/ASB-19 Angle Rate Bombing Set computer. He started releasing chaff to confuse any radar guided missiles or anti-aircraft guns the enemy may have set up. Beads of sweat popped out of his face. In rapid succession Hill released his six bombs.

"Mole! Mole! SAM launch! Two, three SAMs coming at you!" Snake cried.

Not unexpected. Hill pulled back on the stick and released flares to decoy heat-seeking missiles. The laser warning tocsin sounded. *Damn.* "Laser warning, I have laser warning!"

Dockside, next to the emptying Chinese freighter, a specially equipped PLA anti-aircraft team had just let loose with a Starburst shoulder-fired, laser-guided SAM. Starburst, made in Northern Ireland, has been around since 1991. It wasn't supposed to be in China, then again, there were quite a few things that managed to make their way to China, the lure of cash being what it is. The laser-guided system was nearly impossible to decoy. Immune to chaff or flares, the missile was guided to its target by a laser beam. Once the system acquired the target, the shooter simply kept the target in his sights while the system's computer held the laser beam on the target until the missile impacted. Designed for use against helicopters or low-flying aircraft, the missile was tremendously accurate.

The missile exploded just under the engine inlet, knocking out the Rolls Royce Pegasus turbofan engine. The Harrier shook madly as Captain Hill fought to recover control. Hill's leg felt numb. He looked down. *Oh shit!* The missile had torn a fragment of metal loose from the aircraft and sent it up the inside of his right calf, shredding the lower half of his leg. He no longer had rudder control (if the aircraft still had rudder control to lose). Two conventional heat seeking missiles streaked by his canopy, decoyed by the flares. The aircraft had been kicked over on its side by the explosion and subsequent aerodynamic forces. He could see the freighter below him. Hill knew he had about six seconds of flight remaining before his aircraft crashed. He reached to pull the ejection handle. A shard of metal obstructed it. *Oh God. Forgive me.*

Hill pushed the sluggish stick to the right and rolled his aircraft upside down. He was now diving straight onto the ship. He gritted his teeth, "Snake, I'm hit hard. Tell my wife I love her."

The first 1,000-pound bomb hit the ship in the stern smack on top of its superstructure, penetrating two decks down before exploding. Just before the ship's portals and hatches began to shatter and belch fire, the second bomb hit. The dry bulk carrier had five small mounds of crushed ore visible on deck, one pile for each cargo hold. Hill didn't know it, but there was nothing but air under the piles—more specifically, air, a specially built-up interior lattice structure and about 3,500 of the 4,000 PLA conscripts that were to take Kaohsiung still inside, slowed down by heat exhaustion and confusion. The second bomb passed between the rear two piles of ore and exploded in the ship's hold. The ship's hull buckled outward and more than 1,000 soldiers died instantly. The third and fourth bombs hit the piles of ore on the deck and exploded in a great shower of dust, collapsing both piles into the ship's interior. The fifth bomb hit the bow section and exploded inside the ship, just below the water line. Another 500 soldiers perished. If Hill had any doubt that his target was legitimate, he finally noticed two gangplanks extending from the ship to the dock. The first bomb explosions having cleared the soldiers off the ramps like a broom clearing ants off a sidewalk. At 1,000 feet with less than two seconds remaining in the last dive of his life, Hill toggled his 25mm cannon to life (he hoped it would work) and selected an aim point at the middle of the ship, between the second and third pile of ore.

The 22,000 pounds of mostly-fueled Harrier tore through the ship and exploded beneath the deck. In less than 10 seconds of combat with the US Marine Corps, the PLA lost 3,500 men from the 3rd Regiment of the 97th Infantry Division. The Marines had a long way to go to avenge the losses dealt to their Navy brethren, but they counted this a beginning.

*   *   *

The private was barely able to move. He and his platoon were in one of the buildings at the end of the wharf when he heard the unfamiliar *whoosh* of the outbound Chinese SAMs. He stiffly stood up to refill his canteen in the restroom and decided to hazard a look out the ground floor window. He noticed the diving Harrier but didn't process its significance until the first bomb ripped at the dry bulk cargo ship he called home for the last three days. The conscript simply stood at the window, mouth agape. Finally, the blast shock wave reached the private's building. Unfortunately for the young private, the window faced down the wharf at a 90-degree angle to the direction of the shock wave. The plate glass window shattered, shredding his face and cutting his jugular. Within five minutes, the 19-year-old was dead.

*   *   *

Donna Klein had been in the National Military Command Center once before on an orientation visit for CIA employees. The NMMC was on the second floor of the Pentagon. The third floor had been removed over the command center to provide room for large overhead displays and other equipment. The first time she saw it she was amused at how crowded it was with wires and TVs and displays. It looked nothing at all like the huge and lavishly equipped command center Hollywood portrays. She remembered that just to the right of the main door, up in a corner, was a lighted display of the DEFCON status for the various regions where

America's troops were stationed. During her first visit every location was at DEFCON 5 except the Korean Peninsula—it was at DEFCON 4 because of the hair-trigger readiness of the North Korean People's Army to attack the south and the 37,000 US troops stationed there.

After signing in at the entrance she walked through the two sets of doors and began to look to the right to check the DEFCON status. Before she could find the display (did they move it since her last visit?) she saw General Tim Taylor. She found herself looking at him for a moment, studying how he interacted with those around him—*confident, but respectful.*

Seeing her, General Taylor jumped out of his front row chair in the theater-like seating and called out, "Donna! I'm glad you could make it on such short notice. Do you know how hard it is to find the 'A' team on a Washington Friday night? Please sit down." He gestured to the empty chair next to his, "Admiral Gordon here was about to update me on what we know so far in Asia."

"Thank you, sir." Only distracted for a second by her lingering attraction to Taylor, Donna became completely focused on the crisis at hand.

The admiral, white haired, but otherwise young looking, cleared his throat and began, "There is no new information of significance out of Taiwan since we first detected the Chinese attack two hours ago. We have not reestablished contact with the *Belleau Wood* Amphibious Ready Group. An hour ago we dispatched an already airborne RC-135 reconnaissance aircraft based in Okinawa to investigate. A few minutes ago it was intercepted by three Chinese fighter aircraft just inside the north entrance to the Taiwan Strait. They demanded that the RC-135 turn around. Our aircraft is returning safely to base."

Donna looked around. She was the only civilian in the room. She decided to say something, "I trust the aircraft was over international waters in an approved air corridor?"

The admiral wasn't used to being interrupted on his stage, "Why. . . Yes, of course."

Donna's face flushed with anger, "Turning around was a mistake, a huge mistake. We have now set precedence that the Chinese can close the Taiwan Strait to legitimate air or sea traffic. We have also shown them that we are a paper tiger. Who ordered the aircraft to turn back?" Donna said the last accusingly. It was bad enough she didn't see this war coming until it was too late.

Now her error was being compounded by others.

The admiral looked Donna straight in the eye, "The White House."

Donna paused, "Buildings can't order anyone to do a damn thing. *Who* at the White House? The President?"

Taylor stiffened slightly in his seat.

The admiral was trumped, "I. . . I don't really know. The pilot radioed his situation to CINCPAC. CINCPAC called up the chain of command. No one would take responsibility for provoking the Chinese into an open conflict so the ball was passed to the White House. That's all I know. Besides, our latest guidance specifically dictates a hands-off policy on Taiwan."

"Where were you General?" Donna asked quietly.

"Unfortunately the secure comm link in my car went down on the way in. . ."

Donna slumped in her chair and mumbled, "What is this, the amateur hour?" She sat forward and turned to Taylor, "General, on a Friday night, who's minding the store over at the White House?"

"Probably some mid-level NSC functionaries—many of whom come from this building." Taylor knew where Donna was taking him.

"Do you think they could use some reinforcements? After all, what can we do here? We can get information all the same here or there. What matters most now is what is done with that information. Besides, you're the President's second-ranking military advisor."

"Right, and the Chairman's in Kosovo visiting the troops. Let me make a call." Taylor got up to use one of the room's many secure phones.

The admiral stood ignored behind his podium.

Donna spoke, "Admiral, the *Belleau Wood* Amphibious. . ."

". . .Ready Group."

"Thanks. What is that?"

"Today it is a force of four naval ships, it has three amphibious assault ships and an Aegis-class destroyer. It is a self-contained fighting force of about 2,200 Marines and support aircraft."

"What is US policy in the event of an unprovoked attack on the high seas?" Donna asked.

The admiral replied, "US forces have the right to defend themselves without orders from Washington."

"Do we know how far the *Belleau Wood* was from Taiwan

when the Chinese attack began?"

"Of course, they were 14 miles off the southern coast of Taiwan in international waters.   I can give you an exact location. . ."

"Admiral," Donna looked squarely at the officer, "If you were the commander of that task force and you were attacked by China, what would you do?"

"Defend myself and turn around and head for the open ocean."

"And if you were too heavily damaged to flee?"

The admiral winced at the word "flee" and said, "If I was badly hit I suppose I'd seek safe harbor on Taiwan."

"We have to find out where those ships are ASAP.   Not knowing puts us at a disadvantage." Donna sat stroking her chin.

Taylor hung up the phone and turned towards Donna, "Let's go! The White House wants us over at the Situation Room right away."

Donna smiled weakly at the admiral and softly said, "Quite talkative for a house, isn't it?"

Donna had never before been in the White House, not even as a tourist. The Situation Room, at least the one she was shown into, was a small hole in a subfloor of the White House's West Wing. It had one large rectangular table with enough room to seat a dozen people. Behind the chairs at the table were another set of chairs pushed up against the wall.   There was so little room between the chairs, that if both rows were occupied, no one could maneuver between the chairs without stepping over people's knees.   Donna was shocked at the small size of the meeting room—not at all like the public perception of the White House.

The room was dominated by two televisions, one was turned to CNN, the other, MSNBC—a tribute to the immediacy of modern news gathering organizations.   Curiously, neither network had caught on to the war that had just ignited in the Taiwan Strait.

Donna recognized the faces of the National Security Council Advisor as well as two of the three young NSC staffers.   Very junior team—*not good.*

Bob Lindley, the NSC Advisor was dressed in a tux and still had on a bow tie. *The social obligations of the well-connected,* Donna thought, *I hope he hasn't had too much to drink.* He hung up one of the five phones on the table and turned to the CIA staffer and the Defense Department official, "Thanks for coming over, we can use your assistance right now." His voice was clear and strong.

She wondered where some of the other NSC personnel were. She knew many of the civilian staffers had already left the Administration, now in its last half-year of life, to seek jobs in academia, banking or business. That would leave much of the NSC's work to military personnel assigned to the White House. With the famously low level of mutual confidence between the military and this White House Donna calculated that a military staffer here rated just above a White House gardener and just below an intern on the pecking order.

Klein and Taylor edged between the chairs to take their seats opposite the NSC chief.

Lindley looked at Donna, then asked Taylor, "Who's your colleague?"

"Donna Klein, CIA, China desk." Donna spoke in a measured staccato.

"Excellent. What does Defense know about the situation so far?" Lindley was very cool, almost too cool for the potential enormity of the events.

Taylor began, "When we last spoke less than 15 minutes ago my understanding was that the White House had all the data we did. We've been in transit since then. Has there been anything new?" Taylor looked at the NSC staffers.

"Nothing," the senior staffer replied, "We really don't have a grasp on the situation in China yet. We were focused on the situation in Kuwait. The Iraqis just seized three Kuwaiti border crossings. At least one Kuwaiti border guard was killed."

Another staffer volunteered, "And North Korea is heating up as well. Maybe the Chinese are conducting a feint to draw our attention away from a potential North Korean invasion of South Korea."

Donna's stomach tensed. *Time was wasting away; decisions needed to be made.* "Look, gentlemen, the actions by Iraq and North Korea are in support of China's actions, not the other way around. I believe we know enough. First, we know that the PRC has launched a large-scale assault on Taiwan using nuclear weapons. . ."

"Hold on there!" the senior staffer cried, "we don't know that for sure. You can't. . ."

"What is your name again?" Donna asked with a hint of femininity, brushing back a renegade strand of curly red hair.

"Ken Maus. . ."

"Mr. Maus, none of us knows for sure anything about the situation. We're not there, now are we? Even if we were on the ground, there is no possible way we would know everything—we would only know what we thought we saw at a particular place and time. I'm simply giving you what the CIA knows to be happening right now. You have a different analysis. May I continue?"

Lindley looked intently at Klein, "Yes, Ms. Klein, please. . ." Lindley looked at Maus disapprovingly.

Donna wanted to push herself away from the table and give a stand-up briefing, but the chairs were too confining to easily get up. She instead squared her shoulders and began to address Lindley with an occasional glance to the other three staffers, "We know China has launched an assault on Taiwan, *probably* using nuclear weapons. These weapons were exploded high in the atmosphere over Taiwan, most likely to minimize casualties on the ground and maximize the EMP effect. In fact, one of our nuclear early warning satellites was damaged by the explosion as were some commercial communications satellites. We also know from the last transmissions of the *Belleau Wood* Amphibious Ready Group that they were observing a probable Chinese air strike on Taiwan—an air strike involving several hundred aircraft at the least. The *Belleau Wood* was sailing with 2,200 Marines just outside of Taiwan's territorial waters. The major news organizations have not yet caught on to the war," Donna said nodding at the televisions, "Which probably means that the EMP knocked out Taiwan's ability to communicate with the outside world. Lastly, we know that we sent an RC-135 electronic recon aircraft from Okinawa into the Taiwan Strait to establish contact with the *Belleau Wood*. It was intercepted by Chinese fighter aircraft over international waters." Donna paused, "Does the President know about this?"

Lindley looked at Maus. Maus looked back.

"Well," Lindley demanded, "Does the President know?"

"About what? Unconfirmed rumors? Hell, it's not even on the news yet," Maus protested. "Besides, he's at a $10,000 a plate fund-raiser in Philadelphia right now."

"Well, if it does get on the news and the President is caught flat-footed and unaware by a reporter I think he will have wished he was informed." Lindley was agitated—he could lose his job over this if it got out of hand.

Donna wondered how to ask the key question that was troubling her. Like most things she did, she decided on the direct approach. "I was wondering. Our RC-135 turned back when it was challenged. Who ordered the aircraft to turn around?"

Maus looked at Donna and leaned over to whisper in Lindley's ear.

Lindley gave a strained smile and said, "Ms. Klein, the CIA itself recently indicated that China's military build-up opposite Taiwan was more likely for show than for substance. When Taiwan began warning us of a possible Chinese attack on Quemoy the President gave standing orders for the military not to interfere in the opening stages of any potential cross-Straits crisis. He didn't want to limit his freedom of action. If China was simply saber rattling he didn't think it prudent to react aggressively, especially since Sino-American relations are still on the mend since the embassy bombing. If China were to invade Quemoy as the Taiwanese fear, the President thought our remaining uncommitted would enhance our ability to mediate the conflict diplomatically."

"What if China were to invade Taiwan itself?" Donna demanded.

Lindley was unshaken, "Well then, that would take a fair bit of time to accomplish, wouldn't it? I don't see how an early and modest American military response could do anything more than tip our hand to the Chinese that we intend to support Taiwan."

Donna sadly shook her head once, "To the contrary, Mr. Lindley, I'm afraid our actions in ordering the RC-135 to return to base have just given China the green light they need to know that we won't intervene on behalf of Taiwan."

"That's your opinion."

"No, sir, that's my considered analysis. My analysis is that China intends to conquer Taiwan. If they're successful, my analysis is that American power in Asia will evaporate. If American power in Asia evaporates, my analysis is that China will dominate the world in the 21st Century. . ." One of the secure phones began ringing. ". . .My *opinion* is that the decision was flawed and we'll pay dearly for it."

General Taylor gave Donna a modestly approving sidelong glance then cleared his throat, "I agree with the CIA's analysis of the situation. There is one more very important factor you need to tell the President: it is very likely that US forces have already engaged the Chinese and may in fact be on Taiwan itself."

Maus looked ill. Lindley was in an almost blank-stared denial. "What. . .?" Lindley managed to mutter.

"It is highly likely the *Belleau Wood* and the three ships with her were attacked. Our forces have standing orders to defend themselves in such a situation. We may have already exchanged blows with China."

"Oh my God. . ." Lindley blanched. A staffer handed the phone to Maus who quickly handed it to Lindley.

"Lindley here. . . What! You're absolutely sure? Shit!" Lindley was hit hard by the news on the other end, "Okay, right. We're already on it over here. We already have a team assembled. . . The Vice Chairman of the Joint Chiefs is here. . . We'll tell the President immediately. . . This may all be a horrible coincidence but," Lindley looked at Donna, "I think we better treat the incidents as connected."

Just as Lindley was hanging up the phone he was transfixed by a report appearing on MSNBC. "That was the 'Nimmic'," he said quietly while looking at the television, "The Panama Canal has..." Lindley drifted off. The TV was muted but the dateline at the bottom of the screen said Panama. Lindley grabbed the remote and cranked the volume.

There were flames and smoke framed by darkness on the screen. The TV blared ". . .a large cargo ship exploded in the Panama Canal this evening. Many people, perhaps as many as 50, have been killed or injured in the blast that broke windows in Panama City a few miles away. Damage to the canal is said to be extensive. It is unknown at this time what caused the fatal explosion. Unnamed authorities said the ship was a Chinese freighter which reported engine trouble just before exploding. . ."

"Oh God," Lindley moaned, "What do we do?"

The muted television tuned to CNN began to flash a breaking news banner from Tokyo. Lindley grabbed the other remote and clicked off the mute. Both TVs were now competing for attention in the small, now breathy room.

". . .we now go live to our CNN correspondent in Tokyo with a breaking story. Lynn?" The news anchor nodded. The picture cut to a young reporter, "I'm standing here outside Tokyo's Norita Airport where it has been announced that three international flights into Tokyo from points in south Asia are missing. In addition, authorities here report a curious lack of communications with Taiwan's air traffic control system. One aviation safety official here told me that Taiwan's entire air traffic control net went down a little over two hours ago. It's not known at this time if the missing aircraft and the air traffic control system failure are linked. Unnamed US military sources out of Okinawa also report that a flight of four US Air Force cargo aircraft went missing some 300 miles west of Okinawa about two hours ago. . ."

"Shit!" Lindley pounded his fist onto the table. "Taylor, call the Pentagon and tell them they have a leaker! We can't let word of this get out now."

Taylor picked up a phone to call the Defense Department.

Lindley continued on his tear, "What the hell were those cargo aircraft doing so close to Taiwan, anyway? Ken, get the President on the line, I need to talk with him immediately." Lindley turned to Donna and said quietly, "So, you think the Chinese may be invading Taiwan. What next? What do you think they'll do?"

Donna paused. What she said next might well determine America's opening moves in the most important military action of the 21st Century, "China will attempt to conquer Taiwan as quickly as possible. They will also strongly warn us not to interfere in their internal affairs. They will probably threaten nuclear attack on our cities as they last did in 1996."

"What do you mean, 'nuclear attack'?" the NSC staffer asked.

"In March of 1996 when China was launching missiles into the waters off Taiwan to bully them before their presidential elections one of the PRC's generals threatened to nuke Los Angeles if we intervened," Donna coolly replied.

"You can't seriously think they'd do that? We outnumber them better than 100 to one in nuclear missiles," the staffer protested.

Donna shot back, "I take everything the Chinese say seriously. Nothing they ever say officially is by mistake. The leadership in Beijing had the general threaten Los Angeles to see what our reaction was. Our reaction was no reaction—we didn't disappoint them. They took this as a signal that we would not abide by the Taiwan Relations Act and come to Taiwan's aid in the event of an attack."

Lindley looked at his young staffer, "I think Ms. Klein's point is well-taken. China has attacked Taiwan. Let's keep an open mind towards her views right now."

Donna knew she didn't have much time and continued quickly, "As I was saying, they will also seek to intimidate Japan and South Korea. It is important to note that China's invasion effort is extremely vulnerable to a US naval blockade. China knows this and will seek to delay our response by a week or two. That's probably why they attacked the Panama Canal—to delay our ability to surge additional naval forces into the Pacific. Any way, within a week or two they no doubt expect to have secured the island." Donna's eyes were intense, "It is critical that we have a strong response. We also need to initiate a diplomatic offensive with Japan, South Korea, Vietnam, the Philippines, Australia, Thailand and India."

Maus now had the President on the secure line, "Mr. Lindley, the President." Maus gravely handed the phone to Lindley.

"Sir, we have a growing problem over here. . . Yes. I suggest you get over to the White House as soon as possible. . . China looks to have attacked Taiwan. . . No, not Quemoy, Taiwan itself. They probably used nuclear weapons in the attack and US forces may be in the middle of it. . . No, the news is only reporting the explosion in the Panama Canal and the mysterious loss of civilian and US Air Force aircraft in the vicinity of Taiwan. . . The CIA representative here thinks the Chinese deliberately destroyed the Canal. . . Yes, of course. . . Yes, sir. . . Yes. . . Goodbye." Lindley gently hung up the phone and looked at Taylor and Klein. "The President wants to establish a Taiwan crisis ops center. He also wants to prevent any premature leakage of information from the military or anyone else. He wants the White House to control the information flow. He's concerned this could get out of hand very quickly. Taylor, you talked to the Pentagon, right?"

"Yes sir."

Lindley looked at Donna, "Klein, tell your boss at the CIA that we're short handed over here and could use your assistance for a while. In fact, who's your boss?"

"Jack Ramsey."

"Tell Mr. Ramsey that I want him over here too. The two of you will be on 14-hour shifts until we don't need you anymore. I want you to be here tomorrow morning and ready to go at five o'clock. You'll work until seven. I want Ramsey to work from five in the evening through seven in the morning. Call him now and tell him to get over here. He can track the day's events in Asia and brief you on them before we give the President his morning briefing at seven-thirty."

"Yes sir." Donna should have been happy. She would be briefing the President every morning. Instead, she felt as if she was about to play a minor role on the losing side. Tonight was the Sabbath. She decided she'd go home and pray—something she hadn't done for too long.

24
Grapple

Fu placed the SATCOM phone on the table for General Wei to hang up. Wei told him he had a phone for him too, but Fu was embarrassed to ask the general how to use it. Fu remained content to have the general to serve as his secretary. *I'm sure the Chairman doesn't answer his own phone,* Fu smugly thought.

The call to Beijing went well. He spoke to the Chairman, Premier and Interior Minister for three minutes, then spent another five minutes speaking with Soo, the Chairman's military affairs advisor (with the others no doubt listening in on the speaker phone). They were all pleased by the progress and seemed not at all concerned about the unexpected appearance of the American Marines on Taiwan. Detecting their nonchalance about the Americans, Fu decided to press an aggressive idea to further show his martial ardor, "We should demand the Americans surrender their forces. If they comply, Japan and South Korea will be shaken to their foundations and Asia will be firmly in our grip!"

The Chairman loved Fu's advice. Fu wondered what it would be like to rule the world's most powerful nation.

*   *   *   **

The 287 uninjured crewmembers onboard the USS *Curtis Wilbur* had never worked so hard nor so ingeniously in their careers. Seamen, many barely 20-years-old, made decisions and repaired key components without being told to do so. They knew their situation was tenuous at best and did all they could to enhance their chances of survival.

Unfortunately, the massive electronic destruction caused by the E-bomb attack disabled much of the ship's advanced automatic fire suppression and damage control systems. Fortunately, after the Chinese missile hit the engine room, much of the potential for more serious damage onboard was precluded by two members of the ship's crew. They risked their lives, making their way through fire and smoke to activate the engine room's fire suppression system manually. The two seamen were now in sickbay along with ten other sailors. Their actions allowed the crew to restore power to one of the four GE LM 2500-30 gas turbine engines. The propeller shafts were still damaged by the missile attack, but the working engine restored some electrical power to the ship.

After working to rescue 807 sailors and 312 Marines from the USS *Belleau Wood* and USS *Dubuque*, the USS *Germantown* hooked a towline to the *Curtis Wilbur*. Together, the two ships began making their way to Kaohsiung at eight knots. Within another hour they'd be just off shore.

A little more than an hour after the attack, lookouts spotted several fast movers heading east at high altitude. If they were enemy reconnaissance birds it would only be a matter of time before they got some more unwelcome attention.

The *Curtis Wilbur's* skipper, Commander Meade, desperately wanted back both eyes and fang. The crew exhausted themselves, but couldn't get any of the major radar systems up and running. The damage to the receiver circuitry was too extensive to repair at sea. The only functional radar-guided defensive system was a solitary 20mm Phalanx mount. Without a targeting radar, the ship's Harpoon, Tomahawk and Standard missiles were virtually worthless. Commander Meade conferred with his Fire Control and Strike/Missiles Officers on the bridge (with nothing but the Phalanx operational, the Combat Information Center yielded precious little information).

"What's your systems status?" Meade asked of the Strike/Missiles Officer.

The Lieutenant replied, "All the missiles in the VLS (Vertical Launch Systems) must have been shielded from the EMP, they're fine. The Harpoons check out too."

The captain turned to his Fire Control Officer, "Can you get a missile to its target yet?"

The harried Lieutenant JG shook his head, "Everything's still down. But. . ."

"But what?" Meade demanded.

". . .well, sir, it's a crazy idea, but it might work and it's all we have right now. . ."

"Out with it!" The junior officer's hesitancy made the already notoriously impatient skipper even more on edge.

"Sir, one of my Fire Controlmen suggested we send out spotters from the Marine air wing. Two or three Harriers or helicopters might be able to spot ships and call for fire sort of like the Marines do with artillery. . ."

"Hmmm. . ." the captain's sound was uncommittal.

The young officer decided to press on, "Anyway, many of the aircraft have working radios and they all have inertial navigation equipment. Some of them may even have decent targeting or navigation systems that survived the EMP. If we still don't have any radar up by nightfall, the Marines even have some night vision capability that could help us."

Meade pursed his lips, then looked at his officer and grinned, "It looks like your Fire Controlman just invented the 'Mark One Marine' early warning and targeting system. Make it happen!"

It had been a busy two hours. The Marines of the 31st MEU were coming ashore and establishing themselves. The task was, in a way, much easier than it should have been. For one, the Taiwanese were not shooting at them (which might have been the case had the Chinese attack not stunned them so completely). For another, all the Marines had been briefed on the mission prior to the landing due to Colonel Flint's relentless training. The leadership knew exactly where to go (they had maps) and were already familiar with the terrain (due to the practice L-Forms). It was one of the most amazing bits of luck in military history. *No, Flint corrected himself, not luck, you make your own luck in this business.*

Colonel Flint had established a command post in a well-lit (windows and skylights) office of a small hanger with cement walls at Kaohsiung International Airport. The airport was virtually empty and no one complained when they moved in. The war's opening moves must have unnerved the airport personnel and passengers and sent them scurrying for cover in the city.

The XO assembled the staff for a quick situation briefing. The S-2, Major Ramirez, kicked it off. "We expect the weather to become increasingly cloudy today with a rain beginning tomorrow morning from the typhoon to our south. The high today will be about 88 degrees, the low tonight about 82. Humidity will increase from 90% today to over 95% tomorrow. Without 'met' support from the Navy, this will be the last weather report we'll have until we can develop alternate sources." Rez looked at the assembled staff in the hastily prepared command post. He nodded towards the map recently pinned to a wall. Surprisingly, there was even a roll of acetate over the map with the MEU's graphic control measures on it (graphic control measures are the military's version of a football play's Xs and Os). "The enemy situation is as follows. Elements of an unknown PLA force of at least battalion size have landed in Kaohsiung's harbor. Our Harriers have engaged this force, but we don't have any BDA (battle damage assessment) yet. The enemy downed one of our Harriers with a laser-guided SAM of an unknown type. In addition, when Golf Company secured the building next to this hanger they captured a probable PLA operative. He was dressed in a ROC Army uniform. He doesn't speak English. We found these on him." Rez held up a portable SATCOM phone, a GPS receiver, two pistols, three knives and a piano wire garrote. "He was dialing the phone when we found him. His leg was injured too. I think he may have parachuted in. As soon as we link up with someone who speaks Chinese and English, we'll interrogate the man." Rez drew in a breath and began the most critical part of his briefing, "The enemy's probable courses of action are obvious. . ."

Flint loved the way his S-2 was sure of his analysis. A wimpy S-2 who provided too many caveats to cover his ass was worthless to a commander. Rez always stuck his neck out. If his analysis was wrong he'd be the first to correct it, rather than proudly sticking by a faulty prediction.

". . .First, he is trying to seize Taiwan by force. This means he must destroy Taiwan's army, then take Taiwan's center of gravity—in this case, the capital: Taipei. Given the distance between Kaohsiung and Taipei, we are only seeing the enemy's supporting attack. At Kaohsiung, the enemy will seek to engage the Taiwanese army and take away its freedom of action. The PLA must tie down Taiwanese reserves and disrupt their mobilization process. For that reason, I see only infantry and airborne troops being employed on the attack at Kaohsiung. The initial objective will be to seize the harbor, the city and the international airport. Two infantry divisions ought to be sufficient for this task. We'll probably see up to one battalion of airborne dropped on the airport and at least an infantry regiment in the initial assault on the beach. Because the Chinese lack sufficient amphibious assault capacity to lift all they need, I expect that the forces committed to the supporting attack will use improvised transport such as commercial vessels and ferries. To support this attack, the Chinese will have to concentrate air power and missile strikes. We will probably see the use of chemical weapons in the attack. . ."

Flint broke in, "Let's go to MOPP-2 right now." (Mission Oriented Protective Posture-2 would place the Marines into their charcoal-lined chemical protective suits with rubber overshoes, but leave the masks and rubber gloves off—in a hot and humid climate, the suit is extremely uncomfortable to wear.)

". . .I think it is unlikely that we will see additional use of nuclear weapons on the battlefield now that the Chinese are committing their troops to the battle. If there are no questions, I will be followed by the S-3."

Lieutenant Colonel Cook nodded to Rez and took his place by the map, "We have established Echo and Foxtrot Companies at the airport with the Tank Platoon and sections of the Heavy Weapons Company in support. Golf Company and the Amphibious Assault Company remain at the landing site with the remainder of the Heavy Weapons Company. Two sections of the Armored Recon Platoon are in place with the Recon Platoon on the dominating hill mass at Shoushan Park. We have excellent comms with them as long as the couple of working radios they have hold up. The Whiskey Cobras are supporting the recon mission and should return to the airport to refuel shortly. The SEAL team made it out alive with most of their equipment by hitching a ride on the ARG's Bullfrogs. They're at the beach. The Two recommends sending them into harbor to check on the ship that fired on the Harriers. They received the mission about ten minutes ago. We have four Harriers remaining. Two of them are on stand-by here at the airport. The other two have refueled and are currently conducting reconnaissance and anti-shipping patrols in coordination with the *Curtis Wilbur* to our west. The rest of the ACE is involved in lifting surviving Marines off the remnants of the ARG."

Flint inwardly winced at the word "surviving"—it was accurate, but it smacked of defeat. He'd have a private talk with the Three afterward.

". . .We have 18 Sea Knights and nine Super Stallions in the operation. We sent one Huey to coordinate the operation. Priority of pickup is the artillery battery, then any CSS (Combat Service Support) assets we can find. All five LCACs remain operational too. If there are no questions, I will be followed by the S-4."

The S-4 (Logistics Officer), Major Vine walked briskly up. "The good news is, most of the BLT's personnel made it to shore. The bad news is, I can't sustain them for shit. The only asset I have on shore right now is one tactical bulk fuel delivery system. I can fuel the aircraft and the tanks for a day. Fortunately, we're not in East Timor and the level of local support ought to be sufficient to provide us fuel and food. My CSS priority is ammunition, then fuel, then spare parts. The *Germantown's* damaged well deck and stern door is going to make additional equipment recovery tough. I only have very limited CSS personnel assets on shore. I have one section each of the Communications Platoon, the Landing Support Platoon and the Medical Platoon. Most of the Service Support Group and our supplies were on board the *Belleau Wood* when it went down. That's all I have right now. . ."

There was a ruckus at the door to the CP. Flint heard a man's voice say in heavily accented English, "I *must* see your commander!" Flint motioned to Rez to check on the situation while the S-1 (Personnel Officer or Adjutant) began his portion of the briefing. "We can account for 1,099 Marines and 55 Navy personnel. Captain Hill is our only confirmed casualty. Until the recovery operations are complete, I'm listing all other personnel as missing. . ."

Rez poked his head inside the door and motioned for Colonel Flint to step outside into the hallway. Flint began to head for the door, then turned to his staff and said, "You have 30 minutes to work on a plan to repel an airborne assault on this airport, protect Kaohsiung Harbor, and defeat an amphibious assault within a zone ten kilometers south of the southern harbor entrance."

The man who disrupted the meeting was a small, uniformed Taiwanese officer about 50 years old. The officer was weak and coughing constantly. "Sir," Rez said, "This is Major Heng. He is the XO of the 3rd Light Infantry Battalion, 150th Regiment of the Taiwanese Army Reserve. Major Heng, this is Colonel Flint of the United States Marine Corps, the commander of the Marines in the Kaohsiung area."

The officer coughed violently, regained his composure, and bowed. Flint, having been stationed in Okinawa for years, bowed back. The officer said he lived nearby, and was sick in bed watching TV when the electricity went out. He found his phone dead too. When he saw the PLAAF fighters overhead, he knew the Chinese were attacking. He put on his uniform and found a member of his unit who was well enough to begin alerting the battalion of reservists by face-to-face contact. He was pleased to report that most of the reservists healthy enough to walk had reported in to the battalion's mobilization station on their own when they saw and heard the Chinese attack. His battalion's standing orders in a national emergency were the defense of Kaohsiung International Airport. "I would be honored," he labored to say, "If the American Marines would participate in the defense of the airport and my homeland. I will send a liaison officer to coordinate our mutual defense plans."

Flint smiled reassuringly at the officer, "Yes, Major Heng, we would be honored as well to work together. Our only request is that we control the seaward side of the airport. It will make it easier to maintain our lines of communications with our outlying units. We also recommend that your soldiers wear their chemical protective clothing."

"That is our plan." The officer turned to go.

"Before you leave. We have a man in custody who is wearing the uniform of the Republic of China. We think he is a spy. Can you send someone over here to interrogate him?"

"Yes, of course. I should tell you we have already seen PLA motorcycle scouts in the city. Pardon me, I need to go." As if to punctuate the end of the conversation, a series of sonic booms followed by the distant sound of jets was heard. The officer slipped out and weakly mounted the back of a motor scooter. A boy no older than 15 was the driver. The boy smiled broadly at the Marines and waved as he drove off.

Flint waved at them from the door and turned to his Intel officer, "Do you think they'll help or hurt our defense in the short term?"

"I don't think we have a choice, it's their country. If we clearly divide the airport—I suggest straight down the main runway, and send liaisons familiar with the unit's plans to each others headquarters we ought to be okay. . ."

"Hey," Flint's eyes sparkled, "I think I have just the job for Colonel Burl."

Rez looked back down the empty hallway, then cocked his head at his commander, "Sir, you are more devious than you look."

"Thank you, sometimes this job can be fun."

Just outside Flint and Ramirez heard the shouting of a Marine sergeant barking a command. Three seconds later the heavy rhythmic beat of a .50 cal machine gun echoed down the hall from outside.

Major Ramirez drew his 9mm pistol and poked his head outside. The firing "Ma Deuce" was on the roof of the building that stood next to the hanger. The machine gun was pointed skyward. Rez squinted as his eyes adjusted to the cloudy but bright sky. "Sir!" he yelled, "I see parachutes. At least. . ." he stopped to count, ". . .at least a company's wor. . ." The cement pad in front of the major's feet spit chips and white dust. He ducked back inside, "Sheee-it! Mother! Sir, alert the staff! I was right again, we're under attack by airborne!"

Flint was already halfway down the hall, "Worthless prediction, 'Two'. Doesn't count—you never said *when* the enemy was going to attack!"

Major Ramirez didn't have time for a retort—he was emptying half of his 14-round clip at a just-landed paratrooper whose body armor made him one tough hombre to kill. It took Rez three shots to the chest before he realized that the airborne soldier had a Kevlar vest. The Marine's 9mm pistol rounds knocked the just-landed man off-balance. The fourth shot hit the enemy's right forearm just as he was bringing his folding-stock assault rifle to his hip to fire. He went to his knees with a wild look of panic in his eyes. As an intelligence officer, Major Ramirez had never killed anyone before. (He had always joked that if he had to kill someone in combat it was a sure sign that his intelligence skills failed miserably.) Fortunately, as a Marine, he was trained to kill. Rez's fifth shot hit his adversary in the face, knocking the man to the ground on his back where he lay surrounded by equipment, a shimmering drab olive parachute, and dozens of strands of nylon suspension lines.

Rez didn't know whether to retreat into the building to get reinforcements, stay where he was to observe, or get to a roof where he might be able to help other the Marines already positioned. His indecision was answered by 60-plus tons of M1A1 tank that whined and clanked by the doorway at 25 mph.

Boom! The tank's 120mm main gun let loose a round. A moment later there was an answering two-part blast and ball of fire capped by an inky black cloud about 200 meters away visible to the right side of the now stationary tank.

Rez's curiosity got the best of him and he maneuvered himself in the doorway to better see the tank's recent target without making himself a good target. The fire and smoke made it difficult to make out what the vehicle was. Two seconds later, however, there was no doubt.

Just above the burning mystery vehicle Rez saw a Russian-made BMD-3 strapped to a pallet dangling off a huge parachute heading earthward at an alarming rate. About 40 feet off the ground the underside of the pallet erupted with four giant jets of orange flame, burning the formerly wet and green grass underneath. The retro-rocket pallet slowed the vehicle and it landed gently, the released parachute billowing up and towards the

Marine tank, blocking its view.

The BMD-3 is a tracked airborne combat vehicle weighing about 15 tons and armed to the teeth with no less than two machine guns, a 30mm automatic grenade launcher, an anti-tank rocket launcher and a 30mm rapid-fire cannon main gun. It has a track commander/gunner and a driver. An airborne infantry team (half a squad) of five operate its other weapons or can dismount for close assault. The lightly armored BMD-3 was vulnerable to .50 cal fire from any angle other than the direct front, but the people who used it counted on surprise and shock to overwhelm their enemies before they could mount an effective defense. This is why the Russians developed the retro-rocket pallet—it enabled the armored airborne infantry to drop into combat *inside* their vehicles, ready to go as soon as they hit the ground. The system was not without its problems, however; sometimes the rockets failed to ignite leaving the crew either dead or with broken backs. Other times not all of the solid-fueled rockets would ignite. When this happened, the pallet would turn cartwheels in the air before landing, usually upside-down. Needless to say, making a training jump in such a contraption was not viewed as a good use of highly trained airborne soldiers—even by the PLA. Making such a jump in combat was a different story. The PLA generals calculated that the extra dead crew or two was well worth the minutes shaved off the time needed to get into the fight.

Rez decided he had to see more of the situation. An intelligence officer is useless without *some* data to process. He burst out of the building at a low crouch and kneeled next to the tank. His knee sank into something soft. The officer looked down. He was kneeling on the thigh of the airborne troop he killed not a minute before. The tank had run over the head and shoulders of the corpse and blood oozed through its wide metal tracks. Rez didn't have time to get sick. He looked left and right and up—nothing, the tank blocked the view of the battlefield.

Major Ramirez was about to stand up to peer around the tank when he heard Colonel Flint's voice, "What the hell's going on?"

"Airborne! They're dropping armor too! Soviet BMDs!" (Every officer who entered the military before 1991 had a hard time saying, "Russian" when referring to equipment designed and built by the old Soviet empire.) Just as Rez turned his head back towards the tank, the turbine's pitch increased and the tanked lurched ahead leaving him in the open. For split second, just enough to take in the view of most of the airport's runway, Rez had a perfect understanding of the battle. The PLA was in the process of landing at least a battalion of airborne supported by probably a company of BMDs (about 450 soldiers and 10 armored vehicles). If the Chinese could seize the airport then air-landing forces couldn't be far behind. The Marines *had* to defend the airport or all was lost.

Rez ducked, spun around on his heels, and dove for the doorframe just as the BMD charged out from behind its settling parachute. Colonel Flint could see gun flashes from the right bow side of the vehicle. Two holes the size of cantaloupes were blown through the cement wall to the right of the door frame. Rez landed between the colonel's legs. An instant later, the tank, which had rapidly driven off to the right to acquire the small airborne vehicle, fired. A large ball of superheated gas exploded out of the tank's main gun. Not 100 meters away the BMD erupted in a ball of fire. The BMD's small, frying pan-shaped turret went flying skyward along with pieces of something human. Flint stood just three feet inside the doorway, concealed by shadow, gaping at the horribly awesome sight. The turret arced up, spinning slowly like an oblong Frisbee due to the off-center mass of its 30mm gun. The sight was so fantastic, Flint couldn't help but to watch as the turret sailed down and crashed into the cement not 20 feet away from the door. It bounced once, flipping upside-down, and landed on the body of the paratrooper Rez shot two minutes before. Only the man's legs were sticking out from under the smoking turret.

Backing up, Flint burst out, "Shit!"

Rez just lay on the ground for a few seconds, panting.

The opening battle for Kaohsiung International Airport wasn't a fair fight. Most military professionals would rather wage an unfair fight. Their aim is not to go head-to-head with the enemy's strength, but rather to hit him in a fashion that makes it difficult if not impossible for the enemy to hit back. In short order the Marines of the 31st MEU employed four M1A1 tanks, two Whiskey Cobra gunships, and two rifle companies supported by five .50 cal heavy machine guns and four 81mm mortars against the enemy parachute battalion. The result was predictable. The airborne troops, told only an hour before by their recon that the airport was clear, were cut down or taken prisoner (their scout was captured by the suddenly arriving Marines before he could provide headquarters with a situation update). The PLA lost all 10 BMDs, two supporting helicopter gunships that flew across the Taiwan Strait to support the assault, 264 men killed and 103 captured. Of the 448 elite PLA paratroopers who made the drop, only 81 escaped to disperse around the light industrial buildings near the airport. Colonel Flint would ask the soon to arrive ROC Army reserve unit to hunt these men down to reduce the likelihood that any might report on the airport defender's dispositions. In short, the PLA brought a knife to a gunfight.

It was eleven o'clock on Saturday. Over the entire length and breadth of the island the ROC forces began to understand they were in a fight for their very existence.

Communication was almost impossible.

The incapacitating agents temporarily decapitated the civilian leadership in Taipei. If they survived their 12 hours of LSD hallucinations without being killed or captured, they might make a contribution to the war effort, but for now, they were quite literally, insane. On key landing beaches or in ports, a different chemical agent was used to rob the defenders of their mental initiative. Several sites where Taiwan's mobile and armored forces were based were hit with a third type of agent designed to maximize confusion.

China's genetically engineered influenza attack was having the most severe immediate impact on the armed forces. Fully half of Taiwan's military was sick with the flu. Almost half of those were confined to bed rest (many should have been in the hospital but the hospitals were filled to capacity with the very old and the very young).

Lastly, China's conventional assault was going well (with the sole exception of the attack on Kaohsiung). The E-bombs destroyed half of Taiwan's air force and now China's advanced Russian-built fighters ruled the skies over the battlefield. All four of Taiwan's major ports were under assault and some 50,000 troops were on their way by air and sea within the next 24 hours to reinforce the almost 20,000 troops already on the island.

In spite of their disadvantages, the ROC Army still had 195,000 troops on Taiwan—even with half of these ill, they would outnumber the PLA for at least another day, maybe two. To be effective, however, a military force must be able to do three things: shoot, move, and communicate. The first two the Chinese made difficult for the Taiwanese, the last wasn't happening much at all yet.

Taiwan's military forces tried as best they could to restore communications. All across Taiwan the military dipped into their extensive underground bunker network to bring carefully stored radios out of their aluminized plastic wrappings. Within two hours, a series of line-of-sight tactical FM radios began to carry a fraction of the needed communications traffic of modern war. Using airborne electronic warfare equipment designed with the help of Russian engineers, the Chinese jammed some signals and eavesdropped on others (their task made all the easier by the fact that so few radios were working). In spite of the PLA's attempts to shut down Taiwan's radio traffic, some data did get through. The officers in the bunkers asked and answered questions. They shared information. Gradually, a rough picture emerged of the situation. But there wasn't much Taiwan could do about it—yet.

One of the bright spots for the defenders was the sudden and unexpected arrival of the Americans on the scene within minutes of the attack. For the Americans it was fortunate that the Chinese had so severely suppressed Taiwan's defenses—without the initial damage and confusion, the Americans probably would have suffered heavy casualties from "friendly" fire.

It was noon. The *Curtis Wilbur* was now anchored just outside Kaohsiung Harbor's northern entrance. The *Germantown*, waited for clearance to go into the harbor and off-load anything of use for the Marines on shore. In the meantime, a steady stream of helicopters shuttled Marines, excess sailors rescued from the other ships, wounded, and supplies on shore. Normally, the safest place in a combat situation would have been on board ship. However, another Chinese missile attack was highly likely so the shore seemed the safer bet.

With the two Harriers out spotting for the *Curtis Wilbur* the ship's captain decided to go back to the CIC. From there he could track the radioed location of the aircraft and direct any missile attack onto hostile shipping. At 1203 hours the "Mark One Marine early warning and targeting system" found its first target.

"Dragon Two Three to Red Lance, over," it was First Lieutenant Snake Gilbert the late Captain Hill's wingman.

"This is Red Lance," a petty officer Fire Controlman responded.

"Red Lance, I see two large ships. They look like commercial ferries. Do you have a good azimuth to my signal? I read yours as two seven degrees. Over."

"Roger. Wait one on the azimuth, over." Electronic warfare technicians locked onto the Harrier's line-of-sight FM transmission and calculated its azimuth. They reported back to the Fire Controlman.

The petty officer was grinning ear-to-ear. This was his idea in action. "Dragon Two Three, we confirm. We have you at two zero six degrees. We'll split the difference. Do you have a distance? Over."

"Roger Red Lance, my INS (inertial navigation system) says I'm two three point three nautical miles out. Distance to target is about three miles dead ahead of me. I need to get a closer look to get a positive ID, over."

"Roger Dragon Two Three."

Commander Meade paced in the muggy CIC. The missile attack also crippled much of the ship's electrical power and air conditioning capabilities. "Tell Dragon Two Three that we'll fire on his positive ID."

The Fire Controlman radioed back, "Dragon Two Three, as soon as you give the word, we'll launch, over."

High above the Harrier and 11 miles to the west, two squadrons totaling 20 Chinese J-6 fighters were running escort for the invasion fleet. They expected to encounter light resistance from ROC Air Force fighters that may have survived the E-bomb attack nestled deep within their bunkers. They didn't expect a USMC Harrier acting as a forward observer for a US Guided Missile Destroyer.

The USS *Curtis Wilbur* contained 90 Mk 41 VLS (Vertical Launch System) tubes. Of these, 24 held Tomahawk cruise missiles (all designed for land attack) leaving 66 tubes for the SM-2 (MR) (Standard Missile-2 [Medium Range]) anti-aircraft/anti-missile missile. With a range of up to 104 miles, the SM-2 (MR) is what makes it so deadly for hostile air to approach a US task force protected by the Aegis air defense system. The E-bomb burned out the radar receivers on the ship, however, so, except for the small Phalanx radar, all other radar transmitters were turned off. Between the *Curtis Wilbur's* lack of radar emissions and the heavy anti-ship missile attack a few hours before, the PLAN admirals figured the American warships were resting peacefully and harmlessly at the bottom of the ocean.

"Red Lance, Red Lance, this is Dragon Two Three, over!" First Lieutenant Gilbert was checking in.

"Go ahead Dragon Two Three," the petty officer on the *Curtis Wilbur* replied.

"Red Lance, I've got at least 16 inbound bogies six miles off. I haven't gotten a positive ID on the ships yet. Over."

Commander Meade leaned over the Fire Controlman, "We can't fire on the ships yet, they could be civilian. The bogies are another matter; anytime 16 aircraft fly in a mass, they're military. I wonder whose?" The skipper smacked his right fist into his hand. "Damn!"

The young petty officer looked at his commander, "Sir, the Aegis radar receivers are gone but the transmitters work. We could try to illuminate the targets and launch our missiles using the Harrier's general coordinates. With luck, the missiles will home in on the targets and hit some. We can't control them individually so a few aircraft might get hit by more than one missile. It's not perfect, but it's the best we can do."

"Two good ideas in one day! Great job sailor," Meade was beaming, "Tell the pilot what we're going to do and tell him to get on the deck when we fire. I've just decided those are hostile aircraft."

"Dragon Two Three, we're going to target the bogies. We can illuminate them with the radar and hope the missiles home in on the reflected signal. Give us your best guess of where they are, over."

"Roger. . ." replied the lieutenant.

Within a minute the *Curtis Wilbur's* CIC had designated a box some three miles wide by five miles deep by one mile tall some 30 nautical miles away. This was the target box. The captain decided to volley 20 missiles into the box. What the ship's missiles didn't kill, the Harrier could. Then, with the enemy aircraft out of the way, the inbound ships might be IDed and attacked if found to be enemy.

Missiles rippled out of the bow section of the destroyer. They shot straight up then rapidly tipped over at almost a 90-degree angle and headed west. By now the Harrier was only 100 feet above the water, shielded from powerful radar's beam by the curvature of the Earth.

Overhead and now to the east, Snake Gilbert saw trails of black smoke come falling out of the sky. He grinned, called the *Curtis Wilbur*, ran a mental calculation on his fuel burn and gunned the Harrier to engage the remnants of the enemy force before he ran so low on fuel that he wouldn't have time to return and inspect the unknown ships.

As Lieutenant Gilbert thought might be the case, his radar picked up four aircraft heading towards him. *Mothers, I'd run away too if I just got my ass wiped by a blind cripple.* Still configured for ground attack, Gilbert only had two Sidewinder air-to-air missiles at his disposal. He always wanted to shoot another aircraft down—something a Harrier pilot wouldn't be expected to do. *Still, there were those ships to check out.* "Red Lance, Red Lance. We still have four bandits aloft (since they turned back towards Mainland China, it was now a safe bet they were enemy). They're about ten miles closer than they were the last time. They're headed west. I don't have the missiles or the time to deal with these guys, can you take 'em down for me? Over."

On board the *Curtis Wilbur* the skipper nodded. The petty officer called back, "That's a wilco. Missiles on the way."

Less than two minutes later Gilbert saw three aircraft going down in flames. *The last one won't be a problem today.* He edged higher and flew towards the two ships that were now about five miles away. Only 20 seconds later he was certain these ships were part of an invasion force. His targeting radar picked up five smaller ships operating as a picket for the two larger ones.

The targeting solution for the anti-ship missiles was easier than it was for the Standard missiles. First, the Americans didn't have to worry about altitude. Second, the anti-ship missiles had their own radars for terminal guidance and wouldn't have to rely on the crippled Aegis system. Third, ships make a much slower target than aircraft. Even still, the Strike/Missiles officer on the *Curtis Wilbur* had to carefully decide how to use his six Harpoons. The Harpoon's relatively small warhead (488 lbs compared to 1,000 lbs for the anti-ship variety of the Tomahawk) and their small number meant that each missile had to count. (In the bad old days of the Cold War, ships like the *Curtis Wilbur* carried a mix of land-attack cruise missiles and anti-ship cruise missiles. In the age of hyperactive gunboat diplomacy, however, every last one of the 550 anti-ship Tomahawks had been removed from the fleet—both from ships and submarines—and placed into storage. Because of the heavy use of land attack Tomahawks against Serbia in 1999,

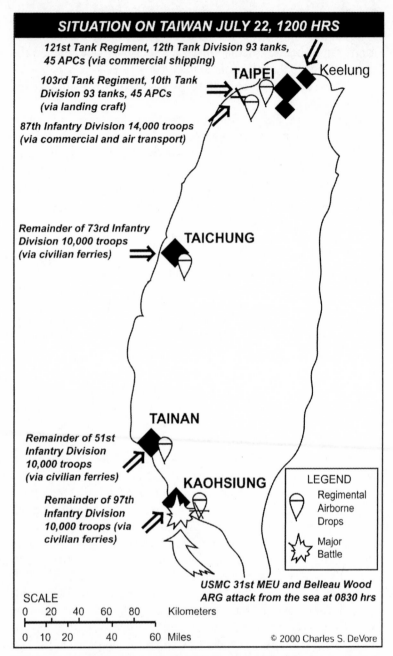

SITUATION ON TAIWAN JULY 22, 1200 HRS

121st Tank Regiment, 12th Tank Division 93 tanks, 45 APCs (via commercial shipping)

103rd Tank Regiment, 10th Tank Division 93 tanks, 45 APCs (via landing craft)

87th Infantry Division 14,000 troops (via commercial and air transport)

TAIPEI

Keelung

Remainder of 73rd Infantry Division 10,000 troops (via civilian ferries)

TAICHUNG

TAINAN

Remainder of 51st Infantry Division 10,000 troops (via civilian ferries)

KAOHSIUNG

Remainder of 97th Infantry Division 10,000 troops (via civilian ferries)

LEGEND

Regimental Airborne Drops

Major Battle

USMC 31st MEU and Belleau Wood ARG attack from the sea at 0830 hrs

SCALE

0   20   40   60   80   Kilometers

0   10   20   40   60   Miles

© 2000 Charles S. DeVore

China expands its toehold while the U.S. Marines attack

200 anti-ship missiles were taken out of storage and were being converted into land attack models.) The Harpoon's warhead was

246

designed to penetrate first, then explode. It was really designed to destroy warships. Given their targets appeared to be large civilian ferries and small patrol boats, Commander Meade wished he had the larger Tomahawks to use. He ordered an attack on the ships using three Harpoons apiece. Meade knew in his current state there was no telling when his ship would be rendered ineffective.

The anti-ship missiles blasted from their canisters on solid rocket motors. The solid rocket motors rapidly accelerated the missiles then burned out, leaving the missiles running at just under the speed of sound on turbo jet engines.

Gilbert was running low on fuel when he saw the first Harpoon streak under him, hugging the waves. He knew there must have been more, but they were hard to see against the increasingly rough ocean which now had white caps. The pilot turned around and made another pass at a right angle to the ships' path. This time he made the run at 1,000 feet. He had a perfect view of the ships about three miles off. Snake hoped their air defense systems lacked the means to reach out and touch him.

The first Harpoon acquired its target, a large ferry dragooned into service from Hong Kong. On board were 5,000 men of the 97th Infantry Division's 2nd Regiment as well as more than 100 trucks and armored personnel carriers.

The heavily laden inland ferry was only making nine knots against the stiffening east wind and rolling seas. It had set sail at 1800 hours the night before from Shantou and was now two hours behind schedule. Its mission was to land the 2nd Regiment in Kaohsiung Harbor, if possible. If the 3rd Regiment had failed to secure the harbor on time, its alternate landing beach was the sandy area just south of the southern entrance to the harbor (north of the harbor was too steep and rocky for a landing). The shallow draft ferry with its powerful and maneuverable engines could slide up on the beach and lower a ramp, allowing its passengers a rapid exit.

The Harpoon went into its terminal dive and hit the ship in the bow. The explosion tore the bow open. This single blow would have been sufficient to sink the over-laden ship within 90 seconds, but the Harpoons weren't smart enough to recognize a dying ship. The second missile dove into the ferry amidships and hastened its demise. Only a few civilian crewmembers survived.

The second ship was the same class of commercial ferry as the first and also from Hong Kong. Modern, sleek and efficient, it normally carried up to 200 cars and 1,500 passengers between Hong Kong Island and Kowloon. Today it was carrying the 1st Regiment of the 97th Infantry Division. Three Harpoons crashed into the ferry's superstructure and set it afire. Fuel and ammunition soon made the ship a very unsafe place to be. The ferry carried only enough life vests and rescue boats for less than a third of the passengers. More than 3,000 soon drowned. Drifting without power, the burning ferry would finally sink about midnight, its huge plume of thick black smoke and intense flames were a half-day reminder to the war's participants that the enemy gets a vote in the outcome of any conflict.

At 1245 hours local time in Taiwan, almost midnight in Washington, D.C., Commander Meade finally reestablished communications with PACOM (Pacific Command) in Hawaii via the INMARSAT (International Maritime Satellite) telephone. Due to blind luck, the INMARSAT was down for routine maintenance during the attack and as a result, was not damaged.

Because INMARSAT calls can be intercepted, Commander Meade didn't want to be too open via unencrypted voice communications. The initial contact sounded like a routine naval communication. The radioman in Honolulu recognized the voice of a signal school classmate of his on board the *Curtis Wilbur*. He could barely contain his excitement at hearing from a fellow sailor he thought dead only minutes before.

Within a few minutes, however, Meade's signal crewmen established a secure voice link over the SATCOM phone. The signal specialist handed Meade the phone, "Sir, I've got PACOM in secure mode. The link may not last as well as with military SATCOM, but it's the best we can do."

Meade smiled at his hard-working sailor and picked up the phone, "This is Commander Meade, captain of the USS *Curtis Wilbur* reporting in. I need to speak with the watch officer. We have been attacked, I say again, we have been attacked."

At the other end of the phone, a four-star admiral let loose a sigh of relief. He had been pacing nervously for almost five hours since two in the afternoon. The news that the *Belleau Wood* ARG was observing what looked like a huge Chinese cross-channel air assault on Taiwan was bad enough. The ARG's loss of comms was worse. The constant calls for information from the Pentagon and even the White House itself were nothing short of a nightmare.

The CINCPAC (Commander-in-Chief, Pacific Command), Admiral Dunbar, measured his voice as best he could as he spoke into the phone (the conversation was routed over a speaker and recorded so the staff would hear everything), "This is Admiral Dunbar. Glad to hear you're alive. Who attacked you and what's your status?"

Commander Meade was relieved to hear the top man himself on the line, maybe now he could get some assistance, "Sir, we have been attacked, probably by the Chinese, judging by the direction of the attack. We have lost the *Belleau Wood* and the *Dubuque* with heavy loss of life. At least 500, although we're still trying to get accountability."

"500 dead!" the Admiral exploded, not only seeing an historic naval catastrophe, but also seeing his career coming to a grinding halt.

"Yes sir, it could have been worse. Both my ship and the *Germantown* were struck by large anti-ship missiles. The defensive systems were all knocked off line by the EMP from a nuclear explosion. The missiles hit us less than 15 minutes later. If it weren't for my crew getting one Phalanx up we probably would have been sunk. . ."

"Why the hell were you in the Strait? The PRC issued a navigation warning. . ."

Meade was shocked. Dunbar was looking for a scapegoat. Fortunately, he was missing and presumed dead. On the other hand, Meade wasn't in the mood for heaping blame on a dead hero and colleague, even if there was an admiral on the end of the phone, "Admiral, we were in international waters. Isn't it the Navy's long-standing policy to ignore such short-notice advisories as illegal? Besides, there is a typhoon building to the southeast and the Taiwan Strait would provide us some. . ."

"Damnit Commander, you just lost more sailors in one day than we've lost on any day since World War Two! Don't tell me about typhoons!"

"Sir, we could use some help here. We have detected and engaged elements of a Chinese invasion fleet heading for Kaohsiung. We think we destroyed the first wave. . ."

The admiral's eyes bugged out, "You've attacked Chinese shipping? Are you fricken insane?"

Meade sighed. He remembered the surprise and the murmuring in the ranks when this admiral was appointed over the heads of more combat-oriented officers. Dunbar's last assignment had been as head of the UN's military observer mission in the Balkans. The appointment as CINCPAC was a plum—he was a politically well-connected officer. "Sir, if we are attacked we have the right to self-defense. We are exercising that right. Sir, my ship is dead in the water, anchored in the mouth of Kaohsiung Harbor, and almost blind and defenseless. I have almost 4,000 sailors and Marines to look after and I'm a damn speed bump in front of a full-scale Chinese invasion. . ." Meade was interrupted by a sailor.

"Sir, the other Harrier reports inbound cruise missiles. . ."

"How many?" Meade snapped.

"More than he can count."

Meade was almost thankful for the deadly distraction, "Sir, I've got to go. We have inbound missiles and only one Phalanx to deal with them. I'll have one of my staff brief you. . ." Meade handed the INMARSAT phone to a stunned lieutenant JG, "Admiral Dunbar wants to speak with you Lieutenant."

*   *   *

The White House Situation Room was abuzz with activity. It was now midnight. The President himself had arrived on the scene from his fund-raiser in Philadelphia and was getting briefed on the latest, largest, and potentially the last crisis to confront his almost completed term.

Jack Benson had come over from the CIA to augment the NSC staff as part of the night shift. Donna Klein would be in at 5:00 AM, get briefed by Benson on the night's occurrences, and assist in providing the President his morning briefing. Now, however, the President was getting his crucial first assessment from exhausted advisors who had too little information to process (the White House's classified and unclassified e-mail and Internet connections had gone down a couple of hours before, overloaded into paralysis by a crack Chinese hacker team). The room's air was one of grim desperation—no one wanted to go down in history as starting and losing a major war with the People's Republic of China.

Bob Lindley, the President's NSC advisor, still had his tuxedo on. The bow tie had disappeared hours ago. Lindley summarized the events of the day, "Mr. President, we know the following about the Taiwan Straits crisis. First, there have been American casualties. Probably 500 sailors and Marines. Second, we think China has used nuclear weapons against Taiwan. . ."

"Nuclear weapons! My God. . ." the President put his hand to the bridge of his nose and forehead and squeezed.

NSC Staffer Maus spoke up, "Sir, they weren't really nukes in the classic sense. They were probably designed to inflict massive electro-magnetic damage. They were exploded in space over Taiwan."

General Taylor interjected, "Very sophisticated use of weaponry, Mr. President. If the Chinese are using the nuclear-pumped E-bomb in this conflict it would severely impact US forces and our technological superiority. We'd be reduced to fighting with Korean War-era technology if they continued using them. We'd have to respond with nuclear weapons to even the odds against their much larger army. Of course, submarines would be shielded from the effects. . ." General Taylor paused briefly, then looked at Jack Benson, "I didn't think the Chinese had the E-bomb yet. Hell, we don't have any in our stockpiles."

"But we designed a few and tested a couple in the late '80s," Benson mumbled, "and a few years ago the Chinese obtained the design and test data." He cleared his throat, "At least we know what we're up against."

There was an embarrassed silence quickly broken by Lindley, "Look gentlemen, we have a massive crisis to deal with here. Let's not engage in recriminations. As I was saying, we think China detonated two nuclear weapons over Taiwan. These weapons severely damaged the communications, radar and computer systems on board four United States Navy ships that coincidentally happened to be in the Taiwan Strait at the time of the attack. When China launched a large anti-ship missile attack, these ships were hit and badly damaged. We think we have lost two ships, the *Belleau Wood* and the *Dubuque*. Third, a flight of four C-17s that were carrying US Army troops to the UN peacekeeping mission in Indonesia are missing and presumed down in the area to the east of Taiwan. There were 104 Army and Air Force personnel on board. We have patrol aircraft out of Okinawa looking for any wreckage or survivors but we have had no luck so far. We think the emergency transmitters on board were probably disabled by the nuclear bombs. There are reports out of Japan that up to nine commercial aircraft are missing in the area too. Fourth, there are reports out of Panama, now confirmed by personnel attached to our embassy there, that the Panama Canal has been severely damaged. It will probably take months to repair. We are working to confirm reports that a Chinese freighter was involved in the accident."

"*Bastards,*" General Taylor had been listening intently, matching every word from Lindley with what he considered truth from the briefing he received a few minutes before in the National Military Command Center. He looked up and remembered he was not in the Pentagon among his own kind, "That was no accident Mr. President. The Chinese are playing this game for keeps. That explosion was meant to do two things, slow down our Navy's ability to reinforce the Pacific and warn us that China will do what it must to win this conflict."

Maus looked at the general, "That's a big assumption for something that could be an accident."

The general shook his head in disbelief at the state of denial that permeated the room.

Lindley drew in a breath and looked at the papers in front of the President, "Finally, Mr. President, we think the US Marines are in Taiwan." The President looked up in shock. "Worse yet, sir, we think the Navy and Marines have attacked and sunk Chinese shipping."

"They *what*?" the President demanded.

"It looks like our military started a war without your permission." Lindley looked at General Taylor.

The President's face lost color. He grabbed a glass of water and took a gulp, "Is that true, General?"

The general, trained to tell it like it was, replied, "Yes, Mr. President. The *Belleau Wood* Amphibious Ready Group suffered an unprovoked attack in international waters. Having been attacked, the Navy and Marine forces are authorized to defend themselves. In the emergency, they retreated to the nearest safe ground to care for their casualties and await orders. Your military is doing fine, sir. They were surprised by the initial Chinese attack but they have recovered as best they can and have defended themselves admirably."

The President and civilian NSC staffers stared at the general like he was a man from Mars. The four uniformed NSC staffers smiled inwardly. The general was getting a first hand taste of what they had to deal with on a daily basis from this White House.

The President looked at the dark wooden table, then locked eyes with Taylor, "What are our military options, General?"

Taylor suppressed a sigh and looked at his Commander-in-Chief, "Not many right now. The Iraqi mobilization has tied down the Marine division stationed in Okinawa. In addition, we have most of the Army's 1st Cavalry Division in Kuwait. Our forces in South Korea are on full alert because of the North Korean maneuvers. Most of the Army division based in Hawaii is now in Indonesia. Our nearest aircraft carrier is in the Persian Gulf watching Iraq. We have two aircraft carriers on the West Coast. One is undergoing repairs and the other just completed a nine-month cruise and is in its training cycle."

"What about your long range bomber fleet?" the President asked.

"Of course, our B-2s could range targets in Taiwan from bases in America, the problem is we can't protect them." Taylor clenched his jaw.

"Can't protect them?" the President looked confused.

"Mr. President, the B-2 is vulnerable to air-to-air attack. The Chinese have developed a system for detecting stealth aircraft. It's not accurate enough to target one with a missile, but it is good enough to scramble fighters to intercept. Without aircover from a significant force, preferably including two aircraft carriers, our B-2s cannot be safely employed against China. It will take at least ten days to assemble the forces we need to respond to China's aggression."

The room was silent. Thankfully, one of the phones rang. Maus picked it up. His eyes went wide and he covered the receiver, "Mr. President, it's the Chinese Embassy. They want to talk to you about the terms for the immediate surrender of US forces on and around Taiwan."

The President started to reach for the phone. Lindley jumped as if snapped out of a stupor. "Wait, Mr. President. You can't discuss surrender terms," he turned to Maus, "Put them on hold for a moment." Lindley turned back to the President, "Sir, no American President has ever directly negotiated the surrender of US forces in the field. You don't want to do this. It's not *right*," Lindley leaned over and hissed in the President's face, "Sir, think of your *legacy*—let the general do it!"

The President nodded and dropped his outstretched hand.

Lindley turned to the general, "General Taylor. Take this call. Find out what the Chinese want. Stall for time. See if we can avoid the term 'surrender' at all costs. There's no need to be drastic. I'm sure we can come up with a solution that's acceptable to both sides."

A stunned general took the phone. He had expected to discuss military options for reinforcing Taiwan or conducting a naval blockade to deny supplies to the Chinese troops on the island—not discuss terms of surrender with a Chinese foreign service officer. What was he going to do? Tell the President to go to hell right to his face?

25
Fog

Commander Meade calculated he had at most three minutes before the first of the cruise missiles spotted by the Harrier found the *Curtis Wilbur*. Meade smashed his fist into his palm and shook his head. If the Chinese had spotted him and targeted him with another volley of their large supersonic cruise missiles he was sure the *Curtis Wilbur* would succumb. His blinded Aegis air defense system and one Phalanx could only do so much. Of course, he could try to target his SM2 anti-air missiles at the threatening missiles as he did with the Chinese fighter aircraft, hoping the radar waves reflected off the missiles would be enough to give the SM2s a target to aim for. The problem was that, unlike the aircraft, he didn't know how many missiles there were, nor did he have a good a fix on their location. Meade made a decision. *Well, the Standard Missiles aren't going to do any good sitting in their launch tubes.*

"Fire Control! I want the Aegis to illuminate to the west. I want a spread of 12 Standards, two each, running every two degrees from 262 degrees to 272 degrees. Launch with a four second separation between missiles set at the same course. Tell the Harrier to hug the waves, no use having him draw fire."

Commander Meade's words sent the CIC's activity level ratcheting up yet another notch. Half the computer stations in the critical nerve center seemed to have their guts exposed with two heavily sweating sailors working on each one. Everywhere else, sailors were trying to do their jobs with equipment of uncertain functionality.

Not a minute after a dozen SM2s rippled out of the bow of the *Curtis Wilbur*, Meade heard the first indication of an inbound missile: the chaff dispenser system firing clouds of aluminum strips into the air—*A lot of good that will do us while we're dead in the water.*

There were eight missiles bearing down on the American destroyer (the SM2 volley had already downed two). They were unlike anything the Americans understood the Chinese to have in their arsenal. As with much of China's high tech military gear, these missiles had their origins in American engineering. Relatively simple in design and concept, these missiles zeroed in on the radar emissions of a target ship. Specifically, these missiles sought out the radar signatures of the famous American Aegis

System or its junior partner, the Phalanx Close In Weapon System (CIWS).

The missiles came in, one right after the other, at 1,000 feet— very high for a missile designed to attack a ship. The employers of these missiles wanted them to be seen and engaged by the ship's defensive systems, especially the SM2 missiles. The reason for this was two-fold: one, the missiles needed to have an active radar signal to track and target, and two, the missiles were very cheap to manufacture, costing less than one-fifth of an SM2. Thus, in a war of attrition against a high-tech opponent, the Chinese could afford to lose many missiles to the more expensive anti-aircraft missiles and still come out ahead.

One by one, the Phalanx acquired and downed the missiles, each missile making it a little closer to the jury-rigged and now over-worked system (looking somewhat like a white R2D2 of Star Wars fame rocking wildly to and fro).

The seventh missile detonated only 300 yards astern, its unburned fuel exploding with a frightening warmth of things soon to come. The CIWS belched its last torrent of tungsten darts and fell silent, out of ammo, its radar still tracking the last incoming missile.

Missile number eight drew a bead on the Aegis phased array radar and dove on the *Curtis Wilbur* at a 45-degree angle. Only 30 yards away from the large radar panel the missile's warhead detonated, sending thousands of steel balls hurtling forward, shredding the radar and the superstructure underneath. The unburned jet fuel in the missile ignited into a fireball, burning and peeling the *Curtis Wilbur's* gray paint. Some of the burning fuel made it into the ship's vulnerable interior; fortunately, not so much as could be quickly dealt with. Only two sailors were wounded in the attack—but the *Curtis Wilbur* lost its only functional Phalanx system as well as the stern Aegis radar transmitter array.

Commander Meade decided he could use some good news right about now. He considered his career as an officer, a husband and a father. The ship's chaplain once told him that God wasn't much for making deals, "God, if you get me out of this one, I'll. . ." So Meade just said, "God help us," under his breath and drove on, not really knowing what else to do.

A phone rang. A young and tired-looking sailor's face broke into a broad grin, "Sir! Commander Meade! We have power to one of the shafts! We can move!"

Meade looked up the ceiling, *Thank you.* He smiled. Deals or no deals, he knew he owed God big time for that one.

Meade grabbed the phone, "Meade here, what kind of power we got?"

"Sir," it was Lieutenant Commander Clarke, head of engineering, "I've got one turbine and one shaft operational. The other shaft is beyond help. I can probably get you six, maybe seven knots. We're working on getting another turbine up. The fuel system was scorched pretty bad by the missiles a few hours ago but we're cannibalizing the other two turbines as fast as we can strip them of anything useful."

"Excellent. You earned your pay today Clarke."

In a curious way, mobility added to Meade's problems. Remaining at anchor just outside of Kaohsiung Harbor was an easy decision—he could either stay there or abandon ship and move his flag to the *Germantown.* Now he had a choice. Stay in Taiwanese waters or make for international waters and presumed safety south of the 21st parallel. At six knots that would take no less than ten hours with the Chinese most likely trying to sink him the entire way.

Meade's eyes narrowed. *Abandon ship, try to run, or wait for the inevitable missile strike.* He looked at the navigational charts for Kaohsiung, noting the depths and calculating where it made sense to land amphibious forces—*where the Marines landed, of course.*

Meade thought of a desperation maneuver the Japanese Imperial Navy tried in World War II—calculating the Americans would eventually weary of high losses, the Japanese decided to sortie the super battleship Yamato at the island of Okinawa during the American assault of that island. The Japanese hoped to beach the massive ship and create an unsinkable battleship that would then proceed to pound the US invasion with its 18.1-inch guns. The Yamato never even reached sight of the island—it was quickly spotted and sunk by American aircraft. *Might as well take some more of the bastards with me.*

Meade gave the orders: with only a skeleton crew remaining he would beach the *Curtis Wilbur* on Chichin Beach at high tide—stern first, the ship's lone 5-inch gun pointing defiantly to the west. *Too bad they weren't defending Okinawa today—the Japanese would really be annoyed that the Americans successfully executed one of their most valiant last-ditch naval efforts.*

Protecting the airport, the prime landing beach just south of the harbor and maintaining a force on top of the big hill overlooking Kaohsiung was a job for at least a division of 14,000 Marines. Flint had less than 2,000 and now, after the recent enemy airdrop that they repulsed, the enemy knew the Marines were there.

Flint turned to his S-4, Major Vine: "Logie, forget about getting more beans and band-aids off the *Germantown*, just get all the bullets you can. I want every weapon, every stick of explosive. We're going to find ourselves in a helluva fight here and I want everyone, even what's left of the service company, armed to the teeth." He smiled grimly, "This is not a humanitarian mission."

Every Marine was trained to be a rifleman. Vine returned the grim smile, "We're on our way."

"Bring back some of those fat Navy chiefs as well. They're not going to like it very much, but they can carry guns, too."

"Now you're talking, sir!" Vine turned to go pressgang some squids into being ammo bearers. *If I live through this,* Vine thought, *this will make a great sea story.*

*　　*　　*

Fu Zemin swept into the Cathay Pacific office in Chaing Kai-Shek International Airport, the intelligence officer, Major General Wei, right behind him. The office and the adjoining offices of other airlines were appropriated by the commander of the Taiwan operation, General First Class Deng Yen-hsi.

General Deng, was pacing the floor and yelling into his SATCOM phone. He nodded at the presence of the two men but continued his tirade, "You stupid dogs! I cannot believe you've let a division of sick foot soldiers and a brigade of tanks that isn't even close to the area of operations prevent you from reaching your first day's objectives!" The general listened to the reply impatiently, then lowered his voice to a growl, "I don't care if the Americans disrupted your effort. China has given you every tool you need to succeed. In fact, you have more than enough to ensure victory. Perhaps what is needed is your own personal leadership. Why are you not at the front with your men in Kaohsiung?"

Deng's eyes were burning with the fires of military leadership. Fu could tell this man savored command in war—even if everything wasn't going according to plan. Men like this could lift

China to its rightful role as the world's hegemon.

"I will give you six hours and the 202nd Air Mobile Division to help you get your follow-on divisions ashore. By 1800 this evening, if you're not in Kaohsiung engaging the enemy yourself, I will personally sign the order for your removal for dereliction of duty! Is that understood General?. . . Fine then, Deng out!"

General Deng clicked the phone off and turned to Party Liaison Fu. He smiled and bowed. "Sir, I am honored by the presence of the Party's trusted representative and the architect of this most excellent operation."

Fu was momentarily stunned—*a General First Class with four stars on each shoulder was bowing to him! Of course, that was as it should be*, he reminded himself, he was, after all, the Party's representative on Taiwan and therefore the highest-ranking political officer on the island.

"You're too kind General Deng. The honor is mine. Please, give me a brief update on your progress. I last had a briefing from General Wei at about 10:00 AM and have since made a tour of our positions around the airport."

"Excellent. Major General Wei is a fine officer. He once worked for me as my Chief of Intelligence when I commanded the 12th Group Army. The situation is simple. We are crushing the Taiwanese and making all of our objectives on or ahead of schedule. . ."

"What about Kaohsiung and the Americans?" Fu decided he would be demanding. He had a reputation for being smart and aggressive, now he wanted to enhance his reputation as a hard nose among the military.

If the general was fazed, he didn't show it, "The Americans have managed to inflict some significant damage on our Kaohsiung operations. They have destroyed the 97th Infantry Division and the 2nd Regiment of the 3rd Airborne Division—12 battalions of infantry. Interestingly, they managed to achieve surprise against the 14th Group Army commander. He expected nothing but virus-weakened Taiwanese troops. He failed to react to the initial indications that his landings were in trouble. I am still not concerned, though. As far as the Americans go, there are not many of them and now we know where they are. I hear our Foreign Ministry is now working out the terms of their surrender. I, for one, almost wish they would fight to the last man so we could exact revenge." The general clenched his fist in front of his barrel chest and squeezed.

Fu nodded, "If we could force a surrender that would be exceptionally good. An American surrender would cause Japan and South Korea to swiftly acknowledge our unquestioned primacy. Is the American presence in Kaohsiung the reason why you risk reinforcing failure?"

Deng arched his eyebrows, "Ah, yes, the 202nd Air Mobile Division. As for Kaohsiung, you are correct, it is only a supporting attack. Our goal is to tie down Taiwanese reserves and mobile forces along the length of Taiwan so they cannot interfere with our landings and build-up around Taipei. By the time the Taiwanese eliminate our southern beachheads and break free to rescue Taipei, it will already be too late, we will outnumber them in the decisive area of operations!"

"General, if I may, if it is only a supporting attack and it is not going well, then why are you willing to reinforce failure with another division?" Fu felt satisfied that he asked a good, militarily relevant question. After all, he was here to be more than just a wall decoration.

General Deng stopped a half-beat, not out of frustration, but out of respect for the younger man's position. A hasty answer would indicate a lack of respect, "Comrade Fu, in most military situations, you would be correct. In an offensive effort, one does not reinforce failure. On the other hand, you have no doubt heard of the axiom, 'one man to the enemy's rear is worth ten men to his front'?"

"Yes, yes, of course I have." Fu also tried not to act impatient.

"Well the landings of the 14th Group Army in Kaohsiung are critical to our success. Even if only two regiments out of the ten we have assigned to that attack make it, they will serve to tie down a regular infantry division, a reserve infantry division, and a tank brigade. Taipei can ill-afford to miss these forces during the coming key battle. Further, we have done so well elsewhere I can now afford to release some of my reserves. The 202nd Air Mobile Division is one of two special purpose, quick reaction divisions at my disposal. Using one to ensure success in the south is a small price to pay. And, now, as you say, additional power at this juncture may force the Americans to surrender. That alone would be a strategic victory far in excess of any lives lost to achieve it."

Fu looked impassive. He refused to endorse or oppose the decision.

"Comrade Fu," Deng smiled like a father preparing to tell a story about his only son, "Have you heard about the Air Mobile

Divisions?"

"No general. I would assume they are like their American counterpart except that I didn't think we yet had enough helicopters in our inventory to lift an entire division." Fu was now curious. Deng now tightly held Fu's interest.

"Well, comrade, let me tell you. . ."

*   *   *

It was 1600 hours. The Marines had been in Taiwan for the better part of one civilian workday. During that time, the Marines killed or captured six battalions of infantry totaling 6,000 men while their Navy teammates sunk or scattered another six battalions. Not bad for a day's work where the highest paid among them received about $70,000 per year in pay and benefits. Colonel Flint cocked his head, *I wonder what they'd have to pay the CEO of a Fortune 500 company to kill, maim or capture 6,000 men?*

Flint was flying out in his UH-1N Huey command and control chopper to inspect the sunken freighter in Kaohsiung Harbor, then visit the Marine recon elements up in Shousan Park. The SEAL team's scouting a few hours before had uncovered a fascinating new twist on the Trojan Horse theme. Flint grudgingly admired the Chinese for their inventiveness. If it wasn't for blind luck, a PLA regiment would own the harbor right now. As it was, only a battalion made it off the ship before it was sunk—*God rest Captain Hill's soul*—and that battalion, bloodied and demoralized by the sudden loss of their comrades, surrendered to a dozen surprised SEALs and a couple of bemused Whiskey Cobra gunship pilots.

Flint's Huey swooped low over the harbor. Some movement to the left out of the overcast afternoon sky caught Flint's attention, "What the hell is that," Flint said to no one in particular, stabbing his finger at the western horizon out of the open side door of the helicopter.

Major Ramirez scratched the back of his neck under his fiberglass CVC helmet. Usually quick with an answer, he said, "It looks like a big flock of birds. . ." Rez squinted, "Is that more over there?"

Flint addressed the pilot over the mike attached to his CVC helmet. "Take us up a bit and fly closer to that," he pointed.

Rez strained to see, then keyed his mike, "They're not birds."

The helicopter rose another 100 feet and edged west towards

Chichin Island.

Flint was squinting too, "They're too small and too slow to be fighters or helicopters. . ."

Rez's voice cracked like a teenager's, "*Hell*, they're hang gliders. Motorized hang gliders!" Rez was amazed, not yet processing the military importance of what he was seeing.

Flint put out a net call designed to alert all Marines and even the now beached *Curtis Wilbur* and the *Germantown* to the new threat. *Commander Meade beached his ship*, Flint thought, *he would have made a great Marine.*

"Attention all Bulldog elements, all Bulldog elements. We are observing some motorized hang gliders coming in from the west. They are probably carrying light infantry. Estimated strength is two groups of ten to 15 gliders. They look like they can only carry one or two men. . ." Flint was about to request an acknowledgment of his transmission when he observed the low gray fog in the distance begin to resolve itself in to tiny specks. Flint keyed off the mike.

"*Holy*. . ." Ramirez muttered from behind his binoculars. He switched the intercom on and smacked Flint in the arm, "Sir, that fog bank over there is. . . What I mean is that. . ." The magnitude of what Rez was seeing prevented an easy description, "Damnit sir, it looks like the whole friggen' PLA is riding in on motorized hang gliders. Can they do that?" Rez knew the question was silly and rhetorical. Rez remembered a small media report in 1999 or 2000 about the Chinese holding a military exercise in Tibet using motorized hang gliders, GPS devices and special communications equipment. He shrugged it off as a typically weird report from China. *Certainly motorized hang gliders had no large-scale military utility.*

Of course, that's what the Western Allies thought in May 1940, just before German paratroopers conducted a massive vertical envelopment of Holland and executed the surprise capture of a formidable fortification in Belgium. Up to that time, the German (and Soviet Russian) preoccupation with sport parachute and glider clubs was deemed by some a healthy outlet for warrior-like impulses. Certainly, the experts thought, men dropped by parachute could do nothing more than serve as spies, scouts, or harassment forces. Having lost the last war, the Germans felt compelled to innovate. They proved the experts wrong.

After a few centuries of Western and Japanese domination, the Chinese similarly felt compelled to innovate. They knew it would be hopeless, at least in the short term, to match America and Japan dollar-for-dollar with high-tech equipment. But, if one was willing to accept something less than the state-of-the-art in the pursuit of military capabilities, then arriving at the use of motorized hang gliders in combat was a natural for the Chinese. The Chinese recognized the utility of vertical envelopment. For years they maintained three airborne divisions, although they lacked the lift to send all three into combat at once (at least without pressing the civilian air fleet into service). Unfortunately, airborne forces could be used safely only when the enemy was not capable of downing a large number of them before they made it to the drop zone. For this reason, the Chinese became intrigued with the American concept of the airmobile division (first employed against China's neighbor, Vietnam, in the mid-60s). Fielding enough helicopters to move an entire division, then training the division to fly and fight as a unit would be time consuming and expensive. Helicopters were also vulnerable to being shot down or bombed at their bases. After years of thought and internal debate, the PLA decided on a third course, neither airborne nor strictly air mobile, they decided to create two divisions of motorized hang glider troops.

Each motorized hang glider cost the Chinese $500 to produce (the equivalent model sold for $10,000 retail in America). A few tubes of aluminum, some cable, some nylon and a motor-scooter motor and presto—a machine capable of carrying up to two soldiers 250 kilometers (150 miles) at a speed of 120 KPH (75 MPH). To lift an entire division of light infantry (with some gliders carrying only one soldier and a heavy weapon or extra supplies) it took 7,500 gliders costing less than $4 million. The hang gliders were small and easy to operate. They were easy to conceal on the battlefield and they were almost impossible to shoot down *en masse*. Even if the enemy knew an attack was imminent, short of using a nuclear bomb, how could they down thousands of moving targets? Even their infrared signature was cool enough to avoid being acquired by heat seeking missiles. Add a few commercial GPS navigation devices for the platoon leaders and some lightweight communications equipment, and the force would know where it was and be able to send and receive orders. The motorized hang glider was nothing short of a revolution in military affairs. It was perfectly suited to an infantry-rich and comparably low-tech army such as China's. And, just as with Germany in May, 1940, the first widespread use of the tactic in combat was calculated to shock an unprepared enemy.

High above the hang gliders in the overcast sky Rez saw the swept back wings of Chinese jets, "Fighters! We need to get out of here. I think the Chinese want to make this landing a success."

Flint's calm voice came over the intercom, "How many you see?"

Rez panned the sky, "I can see about 20 fast movers—it's the ones I can't see that worry me."

"Let's get back to the airport and see how many Taiwanese have shown up to help us defend the place." Flint ordered.

The pilot dropped back down to the water and spun the helicopter around to the southeast.

Ramirez clicked the intercom on, "Sir, how do you shoot down 10,000 hang gliders?"

Flint's eyes looked intensely distant, "You don't. Wait until they land then hit 'em with artillery. With no overhead cover they'll be dead meat for the cannon cockers."

The first wave of 100 Chinese airmobile infantry came low off the waves and swept up the steep sides of Shou Shan Hill. The few Marines on the hill could only see the gliders intermittently through the trees until at last they headed for the open ground around the Martyr's Shrine and began to assemble.

One of the LAVs from the armored reconnaissance company opened up with its 25mm cannon, hitting several motorized gliders in the air. Most of the hits went unrewarded, however, as the cannon simply made small holes in the nylon, which, at 50 feet off the ground and only going 30 mph, were not fatal to the light aircraft. Some of the rounds hit gliders' engines (again, not fatal—they were essentially gliders, after all) and some hit the infantrymen/pilots on board (definitely fatal).

In spite of facing an armored vehicle, the Chinese rapidly began to form up and maneuver against the Marine LAV. Within minutes, a heavy machine gun crew was in action and three RPG teams were found and sent, two to one side and one to the other, to get into position to take out the LAV.

The LAV commander called for help from his company commander and the commander called the 31st MEU looking for artillery or air support. All of Shoushan Park was within range of the six 155mm guns now emplaced at the airport. In less than a minute, the battery was firing rounds down range.

The victory in battle usually goes to the side that can pose more problems then their enemy can react to. This can be achieved through large numbers, simultaneous attacks, or multiple means of attack (i.e., artillery, armor, chemical agents, and air strikes). Up to this point, the Chinese had not yet displayed battlefield synchronization against the Marines, in part, because their intelligence/operations cycle had not adequately detected the unexpected threat, then compensated for it. To give the PLA credit, they had adequately planned for the systematic destruction of Taiwan's armed forces and the swift occupation of the island— they just hadn't planned on American forces being there at the onset of the invasion. Once the PLA chain of command overcame its initial denial of the situation, it was quick to respond.

Colonel Flint heard the chatter from the recon units atop Shou Shan hill on the MEU's command net. A few moments later he heard a frantic call for fire from his units on the beach to the south of the harbor entrance. Flint furrowed his brow, *Damn, the recon elements have priority of fire. I hope the beach can hold out.*

They paralleled the highway back to the airport. Occasionally the pilot would jerk back on the collective to clear power lines or an overpass. Flint was glad they weren't flying at night or in bad weather.

A mile from the airport the pilot pointed to the front. Three dark forms were diving on the airport. They pulled up about 1,500 feet above the runway. At the very edge of the eye's perception, small, dark and evil forms were seen falling away from the jets. The militarily trained eye knew what they were. The eye that beheld close friends and colleagues wanted to deny their purpose. A few moments later denial was met by harsh, red-hot reality as an impossibly large fireball erupted over the airport. The faces of those in the helicopter could feel the heat through the cockpit screen. Five seconds later a sonic boom and overpressure wave lightly rocked the helicopter. As a defiant and almost absurd afterthought, one of the three jets was found by a defender's missile. A small flash (insignificant compared to the inferno below, but significant enough to cause the pilot to eject shortly afterward) was followed by a puff of gray, then a dirty smoke trail as the now pilotless J-6 spiraled to its death below.

"Looks like the airport is under attack," the pilot said matter-of-factly.

Rez joined in, clinically commenting, "Fuel-air explosives. We probably have a lot of casualties there." The tone of his voice changed to quiet concern but he kept the mike on anyway, "God, I hope they had a chance to dig in. . ."

"Rez, I'm going to tell you something I heard from an Army Colonel a few years back in a place called Saudi Arabia, 'Hope is not a battlefield operating system.' Our Marines either dug in or they paid dearly for not doing so. My bet is they dug in because that's what they were trained to do."

Rez was silent. For the first time in his Marine career he saw an enemy use a potent means of destruction aimed at American fighting men and women. Snipers, mines, light weapons fire, even the automatic grenade rounds from the BMD a few hours ago all seemed to be manageable threats, easily overmatched by American technology, firepower and training. This was different and terribly sobering. They were in a war and they weren't necessarily the biggest and toughest guys in the fight.

The helicopter closed in on the airport and began to set down across the street from the main parking lot, a vacant lot filled with mud puddles and overrun with weeds.

They came down hard, bouncing once before settling down. The pilot switched off the rotors, and the two officers ran for the temporary command post. Behind them, camouflage netting was draped over the Huey as soon as the blades were still. The helo disappeared into the landscape, virtually invisible from above.

In the relative safety of the pre-cast concrete walls of a small electronic components factory, Flint and Rez absorbed a quick situation update from one of Rez's staff NCOs. The Chinese were attacking in regimental strength on Shou Shan Hill while the beach was being pounded by air strikes and overrun by at least two regiments of infantry. The *Germantown* was reported hit in the harbor and was on fire while the *Curtis Wilbur* had taken several direct hits from iron bombs on the beach. Its stern was now resting on the sand as the tide was going out (the bow was kept pointing to the sea by the anchor the skipper dropped on his way in to beach his beloved ship). From their previous successes, the Marines now held about 750 enemy prisoners of war from the failed harbor and airport attacks. There were two pieces of good news: their last temporary command post was now a crater (they decided to move after the airborne assault at the airport) and, the ROC Army was now stirring to life.

With that, the S-3, Lieutenant Colonel Cook broke in and quickly explained that the Taiwanese had mustered a battalion of M-41D light tanks (almost 50 vehicles) in the hills only five kilometers east of the airport while almost two full battalions of the reserve 17th Infantry Division (Light) had now taken up positions on the northeast side of the runway.

When it seemed no one was going to mention the huge fireball caused by the fuel air explosives only minutes before, Rez could no longer contain himself, "How hard did we just get hit?"

Cook paused, "Oh, that. Well, first of all, everyone checked in A-okay. We have either landline or FM to every platoon now." Cook was speaking excitedly, "But you didn't see the half of it! Ten minutes ago we got hit with cluster munitions. Destroyed one of the Harriers. The FAE singed our eyebrows but the bombs actually fell short. I guess the anti-aircraft fire unnerved the pilots enough that they missed their mark. I'd imagine they'll be back."

Flint needed some extra cards in his hand right about now, some *good* cards. He addressed Cook, "You mentioned the ROCs. How's our liaison with them right now?"

"Excellent. I take it you missed Captain Ho here behind you when you walked in?"

An officer in his mid-30s walked up, hand outstretched in a Western-style greeting. "Colonel Flint. I am Captain Ho of the 17th Infantry Division. May I be of service?" The officer spoke solid English. He had an accent, but was obviously a veteran of business in the States.

Flint didn't have time for niceties, "You heard about the motorized hang gliders. Have you communicated that to your headquarters?"

"Yes sir, I have."

"We're running low on Marines, what can you do?"

"We intend to put our plans into effect for repelling the enemy off our soil. We will attack at first darkness when the enemy air power is less effective. That will be three hours from now. If I may be so bold, I suggest you pull your forces off the beach and Shou Shan and consolidate at the airport. It will be very difficult for our two armies to coordinate their actions, especially at night. I would rather only kill Mainlanders on purpose than Americans by mistake."

Flint smiled and said, "Captain Ho, you are correct. Cook, call Colonel Bailey and tell him to pull back to the airport. Captain Ho, do you have any artillery support that can be made available to us?"

"That can be arranged." Ho smiled in return.

"Cook, Ramirez—get this gentleman some good targets ASAP. Rez, how's the enemy air-to-air ability against our Cobras?"

"Not exceptional. I don't think the aircraft I've seen so far would even try to down a Cobra."

"Cook, get the Cobras in the air to help our forces at the beach break contact with the enemy. Send all of them to the beach. The recon guys can handle themselves at Shou Shan. Those sailors and wounded Marines are my main concern."

"Roger." Cook was already on the radio sending out the warning order to pull back.

*　　*　　*

Commander Meade stood on his bridge. The deck under his feet was at a 20-degree angle, sloping forward and to port side. He knew the ship's stern was now out of the water due to the low tide. The fires from the four previous bomb hits were now extinguished, but the *Curtis Wilbur's* hull was so shattered that she would never again freely ply the ocean swells. He now had less than 50 crewmembers remaining on board. The rest he sent to join up with the Marines and other sailors on shore. All 50 of the crew were handpicked volunteers and their sole purpose was to care and feed the 5-inch gun mount. They had already rigged up a series of portable generators to maintain power to the rapid-fire gun (the engine room was now a complete loss). The initial motorized hang glider assault caught Meade by surprise, but once he realized the nature of the threat, he decided to remain silent and hope his ship would be ignored as a lifeless hulk. It was.

Evening approached. Thunderstorms were beginning to build in the growing humidity, forming inland, then moving rapidly out to sea. Just before 1800 hours he saw another flight of at least 100 hang gliders about a mile off shore. A growing thunder cell loomed over the would-be Icaruses. Lightning danced from one cloud to another, then flashed towards the ocean. A man of the sea, Meade knew what was coming and he felt pity on his enemy. Heavy, large drops of rain began to pelt the ship. At first, the bridge's windows were untouched, the wind rising from the stern was carrying the rain out to sea at an almost horizontal angle. The men in the gliders were soon obscured by the driving rain. Within ten minutes the cell's center had passed overhead and the rain was now pounding against the window. *Microburst*, Meade thought, *poor bastards are fish food now*.

The storm cell cleared out to sea. For a moment, the sea was devoid of a human presence. Nothing but waves breaking against the *Curtis Wilbur's* bow and foam capped seas beyond. Then he saw it, a gray form surging through the white caps, then another, and another. Three ships were making for the beach to his port side. The ship's radio crackled to life. It was the Marines. The 31st MEU reported that the enemy now held the beach south of the port entrance and the dominating hill mass to the north. The sailors were to be on their own for a spell. Observing a type of radio silence since he beached his destroyer, Meade's signalman (a 22-year-old woman actually) simply broke squelch twice to acknowledge receipt of the message (if there was something really important to transmit, Meade would have done so).

Meade called his guncrew on the intercom and told them about the targets. He ordered them to withhold fire until they were two miles off shore. Assuming they were moving at less than ten knots, it would take them about ten minutes to close to the beach. Within five minutes, Meade calculated his rapid-fire 5-inch gun could acquire all three targets and inflict critical damage on them. This would present the enemy captains with a choice: steam on and get more punishment, or turn around. If they turned tail, Meade would target and destroy their engine rooms. With the prevailing winds and currents, the ships would then drift harmlessly to the southwest (assuming they didn't sink or explode). If they came on, he would still have a few more minutes to shoot. In the back of his mind he wondered why the ships had no escort in sight. In combat, however, one rarely questions good fortune.

The ships pressed on. A flight of three jets appeared behind them and roared on over the beach. Meade heard explosions in the distance. He winced, thinking of the jarheads he secretly admired. Peering through his binoculars, Meade could now see that the ships were large innercoastal ferries, probably used in the Pearl River region serving cities such as Hong Kong and Macau. He gave the order to open fire, starting with the ship furthest to the port (if he hit the starboardmost ship first and it caught fire, the smoke might obscure the other two—being sensitive to wind direction was one attribute of a good naval officer).

The first shot went long, sending a geyser of water high to the stern of the oncoming ferry. The second shot hit the ship's superstructure, maybe killing the captain (Meade wondered if this was the kind of ferry that reversed direction, giving it a second bridge to the stern). The third and fourth shots hit low to the waterline right where Meade wanted them. He saw a large wave break against the ferry and the gaping hole left by his gun. The waves greedily found the opening and entered. The ferry began to founder. A warship in combat could recover from such a blow with pumping and counter-flooding. An over-laden ferry could not. By the time the Curtis Wilbur's 5-inch gun was trained on the second ship, the first was already listing ominously forward.

The skipper of the second ferry, reacting to the hits against the first, thought he'd try evasive action. He turned to port, presenting Meade's gunners with a larger target. It only took eight shots to land five of them at the waterline and two in the engine room. The ferry quickly capsized. Meade actually saw little human forms falling off the ship as it rolled, showing its topside to the beached Americans as it settled upside-down.

The third ferry captain pressed onward. Meade saw the spray pound off his bow and blow over his low-slung deck. Meade muttered, "If we didn't sink the brave fool the sea probably would on his return trip."

The first shot hit the front of the superstructure, directly over the vehicle ramp. The gunners adjusted and. . ."

Ka-bamm! The *Curtis Wilbur* shook. Two more tinny-sounding blasts shook the ship.

Meade felt the vibrations under his feet, "What the hell?"

The intercom cracked to life, "We're under attack. We're under attack from the landward side! There's a group of infantry off our portside stern and they're firing at us with crew served weapons."

Meade responded, "Get some crews up on the .50 caliber stations. Continue to engage the enemy ship. Whatever happens, don't stop firing until he's sunk."

Meade heard shots outside the bridge's starboardside hatch. A second later several rounds pinged against the hatch and bulkhead. He unholstered the 9mm pistol he really didn't know how to use very well. *At least they'll be close*, he thought, *hard to miss*.

A mile out to sea a 5-inch round exploded off the side of the ship—too high to let the heavy seas enter.

Meade could see a group of men run towards the 5-inch turret mount. They were setting something on the deck next to the gun. "Where's the .50 caliber crews! We have a boarding party on the bow, they're trying to take out the gun!"

The gun fired again. The shot fell short and exploded harmlessly in the water just in front of the ferry.

Meade yelled, "Everyone with a personal weapon, follow me!"

He burst out of the hatch and onto the superstructure that overlooked the main deck about ten feet below. The gun mount was about 40 feet away. He steadied his pistol on the wire railing and fired. His officers and sailors joined in behind him. Three of them had M-16s. Four of the enemy fell in the first volley. One pulled the pin on a grenade by the mount's base and dove away. The smooth, featureless deck provided no cover and the man was quickly killed. The gun fired. Meade stood motionless, watching the ferry off in the distance. The shot hit the ferry's bow at the waterline. *Excellent!*

The grenade exploded, sending fragments into the turret's ring and freezing it in place. A fragment found Meade's left leg, gouging his shinbone and tearing out a piece of his calf. His pistol flew out of his hand as he caught himself on the cable of the railing. The pistol was dangling off the cable from its lanyard. Meade began to pull himself up when an explosion rocked the side of the 5-inch turret, blasting a hole the size of basketball in its thin skin. He looked up the beach and saw a Chinese anti-tank missile team reloading its wire-guided weapon mount not 150 yards away.

A small explosion reverberated off the deck in front of the gun mount. Another crashed into the deck between Meade and the gun mount. An instant later, Meade's ears were ringing and he felt suspended off the deck. A weird swinging sensation briefly captured his attention and overrode the dull pain he felt in his chest. He looked up. His pistol lanyard had wrapped around the cabling and he was hanging by the waist from the lanyard. He tried to grab the cabling. His hand wouldn't move. It was strangely silent with only a light ringing in his ears. With a great effort he lifted his head up. In the distance Meade saw his final quarry sink beneath the waves. He had just enough consciousness left to smile. Commander Meade died a minute later.

*   *   *

The latest battle had not gone as well for the Marines. The airmobile infantry had hit hard and in large numbers. They were a lightly armed, but determined foe. The Chinese drove the Marines off of Shou Shan Hill, inflicting moderate casualties: the Marines lost 11 men and two of four LAVs. Another five Marines were MIA. More importantly, the Chinese soldiers successfully destroyed the partially manned coastal defense emplacements along the bluff (partly staffed due to the combined effects of the chemical, electronic and biological attacks). At the beach, all the remaining LCACs had been destroyed and the field hospital had almost been overrun. If it weren't for the Taiwanese 105mm howitzers from the reserve infantry division's artillery battalion, they would have been killed or captured. As it was, the mixed force of Marines and Naval personnel barely broke contact with the enemy in one piece. At the beach they lost 46 Marines and 84 sailors. Another 65, mainly sailors, were unaccounted for.

Colonel Flint was bruised, but he hardly considered himself battered for what could have happened. And now, the Taiwanese were preparing a counterattack.

He owed a lot to the crew of the *Curtis Wilbur*. The last transmission from the overrun ship still haunted him. The female seaman calmly reported the loss of her skipper and the destruction of three large ferries bearing enemy troops. She then reported the ship had been boarded and that she could hear the enemy outside the bridge. The sound of demolitions blasting through a hatch was the last anyone heard from the *Curtis Wilbur*.

It was now 1900 hours local. With the situation somewhat stabilized, Lieutenant Colonel Cook turned to his commander, "Sir, I forgot to tell you. While you were out burning up fuel, you'll never guess what we managed to do. Remember that phone we lifted off the enemy scout? It works fine. We were able to get a call through to PACOM. They wanted to talk to you ASAP."

Flint narrowed his eyes, "Excellent. We can use some help."

Cook handed him the SATCOM phone, "Just push this button here, it's a redial."

The phone rang once then the line picked up, "Pacific Command."

"Colonel Flint here. . ."

Outside, an enemy jet was tearing across the sky making it sound like the Marines were inside an envelop being ripped open.

"Stand-by, we're patching you through to the General Keagan." Flint heard some clicks. A few seconds of static and a voice Flint recognized as Chairman of the Joint Chiefs of Staff came on the line. (The first Marine Corps General ever to be made Chairman of the joint chiefs, General Keagan was a hard-nosed warrior.) "What's your situation Colonel?"

"I am commanding combined elements of the 31st MEU and the *Belleau Wood* ARG in the Kaohsiung area of southern Taiwan. All four ships of the group have been sunk or severely damaged. My Marines have taken about 350 casualties. We have about 600 sailors ashore as well. We have killed, captured or sunk about 12 enemy battalions and at least four transport ships. I think we have seriously disrupted enemy war plans in our sector but we probably can't withstand another coordinated assault. I am consolidating my forces at Kaohsiung International Airport where we are under aerial attack. Local ROC forces are attempting to gain contact with the enemy."

In the White House Situation Room the President and several staffers listened transfixed to the Colonel's briefing to General Keagan in Kosovo. They regarded the speakerphone on the table's center with unwelcome frowns.

A familiar folksy southern accent came over the line, interrupting Flint. There was nothing friendly about the tone. "Colonel . . .uh . . .Flint, I believe it is. I understand that you and some of your Marines are ashore on Taiwan."

The President himself, Flint thought. In different circumstances he would have been amused. *Damn, it must be five or six in the morning in Washington.*

"Yes, sir." Flint was instantly on guard. Never trust someone in authority when they ask you a question to which they already know the answer.

As if to punctuate Flint's reply, the crackling explosions of cluster munitions could clearly be heard in the distance. A moment later there was a large, reverberating explosion. A Marine at the door yelled, "There goes one of the airport's fuel tanks!"

If the President heard the explosion, he was unmoved, "Who in the hell gave you permission to do that? You know the island is off limits to American troops. What is Beijing going to think?"

"Sir. . .?" Colonel Flint stopped himself and another explosion thankfully muffled his insubordinate response. He started again, "We didn't really have any choice, Mr. President. The Chinese sunk our ships."

There was a long pause at the other end of the line. A sonic boom shook a broken piece of glass loose from the window in the factory's front office.

"This is not our fight, Colonel Flint," the President's voice came back on the line. "This is all a terrible misunderstanding. We will protest the sinking of the *Belleau Wood*, of course. But don't engage in any hostilities."

"It's too late for that, Mr. President. We've already engaged elements of three different divisions of the enemy."

"What can a few hundred Marines do against so many?" came the response, dripping with sympathy. *Phony sympathy*, Flint decided.

"I think you'd better try and end hostilities, Colonel," the President continued, "After all, we don't want to find ourselves in World War Three."

"You mean surrender, sir?" Flint's voice was icy.

"Now hold on, Colonel. That's your word, not mine. But. . . yes, find some way to sit down with the local Chinese commander and work out your problems."

"I'm afraid that's impossible, sir."

"Now listen here, Colonel!" the President shouted. "I am your commander-in-chief. I order you to surr . . . er . . cease firing."

"Sir, a cease fire would be difficult. We are being attacked by aircraft at the moment here at the airport. At two other locations my Marines have successfully broken contact with enemy air mobile troops. Surrender is not a viable option right now. . ."

"Why not?" A different voice was on the line. Flint knew he was on a speaker box now.

"Because, to surrender, you have to have someone to arrange a surrender with. Right now, the only officers who may have been able to accept a surrender are either dead or are our prisoners. Lieutenant Colonel Chen, the senior surviving officer of the PLA's 97th Infantry Division, and Major Wu of the PLA's 3rd Airborne Division, have both surrendered to me. Several other cargo ships and ferry boats carrying follow-on troops have been sunk or severely damaged as well."

There was dead silence on the line. Colonel Flint shrugged at

Major Ramirez and continued with his briefing. "We have inflicted something on the order of 7,500 casualties on the enemy, probably double, maybe triple that if you count the shipboard losses. We have taken approximately 750 prisoners. The MEU— that's Marine Expeditionary Unit, sir—has sustained approximately 350 casualties, half from close-in fighting with the paratroopers and air bombardment and the other half at sea when we were hit by Chinese anti-ship missiles. The Navy has sustained many more casualties, but there's no way for us to know exactly how many. We managed to get 600 or so sailors ashore," Colonel Flint smiled, "and are trying to make them into Marines."

There was still silence. Flint drove on, "We have established contact with the ROC forces, who have been hit hard by some kind of combined biological and chemical weapons attack. Their reserves are being mobilized and they may have enough combat power to defeat the last Chinese assault that just pushed us off the beach."

Colonel Flint concluded, "We will continue to hold the airport Mr. President, unless, that is. . ." Flint gave a wicked grin to Major Ramirez, "you order us to join the ROC assault on the commie forces at the beaches."

Flint heard a gasp on the other end of the phone. Two more sonic booms sounded overhead.

"The US Marines are holding Kaohsiung International Airport, sir!" Colonel Flint didn't even try to keep the pride out is his voice. "There will be no throughput from the PLA forces here sir! I doubt if they'll try another motorized hang glider attack. We handed the enemy his head today sir!"

Flint heard some shuffling at the other end of the line.

"Uh, right, Colonel Flint." It was a female voice. The phone clicked at the other end. The phone was obviously off the speaker box. "The President is indisposed. Motorized hang gliders you say?" The voice was soft and quiet. She sounded loathe to disturb the President and those around him.

"Yes, hang gliders. Who is this?" Flint demanded.

"That's not important—remember, this is an unsecure line." The voice sounded uncomfortable and reluctant.

Flint knew he was dealing with a non-political type—probably an NSC, State, DoD, or CIA staffer, "Why the lack of interest in my situation over here?"

"Umm. . .", the woman's voice got very soft, "Suffice it to say that the President is very concerned about the situation."

Flint heard the phone system click over to the speaker box. "Colonel Flint, this is National Security Council Advisor Lindley. It's six in the morning out here. The President has been up all night following your situation. Needless to say he is exhausted. Continue to hold the airport. . ." the phone spit static and faded out.

"Hello, can you hear me?" Flint pulled the phone away from his ear and looked at it. The low battery light shone on the phone. *Damn!*

Half a world away, Lindley was finishing up his instructions to the Marine colonel, his tired mind half looking at CNN and half trying to direct the conversation. ". . .Continue to hold the airport if you can. Minimize your contact with the enemy, if possible. The President wishes to maintain flexibility in this crisis. Is that understood?" The other end was dead. "Hey, the line is dead! Get the Pentagon and get the colonel back on the phone! *Shit,* I wonder how much he heard?"

Donna Klein smiled from behind her hands. *The colonel probably heard what he wanted to hear.* She hadn't liked the tenor in the White House since she arrived at five in the morning shocked to find the President and his key advisors pulling an all-nighter while spiraling down into a deeper pit of defeatism. *The Marines may win this thing in spite of the White House,* she thought.

*   *   *

Colonel Alexander was nearing the end of the longest day of his life. It started that morning with a wake-up at 0300 in Alaska, crossed seven time zones and the International Date Line, and almost killed him twice (first the E-bomb, then the nervous Taiwanese airport security troops). It was now 7:00 PM in Taiwan some 23 hours later.

For the first time since boarding the C-17 that morning, Dan was eating. It wasn't really his idea, but rather one of his NCOs, Staff Sergeant Peña, *Traveller's* (Alexander's M1 *Abrams*) gunner. Examining his tired officer, Sergeant Peña said, "Sir, you have to eat something."

"Yah, yah, I'll get to it. I'd like the ACE (Armored Combat Earthmover) to dig one more position. . ."

"Sir, they can dig without you. You need to eat. Now, sir." Sergeant Peña was persistent.

Dan knew when he was defeated, "Yes, sergeant! What's for chow?"

"Room temperature MREs, sir," relieved that he talked his officer into conducting personal body maintenance, the sergeant smiled.

Dan let out a sigh as he ripped open the tough light brown plastic bag. It was marked as a "vegetarian" meal. The men often joked that the "namby-pamby" vegetarian meals were unfit for warriors, but Dan was secretly glad for the variety. MREs had too much meat and fat in them. At home, Dan was used to pasta several times a week—too much meat made him feel sluggish. "Sergeant Peña, what's the word on Colonel Giannini?"

"Sir, last I heard the Taiwanese took him off to a local hospital. His copilot went with him."

That squared with Dan's recollection too. He was starved for information. A war was swirling around him—he could hear it in the skies above him, but he really knew very little about the situation. He and his 82 men were in Taipei along with eight Air Force crewmen. They had one operational tank, an ACE, four scout Humvees, four MP Humvees, and a medical track. None of the three surviving C-17s had an operational radio. He knew that Taiwan had suffered both chemical and nuclear attack. One of his men bummed a couple of city maps from a Taiwanese security officer, so at least Dan and his men knew where they were in relation to the rest of the city. They also knew which way the enemy would come from (assuming they didn't jump out of the sky right on top of them).

Dan thought about his last assumption—*where the enemy will come from. Did they have an enemy? Was his nation at war with the People's Republic of China? If they weren't at war, what were the implications of his actions?* Dan recalled Taiwan's increasingly independence-minded rhetoric. He knew that the US was somewhat committed to Taiwan's defense—especially if the PRC attacked a Taiwan seeking the status quo fiction of "one China, two systems." Taiwan was moving away from that policy—*and rightly so*, Dan thought, *if they wait any longer, China will be too strong to resist.* Dan stopped himself realizing it was all a moot point. China had already moved to head off a full Taiwanese declaration of independence—any other thoughts were now academic, it was war, and he was in the middle of it. All of this once again begged the question, what should he do?

Dan was taking another bite of his vegetarian crackers and cheese on the turret of his M1 tank—*pretty good stuff, nicely spiced*—when two young Taiwanese men with a TV camera and a small communications relay unit walked up to him followed by one of his NCOs.

"Sir, these men claim to be reporters with a local affiliate of CNN News."

In spite of his misgivings, Dan smiled for the reporters (he was a courtroom attorney, after all), "Oh?"

"Yes sir. I figured since I saw them talking to the airport security troops they couldn't be all bad."

"Good assumption sergeant. Thank you," Alexander nodded at his NCO and turned to the reporters, "How may I help you gentlemen today?" As he was talking, he reluctantly put his MRE down on the turret. He stood up, got dizzy for a second, and hopped off the tank (normally about a five foot jump, made only a foot-and-a-half due to the three-and-a-half foot hole the ACE dug for the tank in the grass strip between the two runways).

The man carrying the relay unit knelt to place the box carefully on the ground, then spoke. "Sir, my name is Wong Kwok Pui. I go by Edward when I'm on TV for English speaking audiences," he said this a bit expectantly, as if he thought Dan would recognize him. His English was near flawless.

"My name is Lieutenant Colonel Dan Alexander, California Army National Guard."

"Welcome to Taiwan. I wish it were under other circumstances. Mind if I interview you for CNN?" By this time the cameraman had set up a tripod, placed his videocam on it, then broke the communications unit out of its box.

"Sure. Mind if I ask, how can you get a signal out? Isn't your equipment damaged?" Dan was curiously hopeful.

"Well, this camera and commo box were in storage in the basement of the television studio. I don't know what happened. There's no electricity anywhere in Taipei. Our backup generator works, but the studio's electronics don't work. With this setup we can get a direct signal out to the low Earth orbit satellites that CNN leases time on. If they want to, we can go live from the scene. Pretty neat, huh?" Edward grinned broadly. It was obvious he went to school in the US.

"Well, let's do it, what do you want to say?" Dan figured this was the only way he had a chance of showing America—and his wife and children too—that he was alive.

Dan absent-mindedly grabbed for the bottom of his BDU blouse to straighten it, only realizing after a few fruitless pulls that he was still wearing his bulky green chemical protective overgarment. *So much for looking the poster boy soldier.* Dan heard the three by five foot American flag snapping in the easterly breeze from midway up one of the tank's whip antennas. Dan and his men put the flag on the tank reasoning that the Chinese might think twice about shooting at an American tank if, in fact, they hadn't intended to make war on the Americans. The flag would now serve as a nice backdrop for the TV interview. The task force operations sergeant major's Humvee was parked next to the tank. Strapped to the back of the Humvee, facing the camera crew, was Task Force Grizzly's unofficial guidon: a long yellow surfboard with the tank and crossed saber emblem of the US Army Armor Corps. Emblazoned around the Armor Corps emblem was the slogan, "TF Grizzly—Charlie Don't Surf".

Dan heard the TV reporter begin his lead in, "This is Edward Wong with CNN reporting from Taipei, Taiwan. A few hours ago China attacked Taiwan in a sudden and crushing attack. We have very little information from areas outside the capital, but here's what we do know: early this morning at eight o'clock, China sortied hundreds of jet fighters across the Taiwan Strait, as Taiwanese fighters moved to intercept the air attack, China detonated two nuclear missiles over Taiwan. This nuclear attack disrupted power and communications over much of Taiwan. Several civilian aircraft were also destroyed or crippled. Joining me here right now is Colonel Dan Alexander of the United States Army. Colonel Alexander, can you tell me, why are you in Taiwan right now?"

Dan was suddenly nervous, "Well, the four aircraft my soldiers and I were on were attacked by the Chinese. We were forced to land here at Taipei." By the time he finished the sentence, Dan was much more at ease—*No different than the courtroom.*

"So the People's Republic of China attacked the US military?" Edward Wong was inwardly smiling, this colonel was giving him and his people an excellent propaganda boost.

"Yes. I don't know whether it was by design or not, but the net effect of it was that we probably lost two aircraft, a C-17 and a KC-135. In addition, one person died on board the aircraft I was riding on due to a massive electrical surge caused by the nuclear detonation."

"So there have been American casualties?"

"Yes."

"What will you do now?"

"We have been attacked, we will defend ourselves until otherwise directed."

"Does this mean you will. . ."

Machinegun fire punctuated Wong's next question. It sounded like it was coming from about 300 meters away to the northeast— probably from atop the roof of one of the buildings abutting the airport. Alexander knew the Taiwanese security troops had set out a perimeter to protect the airport from a modest air assault or parachute-landing attempt. He hoped it was outbound fire even as he was climbing back on to the deck of the tank yelling over his shoulder, "Mr. Wong, I suggest you take cover!"

*   *   *

Someone turned up the volume on the TV and all eyes in the Situation Room were fixed on the set. ". . .up next, we have breaking news from Taipei, Taiwan," the anchor said. Then a commercial came on. Most eyes turned away and someone moved to turn down the volume a notch.

"No, turn it back up," Donna said, "I want to see this."

The TV was beaming forth an inspirational montage of ships, aircraft and computers, ". . .America's strategic trade partnership with China benefits America in many ways: a stronger economy, better jobs, more opportunity for people on both sides of the Pacific. . ." *It was a damn ad for China on CNN!* Donna was shocked, then suddenly filled with admiration at the timing and boldness of it all—*The coincidence is too great, this had to be planned.*

"I wonder how much money the Chinese poured into our media outlets to affect American public opinion on the eve of their war?" Donna said it loud enough that even the President looked up from his quiet conversation with Lindley. "Isn't there an easy way to find out? Political campaign media specialists can get the data quickly—is there anyone here who can find out when the Chinese made the media buy, how much they spent and how long the spots are supposed to run for?"

Another NSC staffer, a military officer in civilian clothes, picked up Donna's cause, "We ought to shut down those commercials right now! Our enemy is seeking to deliver propaganda right to our own people."

Lindley spoke up, "The term 'enemy' is little premature. . ."

The President stepped on his advisor, "Still Bob, I think he's right, call the FCC and tell them to get the stations to pull the ads. Also, get the information the young lady requested—even I'd be interested in that."

The commercial promoting Chinese-American trade ended and the TV showed a young reporter summarizing the situation from Taipei. General Taylor started taking notes. The scene panned from the reporter to an American military officer whom he began to interview. The officer looked tired, but poised, even photogenic, ready for battle in his chemical weapons gear with an American flag occasionally fluttering into view in the near background.

"What the hell is that?" someone asked, pointing at the surfboard. The man was hushed to silence when the realization hit everyone in the room that this American officer was in Taipei and had said he had been attacked by the Chinese.

"Damn!"

Donna didn't see who said this, although it came from close to where the President was sitting.

Machine gun fire was heard in the distance on the TV. The colonel quickly jumped aboard his tank. The camera shot followed him into the turret then began to shake, wildly at first, then rhythmically as the cameraman took the camera off the tripod then shouldered it and began to back up to get a good wide angle view. The reporter kept up a commentary as the tank's engine could be heard starting up with a whine. Suddenly, a figure appeared at the turret roof three feet from where Colonel Alexander's head and shoulders could be seen. The form grabbed at a machine gun mounted to the turret. Colonel Alexander pointed up. The crewman aimed the machine gun skyward and began firing. The noise level shocked the Situation Room into silence. It was very hard to adjust to the fact that this was live television and not a war movie. Not a word was spoken; everyone just stared at the TV.

"Oh my God!" the President said.

*   *   *

Moments after climbing into the tank, Dan saw a small unmanned aerial vehicle (UAV) circling over the airport at a low altitude.

Alexander yelled at his loader, "Jones, damn it, you're supposed to be pulling air guard! Get up here and shoot the damn thing down!"

Jones popped up through his open hatch, chambered a round and acquired his target. It took about ten five second bursts, but Jones finally hit the little reconnaissance drone enough times that it sputtered silent and fell out of the sky, crashing like a large toy on the cement of the runway.

At the east end of the runway towards a couple of bridges over the Keelung Ho river, Alexander saw a green star cluster arc up and lazily separate into several green balls of fire. His scouts had just sent the signal that an enemy force was crossing the river some two kilometers from his tank. Alexander couldn't see anything moving on Sun Yat-Sen Freeway bridge to the east. *They must be coming down Pingchiang Street bridge*, he thought, *at six kilometers per hour I should see them in ten minutes.* Dan didn't know why he expected the Chinese to move at the doctrinal rate of march for movement in the enemy rear, but, without a lot of information, he had to make some basic assumptions. As he sat thinking about the enemy's sophisticated used of reconnaissance drones and what exactly the downed drone may have seen and transmitted back to its controllers before being shot down, another green star cluster rose up, this time unexpectedly from the north. *A two-pronged attack from the north and east.* He slouched a little lower in the turret. Alexander keyed the tank's intercom, "Keep your eyes peeled for more aircraft Jones," he reminded his nervous young loader. Machine gun fire erupted from rooftops to the tank's front (east) and left (north). Alexander caught movement out of the corner of his eye—one of his scout Humvees zipped onto the runway from behind the low-lying hanger buildings to the north and sped towards *Traveller.* Dan wished he had some working radios, but, only the sets in the tank appeared to work, and those only marginally (his crew confirmed that both of the tank's two radios could talk to each other, but further experiments were overtaken by other, more important activities, such as boresighting the tank and digging in).

Given the pace of the scout Humvee Alexander figured there must be something in hot pursuit. He grabbed the TC's turret yoke and sloughed the turret to the left. A vehicle appeared between two buildings. From the front it looked like any one of a thousand different armored personnel carriers (APCs) with a sloped front, a small turret and wheels. It was only 300 meters away.

"Jones, get below and button up. You may have work to do in a second."

The private first class vanished and shut the hatch behind him like a prairie dog diving for cover from a hawk. Alexander was alone up top. He visually inspected his .50 caliber machine gun, then swung it around to face the nearby intruder.

He saw muzzle flashes on the turret of the APC then heard the unmistakable whooshing sound of small arms fire clearing his head by a few feet. Alexander ducked below the line of the turret and fairly screamed into his CVC mike, "Gunner! Sabot! APC! Fire!" Heavy machine gun slugs splatted against and ricocheted off the turret.

Staff Sergeant Peña had already laid the gun and lased the target (at 300 meters you had to try to miss).

As the colonel finished yelling "fire" Peña barked, "On the way!" the tank rocked slightly, the breach of the 105mm gun slammed back and ejected a large, steaming brass shell casing. The shell casing slammed against the ammo blast door with a clang. Some 300 meters away, at the same instant the casing struck the door, the enemy APC was struck by a two-foot long dart of depleted uranium traveling a mile a second. The dart easily penetrated the APC's armor (Alexander could have killed the APC with his machine gun, but hindsight is 20-20). The super dense dart pushed aside 14 millimeters of rolled steel, vaporizing the metal in close proximity to it as well as a small amount of metal from its tip. Once the incandescent steel and uranium hit the open air of the crew compartment it oxidized, combusting everything in the APC at a temperature not too much cooler than the surface of the Sun. This inferno only lasted for the briefest of instants as the pressure in the vehicle surged, then plummeted as the sabot round traveled about 15 feet to the back of the APC and exited, creating a tremendous vacuum in its wake that sucked out much of the carbonized members of the crew. All that remained of the crew was three sets of charred boots if anyone cared to look inside after the burning hull cooled down. As the sound of the exploding APC reached the tank the shell casing hit the floor of the turret and clanged around noisily, ending up next to Peña and almost burning his left arm.

Peña pushed the shell away from his arm and glared at Jones, yelling above the din without using his CVC mike, "Aye! Jones, get that *chingadera* down you fuckin' idiot!" Peña jerked his left thumb over his shoulder.

Red-faced at forgetting to deploy the heavy cloth backstop that absorbed the initial energy of an ejecting round and kept it from bouncing around the inside of the tank, Jones moved to untie it.

Alexander would have preferred engaging the APC with a HEAT (High Explosive, Anti-Tank) round but common practice was to always have a more powerful armor-piercing fin-stabilized discarding sabot-tracer (sabot, for short) round in the breach and ready to go. Using a depleted uranium "Staballoy" sabot round against an APC was a waste and if the round hit a non-vulnerable spot, it might have passed harmlessly through the vehicle.

Jones tugged at one of the backstop's straps when Alexander saw movement to the right. He swung the turret to the right and lined up the gun with the target. This time he yelled with a little less urgency and a little more professionalism, "Gunner! HEAT! APC!"

This APC was almost a mile away at the end of the runway to the east. Peña lased the target with the AN/GVS-5 laser rangefinder. The tank's computer took the information from the laser and calculated the distance to the target. Other information was automatically fed into the computer and calculated as well: wind speed, direction and air density, the type of round and its trajectory, and the droop of the gun barrel due to repeated firings and or temperature. The tank did all this for its crew in less than a second, adjusting the barrel's elevation so that the round would impact within a few inches of where Sergeant Peña put the recticles.

Jones stopped what he was doing and smashed his right knee against the ammo compartment blast door knee switch. The door slid open, revealing almost half of the 50 rounds that were stored in the back of the M1's turret. Jones selected a HEAT round. He grabbed it by its base with his left hand, pulled it out, and flipped it over in one smooth motion, ramming the 40 pound round home up the breech and fluidly following through to avoid being caught by the quickly closing breachblock. Jones yelled, "Up!" and his knee came off of the knee switch, causing the door to slide shut in a second. It sounded like a vault door closing. It would easily sever a careless finger or hand left in its path.

Alexander was already scanning for his next target when he said, "Fire!"

Peña said, "On the way!"

The HEAT round burst out of the gun tube and arced towards

its target (HEAT rounds are much slower and heavier than sabot rounds). The HEAT round's spike and switch assembly (about a six inch long probe) struck the APC's sloped hull. This initiated an explosion in the conically shaped main charge. The explosion heated and compressed the charge's metal liner, forming a jet of metal moving at about 24 times the speed of sound. This round too was overkill for an APC's modest armor. The three crew members and anything else capable of being oxidized began to burn violently in less than a blink of an eye.

The 105mm shell casing bounced crazily around the crew compartment. Peña roared at Jones, "Shithead, I'm going to kill you!"

Jones reached for the dampener and finally untied it. It rolled down like a scroll and hung limp, ready to receive and temper the next blow from an ejecting shell casing.

Alexander reached up and pulled his commander's hatch shut. As his chest was exposed to the battlefield (nametag defilade as tankers call it), he again saw movement, this time to the left. He slammed the turret down over his head just as he saw the backblast of an anti-tank guided missile taking off and no doubt headed for *Traveller*. The operator of the wire guided missile with a large HEAT warhead barely had time to stabilize the missile's flight path and guide it to the target. The missile flew high and detonated against the wall of the terminal building 500 meters to the tank's rear.

Feeling calmer and more confident, Alexander decided to personally engage the thin-skinned APC that had just fired upon him and his crew. He telescoped the commander's hatch up a few inches to the "open protected" position and peered out of the crack. He lined his .50 caliber machine gun up to the target using one hand to spin the .50 cal around from the safety of inside the tank. Using a hand dial, he lowered the machine gun's elevation and pulled the dial. The heavy machine gun rewarded him with a steady beat of four rounds per second. He fired low and to the right. One slight adjustment and his rounds hit home. Many of the half-inch thick rounds penetrated the armor, wounding the driver and killing the TC. The incendiary rounds soon set the APC smoldering. Flames soon began to shoot out of the vehicle, resting not ten feet from its still burning cousin. Alexander clenched his jaw, *there, that made up for the wasted sabot round.*

He looked around for another target. He looked into his tank thermal sight (TTS) tube picture tube and started scanning at x3 power. *There, what's that, just to the left of the burning APC at the end of the runway just beneath the lip of the apron?* Alexander flipped the TTS to x10 power and looked again. The smooth arc of a turret top, its outline broken by its heavy machine gun mount, revealed itself as white hot against a cooler black background in the super heat sensitive scope. The TTS' incessantly chattering cooling system coursed liquid nitrogen through its veins to cool its sensors and optics. It could detect temperature differences of less than one degree Fahrenheit. Just as he was confirming his suspicions about an enemy tank trying to creep up to a hull down position (a position from which the tank's hull is protected, usually by terrain, and only its turret shows—making for a very small target), Alexander saw the heat signatures of two more tanks roll up to the right. "Gunner, sabot, three tanks, left tank first!" the colonel called.

Jones clicked open the blast door, grabbed one round and slammed it home. He clicked his mike on and said, "Up!" The blast door closed.

Alexander said, "Fire!"

Peña lased, called, "On the way!" and squeezed the trigger.

Knowing there were other tanks out there, as soon as Peña fired, Jones opened the blast door and reloaded, saying, "Up!"

The crew was calming down and moving towards a deadly efficiency. Training and adrenaline began to grip the four men. After 90 seconds of combat, the American tankers had fired their main gun eight times and used the .50 caliber once. Three Chinese tanks and five APCs lay burning as testimony to the Americans' speed and accuracy. Other than some scratched paint from a few machine gun rounds, the M1 was untouched.

*   *   *

The mood in the Situation Room was somber. CNN had just broadcast to the world images of an American tank utterly destroying several Chinese armored vehicles. The speed and violence of the action was overwhelming. The room was silent. When the phone rang, several people, including the President, jumped. Someone handed the phone to Lindley, whispering in the key advisor's ear as he did so.

"Mr. President, it's Han Wudi, the President of China on the line. He has an interpreter." The President nodded to Lindley and pointed at the speaker box.

Someone turned down the TV. CNN had lost the live signal from Taiwan and was now playing the recent military footage over again.

An angry Chinese voice came over the speaker box. Donna listened carefully, understanding every word. The Chairman of the Communist Party of the People's Republic of China was talking down to the leader of the free world. *This is not a good sign,* Donna thought.

The translator began, "I demand that American forces illegally on sovereign Chinese soil immediately surrender. Anything less is unacceptable. Do you understand?"

The President was silent. His gaze shifted from the speaker box to the war scenes on TV. The M1, Old Glory snapping in the breeze above the tank, dispatched another enemy tank in the third repeat of the 90-second segment.

More angry words spat forth from the box. Donna's eyebrows arched. Chairman Han was in a rage. The translator enthusiastically intoned, "China demands the immediate unconditional surrender of American forces illegally interfering in our domestic affairs. You will pay a stiff price for continued resistance!"

The President heard his Chinese counterpart. As the savvy leader of a democratic republic, he knew that he faced a far greater menace than an incensed Chinese dictator: the American public. Were he to order a surrender now after the images on CNN of the American tank victoriously destroying Chinese armor, he'd be run out of office and his hand-picked successor defeated at the polls in half a year. "Mr. President," he said slowly to the Chinese leader, "Let me get back to you on that." And very deliberately, he hung up the phone.

Bob Lindley's eyes were as round as saucers.

Donna smiled approvingly from behind her clasped hands.

Ten minutes later the first focus group results came in followed quickly by the White House polling unit's InstaPoll numbers: the American people strongly supported military action against China by 73% to 19% with 8% undecided. Donna shook her head. *I wonder what the numbers would have been if the American tank was destroyed on the first shot?*

*   *   *

Lieutenant Colonel Dan Alexander did a quick 360-degree scan using the TTS on three-power. He scanned again using his eyes from under the safety of the commander's hatch. Nothing was visible except the burning hulks of his enemy. "Jones, cross-level some ammo ASAP! I'm going to have a quick look around."

Alexander pulled his hatch down to the locking position then swung it open on its thick hinge.

The loader immediately got to work taking rounds from the ammo compartment behind the gunner (where they were very hard to get to in combat) and transferring them to the compartment he just took the six rounds from a couple of minutes before.

Alexander hopped off the tank and swept his gaze from building to building, looking for any of his Task Force Grizzly soldiers. He saw the news reporter's small satellite communications unit with its stubby omnidirectional antenna still on the ground near his tank. The tanker saw a patch of color next to a Boeing 737 landing gear assembly—*there they are.* He walked towards a small jet aircraft that was parked on the taxiway about 50 meters away. "You guys all right?"

Edward Wong stepped out from behind the jet's landing gear, "Yes. I believe we are. Is it safe?"

Alexander seemed strangely calmed by the recent action, "No, I expect we just destroyed their forward security element. In a few minutes I would expect many, many more—and artillery. You should find overhead cover right now. You won't last two seconds out here when the artillery starts falling."

"Thank you. We will seek shelter. What will you do?"

"Keep fighting, stay alive. I have nowhere else to go. Any help or evacuation will come through this airport." Alexander paused, "Are you still filming?"

"Yes, we are remoting our signal to the commo box. My cameraman says we just reestablished our connection, although I still can't hear CNN headquarters." The reporter, realizing he had fallen out of character during the fighting straightened himself and said, "This is Edward Wong with CNN. You have just seen an amazing sight as the American Army here in Taiwan destroyed about ten enemy tanks in less than two minutes. You can see the tanks burning brightly in the background."

Seeing the reporter had recovered enough of his senses to function, Alexander waved and said, "God bless America! I love you honey!" He turned and walked back to *Traveller.* He wished he could have known for sure that the signal was getting out. He constantly scanned the north and east sides of the airport. Alexander knew his troops were probably safe. He told everyone except the scouts to stay inside and cover the tank's rear, keeping any infantry off the more vulnerable backside of the tank. He heard one of his Humvees rev up. A second later it appeared from under an overhang next to the passenger terminal and sped up to him. "Everyone okay?"

"Hoo-Wah!" First Lieutenant Robby Mundell, the scout platoon leader, grunted cheerfully. He was a recent addition to the California Army National Guard from the great state of Texas. He worked for the federal government as a DEA agent when he wasn't practicing being a soldier on the weekends (his job transferred him out to California half a year ago). "Sir, you done opened up a Texas-sized can of whoop-ass on the enemy bastards!"

Alexander laughed, then smacked the young officer playfully on the side of his helmet.

"Hey, sir, look what someone gave us in the terminal." The lieutenant held up a pair of small brightly colored plastic two-way radios, "They're a pair of those little Motorola radios like we used during AT (Annual Training). They work fine. I bet we could communicate a mile or two away with these!"

Alexander smiled and shook his head approvingly at the scout platoon leader, "Looks like you're in business again, trooper." He reached out and took one of the radios. "Mundell, take your skinny ass out there and check on your other vehicle, I saw them pop a star cluster at first contact. Once you find them, go reestablish contact with the enemy and report back. Don't be a hero—we aren't getting any replacements anytime soon. Take some of the MPs with you. I expect that we'll see about a company of tanks and a battalion of 'mech' backed up by some self-propelled artillery in about five to ten minutes. I hope that will be all the enemy brings with them. We don't have any more ammo other than what we have on board. If more come and we run dry, I want you to take charge of the advance party and move out to Yangminshan Park as we previously planned."

Mundell was suddenly serious, "Yes sir. That was really good shootin' you did." He turned to his driver, "Let's go!"

Alexander watched the three scouts roar off in their Humvee— the lieutenant, his driver, and the .50 caliber machine gunner suspended from a webbed seat of nylon secured to the roll cage.

*   *   *

Back at the White House the Situation Room was filled with silent men and one woman. Most had conflicting emotions. On one hand, the Americans did very well against the Chinese on national, no *international* television—on the other hand, the Americans did well against the Chinese. This presented the White House with a huge problem. The Chinese wanted the Americans out of the way. They wanted free reign in Taiwan.

Due to a variety of unforeseen circumstances, America's leadership found themselves confronting a very angry enemy on terms and timing not of American choosing. It would be at least two days before the first attack sub could be in place to interdict Chinese shipping. Beyond that, the nearest aircraft carrier battlegroup was a week away with reinforcements another week beyond that. America had few options—an early commitment to combat was a nightmare for the Administration. Now, the very public display of American resistance to the Chinese aggression put the policy makers in an even tougher spot. A retreat or surrender would be seriously questioned by the American public and might erode support for any further action.

Continued resistance, if unsuccessful, would embolden the Chinese and demoralize the public anyway. They were damned either way. To top it off, the Chinese wanted a quick answer to their surrender demands.

The President turned to Lindley, "Bob, we need to send a negotiating team to Taiwan to deal with this crisis immediately. The team needs to be high enough ranking to deal on equal terms with the Chinese, but not so high that we risk embarrassment. The Chinese will accept a team of three. Who do we send?"

Lindley looked at his boss, "I think I should go as your personal representative. . ."

The President thoughtful demeanor seemed only a bit dulled by his lack of sleep, "Yes. Yes! And General Taylor can go as the chief military representative. Perfect!" General Taylor looked up from the table, resigned to the fate his C-in-C was giving him. "Who else?"

"How about Maus?" Lindley asked.

Taylor regarded the young staffer with a poker face. The President's eyes drilled into the table just in front of his resting hands. "No."

Donna was uncomfortable with the real-time creation of the

negotiating team in front of team's potential members.

Taylor cleared his throat, "How about Donna Klein?" Most everyone in the room looked at the analyst with surprise. Lindley raised an eyebrow and turned to whisper in the President's ear. The President nodded. The President pushed himself back from the table and got up, making his way up the narrow set of stairs to the hallway above.

Lindley addressed Donna, "Ms. Klein, can we see you in the hallway for a moment?" Lindley got up and walked upstairs.

The confined spaces of the Situation Room made it difficult for Donna to get quickly upstairs. Her heart raced as she picked her way through the tangle of legs and chairs. *I hope everything's okay. What could possibly be wrong?*

She got to the top of the stairs and saw the President and his National Security Council Advisor standing there, shoulder-to-shoulder. Lindley spoke first, "Ms. Klein, I don't think you should go to Taiwan with the negotiating team. You don't have enough experience."

The President's face betrayed a bit of hesitancy with Lindley's words. Donna took the offensive immediately, "I respectfully disagree. Thousands of more senior analysts failed to see this coming. I did. I think I know China's objectives—how they'll act. I'm the woman for the job." Donna's face was firm and confident. She looked straight at the President. He looked straight back at her, weighing his trust in the young CIA analyst.

The President's gaze turned into a stare. He frowned and examined his fingernails for a moment, "Bob, I have to overrule you on this one. I still want Ms. Klein to go with you. I like her fire. The three of you will make a balanced team. Besides, she speaks fluent Chinese. If we can only send three people, you, Donna, and General Taylor are the three to send. . ."

Lindley started to protest.

The President put his hand on his aide's shoulder, "Look Bob, my mind is made up on this one. I have to trust my instincts. I didn't get to be President by always following advice." The President smiled at Donna.

She never really liked the man—as a leader or as a person—but at that instant, she found herself engaged by his presence and his charm—and the fact that he overruled Lindley to make her part of the team. "Thank you Mr. President, I won't let America down."

*   *   *

Jones had just topped off the ammo compartment and tossed the seven empty shell casings out of the turret when Alexander climbed back on the tank. Alexander grabbed the antenna with the flag on it and untied it. *No sense in advertising our position now that we know the Chinese want to fight.* The commander connected his CVC helmet to the tank's intercom system. "Driver, take us down to the end of the runway to the position we have there. Stay on the grass."

Specialist Hernandez spun up the turbine engine and eased into gear. *Traveller* leapt from its muddy, shallow hole and smoothly closed the distance between its old fighting position and the one a mile to the east. Alexander was always amazed at just how fast and nimble a 60-ton M1 tank could be. The tank slowly rocked back and forth as it sped up to 40 mph, leaving a rooster tail of mud and churned up grass behind it.

Alexander unzipped his chemical protective suit a few inches and reached into his left breast pocket, pulling out the call sign cheat sheet. He palmed the little radio, "Sidewinder Five Niner, Sidewinder Five Niner, this is Thunderbolt X-ray, over."

"This is Sidewinder Five Niner, over."

"Give me your status and location, over." The little radio's reception was crisp and easily audible above the whine and clanking of the tank.

Lieutenant Mundell reported back, "I found my other scouts. They're okay. I'm attaching one MP vehicle to each scout vehicle. I'll visually control the other scout section. That gives me six Humvees total. I'm in an alleyway running into the north side of the airport, just about lined up on the center of the runway. I've seen about ten lightly armed Taiwanese security forces. I don't see any enemy and I can't hear any vehicles except for probably yours, over."

"Roger, I'm heading for the east end of the runway. Recon Pingchiang Street and the bridge over the Keelung Ho River. I'll be able to watch the Sun Yat-Sen Bridge. Report first contact, out."

As they approached the other end of the runway, Alexander heard what sounded faintly like a freight train overhead. Behind him the earth erupted in dirt and fire—artillery! He slammed his hatch shut and pushed it back up to the open protected position.

The tank splashed into its easternmost pit (earlier in the day it rained at least an inch, if not more) and settled in. The tank's profile was almost cut in half. Most importantly, its most vulnerable components, its treads, were safe behind a wall of dirt.

Alexander set to scanning about his new position. He did a 360 in the evening light with his eyes, then took control of the turret and swung it around, looking through the TTS on three-power magnification. What he saw next made his blood run cold. Atop the Sun Yat-Sen Bridge there were two tanks and an APC. The APC had a thin, long gun tube—probably a rapid-fire 30mm gun like the one on the American Bradley IFV (Infantry Fighting Vehicle). The vehicles were moving west, closing diagonally on his position from right to left. They careened in and out of the abandoned cars clogging the bridge, occasionally clipping some or pushing them out of the way. Just behind and hovering above the tanks he saw two helicopters, probably armored HIND-D helicopters carrying an array of anti-tank weapons. As the lead tank disappeared behind the freeway embankment, presumably taking the off ramp to the airport, another rapidly moving tank took its place on the far side of the bridge.

"Sidewinder Five Niner, Sidewinder Five Niner, this is Thunderbolt X-ray, over."

"Go ahead Thunderbolt X-ray."

"You've got two tanks coming from behind you off the Sun Yat-Sen Freeway, over."

"Roger, I can hear 'em."

"Stay low. Thunderbolt X-ray, out."

More artillery struck a mile behind the American tank. This time, instead of the basic point detonation rounds that tear up the ground, the enemy had switched to the much more sophisticated and deadly DPICM round (Dual Purpose Improved Conventional Munition). DPICM is a terrifying tool of modern warfare. Instead of containing one large warhead, a DPICM round disperses dozens of little HEAT rounds on streamers. They kill two ways: if they strike the ground, they blow up, acting as grenades, if they strike the thin armor at the top of a tank or APC, they burn through the armor and usually destroy or disable the vehicle. Two aircraft were on fire now at the other end of the airport, including one of the C-17s. Alexander thought about the artillery barrage, *the enemy still thinks we're back there, between the brief communications they received from the vehicles we killed and the images that UAV sent back before we shot it down—good, maybe this will give us the advantage of surprise for a moment.*

"Gunner, sabot, two helicopters, right helicopter first!"

Alexander decided to down the trailing helicopter. Their wire-guided anti-tank weapons threatened the thinner top portions of his armor. Moreover, the helicopters would serve the enemy as valuable observation platforms. His survival hinged on stealth and speed. He couldn't afford to have the helicopters reporting his position like the police and news choppers did back home during the innumerable LA freeway chases seen on local TV.

Fortunately, one of the best ways to kill a helicopter was with a tank main gun sabot round. The sabot dart traveled so fast and with such a flat trajectory, that hitting an exposed helicopter was no more difficult than hitting a moving tank.

Peña found his target immediately, flipped the TTS to x10 power, and lased the rotary wing aircraft to determine its distance.

Jones stuffed a sabot round in the breach and called, "Up!" He grabbed another sabot round while the ammo blast door was open and cradled it between his knees—with two helicopters airborne he wanted to be able to load the gun a couple of seconds faster.

"Fire!"

"On the way!" Peña pulled the trigger and, without waiting for results, switched to three-power, found the other helicopter, narrowed the field of view back to ten-power, and lased.

Jones yelled, "Up!" in record time—at 19, the youngest member of the crew was still very hyped.

Alexander watched as the first helicopter keeled over and headed for the ground. He could see no smoke or evidence of damage. "Fire," the command was almost routine now.

"On the way!" Peña fired, and in less than one second, the sabot round struck the other helicopter square in its left engine. The shot tore apart the turbine. The combination of burning metal and fuel generated a fireball that consumed the entire aircraft. Just as this airborne fireball was heading earthward, its twin rose up from the ground just to its right. The two infernos passed each other. Both helicopters had been dispatched.

Alexander turned his attention to the bridge. The second tank was almost off the bridge and would likely dip out of sight in a few seconds. The APC would follow less than ten seconds later. He decided to get the APC, then the third tank. With luck, he could choke off the bridge, or at least make traversing it a slower process. "Gunner, HEAT, APC," the commander called.

Peña smoothly went through the motions.

Jones grabbed the appropriate round of ammo and slammed it home. The breach snapped shut with a satisfying metallic sound.

Jones barked, "Up!"

"Fire."

"On the way."

The HEAT round sped out and hit the Russian-designed and built BMP-2 tracked infantry fighting vehicle square in the flank. The warhead devastated the lightly armored vehicle, killing the three crew and seven infantrymen inside.

The Abrams tank now had three shell casings loose on the floor of its turret. The acrid smell of burnt propellant was once again filling the air. The tank crew was now one with each other and with the tank. Each crewman performed his job with little thought—to think meant delay, delay meant death. This precision was the result of intense military training, drill, repetition and discipline—all of those things a free society finds distasteful about the military. Paradoxically, it was by sacrificing a bit of their freedom that these soldiers were capable of defending freedom for themselves and their fellow citizens.

From his open protected position just underneath his partially raised hatch Alexander called out the next fire command, "Gunner, sabot, tank."

Jones opened the blast door, grabbed a sabot round by its base, and rammed it home. He clicked on his intercom, "Up!"

"Fire."

"On the way."

There were now two large fires on the bridge, one at the near end and one in the middle. Combined with the smoke of the burning helicopters, the evening battlefield was growing darker. Alexander wished for nighttime—a dark, cloudy night where his advanced TTS would give him a huge advantage over his opponents—*if we can't be seen, we can't be killed—easily*.

The laser warning signal went off. Alexander saw movement at the far end of the bridge a mile away. He sealed his hatch shut and scanned the bridge with the TTS. Just above the cement guardrail he saw a tank turret. "Gunner, sabot, tank."

Jones began to load the 105mm gun.

Suddenly, the image on the TTS blossomed white. Alexander knew that he was the only American on the battlefield to have an anti-tank capability, unless the Taiwanese were shooting at the tank, this could only mean one thing. . .

A second after the thermal image of the tank was momentarily obscured, a piercing, horrible sound grated against the outside of the tank, causing the massive vehicle to jump, then vibrate briefly like a struck gong. A Chinese Type 85-II tank with its 125mm main gun fired a sabot round at the American tank. The shot hit the Abrams on the front of its turret, where the thickness of the armor had the equivalent effectiveness of more than three feet of steel. The Chinese tungsten dart impacted *Traveller* and deflected just enough to cause the dart's long, thin shaft to shatter. The fragments hurdled onto the tank's exterior, gouging small holes in the metal surface.

Jones only hesitated for an instant. In the back of his mind he knew they had been hit. He also knew that he was still alive and had a job to do. Modern tank warfare is violent and sudden. Until he was killed or injured, he'd stay at his station and load his gun. "Up!" Jones cried with the grin of a teenager who has just realized he cheated death and once again feels like he just might be invincible.

Peña ranged the enemy tank. On one level, he simply went through the steps he knew so well. On another level, his brain processed the fact that they had been hit and that, so far as he could tell, all their systems were still functional—for this, he was thankful. If they had lost a system, the laser rangefinder for instance, he would have compensated for it automatically, without thought. "On the way!"

The American sabot round with its extremely hard depleted uranium bolt shot out and struck the Chinese tank on the front of its turret in the same general spot as the Chinese tank had hit its enemy. There, all similarity of outcome ended. The superior American ordinance impacted the inferior Chinese armor (armor that was adequate by regional standards but wasn't nearly as advanced as that sported by the M1). The metal dart penetrated through the bolted-on reactive armor boxes (meant only to defeat HEAT rounds and anti-tank missiles) and began to push aside the case hardened steel. When it reached the hard but brittle ceramic laminate, it simply pulverized it and drove on, only somewhat dented for the effort. Once the dart reached the last of the armor, it had shed many flakes of now white-hot uranium. When this material reached the tank's crew compartment the result was spectacular, if predictable. The overpressure caused by the rapidly expanding gasses in the exploding tank caused the fifteen ton turret gun assembly to pop off the tank's hull, up and over the bridge's guard rail, and go crashing down to the river bank below.

Before being destroyed, the Chinese tank commander did manage to radio his battalion commander and advise him of the enemy tank and its location. The commander's attached battery of six self-propelled 122mm howitzers was just coming to a halt on a secondary school playfield about three kilometers away. When called, they would be able to suppress or kill the enemy armor.

Alexander considered his situation. He knew the enemy had artillery support—fairly quick responding and accurate artillery support. He also knew the enemy had another bridge they could cross just a kilometer down river from the Sun Yat-Sen Bridge. This bridge was not visible from his current location but he knew his scouts were there. Finally, the enemy had managed to cross at least two tanks on to his side of the river. While his small contingent of scouts and MPs might manage to keep enemy infantry off of his tank if he pulled them back in, he knew that by himself from his current location, he could not keep enemy armor and artillery off of them. It was time for bold action. "Driver! Guide on the gun, move out!"

Specialist Hernandez launched *Traveller* out of its shallow hole and simply followed the direction that the gun tube pointed. Colonel Alexander threw open his hatch and went to name tag defilade. Speed would be his primary means of protection now— and while traveling 20 to 40 mph through city streets, he needed more visibility than he could get with the hatch closed.

"Sidewinder Five Niner, Thunderbolt X-ray, over."

The little radio's response was barely perceptible, "This is Sidewinder Five Niner, over." Mundell was whispering.

"Sidewinder Five Niner, I'm heading north alongside the river bank. I'm going to pass under the bridge. What's your situation, over?"

"My vehicles are just south of the freeway embankment, I'm dismounted with some of my crew under the freeway overpass on Pingchiang Street. I see two tanks covering for a least a company of BMPs that are coming up in a coil about 300 meters north of the freeway. They're moving off of Pingchiang Street bridge. I don't see the infantry dismounting yet, over."

Alexander narrowed his eyes in concentration, "Roger. You have any smoke grenades?"

"I've two, a purple and a green."

"Pop them and toss them out in front of you on the street right now! I'm coming in and I want a diversion. Get back to your vehicles. After you hear the first few main gun rounds I want you to get on the freeway and suppress the infantry with your .50 cals and grenade launchers from behind the guardrail. Do you understand? Over."

"Yes sir!"

"Thunderbolt out." Alexander took a deep breath and let the radio dangle from his wrist on its strap. "Driver, stop under the bridge. Loader, do we have a sabot round up?"

Jones replied, "Yes sir."

"Okay everyone, listen up. The Scouts report that there's at least two tanks and a company of 'mech' out there about two to three hundred meters to our left front. The infantry hasn't dismounted yet. We're going to destroy the two tanks first, Jones, get another sabot round ready, then we're going to engage the APCs with HEAT rounds. Peña, once the tanks are down, I'm going to suppress the APCs with my .50. I want you to fire at will then. If I see a more dangerous target I'll let you know. Hernandez, we'll stay as close to the bridge as we can and still engage the enemy, if we have to come out from under the bridge to kill them, I want you to move parallel to the river bank at about ten miles per hour. Everyone understand?"

"Roger," Peña spoke.

"Yes sir," Hernandez sounded confident.

"Ready sir," Jones looked up at his commander while cradling the 105mm sabot round he would shove into the breach as soon as the gun fired.

"All right then, let's go! Driver, move out 20 meters then guide left until I say halt." Alexander could hear the APC cannon and machine gun fire. The Chinese were reacting to the sudden appearance of Mundell's smoke grenades. The tank edged up to the lip of the river's bank, "Halt!" *Perfect*. With *Traveller's* gun tube on stab, it was already depressed, lowering the profile of the tank. The only portion of the tank that was visible from the enemy's vantage was the 105mm gun, the two machine guns on the roof, and Alexander.

The TC quickly found the first tank and jinked the turret to the left to line up the gun with the target. He began the familiar litany, "Gunner, sabot, two tanks, left tank first, fire!"

Peña didn't need to lase or switch to ten-power—the enemy was too close for that, "On the way!"

The sabot round penetrated the Chinese tank in the left side of its hull. It immediately burst into flames and began exploding as the ammunition inside of it began to cook off.

Jones yelled, "Up!"

Peña pulled the gun to the right. The Chinese tank was already swinging its turret to face the Americans. Puffs of smoke appeared on both sides of the tank's turret and in an instant it was obscured in a thick cloud of smoke. The smoke blotted out the TTS image.

Alexander called, "Gunner, sabot, tank, fire!"

Peña was sure he had already lined up the gun to hit the enemy tank. Unless it already moved out, he would hit it, "On the way!" He squeezed the trigger just as the Chinese tank charged out of the smoke.

The round hit the side of the turret with a shower of sparks. Inside the tank, hundreds of metal flakes knocked loose by the shot peppered the gunner, blinding him. The Chinese crew was stunned but not dead.

"Gunner, HEAT, APCs, fire at will!"

"Up!"

Alexander set to work with his .50 caliber heavy machine gun. *Traveller's* muzzle flashed as a HEAT round reached out to its target. A BMP-2 exploded in a ball of flames. The muzzle flash hurt his eyes, even from behind his goggles, but he knew it was much better behind the flash than in front of it. He saw some infantry come boiling out of the BMPs, seeking cover and orienting themselves on their enemy. Small explosions tore at their ranks and several fell from an invisible hand. Alexander grunted to himself—the Scouts and MPs had now gone to work.

The tank's gun erupted again, and once more they were rewarded with a burning enemy vehicle. Alexander heard the sting of bullets rip the air around him. "Driver, move out. Stay on the river's bank."

The tank's gun remained locked in place, perfectly stabilized, even as the tank moved out at a 15-degree tilt along the river's edge. Motion offered some protection to the TC. Alexander weighed going to open protected but rejected it. He needed to see and was willing to accept the risk. Alexander heard DPICM rounds impacting behind him near the edge of the airport less than half a mile away.

The tank moved north, then crossed over Pingchiang Street and followed the river's path as it looped back around to the southwest. After two minutes of action, the tank fired a dozen rounds and hit a dozen vehicles. The broken bodies of the enemy infantry littered the compact killing ground. Some soldiers raised their hands in surrender. Alexander picked up the portable radio, "Sidewinder, Sidewinder, we have enemy trying to surrender in here!" No response. "Sidewinder, Sidewinder, do you copy?"

"This is Sidewinder, go ahead Thunderbolt."

"Sidewinder, I see about 20 enemy infantry trying to surrender. I'm going to drive slowly towards them and push them up your way, get the MPs ready to secure them. Have them march them down to the airport and turn them over to the security forces there."

"I don't like this sir. It's too dangerous."

"I'll be buttoned-up. They don't have anything that can kill the tank from close in. Just cover my rear and make sure no one shoves an RPG up my ass."

"Roger," a reluctant lieutenant said.

Alexander pulled the hatch shut above him, "Driver, move out at a walking speed to the south." He began slewing the turret back and forth slowly. Within five minutes they rounded up 26 dazed Chinese infantrymen, half were wounded. The six MPs in their two Humvees led them off on Pingchiung Street under the freeway overpass towards the nearby airport.

Alexander noticed his knees were beginning to shake and that he was getting a bad headache. His mouth was tremendously dry. He reached inside the turret for his web gear and canteens, found one and drained the quart of water in one long gulp. He went back on the vehicle intercom, "Everyone take a water break, we've been in some hard fighting. Good job men. Damn good job!"

*   *   *

In small city of Hsichih, midway between the Taiwanese port city of Keelung and Taipei, the commander of the 12th Tank Division was simultaneously pleased and disturbed. He had much to be pleased with. Since landing the 93 tanks and 45 infantry fighting vehicles of the 121st Tank Regiment at noon, he had quickly assembled them and moved them to the outskirts of Taipei, losing only three BMPs in the process to a Taiwanese tank platoon. His forces destroyed one enemy tank and the other two beat a hasty retreat to the northwest.

A few minutes before 1700 hours, with the other two regiments of his division now landing at Keelung, he decided to send a reconnaissance-in-force into Taipei with the limited mission of capturing Taipei's airport to deny its use to the enemy. The area around the airport was open enough that he wasn't worried about getting bogged down into house-to-house fighting with his mechanized forces. Further, if the enemy perceived a threat to his capital, it would make his true task—a link up with elements of the 10th Tank Division in the vicinity of Hsintien eight kilometers south of Taipei—all the easier. With the battalion at Sungshan Airport, the remainder of the 121st Tank Regiment would then be able to roll down Highway 3, skirting the eastern edge of Taipei with little fear of a Taiwanese counterattack.

Within two hours his plan was proceeding well. The lead elements of his main effort had already made it to the Taipei suburb of Musha and the town of Shenkeng two klicks to the east. Hsintien was only seven kilometers southwest of his armored spearhead making him 12 hours ahead of schedule (his armor was to arrive at Hsintien no later than noon tomorrow and link up with the 1st Airborne Division which was to begin dropping onto the city early tomorrow morning).

Meanwhile, the supporting effort had just reported reaching the bridges on the Keelung Ho. Sungshan Airport was in sight at the cost of only three BMPs from the combat reconnaissance patrol (knocked out by a solitary Taiwanese M60A3 tank that retreated to the northwest as the Chinese armor began to arrive). Then, chaos descended on the battalion. Within minutes, the battalion's forward security element reported sighting a platoon of tanks— American tanks, flying American flags! The battalion commander lost contact with his forward security element in only two minutes. The general suspected the Americans were at the airport in greater numbers than the forward security element reported and called his commander, the chief of the 12th Group Army, to tell him so.

The 12th Group Army commander called him a coward and assured him that the Americans couldn't possibly be on the island (but, just in case, he called PLA command in Beijing and demanded reinforcements to contend with the American threat). The 12th Group Army chief then ordered him to take the remainder of the battalion he committed to take the airport and finish the job before nightfall—hence his discomfort. In war, a thousand praises can be wiped clean by one failure. He listened intently as the battalion's main body approached the airport. With 28 Type 85-II tanks, 11 BMP-2s, and six 122mm self-propelled howitzers, he knew this was a force to contend with. Monitoring the battalion's radio net he was shocked to hear the battalion's mechanized infantry company team get annihilated in less than ten minutes.   The intelligence map displayed the sightings of American M1 tanks. A platoon at the center of the airport, another two tanks at the east end of the airport, still more north of the Sun Yat-Sen Freeway—at least a company of heavy American armor!

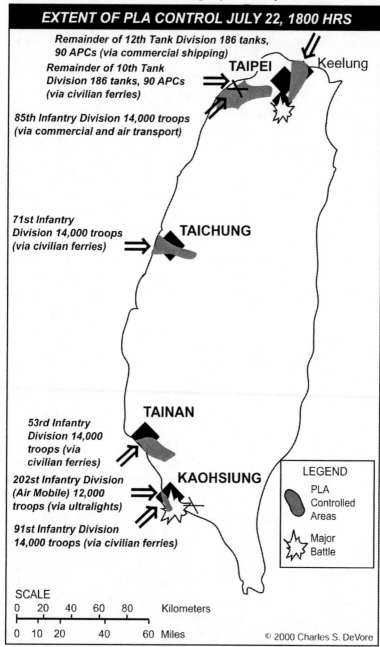

EXTENT OF PLA CONTROL JULY 22, 1800 HRS

Remainder of 12th Tank Division 186 tanks, 90 APCs (via commercial shipping)

Remainder of 10th Tank Division 186 tanks, 90 APCs (via civilian ferries)

85th Infantry Division 14,000 troops (via commercial and air transport)

TAIPEI

Keelung

71st Infantry Division 14,000 troops (via civilian ferries)

TAICHUNG

TAINAN

53rd Infantry Division 14,000 troops (via civilian ferries)

202st Infantry Division (Air Mobile) 12,000 troops (via ultralights)

KAOHSIUNG

91st Infantry Division 14,000 troops (via civilian ferries)

LEGEND

PLA Controlled Areas

Major Battle

SCALE

0   20   40   60   80   Kilometers

0   10   20   40   60   Miles

© 2000 Charles S. DeVore

The PLA attacks to cut-off Taipei

This was far more than his remaining two tank companies could be expected to handle, yet. . . there was the 12th Group Army commander to deal with.

*   *   *

Alexander's knees were still shaking, although now somewhat less. He was slightly nauseated too—he knew he downed his canteen too fast. The Chinese prisoners and wounded had been rounded up and he was about to head back towards the Keelung Ho and pass under the Sun Yat-Sen freeway bridge when he caught movement out of his left eye. It was one of the Chinese tanks only 50 yards away! As its turret was rotating towards him, Alexander dropped inside his tank in what seemed like a maddening eternity. He grabbed the turret control and jerked the turret around to face the threat, he used his other hand to steady himself and wasn't able to use the intercom. He screamed, "Gunner, sabot, tank!"

Peña, still cradling his canteen of water, spilled it in his lap as he seized the control yoke.

Jones yelled, "We have a HEAT round loaded."

Alexander roared, "Fire! Fire the damn thing!"

The enemy tank fired, its sabot round hit the American tank square on the front of the turret and penetrated through four inches of armor before stopping. The reverberating *clang* was brutally loud.

Peña called out, "On the way!"

The breach slammed back and nicked Jones's protective suit, tearing a small hole in the hip, "Shit!" The young soldier realized how close he came to getting his hips pulverized.

The HEAT round exploded against the enemy tank with tremendous sound and fury. The tank's bolt-on reactive armor did its job, however, and the shot's only effect was to shake up the enemy crew. Reactive armor, pioneered by the Israelis and the Russians, is a fairly cheap way to harden tanks against HEAT-type rounds. Reactive armor is a small metal box with sensitive explosives inside. Dozens of them can be bolted onto the side of a tank. When a HEAT round triggers the box (no other type of ammo will), it explodes outward, disrupting the shaped jet of super hot and dense metal formed by the HEAT round. Once triggered, however, it leaves a vulnerable spot where the box and its nearby

303

companions are blown free of the tank.

Alexander, knowing that the HEAT round probably didn't do the job yelled, "Gunner, reengage, sabot, fire at will! Driver, pull left and face the tank. Go! Go! Go!"

The Chinese tank crew, now down to two men since the gunner was blinded earlier in the battle (the Type 85-II tank had an auto loader so the tank only had a three man crew) shook off the HEAT round's impact (with the gunner out of commission, the TC took his place while the gunner sat uselessly at the TC's station). The TC selected another sabot round and depressed his gun tube, aiming for the more vulnerable flank of the M1's hull.

Jones opened the blast door, grabbed a sabot round and slammed it home. He got out of the way and yelled "Up!"

The Chinese gunner was dismayed to see the M1's hull pivoting around. He raised his gun tube and aimed for the vulnerable turret ring (the spot where the turret meets the hull). His autoloader finished ramming first the sabot round home, then the charge (unlike the American tank, his main gun did not eject a shell casing). He began to squeeze the trigger.

Happy with where he placed the last shot, Peña only slightly adjusted his aim to compensate for the just pivoted tank and yelled, "On the way!" as he pulled the trigger.

The American long rod penetrater poked its way through the Chinese armor and completely wrecked the interior of the enemy tank. A few seconds later the ammo started cooking off, confirming the kill before the American tank crew wasted another round on the tank.

Alexander felt bone tired, "Let's get out of here before his friends show up or the artillery starts falling. Hunting will be safer tonight." He grabbed the handheld commercial radio, "Sidewinder, Thunderbolt."

"You all right Thunderbolt? I heard some serious shootin' a few seconds ago." Mundell's southern accent was measure of home in a strange land.

"Yea, one of the tanks wasn't quite dead yet. You have those EPWs secured, over?"

"Roger. We even have our medics tending to them, over."

"Right, get your scouts out and cover the bridges. We need to conduct some maintenance." Alexander clicked off the transmitter and switched to the intercom, "Hernandez, take us back to the airport via the route under the bridge by the river. Move out fast."

The tankers closed on the airport. Alexander ordered Hernandez to pull *Traveller* into an aircraft hanger near the ACE dozer. The crew got out and stretched. Dan noticed a large wet spot on Peña's crotch, "So, the Chinese scared the piss out of you, eh?"

Peña looked down. Hernandez and Jones crowded to look at him. The gruff old sergeant said, "Oh, no sir! I spilled my canteen during that last engagement!"

Hernandez ribbed his senior NCO, "Sure, Sarge, we know you wet yourself. . ." he turned to the colonel, "Sir, does this mean he doesn't get any medals?"

Jones finally smiled, "If he doesn't get any, can I have his?"

Peña laughed, "Okay, okay, I pissed my pants—but tell anyone and I'll rip your heart out!"

Everyone laughed hard, then got to work preparing *Traveller* for a long night of work.

26
Ghosts

It was Sunday morning, July 22. Commercial and military Chinese aircraft had been landing follow-on forces at CKS for 22 hours now. Where only a battalion of commandos were the day before, some 34,000 infantry and 10,000 People's Armed Police paramilitaries were now concentrated.

The ROC Air Force was nowhere in sight. The one feeble airstrike the Taiwanese did try to mount was detected by one of the new Chinese airborne early warning aircraft (featuring an Israeli Elta Phalcon phased array radar on a Russian-built Il-76 cargo aircraft). The Chinese AWACS vectored fighter aircraft to intercept and destroy the attackers.

The only moments of true concern occurred a few hours before when the airport began to receive some artillery fire. PLA artillery and American-built counterbattery radar systems rapidly answered the enemy and silenced his artillery.

In spite of all this success, Lieutenant Colonel Chu Dugen felt little consolation. Instead of soaring at the height of his professional military career, Dugen's thoughts returned to his father and mother. His father: dead. His mother: languishing in a jail, probably in Lipu County. He thought of the reasons why his mother was in jail—his father's brave, but foolish stand against the Party's corruption and his mother's silent faith in something larger than herself, the Communist Party, or even China. He had never attended church with his mother—he never even knew she was a Christian until she told him during his last, brief visit home (although, in retrospect, he had his suspicions). Dugen pondered the words of the regimental political officer before he left for Hong Kong, "Do well in Taiwan and the State may show your mother leniency." He knew his mother and the God she held so dear would not approve of his actions—and yet, he had his military duty and honor to uphold. And, if the State wished to spare his mother because he simply did his duty to the best of his abilities, then so be it.

Dugen sighed and reported in to 10th Group Army headquarters in the basement of the modern CKS terminal. "Lieutenant Colonel Chu of Jia Commando Battalion reporting for orders." He announced himself in the operations center, saluting the senior colonel seated behind a commandeered civilian office desk. He glanced over the colonel, trying to observe one of the situation maps. A major general and a civilian, no doubt a Party official by the looks of his grooming, partially blocked his view.

The colonel stood up, and smiling, took Dugen's hand. Dugen was taken aback as the colonel shook his hand and said, "Excellent! Well done, Colonel Chu. I have orders here promoting you to colonel!" The senior colonel reached into his pocket and pulled out two new colonel's epaulettes, their three stars almost filling the length of the small pieces of cloth (the senior colonel's own four stars looked cramped for space by comparison). He then unbuttoned Dugen's epaulettes and replaced them with the new rank insignia.

"I was just performing my job, sir." Dugen felt a rush of conflicting emotions. He hadn't even been shot at and now he was getting promoted.

The major general by the map tapped the civilian on the shoulder and pointed at Dugen. Dugen was growing increasingly uncomfortable. He simply wanted to get his new orders and get back to his men.

The civilian stepped forward. "Congratulations Colonel. . ." he stopped, looking for the nametag which wasn't on the commando's uniform.

"Chu, sir. Colonel Chu."

The man paused briefly, "Congratulations Colonel Chu. I am Fu Zemin, the Senior Party Representative on Taiwan. On behalf of China and the Chinese Communist Party, I thank you for your commendable efforts."

"Thank you Comrade Fu. I will personally convey your thanks and the thanks of the Party to my men."

Fu and Dugen both thought of each other's last names. They both dismissed as highly improbable that they could be somehow connected by their fathers: counter-revolutionary assassin and heroic victim, aggrieved farmer and corrupt Party boss. Fu Zemin smiled, turned on his heels and went back to the map. Dugen exhaled.

"Sir, my orders?" Colonel Chu was now completely focused on the present.

A few minutes later Dugen had received an overview of the situation around Taipei (better than he thought it would be at this point in the campaign) as well as his mission. Using "requisitioned" civilian vehicles from the CKS International Airport parking lot his commandos would drive as far east as Taishan, securing key road junctions along the way. Taishan was a bedroom community of Taipei. It was situated on a low lying ridge only nine kilometers from the Tamsui Ho River which marked the western boundary of Taipei. From there Jia Battalion would report back to headquarters, take up defensive positions, and await further orders.

Dugen returned to his assembled battalion at the baggage claim area. He looked forward to the mental concentration required by military operations. Soon he would forget about his mother and the nagging doubts he had about his purpose in life.

*   *   *

Colonel Flint's Marines were exhausted and battered, but not defeated. After a full day of intense action, they dealt out more than enough punishment to make the enemy wish they never saw another US Marine again. More importantly, they happened to be in the right place at the right time to completely frustrate China's finely tuned invasion plans—at least in the region around Kaohsiung.

The Marines' success in blunting China's early efforts at taking Taiwan's largest port gave the local defenders valuable time to recover. That night they launched a determined attack and retook the beaches from the Mainlanders. By the morning light, only sporadic pockets of Chinese resistance remained to be cleaned up. China still owned the skies and had made headway at three other ports to the north, but at least in the south, the threat was beaten back.

Curious at how the Taiwanese could bag such a large number of invaders overnight, Colonel Flint sent Major Ramirez over to the 17th Infantry Division's headquarters to investigate. The major came back without any official information (the Taiwanese refused to divulge "state secrets"). But, what he did see aroused speculation that Taiwan had a trick or two up its sleeve as well. On his way back to the Marine's airport HQ, Rez spotted a column of enemy prisoners of war. Judging by the way they stumbled along and the strange looks in their eyes, Rez guessed that they had been blinded by some agent or weapon. *All's fair in love and war*, Rez thought, remembering the aborted Combat Laser Assault

Weapon from the early 90s. The idea behind the CLAW was to use a computer controlled laser weapon that would sweep a laser beam across the battlefield, permanently blinding enemy forces. The US decided not to deploy the system, reasoning that it was too inhumane and that if America forewent its development, other nations would follow suit. This was a false pretense. Rarely have nations refused to deploy weapons they viewed as being in their national interest just because another nation refused to do so. With China's huge advantage in infantry and Taiwan's advantage in technology, it was only natural that Taiwan would seek to use capital to offset its opponent's advantage in labor.

When the intelligence officer got back to headquarters and reported to Colonel Flint, the senior officer considered the latest information for a long moment. Flint finally sat down wearily, looked up at Ramirez and said, "Rez, this is going to be one hell of a vicious war. There will be no rules. The last nation left standing will rule the world for a hundred years. You think America's ready for that?"

Rez was surprised at his boss' sudden bout of melancholy. He tried to put a good face on things, "Well sir, we were ready in World War Two."

Flint shook his head, "That was a different generation and these are different times. In a couple of days the Chinese have used chemical, biological and nuclear weapons. You can't beat China with two months of high altitude air strikes and cruise missiles. Do you think America can go toe-to-toe with these bastards and do what it will take to win?"

"We did."

"We're Marines, Rez, that's what we do. It's the home front I'm concerned about."

*   *   *

Donna Klein had returned home for a lightning strike to gather some clothes in preparation for her trip to Taiwan. She had huge misgivings—not about her participation, but about the trip itself. *Why send a team to Taiwan at all? What could be gained through negotiations?* The Chinese expected unconditional surrender. The President wanted to stall for time until greater forces could be mustered to provide him with more leverage. *Would negotiations in bad faith be worse than none at all?*

The whole mission had an unusual air about it. Three people: the National Security Council Advisor as the President's representative, Vice Chairman of the Joint Chiefs as the lead negotiator of the surrender terms, and a low-ranking China expert from the CIA—three people attempting to diffuse a potential war between the two most powerful nations on the planet. The State Department was completely opposed to the mission from which they were excluded. However, the Chinese set the terms: no more than three people, including translators, were to fly into Chaing Kai-Shek airport no later than Tuesday and deal directly with the senior Party representative on Taiwan.

Donna knew the Chinese were carefully controlling the venue to their advantage. First, by getting the Americans to agree to meet them on Taiwan, the Chinese had already established the concept that Taiwan was just as much a part of China as was Beijing. Second, by limiting the numbers of the delegation, the Chinese were able to limit the Americans' potential for mischief. Third, a small delegation was an outward sign of weakness. Such a delegation would lack the stamina to do anything more than capitulate to Chinese demands for the surrender of US forces.

The White House began to get a clearer picture of the extensive Chinese preparations for war. With information hastily pulled together from America's intelligence agencies—Donna's own CIA, the DIA (the military's counterpart), the NSA (an agency that gathered signals intelligence), and the State Department, it became obvious that China had secretly prepared for a crushing assault on Taiwan for an entire half year. Had they looked with their eyes and not blanketed the facts with their preconceived notions, any one of America's information gathering agencies could have foreseen July's events. Instead, they were all playing catch-up.

Donna had already moved beyond the finger pointing. She had come as close as anyone in the CIA to discerning China's true intentions before the attack. Had she been free to work full-time at the China desk instead of being diverted to assist the overworked Indonesia section during the humanitarian crisis there, she might have called it—not that anyone would have listened to her.

What wasn't easy was determining what China's intent was after taking Taiwan. Understanding the nature of this conflict was essential. Was it a regional conflict or the opening move in a larger, more ambitious game plan? Knowing was essential for US planners trying to formulate an appropriate response—this was the question that occupied Donna as she packed. *Taiwan today. Tomorrow...?*

*   *   *

Dugen had only been on Route 4 for a few minutes when he saw it: the Goddess of Democracy! Dugen's mind raced as he tried to suppress the walled-off emotions of that brutal day in '89 at Tiananmen Square. The terrified look on the faces of young men and women—people no different than himself, people who believed in a better China, people he gunned down in cold blood without remorse. Dugen stared at the five-meter high statue. Dugen's driver pressed on, oblivious to the symbol that had come to haunt his commander's dreams.

Only three hours later Colonel Chu had met his objectives and had taken up positions in Taishan. He had seen two more Goddess of Democracy statues along the way, each sending him deeper into thought.

The last one they saw during the road march his political officer halted the convoy and ordered a squad to destroy it. Chu countermanded the order, claiming they neither had the time nor the ammunition to waste on destroying a statue. The political officer relented and returned to his car to sulk, not wanting to challenge the popular commando officer.

Dugen made his command post in a small office building overlooking Taipei. He viewed the enemy's city through his Japanese binoculars. Taipei gleamed and sparkled in the shafts of light that shone through the clouds. He placed the field glasses down for a moment to rest his eyes, then noticed a scuffle on the street below between one of his men and a civilian motorcyclist. The commando had forced the man off of his motorcycle and was binding his hands behind his back, when Dugen noticed a slender white form in the small park beyond the street. *The Goddess!* The PLA colonel sat in a leather executive's chair and stared slack-jawed out the window. On the street below, the young, now helmetless man sat tied to a lamppost with his head bowed, crying. Dugen's gaze passed from the young man to the Goddess of Democracy and back to the young man. Dugen's thoughts returned to 1989. Could he ever regain what was lost?

*   *   *

Alexander talked a couple of Taiwanese airport security officers into finding *Traveller* a truck full of jet fuel. A few hundred gallons later, *Traveller's* thirst was slaked and the tank was ready for an eight-hour night shift (until it would have to be refueled again).

Traveller and its crew were now in their element—nighttime in the tank with the best night vision on the planet. Alexander worked the patch of open ground and highway bordering the river northeast of the airport. The uncharted city further to the east over the river was too dangerous and constrained for a tank to operate.

Peña had just bagged his latest victim, the fourth tank of the evening, when Alexander's radio broke squelch, "Thunderbolt X-Ray, this is Sidewinder Five Niner, over." The voice was hushed.

"Go ahead Sidewinder, over," Alexander responded.

"Thunderbolt, I'm hearing some tracks due east of the airport. I think they're fording the river."

"Roger." Alexander was just about to order Hernandez to move out to investigate when he saw the flickering whiteness of a far-off flare. The light streaming in through his TC's periscope increased in intensity. Alexander looked up from the TTS scope and peered through the thick glass prism. The landscape danced under the light of at least half a dozen large flares—*Traveller's* cloak of darkness was stripped away, they could be seen.

"Driver, let's pull back behind that berm about 50 meters to the left," Alexander ordered with some urgency.

The tank's turbine wound up and they began to move forward. *Traveller* violently lurched forward and an eardrum-popping concussion swept over the crew. Alexander was knocked off his seat and barely caught himself before falling onto the back of Peña's seat. Alexander wiped blood off his nose.

Jones started screaming, "Shit! Shit! Oh God, we're going to die!"

"Shut the fuck up!" Peña yelled. Peña jacked himself around to look at his commander, "You okay, sir?"

Traveller shuddered again as explosions rocked the air just outside the tank.

Alexander steadied himself and looked at his gunner in the dim red light of the tank's interior, "Yeah, I'll be. . ."

"Ow! Shit! My hand!" it was Jones again, "I burned my hand on the blast door. We're on fire! Bail-out!"

Alexander reached out and grabbed the edge of Jones' fiberglass CVC helmet, pulling the young loader's head toward his chest, "Stay inside! If you open the hatch now we'll all die!"

"What's. . ."

"We've been hit in the rear of the turret. Our ammo's blowing up and the explosions are venting out like they're supposed to. Now calm down and load a sabot round so we can kill the son of a bitch that shot us." The M1IP carried 13 rounds in various nooks and crannies inside the turret itself. It wasn't much, but it was more than enough to kill their attacker and get back to the airport (assuming the engine still worked).

Only 500 meters away from the American tank, a Chinese tank crew was celebrating. They had finally done what no tank crew had ever done in the history of warfare: killed an American M1 Abrams tank.

The disciplined crew quickly quieted down. Intelligence said there were other American tanks out there. The commander turned away from the brightly burning American tank and looked for more targets under the canopy of flares fired from four of the battalion's mortar tubes.

Loading the main gun gave Jones an opportunity to calm down. He broke loose another sabot round and held it at the ready between his knees.

Alexander took a slow draught of air and began, "Gunner, I'm going to swing the turret around. Driver, as I do, I want you to neutral steer us around to the right. Do a 180. I want everything to happen fast. Ready?" Alexander didn't wait for the question to be answered. He whipped the 20-ton turret around, Hernandez following quickly with the hull. *There.* "Gunner, sabot, tank, fire!"

Peña saw the enemy tank was almost close enough to touch. He didn't need to lase, which was a good thing, because he noticed the laser was inoperative only seconds before. Peña pulled the trigger. Traveller gently rocked back as the 105mm gun recoiled. They were rewarded with a blinding flash as the sabot dart penetrated its target and incinerated everything combustible inside.

Alexander collapsed in a heap on pile of used small aircraft tires in the hanger *Traveller* was parked in. Their first night in Taiwan was very productive. The American tank's TTS allowed his crew to identify and kill four enemy tanks without a return shot. The fifth tank almost killed them, but almost didn't count in war. By the early morning hours, the enemy was in full retreat. Alexander failed to pursue the enemy. Not that he didn't want to, but between his crew's lack of rest, *Traveller's* lack of fuel, lack of ammo, and battle damage, pursuit didn't seem like a prudent option.

Thankfully, his scouts linked up with a Taiwanese tank company commander and filled the ROC officer in on the Americans' ongoing actions. The commander had six M60A3 tanks at his disposal—tanks with the same gun and largely the same TTS as the Americans' M1IP. Compared to the M1, the M60A3 was a lumbering beast. But at night, in the darkened city with thermal sights, speed was not the deciding factor; hitting the target was. The Taiwanese destroyed another 12 tanks, only losing one in the fight. By morning, the immediate threat to Taipei was blunted and the Taiwanese had erected an effective defense of the city proper.

With three of Task Force Grizzly's MPs in a Humvee standing watch, Lieutenant Colonel Alexander, Staff Sergeant Peña, Specialist Hernandez, and Private First Class Jones passed out for a well-deserved rest. They had been awake for the better part of 36 hours.

*   *   *

In the medium-sized Orange County city of Tustin, some 30 miles southeast of LA, Judy Alexander pulled into her driveway. The Chevy Suburban was loaded with groceries and children. She immediately noticed the three news vans parked on the street. Three news crews stood on the sidewalk in front of her house like circling vultures.

After seeing Dan on CNN, then on all the networks earlier in the day, she had to admit she wasn't surprised by the media finally tracking her down. Not being intellectually surprised was one thing. Actually seeing the reporters and their cameras was quite another.

The automatic garage door swung open and she immediately hit the button to close it after her. One of the reporters set foot in her garage, tripping the infrared sensor that prevents garage doors from crushing little children. The door immediately stopped. All three news crews stood there; eight people waiting expectantly.

Judy froze. She didn't know whether to back out of the garage and flee—*flee where?*—or get out and face the media. She sat there. Dan Junior, age two, started to cry from his car seat. Judy settled on her plan of action.

She opened her door, "Hi there!" she said cheerfully, "Absolutely *no* interviews. . . until all the groceries are put away. If you help, I'll be done quicker and I'll let you conduct the interview in the house. If you're nice, you might even get cookies and coffee."

Not accustomed to their quarry taking the initiative *and* being friendly, the news crews set their equipment aside and enthusiastically pitched in. The kids, food, and cameras were inside within a few minutes.

Judy made a pot of coffee and sent the children in the backyard (for safety's sake, she refused to let them be seen on TV). The three of them pressed their noses against the French doors, angling for a look at the reporters about to commence the interview. By mutual agreement, Judy got the reporters to agree to rotate their questioning. The result was a fairly dignified and somewhat organized interview of the wife of America's newest hero.

27
Maneuver

It was the start of Fu Zemin's third day on Taiwan. He even had a restful night's sleep. In general, the operation to recover China's wayward province was going quite well. The senior officers around him smiled and even joked occasionally. So far, this was nothing like he feared war would be. He settled into his seat with a hot cup of tea for his morning briefing. His military counterpart, General First Class Deng Yen-hsi sat to Fu's right, smoking a cigarette. Major General Wei sat just behind Fu.

The Chief of Operations for the Taiwan invasion began the briefing, "Comrade Fu, General Deng, comrades, as of this morning at 0600 hours, we have 17 divisions in action on Taiwan. This includes two tank divisions, two mechanized infantry divisions and an artillery division in the vicinity of Taipei. The Chief of Intelligence will provide you with details, but let me say that the enemy can now only muster 14 partially manned divisions against us. We destroyed a division of ROC marines at Keelung on the opening day as well as the 12th Infantry Division yesterday in heavy fighting around Hsintien. Other enemy divisions have retreated before the face of our stronger forces. In addition to our 17 divisions, we have landed about 40,000 soldiers of the People's Armed Police. They are proving extremely effective in keeping our rear areas secure and suppressing any resistance among the civilian population. We expect to have some 250,000 PAP in the province within a week." The general paused for effect, "As of yesterday at noon, we isolated Taipei from the rest of Taiwan. From now on, enemy forces in Taipei will grow weaker while we grow stronger. We will now concentrate on forming a series of defensive positions beginning at Taichung and extending north to include a double ring around Taipei: one facing outward, the other inward. Once we have defeated the enemy's mobile formations in the inevitable counterattack they must launch to relieve their besieged capital city, we will simply march into the defeated city. If there are no questions, I will be followed by the Chief of Intelligence."

Fu felt this plan was sound, and his lack of formal military training left his no firm grounds to criticize it, still, there was the nagging issue of the Americans and the spectacular failure in the south. Fu placed his tea on the low table in front of his knees and said, "General, could you please help illuminate something for

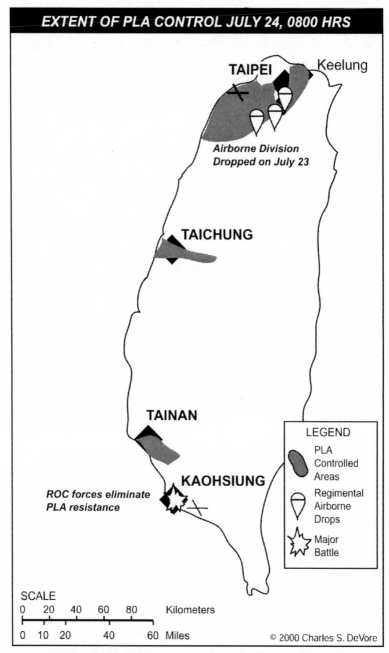

EXTENT OF PLA CONTROL JULY 24, 0800 HRS

TAIPEI Keelung

*Airborne Division
Dropped on July 23*

TAICHUNG

TAINAN

KAOHSIUNG

*ROC forces eliminate
PLA resistance*

LEGEND

PLA
Controlled
Areas

Regimental
Airborne
Drops

Major
Battle

SCALE

| 0 | 20 | 40 | 60 | 80 | Kilometers |

| 0 | 10 | 20 | | 40 | | 60 | Miles |

© 2000 Charles S. DeVore

The PLA consolidates gains around Taipei

me. Why are you not mentioning our reverses in Kaohsiung nor the presence of so many American troops?"

The Chief of Operations stopped only briefly to formulate an answer, "Comrade Fu, the issue of the Americans will be addressed by the Chief of Intelligence. As far as Kaohsiung, yes, it is true that we lost four divisions and an airborne regiment in our assault there. It is important to note, however, that this action tied down Taiwan's 4th Armored Brigade and allowed the successful landings at Tainan to take hold and expand. The enemy will now have to fight his way through our defenses there before he can mass enough power to threaten our first defensive line 120 kilometers to the north at Taichung. Remember too, Comrade, that we committed more forces to Kaohsiung in an effort to capture the American Marines who landed there."

Fu was not happy with the fact that the Americans had gotten the jump on them in this war. It was crucial that the PLA quickly develop a reputation for being unbeatable—unbeatable armies were quite useful in conquering weak, fearful neighbors at a minimal cost. "Why were chemical agents not used after the first attack at Kaohsiung?"

"Comrade, it was a matter of weather. The typhoon east of Luzon Island caused strong prevailing winds to blow offshore. In such conditions it is very difficult to build up militarily-significant concentrations of chemical agent." The general was cool and confident throughout the briefing. Fu hated to admit it, but he was unable to pin the blame on anyone for the operation's only major problem to date. He would speak to the Party leadership in an hour and tell them he still had complete confidence in the military's ability to achieve their objective of forcibly reuniting Taiwan with Mother China. Most importantly, he expected to be able to deal from a position of strength with the American delegation that Beijing told him to expect at the airport by next morning. The thought of accepting the surrender of American forces from a US four star general made Fu smile wickedly on the inside.

*   *   *

Donna Klein, General Taylor and Bob Lindley made it to Okinawa in the pre-dawn hours after flying all night from Andrews Air Force Base with only one stop in Anchorage. The three would-be negotiators were exhausted and jet-lagged. Donna argued for spending the day in Okinawa to rest up, but Taylor and Lindley both insisted on immediately pressing on to Taiwan as planned. Both had their reasons that neither cared to share with the woman from the *Company*.

The flight plan made the Air Force general nervous. Flying into contested airspace in the small, unarmed Defense Intelligence Agency executive jet (the DIA maintained most of the DoD's executive jets) without an escort was a good way to get shot down—either by the Taiwanese or the Chinese (either of whom could also have a motive for doing so).

Donna mentally reviewed her instructions one last time: conduct a quality check on the Chinese to English translation being done by the Chinese, overhear any useful bits of information or gain subtle insight into the negotiation dynamics, and serve as a foundation of knowledge about China for Mr. Lindley and General Taylor—*fairly easy stuff when compared to the actual job of negotiating the surrender of US forces—or at least appearing to negotiate their surrender*, she corrected herself.

When the twin-engine jet lifted off the runway, Donna was snapped back into the here and now. Taiwan was less than an hour away. She decided to review one last time her classified briefing material on possible Chinese end games for the conquest of Taiwan. . .

*   *   *

The American officer had been skipper of the USS *Los Angeles* (SSN-688) fast attack submarine based out of Pearl Harbor for six months now. He loved command. He was proud to be a naval officer. While he was also black and was cognizant of his status as a role model to the African Americans under his command, he felt an even larger responsibility to be the best of the best to his entire crew. With 11 officers and 115 enlisted riding a nuclear powered steel tube under the waves, responsibility did not come lightly.

The skipper had been watching the build-up of tensions between China and Taiwan with interest. His interest was motivated by his personal participation in the last run up in tensions in March of '96 he when prowled the Taiwan Straits as part of a US task force. Back then he was finishing up his tour as head of engineering for the USS *San Francisco*. He'd since completed some schooling shore side, then served as XO of the

Los Angeles before taking command. He knew he was marked as a fast burner, but he would have preferred to remain in command of the *Los Angeles* the rest of his career.

When he received orders to make all speed for the Taiwan Strait he wasn't at all surprised. What surprised him was that, as far as he could tell, he was the only American military response to the Chinese invasion of Taiwan. He knew the armed forces were thinly spread around the globe—*but one attack sub was all the world's most powerful nation could send against the world's second most powerful nation in the opening moves of a conflict?* He wondered at the other dynamics in play that limited the US response.

The *Los Angeles'* mission was simple: pass undetected into the Taiwan Strait (they'd already rode the southerly current into the passage, making only two knots against the sea); then await orders to begin sinking Chinese shipping with a priority towards heavy sea lift, then capital ships (warships). The main danger to the *Los Angeles* lay in China's stated threat to mine the Strait to prevent foreign naval interference.

The skipper reread the summary of the recent naval actions in the Strait. One of the Chinese *Kilo* class subs drew first blood, sinking a Taiwanese diesel-electric boat. A *Los Angeles* class with an American crew was more than a match for the Chinese *Kilo*. Still, in the fairly confined spaces of the Strait, shooting and living to tell about it would be a challenge. In spite of the danger to himself and his crew, he smiled inwardly—he loved challenges as much as he loved command.

*　　　*　　　*

On Sunday evening the Speaker of the United States House of Representatives put out the call for an emergency session to consider a resolution for a declaration of war on China. Most of the Members were out of town in their districts and didn't plan on being back until Monday evening. The Speaker wanted a quorum by Monday morning with a vote by Monday evening at the latest. The debate promised to be raucous and the vote by no means unanimous, but the Speaker calculated that China's unprovoked attack on the US Navy would turn enough votes away from China and its powerful business allies to force passage. Then, it would be off to the Senate and a less-certain future. The Speaker and his allies wanted a declaration of war for two reasons: first, to ride the popular wave of support for action generated by the images of the lone American tank making a stand and the news of the Navy's horrible losses in the surprise attack; and second, to make it more difficult for the President to cut a deal with the Chinese and abandon Taiwan before China could be dealt a decisive blow.

28
Eyeball-to-Eyeball

The flight from Okinawa was thankfully short and uneventful. As the small twin-engine DIA VIP jet set down at a rainy Chaing Kai-Shek International Airport, Donna set to work counting Mainland aircraft and aircraft types (the constantly overcast weather had hampered spy satellite operations so the "Company" had asked her to do some old-fashioned spying). Donna also wryly noted that the Mainlanders had replaced the airport's welcome signs so that the airport's new name read *Deng Xiaoping International Airport.*

The aircraft came to a halt at an out of the way portion of the airport, far from any protection from the rain. Within seconds, Chinese security forces swarmed over the aircraft. When the Air Force crew popped the hatch, eight armed Chinese security officers forced their way on board. They seemed to have no mission other than to have a look around and a few minutes later, they left, leaving wet footprints and drips of water everywhere.

General Taylor and Bob Lindley were quiet. Donna noted their demeanor was probably what the Chinese wanted to shape. Both men were stunned by the unceremonious force the Chinese used to establish their unquestioned superiority in this situation. Donna knew the Chinese were trying to keep the American team off-balance and on the defensive—this would make them easier opponents to deal with.

Donna decided to break the ice, "Well, gentlemen, we know what the remainder of this mission will be like. We might as well get used to it. What's the worst they could do to us?" Donna got up and began walking towards the open passenger exit.

"What the hell are you going to do?" Lindley asked incredulously.

"Mr. Lindley, you can simply wait here on the tarmac, if you like, but I think we should take some of our own initiative. Let's grab our briefcases, head for the terminal, and see how far we'll get."

General Taylor smiled. "I like your plan."

"This is insane!" Lindley protested, "You can't do that!"

Donna stopped at the exit, raindrops smacking against her shoes, "Oh well, I guess we won't get to test them this time, here comes the official welcoming party. Nice limo. And look at all those cameras. . ."

*   *   *

The *Los Angeles* had slowly and quietly made its way into the Taiwan Strait two hours ago. Between the ocean current and sub's own creeping pace, they had gone only 10 nautical miles. Still, it was far enough to be inside the PLAN's first anti-sub picket line.

Not long after entering the strait the submarine picked up a message on the ELF communications set (ELF: extremely long frequency, a very slow way of communicating code with a signal that penetrates ocean waters). The coded message was simple: proceed.

Within an hour, the skipper and his crew had sunk a PLAN Jiangwei-class frigate and a Quonsha-class amphibious troop transport (capable of carrying 400 troops). They were now eluding a very determined foe who was using aircraft, helicopters, ships and technical assistance from a battery of Russian satellites to corner, then destroy them.

The commander was too busy surviving to be scared.

*   *   *

The hotel was only a five-minute trip from the airport. When he got to his room, General Taylor placed his satellite pager on the windowsill. Within a couple of minutes it rewarded him by vibrating (he hoped he wouldn't have to hook it up to its antenna attachment). He grabbed it and read the message (the message would repeat itself every ten minutes for an hour). The pager's readout said: MOBILE BAY ACTIVE. Taylor grunted approval. America was responding to China's challenge. It wasn't much— *and the Navy was doing it, not the Air Force*—but it was a start. Taylor wondered how the Chinese would react when the Americans sat down to negotiate with a wild card in their hand. Taylor stifled a big yawn, *talk about Mondays—this will be the toughest Monday of my life!*

After half an hour to stow their bags and change clothes, Bob Lindley, General Taylor and Donna Klein settled into the hotel meeting room to await their Chinese counterparts.

So far, everything was perfect, Fu Zemin chortled to himself. The opening video shots of the American delegation, looking small, wet and scared, would soon be triumphantly projected on

323

televisions all across China. The embarrassing stain of China's 1999 humiliation at the hands of America in Belgrade would soon be wiped clean and then some. Fu couldn't wait for the "negotiations" to start.

The three Americans walked into the large hotel ballroom. Fu sat at one end of a long mahogany table. No other Chinese sat with him. Behind him stood six PLA generals, two minor Party officials, and two translators. Two television crews captured the event on tape for later broadcast to China and the rest of the world (after appropriate editing, of course). Three photographers snapped away. The Americans had simple chairs to sit on, Fu's chair was heavy and ornate.

Perfect, everything was perfect, Fu marveled at his own power.

The Americans sat down. Fu looked at them: Mr. Lindley, a former lobbyist for China, now in the employ of the President himself, said to be still very sympathetic to China and not at all in favor of confrontation. By Lindley's expression, he was clearly looking for mercy and favor from the Chinese. General Taylor, an Air Force officer, more accustomed to flying bombers on almost risk-free missions over virtually defenseless small nations— *definitely not a negotiator,* Fu thought. *Then there was the woman, a contemptible woman from the CIA. Supposedly she knows Mandarin.* Fu harumphed to himself at the thought of a white female actually being fluent in his tongue, *stupid Americans with their weak notions of equality between the sexes. After we conclude the negotiations, I ought to have her arrested as a spy and. . .*

Major General Wei walked into the room behind Fu just as Fu was about to open the charade. Fu held his tongue and his anger. After just a few intense days he was beginning to rely heavily on the intelligence officer—he knew Wei would not interrupt such an important event without good cause. Wei got close to Fu's ear, "Sir," he whispered, "the Americans have sent one of their attack submarines into the Taiwan Strait. It has sunk two of our ships. The Navy is trying, but it will be hard to sink. I thought you should know."

Fu whispered back, "Yes, you are correct. Thank you general." He cleared his throat and then spoke loudly for the cameras in Mandarin, "The Americans are jeopardizing the negotiations for the surrender of their forces on Taiwan by needlessly playing with fire. I am calling a break in the negotiations for two hours until the Americans become serious and desist all resistance on both the land, on and *under* the sea, and in the air around the sacred Chinese island province of Taiwan!"

The Chinese translator flawlessly and with excellent expression turned Fu's words into English. Lindley looked frightened. Taylor held a blank face. Klein simply looked alert, her eyes methodically sweeping the room, looking for useful bits of information. Five tough looking Chinese security guards came into the room and escorted the American delegation back to their suite down the hall.

When the three Americans got back to their suite and the door shut behind them, Lindley wheeled on Taylor and screamed, "What the *hell* was that all about General?" Lindley's veins stood out on his neck and forehead. Donna studied both men.

"General Taylor," Donna said soothingly, "before you answer that I would like to remind you that we are not in a private location."

"Yes, yes, of course," Taylor said, picking up a pad of hotel paper. He wrote in small letters, "We have a sub operating in the Strait. It probably sank something."

When Taylor showed the note to Lindley, the National Security Council Advisor blew up, "Whose dumb ass idea with this? The President's or did *you* dream this one up?" Lindley jabbed the General on his bemedaled chest.

Donna gently grabbed Lindley's wrist and took the note from his clenched hand. She read it then looked at Taylor with an arched brow. She looked around for an ashtray to burn any further notes in before flushing the ashes down the toilet. "Gentlemen, I suggest we stick to our mission—the *negotiations*." Donna knew that they were simply there to occupy the Chinese and stall for time until more force could be amassed, she only hoped she could keep her colleagues in mind of that.

Lindley shook his head and turned on his heels muttering under his breath.

"Why don't we all relax for awhile? We've been up a long time and we won't be sharp when we need to be," Donna suggested. She thought of her role during the last minute—*the junior to both of them, yet the peacemaker. Damn the lack of organization and rehearsal for this "diplomatic" mission.*

While Fu let the Americans worry and wait, he consulted with Beijing on their next move. The leadership was obviously worried about the turn of events with the United States. More than the substantial amount of shipping the US sub could sink, the symbolism of American resistance could rally Japan, South Korea, and other Asian powers to the US-led opposition of China's takeover of Taiwan. Clearly the Americans had to be made to back-down or be quickly destroyed. Beijing properly ascertained that the delegation now on Taiwan had no true authority to negotiate a general surrender of US forces (those forces on Taiwan maybe, but a submarine at sea, never). The leadership directed Fu to "negotiate" for the cameras and the potential propaganda value, but otherwise to await word of further Chinese initiatives designed to force the Americans to give in.

All three Americans checked in with the "office" during their time out. All three did so on their mobile satellite phones. All three knew that their calls (at least the outbound voice portion) were being monitored by listening devices. Other than the fact that the Chinese were reluctant to deal with the Americans while the submarine prowled the waters off Taiwan, there was no news or new directives from Washington. One hour slipped into two. Lunchtime passed. Finally, at 2:00 PM, the famished Americans were served a modest fare in their suite.

*　　*　　*

At 3:14 PM, the *Los Angeles* claimed another victim, this time a 5,000-ton coastal steamer heading to Taiwan with a load of trucks and armored personnel carriers. The PLAN tried once again, unsuccessfully, to sink the attack submarine. The PLAN's admirals debated whether to send their Kilo-class boats after the Americans, but decided it was better to keep the Kilos alive and a threat to complicate the Americans' planning than to waste them on an enemy that was ready and waiting for them. The Chinese redoubled their efforts to find and sink the sub from the air.

Beijing was in a quandary. The war on Taiwan was going well. The generals estimated that within a week, ten days at the most, Taipei would fall and general resistance would cease. That is, if the Americans could be kept out of the war. The introduction of the attack submarine into the fight was a minor, but troubling inconvenience. The military experts knew that more American naval power would soon arrive and that, if nothing was done to check it, the Americans would choke off vital supplies and reinforcements just as victory was at hand. Bold action was needed to seize the initiative from the Americans and save the about-to-be-won victory from American meddling. The leadership made the decision to employ a special stratagem—a secret weapon that was carefully prepared for just this eventuality. A weapon that, if successful, would knock America out of the war and turn all of Asia into China's docile back yard. The timing for the weapon's employment had to be perfect to maximize its effect. The countdown started. . .

*   *   *

On Monday morning at 8:30 in Washington, D.C., the United States House of Representatives was gaveled to order. If most of the Members of Congress were sleepy from the hasty recall to the capital, they didn't show it. The House chamber was abuzz with purpose and a sense of history. The motion to declare war had been drafted the day before in committee (highly unusual for a Sunday) and the rules of debate were decided upon. Each side would have four hours to debate the issue with a final vote scheduled for 7:00 PM. There were to be no amendments allowed—a straight up or down vote would be the order of the day.

The first Member rose to speak. He was a long-time Congressman from New York, very respected, and although not of the same party as the President, was known to be supportive of the Presidency in times of foreign crisis, "Mr. Speaker, I move to suspend the rules and pass the joint resolution to declare war on the People's Republic of China, to support actions the President has taken with respect to Chinese aggression against Taiwan and to demonstrate United States resolve."

The Clerk of the House read the resolution with a clear and unemotional voice, "House Joint Resolution 745.

"Whereas the Government of the People's Republic of China without provocation on July 22 attacked United States Naval vessels in international waters, attacked United States Air Force air craft in international airspace, invaded and occupied the territory of Taiwan, has brutalized the population of Taiwan, and has disregarded the rights of diplomats, all in clear violation of international law and the norms of international conduct. . ."

The resolution ended by calling for a declaration of war on the PRC. The chamber was so quiet that when the Clerk of the House finished speaking and shut off his mike the spectators in the House Visitors' Galley could hear his papers rustling as he tapped them back into a tidy pile.

By eleven o'clock it became clear there were four basic lines of argument, two for, and two against the declaration of war on China. The moderate opposition to the resolution was summed up by a powerful, pro-trade committee chairman:

"Mr. Speaker, Ladies and Gentlemen, I rise in opposition to the resolution. This is madness! This is not some academic exercise! We are debating whether or not to go to war against one of our largest trading partners and the world's most populous nation! China is not our enemy. They have no designs on US territory or world conquest. They simply want to be able to make their ancient and proud nation whole again. Let us not stand in their way. Our relations with China are far more important than to squander them on the shoals of a small and insignificant island. Please, please, please, listen to me! We must not, we cannot, risk war with a major power over territory that even most of us believe belongs to them!

"In addition, I hope the President will ignore the rising chorus of unemployed cold warriors and armchair generals urging him to strike out against China. It is awfully easy to order air strikes on China from the comfort of your living room; it is a whole lot harder when you have to bear the full responsibility of such an action as Commander in Chief. Let us support the President, but let us not goad him into action that may be unwise or unsuccessful. Let us not prematurely set the President's path so that his only choices become failure and certain folly!"

The Member finished his speech to a smattering of applause. His convictions were genuine, although some of his opponents didn't think so and were prepared to use his record of campaign contributions against him (he represented a district where the largest employer was an aerospace company with billions of dollars of exports to China at stake).

Another point of view was expressed by a Member of the House's bloc of traditional pacifists:

"Mr. Speaker, I thank the distinguished gentleman for yielding, and I rise in opposition to the resolution. Mr. Speaker, I find it difficult to oppose my Democratic leadership and the President in this matter, but I believe the resolution is not in the national interest and, as a matter of principle, I am compelled to dissent. America can no longer be the world's policeman. We must come home. It is our own serious economic problems here at home that deserve our attention and our resources.

"While I agree with the resolution's characterization of the reprehensible actions of the People's Republic of China and the resolution's approval of severe economic sanctions against China and the freezing of Chinese and Taiwanese assets in the United States, can anyone honestly believe that our military would be on the shores of Taiwan today except for the Pentagon's deep-seated and irrational Cold War hatred of the Chinese Communist Party?

"There is simply no threat to the American homeland. We are there plainly and simply because old Cold Warriors hate China. And, I believe, no American life is worth sacrificing for this outmoded hatred. Especially since the Asian powers with the most to lose are our economic competitors.

"I am exceedingly concerned that the passage of this resolution will provide a fig leaf of a congressional public relations mandate for the President to accentuate a military resolution of this crisis, rather than sustained diplomatic negotiations with all concerned parties. Before this is over we will put hundreds of thousands of our uniformed military personnel in harm's way. We have an obligation to them, a moral obligation, and an obligation to the American people and people in Asia to achieve a just resolution of this crisis without recourse to further bloodshed and devastation."

The arguments in favor of the resolution were also in two camps: Members who believed China was a looming military and economic threat to America and another group who were perennially disgusted with China's human rights violations and exploitation of low-cost labor (the later motivated, more often than not, by powerful organized labor interests). Both camps drew on the fact that Taiwan was a democracy while China was not.

With only ten minutes remaining on the clock for the pro-resolution side, a big-labor Democrat from the heart of Chicago rose to speak:

"Mr. Speaker. The near-war in which we find ourselves is a classic case of bad policy choices coming back to haunt us. China has a long history of aggression in the region, ask Tibet, ask South Korea, ask the Philippines, ask Vietnam. They have an abysmal human rights record, and have violated international conventions against the proliferation of missile technology and nuclear weapons. Despite that, both Republican and Democratic administrations over the decades of the 1970s, 1980s and 1990s increasingly tilted United States policy toward China. Their bad judgment was compounded, of course, by their failure to develop a consistent fair trade and human rights policy with respect to China.

"This coddling of China's dictators has only served to embolden them to action against a tiny and vibrant democracy. I have visited both Taiwan and China. Let me tell you this: Taiwan is governed by its people—a government of the people, by the people and for the people. The People's Republic of China is governed by a bunch of corrupt old Communist Party thugs.

"Some of you today have blamed Taiwan for initiating this crisis, for effectively declaring independence. Shame! Shame on you! You and your elitist ilk in the State Department fret about hot heads in Taiwan—as if a government freely elected can ignore the will of its people! If the government in Taipei didn't declare Taiwan's independence it would have deserved to be thrown on the street. And I'm sure many of the same people who now tut-tut their moves towards independence would have condemned them for being less than democratic had they ignored the will of the people. Well, you can't have it both ways: either Taiwan and its people are free, free to choose their own path and deserving of our support, or they're not, in which case they are no better than the butchers of Beijing who now rule over one-fifth of the world's population and lust after more!

"I support the resolution and I support freedom for the people of Taiwan *and* the people of China!"

At his last sentence, he pounded the podium in the midst of thunderous applause.

The last Member to speak for the pro-resolution side, a conservative Member of the House Armed Services Committee rose:

"Mr. Speaker, I yield myself the remaining time. Mr. Speaker, I rise in support of House Joint Resolution 745 and urge its adoption. This resolution is the result of intense and urgent deliberations between the majority, the other side of the aisle, and the administration on what must be the most important of the shared powers of Congress and the executive—the issue of war.

"This resolution was crafted by members of the committee in close consultation with the highest representatives of the administration and represents that which can be achieved when there is consensus among Americans with regard to our principles of constitutional democracy and that our traditional role of opposing illegal and naked aggression, be it against Poland in 1939, Pearl Harbor in 1941, Kuwait in 1990, or Taiwan today.

"Simply stated, House Joint Resolution 745 affirms and congratulates the President on the actions he has taken in the past two days with respect to the current situation in and around Taiwan as a result of the Chinese invasion. Congress should indicate that it will stand behind the President's stated objectives to preserve democracy on Taiwan and to protect American lives and interests. The explicit use of chemical and nuclear warfare is a tactic worthy of Attila the Hun, Genghis Khan and Adolf Hitler, and a blatant violation of all norms of international law and civilized behavior. The activities of the Communist Chinese occupying forces in Taiwan must also be a focus of the condemnation of the world. . ." He continued, citing historical precedents and the urgency of the situation.

Soon, the Congressman wrapped up his presentation with a grave flourish. "Let us not be deceived. The Chinese invasion of Taiwan is the opening gambit in a move to dominate the world—to make the 21st Century the Chinese century. If we suffer a failure of nerve at this defining moment, we will pay the price as assuredly as Britain paid the price for Neville Chamberlain's failure to stand up to Hitler."

In spite of the fervor the pro-resolution side enjoyed, the final vote was surprisingly close: 229 in favor, 191 against. For the first time since 1941, the United States House of Representatives had passed a declaration of war and sent it on to the waiting Senate where the more deliberative body was just gathering for an evening of debate. It was 7:40 PM on Monday.

*   *   *

Half a world away from Washington's war of words a different aspect of war, also involving words, was being prepared. In Sichuan province in the southeast portion of China, a Long March 2C/SD ("2" for two-stage, "SD" for Smart Dispenser, a special satellite dispensing device used to place multiple low earth orbit communications satellites into their orbits) commercial rocket was nearing lift off. The rocket was a mainstay of China's lucrative commercial launch vehicle market. How it got to be that way is an interesting story. After NASA's *Challenger* disaster in 1986 there

331

was a string of American launch vehicle failures as the US tried to restart its unmanned space program. At the same time, the European Ariane program was beginning to have success with its launch vehicles. Fearful of a European near-monopoly in the commercial launch vehicle market, American satellite manufacturers lobbied the US government to allow them to launch commercial satellites on Chinese rockets. Unfortunately, Chinese rockets had a disconcerting habit of exploding with their quarter billion dollar cargoes on board. Eventually the satellite insurance industry demanded that Chinese launch vehicles be made more reliable—if not, the satellite owners would have to self-insure or use other, safer (and more expensive) rockets. Rather than fatten Europe's space industry coffers, the Americans decided to improve China's launch vehicle reliability and accuracy.

At T minus zero the booster's engines ignited, sending a tremor through the two-stage rocket. The launch vehicle lifted off on schedule (the launch window was half an hour long) and cleared the pad in a deafening roar. Ten seconds into its flight the rocket began its pitch over maneuver. Instead of heading in the normal easterly azimuth of 94 to 104 degrees (taking the rocket over fairly unpopulated areas in the shortest distance to the South China Sea), the rocket tilted over to the northeast. Normally, this would have been cause for alarm and the rocket would have been command detonated to prevent a civilian catastrophe. Instead, the rocket was allowed to continue its climb for space. Just 122 seconds after liftoff the first stage shut down. A fifth of a second later the second stage ignited, sending the first stage tumbling back to Earth. Less than four minutes into the flight the payload fairing separated, revealing the Smart Dispenser and its cargo of five spherical vehicles.

Had the Chinese launched an intercontinental ballistic missile (ICBM) from one of their established missile fields, US missile launch warning satellites would have detected the launch within seconds. A few moments later, the satellites' data would have enabled the sprawling underground complex at Cheyenne Mountain in Colorado to determine where the missile was headed and whether or not it was a threat. The Chinese weren't willing to risk American nuclear retaliation over this mission, so they chose to use a civilian launch vehicle (stated US nuclear retaliation policy was to wait until confirmation of a nuclear explosion—but the Chinese didn't believe any nation could be so stupid as to wait until a bomb actually detonated before launching a counterstrike).

They even went so far as to have the China Satellite Launch and Control General in Beijing officially communicate to America their intent to launch a commercial satellite sometime during the morning hours.

The ploy worked. The launch was spotted by America's early warning system but it was deemed non-threatening. Concern was much higher for a suspected North Korean three-stage missile test launch that was threatened anytime soon. The Americans viewed North Korea as a dangerous rogue state with less to lose from reckless behavior than a wealthy up-and-coming nation such as China. As was often the case with Western perceptions about Asia, it was wishful thinking backed by a skewed view of history.

The young female US Air Force lieutenant was just beginning her day under a thousand feet of rock at Cheyenne Mountain. A Defense Support Program satellite in geosynchronous orbit had just picked up the Chinese Long March rocket's intensely hot exhaust plume as it cleared the thick cloud deck over southern China. While fairly new to the post, she quickly noted the rocket's trajectory was atypical. Frowning, she called the watch officer over to her console where she was roughing out some preliminary flight paths, "Sir, please take a look at this."

The major walked over to the lieutenant's station with its two large computer screens, "What do you have?"

"Sir, very unusual. This Chinese commercial launch is way outside of its normal azimuth. The flight path will take it just to the southeast of Beijing—fairly dangerous given their safety record."

The major first looked at the technical data on the lieutenant's screen. Satisfied she used the correct sensors and algorithms to draw an appropriate conclusion, he asked her, "Tell me what you think they're doing."

"Hmmm," she was delighted the major asked her her opinion. She had already developed her suspicions about Chinese intentions for this launch and was ready with a well thought out answer, "Sir, the Chinese announced the launch beforehand. This usually indicates a commercial launch. However, given the state of near-war we are in, I think that this is a reconnaissance satellite mission. The bird they're launching is going to keep tabs on our West Coast port facilities."

"Good analysis. But why would the Chinese need to use a spy

satellite when they probably already have at least 50 agents at each West Coast port site anyway?" The major retorted with a slight smile. The rocket advanced another few hundred miles since their conversation began.

"Maybe just to show us that they have modern capabilities too?" the lieutenant was reaching now—the major had blown away her theory.

The major stroked his chin, "Waste of money. No, I'd say the Chinese are launching a commercial photosat. Wasn't a Canadian-Israeli joint venture company going to try to launch a commercial photoreconnaissance satellite and then sell the pictures to farmers over the Internet? As I remember it, the French weren't too happy with the competition for SPOT so they blocked a launch on Ariane. The Russians have had problems at their launch facility recently and we're backlogged for at least two years at Cape Canaveral. All the same, let's call the colonel. Fascinating. . ."

The US Embassy in Beijing had been on the ragged edge for three days now. Every foreign service officer was straining to prevent a wider conflict from breaking out between America and China. The phone call from Beijing's Foreign Ministry was extremely unwelcome news. About 12 minutes after the launch of the Long March rocket, the Chinese called to tell the Americans that one of their commercial rockets had malfunctioned and was heading on a course that might take it over heavily populated areas of America's Pacific coastal region.

No one at the embassy questioned why they would receive the call as opposed to the information going directly to Washington over the Sino-American hotline (a telex rather than a phone). The embassy thanked the Chinese for their consideration and then called Washington with the news.

Each one of the five payload spheres weighed just under 1,000 pounds. The spheres were slightly flattened on one side and covered with a heat resistant ablative material. The flattened side also sported a small solid rocket motor. Called aeroshells, the spheres' purpose was to enable the cargo inside to survive a fiery reentry into Earth's atmosphere.

The Smart Dispenser released the first sphere 100 miles over

Alaska's Unimak Island. A few moments later it released the second. Once clear of the Smart Dispenser each of the spheres' onboard guidance computers oriented the small vehicles and fired their retro rockets. The two packages began their de-orbit maneuver. In a few more minutes the other three vehicles would begin their sequences too. It was all very precise. The Chinese-adapted American technology worked perfectly.

All three kids were terrorizing the puppy. Dan bought it a month before he was called up for duty and the little dog, Moxhe, was barking back, joining in the fray. Judy Alexander was ironing clothes and watching MSNBC with half an eye looking for any fresh news about Dan and Taiwan when her neighbor called to tell her about a car chase on TV. Judy reluctantly changed the channel. She hadn't slept much since Dan's aircraft was forced down in Taiwan—*maybe the local news will take my mind off of Dan for a bit*, she thought.

The chase was about half an hour old when Judy changed the channel. All the local networks were covering the latest Southern California carnival from their news helicopters. Judy didn't know with whom to be disgusted the most: the networks for constantly catering to mindless visual images that had zero impact on her life, the stupid thugs for endangering the lives of others, or herself for being even partially captivated by the spectacle. The chases always ended the same way. The fleeing suspect was inevitably captured—dead, wounded or in one piece—then the news would proceed to replay the most exciting portions of the chase for the rest of the evening. It all had kind of a predictable regularity about it; just another car chase on an LA evening.

Uncharacteristically, just as the chase was coming to its inevitable climax, the station broke into its special coverage to bring an even more important news flash.

The government clerk was hurrying to the deli on the corner of West 5th and South Spring streets in downtown Los Angeles for her customary dinner. She normally took an hour for dinner from her evening shift job at the Board of Public Works office, but today was different—she planned on eating in half an hour so she could take off from work early. Her thoughts were divided between the savory anticipation of the lox and bagel she would order and the date she had planned with her boyfriend at the beach in Santa Monica.

A puff of wind blew the deli's aroma under her nose. She had almost made it to the deli's door when a tiny leaflet came fluttering down right in front of her face. Annoyed, she brushed it away, looking around to see who had been so rude as to thrust a leaflet at her. Everyone around her had stopped. Some were looking skyward. She followed their eyes up to the sky. A small blizzard of white leaflets, each about three times larger than the fortune in the cookie she ate last night, was floating down between the buildings. *What in the world . . ? Probably some marketing gimmick—boy are they going to get in trouble!*

She grabbed at the next leaflet that came floating down and read the tiny text:

A Warning to the American imperialists!
Warning! Warning!
China is engaged in a patriotic struggle to liberate Taiwan from the remnants of Chiang Kai-Shek's forces. Do not let your politicians interfere in this just struggle, America! Withdraw your forces from Chinese territory now, before it is too late!

This message was delivered by China's new and powerful Dong Feng-31 missile to the people of the United States.
Warning! Warning!

As she read the leaflet her hand started to tremble. She had forgotten all about food. Instead she looked anxiously up at the sky. The leaflets had all fallen to the ground, and only the gray haze of a Los Angeles summer afternoon greeted her gaze.

Since moving to Los Angeles from the San Joaquin Valley five years before, she had lived in fear of earthquakes in the Big City. But this was a new and unanticipated threat. She knew from the news that America and China were edging closer to war—*but who would have ever believed such a conflict could come home? What if the Chinese started firing other missiles, this time not loaded with leaflets?* Having a degree in political science from Cal State Fresno, she vaguely remembered that the Chinese had threatened to do just that several years before in 1996 when Taiwan held its first free elections. Then again when the Taiwanese moved to declare their independence after their last election a few months before. She recalled China's fury on the evening news for a few days last March—fury that was muted by the ongoing crisis in Indonesia.

She suddenly decided that she was going to go visit her parents who lived in Fresno half a day's drive away. She would leave the city tonight if the news confirmed the source of the leaflets as being from China and not from some sick pranksters.

She remembered an emotional discussion from high school about the horrors of nuclear war—just before her school voted to declare itself a nuclear-free zone. She paused. *No!*, she said to herself after a second, she would leave now. She had some vacation time coming. She would call her boss from her parents' house after she arrived and make an excuse for not returning to work.

Judy stood, steaming iron in hand and mouth agape, watching the television. Leaflets purporting to be from a Chinese rocket had just fluttered over downtown Los Angeles. An unidentified object dangling from a bright orange parachute floated down just west of the Los Angeles Civic Center. As soon as it hit the street it began belching a deep purple smoke, sending pedestrians scurrying in terror. All five news helicopters assigned to the now-forgotten car chase were en-route to the scene. One sharp-eyed chopper pilot saw a small brush fire on the tinder-dry hillside below the HOLLYWOOD sign. The cameraman shot the growing flames as the helicopter swooped by heading for downtown. Just as the "D" started going up in smoke and flames he had to break away to begin to shoot the more alarming (and presumably better rating) image of the purple smoke fuming UFO.

Remote in hand, Judy clicked through the local stations. All of them were covering the action with growing alarm. She stopped cold at ABC Channel 7. There, coverage featured a picture within a picture with the dateline Everett, Washington. There, as in downtown Los Angeles, a mysterious pod landed and was letting loose with purple smoke. The coverage switched to an ABC reporter on the street in Everett while the LA airborne coverage shrunk to the upper left corner of the screen. The young reporter was almost breathless with her excitement, "I'm here in Everett, Washington, a city just north of Seattle, where a strange and threatening object has parachuted onto a community college football field. About the same time the object appeared thousands of leaflets appeared scattered over several city blocks nearby." The reporter held the leaflet in front of her face and began to read it. . .

Judy's initial thoughts turned towards Orson Wells' *War of the Worlds* broadcast, but she grudgingly realized this was reality—reality that might demand action very quickly. "Kids! Get your shoes on, fast. Mommy's going to get some food and clothes, we're going for a long ride in the car."

The two youngest children shouted in unison, "Hooray!"

Judy turned away from the screen just as one of ABC's national anchors broke in to say that the strange pods had been sighted north of Seattle, Washington, west of Portland, Oregon, in San Jose, California, in downtown Los Angeles, and just across the border from San Diego in Tijuana, Mexico.

Sally, the nine-year-old, had been moody since her father went away on active duty. She'd been watching the news and asked plaintively, "What are we going to do, Mommy?"

"Get out of town and go to a safe place."

*   *   *

The Chinese terror rocket had accomplished its mission. In only one hour the entire calculus of the American effort to support Taiwan changed—just as it had changed the previous day when the defiant images of Lieutenant Colonel Alexander's tank flashed across living room televisions. China correctly predicted that America would not retaliate against an "accidental" commercial rocket launch. Moreover, their war games correctly surmised the US non-response once the rocket was understood to have a politico-military purpose. How could America strike back against a rocket carrying reentry vehicles stuffed with propaganda leaflets and harmless (if theatrical) purple smoke? (Even if the rocket's Smart Dispenser carrier crashed down on the Hollywood Hills and ignited a brush fire—no one was killed after all.)

The genius of the Chinese assault was that it struck at the core of the American center of gravity—the people. Once Americans realized they were vulnerable to Chinese attack and that the Chinese meant to take Taiwan, even if it meant nuclear confrontation with America, American support for continuing the fight vanished. Even if the politicians and generals wanted to stay in the fight, they couldn't. By sending a missile slashing down the West Coast, the Chinese concretely illustrated America's complete helplessness in the face of nuclear attack. The threat of nuclear annihilation was no longer an abstract concept. America's will to resist wilted. China would have its way with Taiwan and

338

sometime in the future—maybe six months, maybe a year, maybe five years—China and America would either come to blows or America would acknowledge China's place as the world's leading superpower. A superpower far more willing to spill blood to achieve its aims than the tired, worn out, and once-proud nation called America.

The Chinese knew they had America on the run and now they aimed to ram home their advantage before the wily Americans could think their way out of the box they'd been slammed into. The Vice Premier for Foreign Affairs himself, Mo Waijiao, called Fu Zemin and relayed to him the good news. He instructed Fu to immediately call the Americans to the "negotiating" table and demand the unconditional surrender of US forces on Taiwan. If the Americans agreed, the television footage of the august event would be broadcast all over the world. Within a day Japan, South Korea, Australia and any other nation of a mind to resist China's rightful demands would be falling all over themselves to make friends with China. China would resume its place as Asia's hegemon and obedient vassals instead of enemies soon would surround it.

*　　*　　*

The United States Senate had the House's declaration of war resolution for all of half an hour when news of the West Coast terror rocket came in. The senior senator from the state of California immediately moved to table the resolution. A somber and uncharacteristically quiet Senate agreed to her motion on a vote of 84 to 10 with two voting present. The declaration of war was dead.

*　　*　　*

Millions of people in Los Angeles—and in Seattle, Portland, San Francisco and San Diego where leaflets had fallen as well—came to the same decision at the same time: get away from the targeted urban areas. The news media didn't make the situation any better. Stunning visual images coupled with grave "experts" predicting the imminent possibility of nuclear war sparked the largest, quickest exodus in the history of humanity.

In Los Angeles and Orange counties and inland, almost five million people got into three million vehicles and added to the tail end of the usual evening rush hour. Many more would soon follow as they saw images of their neighbors leaving town. The Los Angeles Basin experienced its worst traffic jam ever. Within half an hour gridlock set in with all routes leading out of the area packed with panicking people, listening to their radios and trying to out-smart and out-drive their fellow citizens.

Judy, her three children, and the family dog left the house in only 15 minutes. Judy packed a few gallons of water, some food, sunscreen, and a pistol (which she knew how to use better than her husband did—the legacy of fear from a nearly successful rape in a college parking lot many years before). Thankfully, the family always kept an earthquake survival kit. That, and Dan's saved up old MREs that he always brought back from the field, gave the family enough food to last a week. Judy's gas tank was mercifully full.

Judy drove east, taking the new toll road out of Tustin over the low-lying mountains that define the border between Orange County and Riverside County. She knew that if she could get out in front of the masses and stay out in front she'd be able to clear the knot of people who would inevitably try to flee the city.

For almost 15 minutes she made good time. Then the toll road hit the eastbound 91 Freeway. The freeway was choked (actually only slightly worse than for a usual evening rush hour—the freeway was far more congested a few miles to the west). At an average speed of 10 miles per hour Judy calculated she'd make the Cajon Pass on the 15 Freeway in about six to seven hours—sometime after midnight. She prayed that'd be quick enough to clear the clot of city dwellers fleeing east from Los Angeles.

Judy knew not where the other drivers were heading, but she intended to go to Ft. Irwin, some 45 miles northeast of Barstow in the middle of the Mojave Desert. She remembered from a discussion she and Dan had during the last couple of years of the Cold War that Ft. Irwin was to be the rallying point for military personnel and their families in the event of a nuclear war or other catastrophic national emergency. She knew the military installation had other advantages in their present situation as well—it was remote, few people knew about it, and it would be safe from the chaos that would likely result from millions of displaced persons trying to survive in the wilderness.

29
Counterattack

On Saturday, Taiwan's armed forces were shocked and pummeled into paralysis. On Sunday, reeling from the fast hitting Chinese blows, Taiwan struggled to call up its reserves and assess the situation. They knew PLA forces had already isolated Taipei by Sunday morning and, no doubt, would seek to tighten the ring around their capital. By Monday, the Taiwanese army was beginning to fill out its ranks with reservists and returning active duty soldiers who were finally overcoming their mystifying bout with the flu. Monday's action was dedicated to mopping up the last of the PLA resistance in Kaohsiung and cordoning off the PLA beachheads in Tainan and Taichung. Taiwan's light infantry reserve divisions were well suited for this task when reinforced with some artillery. By Monday evening, a rough parity existed around Tainan where the 15th and 16th Light Infantry Divisions (Reserve) had boxed in the Mainlanders. South of Taichung about 80 miles south of Taipei, the Taiwanese 14th Light Division (Reserve) blocked any southward PLA movement while rendering Taichung's commercial airport and seaport unusable with artillery fire.

The Republic of China navy was reduced to a fraction of its pre-war strength. The ROC air force struggled to achieve even local air superiority for minutes at a time. The ROC high command knew that every day that went by was another day the much larger PLA would get stronger in relation to their own rapidly mobilizing forces. Further, for years Taiwan's defense plans called for defeating the enemy at the beaches, then throwing him back into the sea with a swift counterattack before China's numerical superiority could grind the Taiwanese to dust. If there was to be any hope of success (especially now that America appeared to be abandoning its democratic ally) it would have to come within a day or two.

The army leadership outside of Taipei (communications with the capital was still sporadic due to Chinese radio signal jamming) decided on Tuesday morning to launch a counterattack on Wednesday. The counterattack would have three phases.

During phase one, the Taiwanese units in the field south of Taipei would halt their retreat and pull themselves into well-defended perimeters, drawing supplies from the ample quantities of bunkered ammunition, fuel, and food. These forces would pound the ports of Keelung and Taichung. They would employ artillery and rocket fire to make Chaing Kai-Shek International unusable. While the PLA could still bring troops and supplies ashore on the beach to the west of CKS airport, the quantities lifted would be far less than if they had full use of Taiwan's modern transportation facilities. From their battle positions the Taiwanese could also mount a series of aggressive reconnaissance in force actions designed to gain more information about their enemy while keeping him off balance.

Phase two of the counterattack would consist of marshaling all available mechanized infantry and armor forces for a break through at the lightly held passes 12 and 15 miles to the east of Taichung. This would have to happen on Wednesday night (using Taiwan's superior night vision capability to advantage over the Chinese).

Moving at night (and perhaps during the day as well if the cloud cover remained low and thick) the ROC counterattack would gather momentum and strength, then culminate in phase three on Friday night with a battle to pierce the PLA's ring around Taipei. The ROC generals hoped to draw the Mainlanders into a decisive engagement, destroy the enemy's armored forces, then lift the siege of the capital.

The plan had no margin of error and only one armored brigade in reserve (the 4th, way down in Kaohsiung—and it would no doubt be subjected to aerial interdiction during its entire journey north). Unfortunately, it was the only plan the Taiwanese generals had that could seize the initiative from the Mainlanders and win the war. Remaining on the defensive would be prudent, but it would result in a slow and certain death for Asia's newest democracy.

*   *   *

Fu Zemin read the dispatch from Beijing with unbridled glee over his morning tea. His trust in the Party leadership had never been stronger. Their bold and imaginative strike at America's will to fight was as inspirational as it was effective. Most importantly, the mission's success would now ensure that the struggle between China and its wayward province would remain free of outside interference. With the war going very well in the north, it would only be a matter of time before the combined forces of the PLA, the PLAAF, the PLAN and the PAP snuffed out the last of the counterrevolutionary forces on Taiwan.

Still, Fu had the more immediate concern of what to do with the American negotiators. Beijing still wanted a very public surrender—and now the price the Americans would pay for their insolence would be redoubled. Instead of being allowed to surrender their arms and leave Taiwan under an American flag, the American soldiers would now be required to surrender to a "neutral" third party: the Democratic People's Republic of Korea.

Fu moved to summon Major General Wei to his office. He would conclude the negotiations by noon and be done with it. He was about to shout for one of the junior officers to fetch Wei when he heard the unmistakable *crump, crump, crump* of falling artillery in the distance. He was annoyed that pockets of resistance were still so close the airport as to require the use of artillery to root them out. A deafening blast suddenly shook his world, punching the air out of his lungs and cutting the lights. The next thing Fu realized he was on his butt underneath his thick oak desk with a terrible ringing in his ears.

In the Tanshui Ho River valley a few miles south of the Shihmen Reservoir some 35 miles south southeast of CKS International, a little known ROC artillery unit rapidly ran their missile launcher back into the tunnel carved deeply into the side of the ridge. A few moments before they had launched a liquid-fueled Ching Feng missile. The missile, with a range of 70 miles, was a very weak counter to the hundreds of Chinese solid-fueled missiles across the Strait. Based loosely on the obsolete US Lance short-range ballistic missile, the Taiwanese built only 20 of them in the mid-1980s, then scrapped the program under strong US and Chinese opposition. While the Taiwanese built no more missiles, they did keep the ones they already had. Over time the missiles' guidance system was improved—adding GPS terminal guidance made the missiles accurate to within 50 meters.

The ROC army was surprised that the PLA gave them such a lucrative target. All the tactical units from the five group army headquarters on down to the regimental command posts had been carefully hidden and constantly moved during the previous three days of fighting. The overall PLA headquarters for the Taiwanese operation, however, remained fixed at CKS International Airport. Buried deep within the modern concrete and steel terminal building the Chinese must have figured they were safe from anything in Taiwan's arsenal—perhaps they were overconfident from the spotty performance of their adversaries over the last few days. In any event, the Ching Feng's large high explosive warhead was a perfect bunker buster. If the PLA offered such a target to the Taiwanese again, they'd gladly strike at it.

Donna slept at least five hours. Some of the jet lag was shaken out of her system and she began to forage for some coffee in her room. Finding none, she decided to call room service. There was no reply. She debated walking down to the hotel restaurant.

Donna noted that mainly older men and a few women served the thinly staffed hotel. She figured they were dragooned into service from the surrounding neighborhood (accounting for the complete lack of military-age men at the hotel). The hotel was crawling with People's Armed Police and a few junior-grade officers. *Certainly all of these people are getting something to eat somewhere. . .*

She was about to walk down to the hotel restaurant when she heard the muffled sound of artillery fire a few miles away. Mildly surprised that the Chinese put her into a room that looked down upon the airport, she carefully drew back the heavy curtain and surveyed the rainy scene. Wherever the artillery had exploded she couldn't see. *All this rain would suppress clouds of dust and smoke from the bursts anyway.*

Without warning a giant explosion bloomed like a deadly orange flower from atop the passenger terminal. She jumped away from her window seconds before the shock wave hit the building. Her window shook but remained intact. She thought she could hear the sound of glass breaking elsewhere. *So, the Taiwanese still have teeth. I better call home.* Donna took the satellite phone from her purse then walked back to the window to get better reception. She'd figured the office would be very interested in the latest action around the airport. . .

*   *   *

Large sections of Los Angeles and San Diego were burning. Looters roamed the streets virtually unchallenged. The few police who remained on the job were overwhelmed and reduced to protecting their own stations from the threatening mobs. Almost 15% of the California Army National Guard was in Ft. Polk,

Louisiana preparing to go to Indonesia, much of the remainder was scattered throughout the state. Even if the governor called them up, the fear-driven chaos had spread so fast and furiously that it was doubtful 10,000 Guardsmen could do anything at all.

By three AM Judy made it to the Cajon Pass. Her fuel mileage was horrible and she feared that she'd be unable to make it to Ft. Irwin without refilling the tank. Fortunately, the freeway speeds picked up a bit and she began to average 30 mph in stop and go traffic. She hadn't been this exhausted since the birth of her last child, but, with the same life and death issues at stake as in childbirth, she drove on.

Just outside of Barstow she noticed the strip of factory outlets that marked the unofficial end of civilization until Las Vegas (or at least the California-Nevada border where a small city had sprung up to cater to those who couldn't last another hour before commencing their gambling). "No shopping today," she said to herself, mainly to stay awake. KNX news radio out of LA helped her stay alert for a while, but soon the endless reports of increasing violence, arson and looting became repetitive and the news had the opposite effect.

Every motel in Barstow was full, every parking lot packed with fleeing people from the city. Three gas stations in town were still open. The others were either closed or out of fuel. Judy pulled into a line that was more than a city block long. She estimated by the time she'd make it to the front of the line it would be dawn. Her toughest task was staying awake. The kids were asleep and the puppy, long since having relieved himself in the back of the SUV, only occasionally whined.

Minutes stretched into two hours and she was finally at the front of the gas line. The price per gallon was $42.95 and 9/10th of a cent. The fill-up would cost about $800. Judy was shocked, but she needed the fuel. Within an hour or two she'd make Ft. Irwin.

*   *   *

Phase one of the ROC counterattack went as planned. Most units halted their retreat from the advancing PLA forces and dug in as ordered. Several ROC units were quickly surrounded after going to ground, but with hidden supplies to draw upon and the knowledge that holding fast would not be in vain, the men stood firm.

Chinese intelligence misread the Taiwanese moves as the actions of a dying army. They confidently assumed that, with no hope of American intervention and being cut-off from their capital, their foe was simply laying down to die. The PLA concentrated its efforts on the pockets of resistance and began to pummel the Taiwanese positions with artillery. This was exactly what the ROC commanders had hoped for.

With the PLA focusing its energies on eliminating its "trapped" quarry, ROC intelligence was able to gain valuable insight on enemy unit dispositions and strength. Well-placed Taiwanese rocket and artillery fire managed to reduce the rate of supplies coming to the PLA at Keelung, CKS International and Taichung. On Wednesday, for the first time in four days, the amount of supplies used by the PLA outstripped the fresh supplies moved onto the island.

In the gathering gloom of a darkly rainy Wednesday evening, the first deliberate ROC counterattack of the campaign began. Instead of leading the attack with mechanized and armored forces, the point of the Taiwanese spearhead consisted of reserve light infantry, elite airborne soldiers, and mortars for fire support. With a better than seven-to-one advantage over the unreinforced PLA airborne forces at the passes to the east of Taichung, the Taiwanese infantry quickly stamped out opposition. Within an hour the ROCs bagged 139 prisoners of war. Most importantly, their method of attack concealed the more ambitious nature of their offensive intent. PLA intelligence read the setback as nothing more than a local action—another pinprick raid designed to harass PLA forces or help regular army ROC forces in their general retreat from the victorious PLA.

By midnight two Taiwanese armor brigades (104 operational tanks) had maneuvered through the gap and were racing north. If the weather continued to cooperate and stayed rainy with a low cloud deck, the Taiwanese expected to continue their movement north for the most part unhindered by the PLAAF (only the most modern Russian-built aircraft were capable of all-weather operations—and these numbered less than 200 out of thousands of Chinese aircraft). If the weather cleared, the Taiwanese planned to break east for the hills and forest country and wait until nightfall before resuming their dash north.

*   *   *

After racing north to the outskirts of Taipei, Colonel Chu Dugen's Jia Battalion was relieved by a regiment of regular infantry and given a welcome opportunity to rest for six hours. By Monday morning his commandos were restive and waiting for their new orders. The orders weren't much of a surprise for Dugen, and, although of a conventional nature, he knew they would be the most difficult to carry out to date. Jia Battalion was to conduct a night river crossing of the Tanshui Ho and scout enemy positions on the western edge of Taipei. If the enemy was there in strength, Dugen's lightly-armed commandos would have a difficult time in the urban terrain against a prepared foe.

Colonel Chu rehearsed his troops all day Monday, using a wide, but deserted thoroughfare to simulate the river. When he was satisfied everyone knew their part of the mission, he gave his men three hours to eat, rest, and prepare.

The battalion started the crossing at 0124 hours. A thick mist hovered over the river. The sounds of the nearby struggle muffled what seemed to be the deafening roar of the paddles of the assault boats in the river. Halfway across the 400 meter-wide river, Dugen found himself praying for success and the safety of his men. Startled and embarrassed at his faith, he stopped, then he said a prayer for his imprisoned mother.

As Dugen's rubber boat reached the far shore he felt a small breeze blow by his ears. He hopped out of the boat and helped his soldiers drag it up on the shore. The wind picked up another notch. Dugen looked over his shoulder at the river, peering through his American-manufactured thermal sight. It showed nothing but a uniform gray—*the river must be still shrouded in fog*, he thought. The sight began to transmit images of heat on the river. *There!* A dingy with one squad. Dugen smiled that another ten men had made it across. The wind ticked up another notch, suddenly Dugen saw two, then three groups of men in their rubber boats. Dugen flipped the sight off his forehead. The pressure sensitive device automatically went to standby and darkened. He looked up. *Stars!* A sinking feeling gripped the pit of his stomach. Less than half his men were across and the fog was lifting!

Dugen heard a faint pop. He saw it out of the corner of his eye—the faint trail of a rising flare. Three seconds later the nighttime turned to a whitewashed day as a large mortar flare lit up the river, then lazily descended on its parachute. There was a shout from a few hundred meters away, then tracer rounds arced out of a building overlooking the river, piercing the thin rubber hull of an assault raft and the thin human skin of its occupants. In five seconds, more of Dugen's commandos fell then had fallen in the previous three days. Among their number was Jia Battalion's annoying mascot, the political officer.

By Wednesday night the commander of the 10th Group Army authorized a withdrawal of the remnants of Jia Battalion. In 48 hours of hard fighting, Dugen's battalion of elite commandos was down to less than 150 men. Dugen himself was wounded (two flesh wounds, one in each leg) and exhausted almost to the point of collapse.

The Chinese unloosed a modest five-minute artillery barrage mixed with smoke to cover Jia's retreat. Halfway back across the river the smoke lifted and another 50 men fell to the ROC machine gunners. Dugen's anger and the adrenaline rush of fear got him to the other side of the river. When his last commando made it to the safety of the modern steel and cement buildings on the west bank of the Tanshui Ho, Colonel Chu passed out.

Fu Zemin was released from the field hospital at six in the morning on Thursday with a twirl of cotton gauze on his skull and a massive headache. The Taiwanese missile attack on the airport caused him to lose two whole precious days. For two days the Americans just sat at the hotel. He was half thankful Beijing didn't send in a backup negotiator to arrange for the Americans' surrender. On the other hand, a crucial window of opportunity was almost closed.

Fu winced as he got out of the jeep and made his way to the hotel where the Americans were staying. He approved of the decision to move the headquarters to the basement of the hotel. If the Taiwanese found him again, he wanted to make sure the Americans would be the first to die in the attack.

Fu was slowly escorted to his chair in the briefing room. Thinking of himself as the only "hero" to be wounded in the Taiwanese attack, he was disappointed to see several officers and staff clerks carrying on with their duties having suffered wounds apparently far worse than his own. For a moment he was ashamed of his self-centeredness, but he quickly recovered his air of superiority.

An intelligence officer Fu hadn't seen before walked up to the large map board. He was only a colonel (Fu later discovered that the Chief of Intelligence for the headquarters was mortally wounded in the missile attack). The young looking officer began his briefing, "Good morning. My name is Colonel Chung. I am the deputy to the Chief of Intelligence.

"First, the weather. The weather will remain overcast and rainy with a low ceiling for the next 24 to 48 hours. This does not affect our ability to use commercial aircraft but it does severely limit our tactical air operations and aerial reconnaissance capabilities. Off road mobility is also poor. Local flooding caused by the lack of dam and reservoir maintenance as well as damage also limits river crossing operations.

"Now an overview of the situation. We have 18 divisions in the field opposite 13 understrength divisions of the enemy. More importantly, our divisions are in place to accomplish their mission of capturing Taipei. By merely holding our ground we can starve the capital into submission. In addition to the 250,000 troops we now have on the island, more than 100,000 PAP security forces are securing the rear areas. We have had very little bandit activity as a result.

"Moving from north to south then, allow me to summarize current posture of enemy and friendly forces," the colonel began using a small metal pointer, tapping each area with precision as he spoke. "In the vicinity of Taipei in the 10th and 12th Group Army sectors, we have the bulk of our deployed forces totaling two tank divisions, three mechanized infantry divisions, four infantry divisions, an air mobile division, an artillery division, an airborne infantry division and two regiments of airborne infantry. Opposing us in this decisive area are two divisions of infantry, one airborne brigade and one tank brigade in Taipei and the Yangmingshan mountain redoubt to the north. South of the city we have the remnants of the 1st Mechanized Infantry Division, a tank brigade and an artillery brigade. On the east coast we still have an airborne brigade that has not apparently moved from its positions since D-Day. Enemy activity has slowed down in the last 24 hours. Very little movement has occurred in this sector, although we have seen an increase in artillery and rocket fire concentrated on our ports of debarkation."

Colonel Chung paused and gathered his concentration for what he knew to be the rough part of the briefing. "Now then, in the 11th Group Army area we have two divisions of infantry at

Taichung along with a regiment of airborne infantry. These divisions hold strong defensive positions anchored by the city of Taichung and running 20 kilometers west to the port facilities. Opposite these forces are one mechanized infantry division, three infantry divisions, two tank brigades and an artillery brigade. Last night, the 1st Regiment of the 2nd Airborne Division reported a strong enemy attack on a battalion battle position in the hills to the east of Taichung. Following the pattern of the enemy's actions at Tainan and Kaohsiung, the commander of the 11th Group Army expects the enemy to counterattack his forces in an attempt to seize the port. He has given his commanders direction to stay in place, using the extensive urban cover to exact a high price on the enemy. He estimates he could hold out for at least a week under a strong assault. Should the enemy attempt to reduce our positions at Taichung, this would present an opportunity for us to strike south and smash the northern part of the enemy's attack against the 11th Group Army's positions around Taichung."

Fu shifted uncomfortably in his chair. In somewhat less then 48 hours of absence, the ROCs had managed to reverse their misfortunes at yet another major city—first at Kaohsiung with the unexpected American intervention, now at Taichung—*what next?*

"In the 15th Group Army area we have two infantry divisions and a regiment of airborne infantry. The enemy also has two infantry divisions, one to the north and one to the south. . ."

Fu cleared his throat, "Pardon me colonel, but we enjoy interior lines of communication in Tainan. Why doesn't the commander of the 15th Group leave a small holding force to the north or south and move to crush one of the divisions opposite him?"

The intelligence officer stammered, "Comrade, I cannot answer for operations." He looked to the small knot of operations officers standing in the corner to his left.

"Comrade Fu," it was a major general, "The commander of the 15th Group Army is a prudent officer. He has reported a build-up of enemy armor to his east—probably the 4th Tank Brigade fresh from its fighting in Kaohsiung. We all think it appropriate for a continued defensive stance while the possibility of a mounted assault remains. When the weather clears, and we once again have strong air support, we can move against the enemy in this sector."

Colonel Chung looked ill now, "Now, in the 14th Group Army sector. . ."

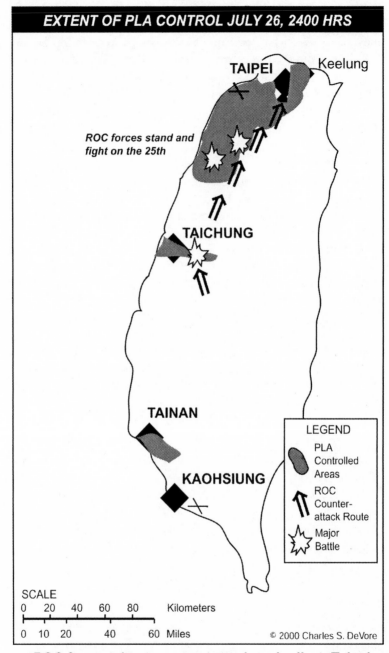

EXTENT OF PLA CONTROL JULY 26, 2400 HRS

TAIPEI Keelung

ROC forces stand and fight on the 25th

TAICHUNG

TAINAN

KAOHSIUNG

LEGEND

PLA Controlled Areas

ROC Counter-attack Route

Major Battle

SCALE

| 0 | 20 | 40 | 60 | 80 | Kilometers |

| 0 | 10 | 20 | 40 | 60 | Miles |

© 2000 Charles S. DeVore

ROC forces plan to counterattack and relieve Taipei

"We have sacked the commander of the 14th for incompetence," the operations major general said, sparing the intelligence officer the agony of explaining the setback to the senior political officer on the island. Colonel Chung was visibly relieved. "We have perhaps 5,000 troops remaining around Kaohsiung from the forces we committed there. We do not expect them to hold out much more than a day or two."

Colonel Chung broke back in, "This, of course, presents a challenge to the 15th Group Army. We estimate that within 72 hours the enemy will have rested and refitted the 10th and 17th Infantry Divisions and will commit these forces to an attack to retake Tainan."

Colonel Chung collected himself, then summarized the situation, "Sir, while we have had setbacks in the south, we believe our position to be so strong around Taipei that it would be militarily impossible for the Taiwanese to dislodge us from our siege. Furthermore, theirs is a wasting position. Every day we get stronger and they get weaker. Without the Americans or the Japanese to come to their rescue it is only a matter of time before their options run out and they will be forced to surrender."

Fu's concussion sent waves of pain into his head. *The military situation was still acceptable, even if the Taiwanese were enjoying some minor success—it was too little too late anyway. In the meantime, he aimed to make the Americans pay for the Taiwanese aggression.* Fu smiled to himself. "Send General Wei to my office, we have some planning to do."

A curtain of hesitancy descended on the briefing room, "Wei's dead," someone said from the back of the room, "Comrade Fu, General Wei is dead. He was killed during the recent attack. We're sorry. We thought you knew."

"No, I was unaware of his death. That is all then. I will be in my office."

Yes, the Americans must pay, Fu thought as he got to his feet, his head throbbing.

*   *   *

The leader of the Falun Gong in Amoy posted a couple of his followers at the door of the restaurant before entering. They would warn him in case a public security detail happened by. It didn't hurt to be careful. The usual persecution had intensified over the past two weeks, as the government sought to lock up potential troublemakers while it moved against Taiwan. The crackdown against his sect, the "Buddhist Law", was continuing as was the crack down against Christian groups. His lunch partner was the pastor of the largest underground Christian church in the city. Many leaders of house churches were already in jail. Both men had to exercise extreme caution.

In pre-revolutionary days, Amoy and the surrounding district had been the home of a substantial number of Western missionaries. Strangely enough, the sudden expulsion of the Christian missionaries from China had an effect entirely opposite of what the Communists had intended. Instead of drying up and shriveling away without leadership, Chinese Christian churches of all faiths proliferated as Chinese laity took over leadership roles once reserved for white Westerners.

Much to the consternation of the officially atheist Communist Party, the harder they cracked down on religions of all stripes, the more religion seemed to flourish. Party experts projected the number of serious religious adherents as outnumbering the membership of the Chinese Communist Party by about ten-to-one.

"Welcome, Master," said the restaurant owner, bowing slightly as the man entered the crowded restaurant. Another follower of Falun Gong, he led the "Master" to a secluded table where Brother Ouyang was seated, then poured tea for them both. Every table within earshot was occupied by a loyal member of the sect.

The "Master" lifted his cup of tea in a silent salute at his tablemate who responded with a salute of his own.

"Both of us believe that the way of peace is superior to the way of the sword," the "Master" began. "But the situation has grown intolerable."

Brother Ouyang nodded thoughtfully, "What do you have in mind, Master Chao?"

The "Master" leaned forward and presented his thoughts to the Christian. If the State knew what was said next, both men would have been summarily shot and their families sent bills for the bullets.

*   *   *

Fu had a medical orderly remove his bandages and apply makeup to his wounds. He looked at his head and his one black eye. *No, this will not do.* "Find me a pair of sunglasses," he snapped, "We cannot allow the Americans to know of my injuries."

With neither reinforcement nor resupply, the American forces were becoming increasingly irrelevant from a military standpoint. Their political utility was still high, however, and Fu was determined to force their surrender. He set a meeting time of noon and instructed his staff to make the necessary final preparations.

Donna knew about the Chinese propaganda rocket. She also knew about the terrible toll the Chinese attack took on America's West Coast cities. Los Angeles was especially hard hit. The Agency told her that damage from looters and rioters was estimated in the billions of dollars (she doubted that the information constituted useful intelligence should the Chinese have been listening in—no doubt both CNN and the Chinese consulate in LA had already conveyed the news). More troubling was the horrific toll on the displaced population in Southern California. With a complete breakdown in the infrastructure of a modern society, hundreds of thousands of people were in danger of death by dehydration in the desert wastes between Arizona and the coastal urban areas. The authorities were trying to move the people back to the city, but with the lack of law and order and the threat of nuclear attack, people refused. Donna marveled at her nation's complete lack of any response—*One unarmed missile and we give up. . .*

She heard a soft tapping on the door, then a barely audible rasp, "It's Taylor, let me in."

She opened the door to the civilian attired four-star general. He immediately went to Donna's bathroom and turned on the sink's faucet. The water pressure wasn't as high as it was the day before, but the noise of the running water was still enough to conceal a whispered conversation.

"I thought you should know, we extracted the Marine force out of southern Taiwan last night. We picked up more than 1,000 Marines and Navy personnel. The Chinese might be a little ticked during today's negotiations."

Donna raised an eyebrow. Now successful retreats were counted as victories. "What about the force up in Taipei?"

Taylor frowned, "Hell, Klein, there's probably only about 40 of them left, besides, the downtown airport is under constant surveillance by the Chinese, there's no way we could extract them, even if we knew where to find them."

"That's a load of bull general, and you know it; you don't need fixed wing aircraft to fly in there and get those soldiers. Helicopters from Okinawa would do just fine."

"Look, I didn't come here to argue tactics with you. . ." Taylor looked very uncomfortable, "There's something else you need to know—Lindley's a mole for the Chinese."

Donna's mouth fell open. She struggled with this new bit of information. "How did you. . ?"

"Find out? I have a secure system two-way satellite message pager. The NSA figured it out a few days ago but only recently did they gather enough evidence to make it official."

"How can I believe you—you could be the spy yourself."

"Damnit Klein! I'm the general, he's the former Chinese lobbyist, remember? I've dedicated 35 years of my life to the military; he made millions in fees from China before he made it to the White House. It's so obvious. Have even you gone blind to how obvious this is? If *Admiral* Klein was here he'd dare call Lindley what he is: a traitor."

Donna flushed briefly. She'd had her suspicions about Lindley, especially when he tried so hard to get the President to keep her off the negotiating team. "What do we do? We can't very well arrest the senior member of our team for treason while on Chinese soil can we?" Donna's face showed the question was merely rhetorical; she was already thinking of what to do.

A loud knock at the door startled both Americans.

"It's Lindley. We have to be ready to go in ten minutes Donna. The Chinese want to resume negotiations. You hear me?"

Donna spoke loudly, "Sure, no problem."

"Taylor in there with you?" Lindley asked.

"Yes."

"Okay, fine, I want to see you two in a couple of minutes in my room." Lindley's tone was curt.

"We'll be there," Taylor said.

Lindley's footsteps could be heard walking away.

"So, what do we do?" General Taylor hissed. He was consumed with contempt for Lindley and loathed the thought of even visiting his room.

"I may have a solution, but I'll need your help. . ."

*   *   *

All day Thursday the rain drizzled down. Low hanging clouds clung just above the base of Taiwan's mountains and hills. The People's Liberation Army Air Force was nowhere to be seen. Maneuvering over familiar terrain and in friendly territory, the ROC army made good time and advanced north in good order.

On Friday afternoon a little-noticed engagement was fought at the intersection of Tollways 1 and 3 less than ten kilometers south of the Touchien Hsi River about 50 kilometers southwest of Taipei. With this key crossroads in hand, the ROC leadership was free to pursue a breakthrough to the north along Tollway 1 or further to the east along Tollway 3 where the terrain was more restricted but the concealment was better.

The ROC plan was simple and aggressive: as soon as darkness fell, seize the intact bridges over the Touchien Hsi River along both Tollways, then, employ overwhelming firepower and armor against the 85th Infantry Division to the east, breaking through to the division's rear command post at Kuanhsi. Leaving behind the infantry to mop up the rear and clear the supply route, the 2nd Mechanized Infantry Division, 3rd and 5th Armor Brigades and the 6th Armor Brigade (Light) would drive north, brushing past the ROC 1st Infantry Division's battle positions surrounding Lake Benevolence and the Tomb of Chaing Kai-Shek. Just before dawn the commanders expected to fight the battle to break through to Taipei, drawing in the Chinese mobile reserve and destroying them piecemeal with superior fighting skills and night vision capability.

Fu Zemin needed a replacement for General Wei. The intelligence officer had quickly made himself indispensable and the political officer missed him as he would his own right hand. Wei would have known what to do when the leader of the American team became violently ill and lapsed into a coma. As it was, Fu allowed the Americans another two hours to recover. Then, two hours slipped into three, and three into four as the military situation south of Taipei became increasingly critical.   Clearly, the Taiwanese were not simply going to give up and die as everyone thought they were going to do just yesterday. By dinnertime Fu had completely forgotten about the Americans—and dinner.

While Fu respected General First Class Deng Yen-hsi, the commander of the operations on Taiwan, he found the general impenetrable and gruff, at least around him. Fu desperately needed a military officer at his side to communicate a clear picture of the evolving situation. General Wei had been that officer, now he was dead. On the positive side, at least he thought of a replacement for General Wei: Colonel Chu. The commando colonel who had impressed him a few days before had been lightly wounded in a terrible fight that claimed three-quarters of his battalion on the edge of Taipei itself. This hero of the People was known to be resourceful and tough. Without a battalion to lead and too wounded to be highly mobile for the next couple of weeks anyway, Fu decided to request the services of Colonel Chu as his personal aide (the PLA's political secretariat had neither the time nor the opportunity to inform the field forces on Taiwan of Colonel Chu's unique status due to his mother's treasonous actions).

Colonel Chu was due to arrive any moment now—and not a second too soon. Fu wanted both the counsel and comfort that the brave commando leader would provide. Stronger Taiwanese forces than anyone had thought could be mustered had just broken through PLA lines east of Hsinshu and were reported to be only 25 kilometers from Deng Xiaoping International Airport. Worse yet, only an understrength airborne division stood between the ROCs and Fu Zemin's small but very Communist body.

30
Rout

All Friday night the Taiwanese spearhead thrust north. By three in the morning the lead elements of the attacking vanguard could see the artillery duels lighting up the low-hanging clouds around Taipei. According to ROC intelligence, the army had only the PLA's 1st Mechanized Infantry Division between them and their beleaguered capital. Taiwan's best tanks, 47 venerable ex-US M60A3s, were brought forward to make the assault, just to the east of Tollway 3 in the secondary road network running between the tollway and the ridge that paralleled it (the tollway itself was known to be mined). The tanks lined up, their engines rumbled behind a low-lying rise that separated them from the enemy some one kilometer away. Behind each tank there were two M113A2 armored personnel carriers, each with two crewmen and 11 infantrymen aboard. In front of the tanks sat 35 LAV-150 Commando armored fighting vehicles (armored cars equipped with a 20mm gun and two machine guns each). Only one kilometer south of this brigade-sized force was another of comparable size (only with older M48A5 tanks, also equipped with thermal sights). In reserve, the Taiwanese held the 6th Armor Brigade (Light), equipped with completely remanufactured M41 light tanks, reinforced with a battalion of mechanized infantry. The 4th Armor Brigade was still on the march some 40 kilometers to the south. Almost two-thirds of Taiwan's remaining armored force was ready to tear loose into the Chinese lines, force a decisive engagement, and wrest victory from the PLA.

On the other side of the lines, 20 kilometers to the northwest in the basement of a hotel near the renamed Deng Xiaoping International Airport, Fu Zemin was watching the Taiwanese advance unfold like an unstoppable tide. His head hurt and he was fearful almost to the point of irrationality. Beside him, standing stiffly due to his leg bandages, his pain, and his discomfort at having to be so close to one holding political power, was Colonel Chu Dugen. The usual activity of any command post swirled about the two—clerks carrying messages, intelligence and operations staff updating information about enemy and friendly units with grease pencils on the thin acetate map overlay, and the crackling din of radio communications parsed from key sectors of the battlefield.

As much as the political officer Fu was worried and unsure of himself in the situation, Colonel Chu was calm. He resented having been pulled out of the field. He hated the Party and this pathetic man who represented all its evils. But, at least he understood the military environment. He strained to turn his easy understanding into calming and straightforward explanations for his latest charge. If Comrade Fu was appreciative he didn't show it.

Colonel Chu saw the battlefield as a living thing existing in all four dimensions. He knew what the Taiwanese were after. He knew victory was within their grasp—he also knew that they would be very vulnerable for an instant. If the PLA could strike at that rich concentration of armor and shatter it, all militarily significant resistance to the Mainlanders would end. Unfortunately, to strike such a target one needed exceptional timing (best achieved by slowing down the breakthrough at the point of entry) and the means to deliver the blow. The method of achieving both the timing and blow were unknown the Colonel Chu—he simply knew the necessity of doing so.

Colonel Chu turned to address the political officer, wondering once again if he was any relation to the man his late father was accused of assassinating, "Comrade Fu, may I confer with you about the current operations?"

Fu was almost glassy-eyed. He fiddled with a small, circular scar in the middle of his right palm. It was 0427 hours. The basement room was stuffy, heavy-laden with cigarette smoke and sweat. Mud covered the floor from the comings and goings of field commanders and liaisons. General Deng hadn't been seen in hours and Fu half expected the general suffered a break down or worse. The chief Party representative on Taiwan turned to his new aide and said hoarsely, "Yes, tell me what you think."

"Comrade Fu, I think we are seeing the pivotal battle in this campaign. All will be won or lost based on the actions of a few thousand brave men and a handful of commanders. We should know the outcome within two hours, three at the most."

The colonel's certainty did little to comfort Fu. Fu Zemin's entire life and career was now tied up in the success or failure of some mid-ranking PLA commander 20 kilometers away. After one week of fighting, Fu decided he didn't much like war after all—it was too messy, too uncertain. Moreover, Fu couldn't manipulate military affairs as readily as he could Party politics. Fu said under his breath, "Colonel, do you trust Deng?"

Dugen was taken aback—*trust Deng? Is this a trick?* "Sir, I have never served directly under General Deng, but I know him by reputation to be one of our most aggressive and resourceful generals. He inspires complete devotion in his men as well. I have the utmost confidence in his leadership abilities."

As Dugen finished his sentence, a map worker erased an enemy unit symbol then redrew the same unit another five kilometers closer to Taipei. The enemy was now only ten kilometers away from the outskirts of the capital. Colonel Chu noted only one battalion of tanks and one battalion of truck-mobile infantry stood between the enemy and his objective. The nearest mobile unit of significance was at least 15 kilometers away—and it hadn't moved from its position for 36 hours. A clerk handed the map worker a message. He quickly erased the PLA tank battalion and advanced it to a position directly opposite the ROC tank brigade.

The commando colonel remained impassive to the new posting. Inside, he questioned the wisdom of uprooting a tank battalion in prepared defensive positions to blunt the point of the thrusting spear during the hours of darkness that favored the enemy. Such a small-scale effort using no more than 30 tanks was doomed to failure and could only slow the enemy's advance for half an hour at the most.

Judging by Fu's hopeful look Colonel Chu correctly assumed Fu really didn't understand the implications of the situation map. With decisions already made and set in motion hours ago, Chu decided not to tell Fu that things were looking worse by the minute for the PLA. Whether he knew now or an hour or two later, it would make little difference: the PLA was very likely going to be compelled to go on the defensive until the long term effects of a costly and demoralizing blockade could bring the island to its knees. Without friends to rescue her, Taiwan was doomed—it would just take more time for China to subdue the province than originally anticipated. Chu decided to attempt small talk to divert Fu's attention, "Comrade Fu, may I ask, how did you get that scar on your hand?"

Fu's face brightened for an instant at the prospect of telling the warrior his war story, then darkened for effect, "I was in our Embassy in Belgrade in 1999 when the Americans bombed it."

Chu grunted admiringly, "Well, that means you've been

bombed two more times than I have!"

*   *   *

Lieutenant Colonel Dan Alexander's tank *Traveller* died three days ago. The lack of logistics support and mechanics coupled with a few direct hits from PLA tanks (all destroyed shortly after challenging the American tank) was too much for the 64-ton tank to handle. By the time Alexander made the painful decision to abandon his steed he and his crew had chalked up 63 kills (it would have been less, but the ROC's M60A3s used the same round as the M1IP's 105mm gun—it didn't take much persuasion before *Traveller* was given another 20 rounds to carry on the fight). The worse part about leaving the tank behind was trying to destroy anything of value inside of it in case the Chinese ended up winning the war and capturing the vehicle (which, from Alexander's viewpoint, was a very real and growing possibility). The crew destroyed the breach with a thermite grenade, placing two unused HEAT rounds under the path of the molten-hot metal they knew would be produced by the grenade. A minute later *Traveller's* insides were a smoky ruin—what four days of continuous combat failed to do, her own crew did to her.

Alexander pulled his remaining force of 67 National Guardsmen off the increasingly tenuous line around Sungshan Domestic Airport (also destroying the avionics of the three parked C-17s) and headed north to the Yangmingshan Mountain district of Taipei. There, at the foot of the thickly wooded mountain, he knew he would find the American Ambassador's residence (the Taiwanese said the embassy itself was evacuated after sustaining some artillery damage). Technically, Alexander knew that the Ambassador was called the Representative of the American Institute in Taiwan—a diplomatic nicety designed to allow the Chinese to pretend that the Americans had no diplomatic relations with an island they considered a renegade province. Practically speaking, however, Alexander knew that the Chinese would understand that little could be gained by violating diplomatic conventions. So long as they were on American soil, Alexander and his men would be safe. Besides, he imagined, the Marine embassy guards would probably welcome the reinforcements.

*   *   *

Logistically, Flint knew his Marines were spent. Too much was lost with the sinking of the *Belleau Wood* and the *Dubuque*. Without spare parts and ammunition, they were quickly reduced to barely more than light infantry with a decreasing number of helicopters and vehicles to call upon. Worse still, an increasing number of the personnel he had were coming down with the flu.

Even so, Colonel Flint had been filled with conflicting emotions since he first received the order to evacuate Taiwan Wednesday afternoon. The Marines of the 31st MEU left Taiwan an unbowed force. With less than half of their original members remaining, the Marines knew that they had performed to the highest standards of the American fighting tradition—more than 15,000 PLA soldiers killed and hundreds more captured were the undisputed tribute to combined efforts of the US Marine Corps and the US Navy. Flint knew that had America enough stomach for a fight, they could have not only cleaned the PLA off of Taiwan, but landed on Mainland China itself and taken Beijing just to show it could be done. But, it was not to be.

On Friday, Flint stopped by his old office on the way to see his Marines at the hospital. It was dusty, but otherwise untouched since he left Okinawa for East Timor more than seven months ago. It felt strange to be in the office. After seeing so much death and suffering, the office—*my office*, he reminded himself—seemed coldly bureaucratic and out of place for a warrior.

As soon as he landed at Okinawa the inquisition began. Everyone of higher rank wanted to know why he did what he did. Did he know that he almost caused World War Three? That the US West Coast had been terrorized because of his decision to fight? That China had demanded his unconditional surrender and internment in North Korea? It was upon hearing this last item that Flint was just damn glad to be off the island. Given the record of his Commander-in-Chief he knew that he and his men probably came very close to being long-term "guests" at the Pyongyang "Hilton". Still, he was left with the feeling that he had unfinished business on Taiwan—he and his Marines didn't leave *after* completing a job; they were forced off the island prematurely by policymakers in Washington.

*   *   *

Just outside the town of Fuqing, about 40 kilometers south of Fuzhou, three Dong Feng-15 missiles were on their final countdown. The orders called for the missiles to be launched at one-minute intervals. The three warheads were targeted to land at four-kilometer intervals in a string eight kilometers long. The first missile lifted off flawlessly and on time, leaving a thick gray-white plume in the early Saturday morning sky.

The neutron bomb is a misunderstood weapon in the West. Touted as a counter to the massive Soviet armored advantage in Europe in the late 70s and 80s, it was developed but never deployed by NATO. Soviet propaganda and the appeasement-minded Western Left killed the weapon. Fortunately, the timely appearance of high-tech American tank killers such as the Multiple Launch Rocket System (MLRS) with 644 tank-busting bomblets in each missile, lessened the military need for the controversial weapon.

The neutron bomb, also known as the "enhanced radiation weapon" is basically an H-bomb without the uranium-238 jacket used to increase the blast effect by absorbing neutrons. Without the dense jacket of U-238 to catch them, the neutrons are free to escape in much larger numbers than in a regular thermonuclear device. What makes the neutron bomb of interest to the military is that it is especially well suited to killing concentrations of tanks on a battlefield. Tanks are tough and can actually withstand the effects of a nuclear bomb—they are virtually crush-proof, so a nuclear bomb's blast effect with its building-collapsing overpressure is not much of a threat—and they are highly resistant to heat. Instead, the neutron bomb's enhanced flow of radiation efficiently kills tank crews within the small radius of blast and heat created by the explosion. A one-kiloton neutron bomb affects a fairly small area: a diameter of about two miles (three kilometers).

South of Taipei, the tankers within a kilometer of ground zero were killed outright, those further away got radiation sickness, some dying within a few days, others within two weeks.

For the Chinese on Taiwan, the neutron bomb held a particular attraction. First, it could be used to negate the Taiwanese advantage in armor in the early, vulnerable stages of the invasion before the Chinese could land their own armor in large numbers.

Second, its effects were very confined and the fallout minimal. Were the PLA generals of the same mind as their 1980s NATO counterparts for whom the bomb was originally designed, there would be a final consideration: with enough warning and preparation, friendly troops could easily survive a close encounter with an enhanced radiation weapon by simply digging in. Unfortunately for the nearby PLA troops, their senior officers had no excess of humanitarian impulse—more than 2,000 PLA conscripts died in the three explosions along with more than 3,500 of their foes in 157 tanks and 256 armored personnel carriers. Complete surprise was deemed more important than sparing the lives of a few common infantrymen.

Moments after the dust from the third blast cleared, the PLA's 10th Tank Division west of Taipei and the 12th Tank Division south of Taipei at Hsintien rolled into action. By the end of the day Taiwan's 4th Armor Brigade would be the only mounted force standing between the Communist forces and the southern three-quarters of the island nation.

31
Gambit

The last two days were a strange mix of boredom and fear. There was little official business to demand Klein and Taylor's time (the Chinese took the Americans' satellite phones; Taylor's two-way pager was their only link—and its batteries were running low).

The downtime led Donna to regard the general in a different light. At first she absorbed his mannerisms. He was calmly efficient. Whenever she came close to him, however, she noticed him tense up. With Lindley out of the way, they quickly became friends.

. Over a Saturday breakfast of boiled rice, stale bread and tea, Donna asked Tim Taylor the question that had been in the back of her mind for half a year, "Tim," the older man looked up from his plate, his pleasant, but distant expression quickly turned to discomfort, "At the war game when our eyes first met, what were you thinking?"

Taylor looked at Donna then looked away to his right, "I was thinking that you were a beautiful young woman. You, ah. . ." Taylor struggled with control, "you reminded me of my late wife and the first time I saw her. You kindled a feeling in me I thought I'd never have again. When I spoke to you after the first day though, I knew you were uncomfortable. I didn't blame you. I'm old enough to be your father and you probably didn't appreciate an old goat hitting on you. In any event, I am thankful for meeting you. You showed me I might still be capable of loving someone."

Donna reached out and squeezed Taylor's hands. She looked at him, "First of all, I was uncomfortable; I saw your wedding ring and I thought you were married. Secondly, my father is old enough to be your father. Thirdly, you weren't 'hitting on me' and you're hardly an 'old goat.'" She squeezed his hands again.

Taylor looked at Donna, "Well, what do you say we get to know each other better?" He chuckled, "I know a great Chinese restaurant. . ."

"Do they serve rice and stale bread and have lousy service?" Donna smiled gently.

"Yes. But they have nice, private tables. . ."

By Saturday afternoon, Donna had spent eight solid hours talking with Tim (as she began to think of him). The war's sounds occasionally intruded on their little universe. It was the longest period of time Donna had ever talked with any man without that man expecting a kiss—or something more.

Their blossoming friendship was forgotten briefly on Saturday afternoon when Tim told her he had received a communication on his message pager that the Chinese had detonated three small nuclear weapons south of Taipei. After that, their relationship took on a sense of urgency.

It was Sunday morning. Donna took it as a positive sign that the Chinese hadn't returned to press their surrender demands for three days now—*the PLA must have its hands full, perhaps they used the nuclear bombs in desperation.*

As for Lindley, she figured he was only now recovering from the drugging she administered to him with Taylor's help. She knew the drug's aftereffects were painful, but she held absolutely no sympathy for the traitor.

A loud banging on the door ended the temporary break from their mission. "General Taylor," the voice demanded in strong tones, "You and Ms. Klein are required to meet with Party Representative Fu within five minutes. Be in the hallway in three minutes and we will take you to him. Do you hear me?"

"Yes," Taylor yelled through the door.

"Do not be late."

Taylor grumbled. All the tenderness Donna saw in him the last 24 hours vanished; the warrior returned. Donna was thankful for the seamless transition—*there was serious work to be done now.*

Donna grabbed her notebook and considered whether or not to take her microcassette recorder. She decided to take it and show it to the Chinese, asking for permission to use it to assist in transcribing the notes from their meeting.

She walked out into the darkened hallway, a half step behind Taylor. She could barely make out the figures of two Chinese military men at the end of the hall. "You come now! You must not be late!" bellowed the soldier to them.

Donna heard Taylor grumbling under his breath—she thought she heard something like, "Come now, my ass!" Fortunately, the soldier's English wasn't good enough to understand the insult.

The soldier, pistol raised, beckoned them towards the stairwell.

Donna leaned over to speak quietly into Taylor's ear, "Are we really going to negotiate a surrender?" Even though they discussed it, Donna still refused to abandon hope.

"Of course. Let me put it to you this way: were we commanding troops out in the field in a militarily untenable situation we could negotiate terms of surrender. This situation is no different. . ."

"Except that the troops in question seem to have no desire to surrender," Donna reminded the general.

Taylor was momentarily reflective, "Well, yes, we do have that minor consideration to contend with, don't we?"

"Assuming we do arrange for acceptable surrender terms, how do we convince the soldiers to give up?"

Taylor sighed before stepping through the stairwell's door, "Hell, I'm still trying to figure the surrender terms part out, I haven't thought about the actual execution of the mission."

The two Chinese soldiers and the two Americans clanked down the metal staircase, everyone held their thoughts to themselves. Donna's stomach tightened. *What if Lindley is conscious? What if he remembers what happened to him?* The drug experts at the CIA assured her that anyone so incapacitated by the drug would have a very difficult time recalling anything around the time of the injection. She hoped so, she could only wonder at what the Chinese would do to her if they knew that their highest mole in the US government was disabled by a lowly CIA analyst.

Donna and the general were ushered into a well-lit room in the hotel's basement. Other than six guards standing around the periphery, there was no one else in the room. The room only had one office-sized work desk and one chair, nothing else. The solitary desk in the middle of the room made the room look much larger than it really was. "I'd say the 'negotiations' are over General," Donna said softly.

"We should have nuked the bas. . ." The door burst open. Two soldiers hurried in, followed by a man wearing large, dark sunglasses. ". . .tards," Taylor finished a beat later.

The man—Donna now recognized him as the 'negotiator' from a few days before—slowly walked to the desk and sat down. A tall, muscular colonel followed stiffly three paces behind him. Another man, a captain, followed behind the colonel. Party representative Fu spoke in Mandarin, "I have a list of demands. . ."

Donna pulled out her microcassette recorder, "May I use this to avoid errors?" She asked in her own excellent Mandarin.

Fu looked up, not expecting to be interrupted so soon, "No!" He turned to a soldier, "Take that device from that woman!"

A soldier stepped forward and gruffly took Donna's recorder.

"*I* will tell you what errors you make," Fu hissed at the analyst. "Now then," Fu comported himself, "Speaking for the People's Republic of China, I have three demands.

"First, all United States armed forces personnel unlawfully on the Chinese sovereign soil of the province of Taiwan will cease hostilities as of 1800 hours Monday.

"Second, said forces will surrender to representatives of the Peoples Liberation Army by 0600 hours Tuesday morning.

"Third, the United States of America will recognize Taiwan as a province of the People's Republic of China's by converting their illegal diplomatic presence into consulates of the United States of America to the People's Republic of China." Fu looked up from his paper. The room was silent.

Donna saw Fu's paper was hand written in large Chinese characters. She also noted an abrasion under Fu's left eye that was partially covered with makeup. Donna began to worry that she would have to translate, and thus be virtually cut-off from the negotiations. The captain behind Fu took a step forward and repeated Fu's words in very good English.

General Taylor's ears flushed, but otherwise he held fast. Taylor cleared his throat, "We need safe passage into Taipei to visit the United States soldiers before we can act on your first two demands."

The captain leaned over and translated Taylor's comments. Fu cocked his head to listen. He nodded, started to speak, then stopped. Fu turned to Taylor and said in Mandarin, "Why only Taipei?"

Donna said under her breath, "They don't know about the Marine evac."

Taylor nodded and waited for the translation a second later. "We have personnel in Taipei who were stranded there when their aircraft sustained mid-flight damage during your surprise attack. We have no one else in Taiwan."

"He's not going to like this," Donna said between her teeth.

The translator finished Taylor's statement.

Fu spat sharply.

Donna said, "He called you a liar."

She finished just as the translator enthusiastically yelled, "Liar!"

Taylor paused to let the room calm down a notch, "Our personnel who sought refuge from your unprovoked attack in international waters in the vicinity of Kaohsiung were evacuated several days ago. The United States has no military presence in southern Taiwan."

Fu intently listened to his translator. His forehead wrinkled with thought. He said, almost smiling, "Ah, you mean the Marines retreated from the field before the face of a superior enemy?"

Taylor bridled at the translation and retorted, "I mean what I said: the United States has no military presence in southern Taiwan. We evacuated."

After the translation, Fu snorted, "I'd say you abandoned your ally just like you did in 1975 in Vietnam after your defeat."

"Touché," Donna said softly, "He's playing for the Asian audience and history and I'd say we've given him most of what he wanted."

Donna's comment overlapped the translator's statement and Taylor took a moment to process both messages. Donna turned from Taylor and said in English, "We are authorized to act on your first two conditions. Your last condition will require consultations with our government. We also have concerns regarding the several thousand United States citizens in Taiwan. What do you wish to do?"

Fu listened, thought for a moment, then spoke through his translator, "You will act immediately on items one and two. After you have successfully executed these items, we will return to issue number three. Citizens of the United States engaged in lawful business activities will be unharmed and allowed to continue operations. We view this as nothing more than a civil disturbance. Business disruption is unfortunate, but should be minimized for the benefit of all sides. You will be contacted when we have arranged for your safe passage. You are dismissed."

All the way back upstairs Donna unsuccessfully tried to think of ways to snatch victory from the dragon's maw. The difficult part of her mission was only beginning.

*   *   *

Three neutron bombs and a crushing PLA armored assault on the dazed ROC survivors eliminated any threat of a Taiwanese counterattack on Saturday. By Sunday the PLA had complete freedom to maneuver on Taiwan. Instead of simply seizing terrain, they concentrated on annihilating their enemy's army one unit at a time. This effort naturally carried them south, but at a speed dependent on the tactical requirement to find and overwhelm their foe.

Another benefit accrued to the PLA as well: both Keelung and Deng Xiaoping International Airport were now free from enemy shelling. In addition to the increased flow of supplies, the Mainlanders shuttled in another 5,000 PAP paramilitaries from Fujian province as well as an additional mechanized infantry battalion from Guangdong.

The PLA's supreme commander on Taiwan, General First Class Deng, was confident that hostilities would cease within ten days—two weeks at the most. The battle was won (as it was even before the fighting started according to the precepts of Sun Tzu), all that was left to do was to formally act out the pre-assigned roles of victor and vanquished.

Deng fully briefed Fu on the situation. In turn, Fu shared his own good news with Deng: the Americans had already begun their ignominious retreat from Taiwan.

Deng was only partially saddened that he would not soon have a chance to inflict the sting of defeat on the Americans. Fortunately, Deng was a strategic thinker, like Fu, he too understood the value to China of America's retreat. Besides, he knew that, in time, he would again meet the Americans in battle.

*   *   *

The odd-shaped black bat winged jet taxied down the runway at the American air base on Okinawa. An impressive feat of Yankee engineering, the F-117A Stealth Fighter had its limitations. While it was nearly invisible to radar, it had to be operated at night to avoid visual detection; if spotted, it was very vulnerable, especially to enemy fighter aircraft. The F-117A was also poorly labeled. It was far from a fighter. Its primary purpose was as a tactical bomber and it was well suited for this role. The F-117A's usual mission was to fly over heavily defended areas at night, dropping 2,000-pound laser-guided bombs on key targets. Tonight, however, this Stealth Fighter had a more unconventional mission to perform.

Since China's invasion of Taiwan, there had been no communications between the de facto US Embassy in Taipei and Washington. This fact, coupled with the Chinese demands for surrender of all US forces on the island, meant that it was imperative to establish reliable communications with the Ambassador—especially since the Ambassador's residence was now home to 67 tired American citizen-soldiers, many of whom were wounded.

Staff Sergeant Michael Heinzleman began his military career as a member of the Army's elite Golden Knights parachute team. Enjoying military life far more than he anticipated, and wanting an even bigger challenge, Heinzleman signed up for a special opportunity to train with the Navy's SEALs. Within a year, Heinzleman was on the Army's secretive Delta Force. He was at Ft. Bragg, North Carolina when he received orders to assemble a HALO (High Altitude, Low Opening—a technique used to clandestinely insert parachutists, usually at night) kit and meet an aircraft at Pope Air Force Base next door. That was 24 hours ago.

Heinzleman now found himself doing something so classified and unusual, that he himself had only heard rumors about it. He was strapped into a special pod inside the bomb bay of a Stealth Fighter.

Deep inside of China's South Central Air Defense Region bunker a yellow blip began flashing on a monitor. Moments before, China's Passive Coherent Location system detected minute variations in civilian radio and television signals caused by the passage of a solid object through the sky. This information was automatically compared with regular radar data from China's fixed ground and airborne systems. Within seconds, the system flagged the location of a probable stealth aircraft. When the Passive Coherent Location system saw something that radar didn't see, it was an indication that American Stealth aircraft were lurking about. Only two minutes later the South Central Air Defense Region radioed an air interceptor division covering north Taiwan and told them to vector fighters to intercept the probable inbound Stealth.

Heinzleman checked his watch, barely readable from behind the protective goggles he wore as part of his completely black, rubberized ensemble. According to the time he ought to be getting close to Taipei. As he looked away from his watch to adjust a strap, the pilot came over the intercom and announced, "Sergeant, I've got 20 seconds to the release point. Everything is nominal. We're at 10,150 feet. Barometric pressure is at 29.95. Temperature is 49 degrees. Humidity is 100%. Wind is at 110 degrees, speed is 15 knots."

Ten thousand feet, won't even need oxygen, the Sergeant thought. "Roger, all my systems check as nominal."

"Opening bomb bay doors."

A kilometer away and just above the cloud deck a pilot in a Russian-made Chinese Su-30 fighter intently scanned his instrument panel and heads up display. He grunted—*Nothing, probably just a spirit in the machine.*

He was about to call for instructions when a flight controller in the nearby ETA Phalcon AWACS broke squelch, "Sea Wind 42, we have a radar return!"

"Go ahead, over."

"I have a return fixed at about a kilometer to your direct front. No altitude reading yet. Doctrinally, he'd fly in the clouds. You better slow-down, you're going to pass him in a few seconds. I have his airspeed at 280 KPH."

"Affirmative. I'm deploying flaps. I still don't see him on radar."

"You may be too close, widen your search beam. Maybe we're getting a return from a different part of the aircraft than you can see."

"Right..." the pilot thought about his situation. He could be the first pilot in history to shoot down an American Stealth aircraft in air-to-air combat. He might even be the first pilot to down an American aircraft since the Korean War. He took a cleansing breath and called the AWACS, "Am I clear to fire a missile? I have an idea."

"We have no friendly traffic in the sky to your front." There was hesitation in the controller's voice, "What's your plan?"

"No time to explain, the target's almost over Taipei. I'll call you after I succeed!"

The pilot was confident in his position as an elite fighter in China's best air regiment—he knew he had some leeway for creativity in combat. He burned up his airspeed and dropped into the cloudbank.

Heinzleman looked down. He could see nothing. The wind tugged a bit at his clothing. He knew that within a few seconds he'd have to leap out into the abyss—every moment that the stealthy aircraft had its bomb doors open was a moment that its famed radar invisibility was virtually worthless.

"Jump on my mark," the pilot warned, "Five, four, three..." A bright yellow glow lit up the clouds under Heinzleman. "What the... Shit!"

The glow was immediately followed by a series of orange flashes, ruining the night vision in the sergeant's left eye (he kept the right eye closed) "We got a heat seeker launch! Decoy flares auto-deployed. Jump now, ride's over soldier!"

Heinzleman decoupled the intercom then hit the quick release buckle. He was free. Within a few seconds he was falling at 110 mph. Using his right eye, he looked down at the softly illuminated face of the GPS receiver strapped to his left forearm. He was falling a little too far to the south. Using his arms and legs as wings, the champion parachutist corrected his path and wondered what was to become of his ride.

The Chinese pilot's hunch paid off handsomely. The launch of his heat-seeking missile caused his prey's decoy system to kick in, automatically dispensing flares to entice his missile off course. The flares backlit the target cruising in the thinning cloud layer, making it stand out as an inky black hole in a bank of orange fog. He pushed his nose down and lined up for the kill—*cannon no less, how poetic. Tonight he would become a hero among heroes.*

Above him, only seconds after he jumped, Heinzleman's remaining night vision was sorely tested by flashes of tracer light followed by an explosion. A flaming arc of debris rained down a mile away. *No one will ever know I made it out unless I land on target.*

Heinzleman deployed his black parasail at 900 feet. He flipped down his thermal sight (already warmed up and on) and searched for the distinctive roof of the American Ambassador's residence.

Less than ten seconds later he touched down, right on the money. Heinzleman released the parachute harness. The chute slowly began to drift off the roof before he could get control of it.

He knew the Ambassador's residence was still within Taiwanese-controlled territory but that it was very likely the residence was under continuous observation by PLA forces. His arrival was supposed to remain a secret.

Heinzleman almost finished gathering his chute together when he heard the crunch of roof gravel behind him. He wheeled about, meeting a rifle butt as it smashed into face, robbing him of consciousness.

*   *   *

The Republic of China's army was crushed before the gates of Taipei, yet, the ROC commander on Quemoy had five divisions reinforced with some armor, artillery and air defense artillery. Other than a handful of minor injuries during the initial PLA bombardment, his garrison had suffered none of the horrific setbacks that had befallen Taiwan. Without Taiwan, however, his position was untenable. Within three months his soldiers would run out of food (the civilians on the two islands were already complaining of rationing).

On Sunday morning the garrison commander put out the word for all of his generals to assemble on the main island of Quemoy by Monday morning to consider their courses of action. The commander wanted to reach a consensus on when and how to surrender with dignity.

Brigadier General Mao, the commander of the garrison on the smaller of the two islands Quemoy, took a small fishing boat over to the main island on Sunday night for Monday's war council. On his way over Mao's grimness was multiplied by a heaving case of seasickness. Curiously, he slept soundly in one of Quemoy's barracks bunkers and awoke refreshed and committed to whatever purpose he was assigned in these, the last days of his Republic.

The meeting started at 0700 hours Monday morning. The 22 generals, along with an admiral and an air force general, snapped to attention as the Lieutenant General briskly walked into the large underground meeting room.

The general wasted no time in explaining the hopelessness of the situation and the honorable defense the garrison had thus far offered. Mao looked around the room. He saw one general, a classmate of his at the academy, crying silently. Mao shook his head and returned his attention to the garrison commander just as the leader was preparing to seek a consensus. Mao cleared his throat and began to stand, saying, "Pardon me, sir, but I feel compelled to speak to this issue."

Normally, such a statement would have been frowned upon. These were not normal times, and, since there were only flag officers in the room, an air of congeniality was possible which would not be the case were lower ranking personnel present. "Yes, General Mao, please continue," the three star said.

"Sir, we have enough food and water for three months—a little less than two if we share it with the civilians. What's the harm in waiting? Even if we are defeated, won't our stand here improve the treatment our countrymen get at the hands of the Communists?"

A murmur coursed through the two-dozen senior leaders. The garrison commander, not expecting a double defiance (to himself and the Chinese), backed off a notch. "Fine, gentlemen. General Mao has a valid point. Still, I see little to be gained by sacrificing ourselves for a lost cause. I suggest we eat, meet amongst ourselves, and reconvene this afternoon at 1500 hours to make our final decision."

Mao grunted to himself—*So the general was going to politick. Taiwan dies and we talk.*

*   *   *

Chu Ling prayed harder than she ever had before in her life. She didn't pray that her life would be spared, but rather the life of her son, Dugen, and the lives of her 59 friends, relatives and the 41 children from the village. She also prayed for the soul of Lee Bensui, the late Fu Mingjie's Party deputy. This evil shadow of a man came by the jail every day to gloat over his captives, until, on the fifth day, he came by no more. Ling decided that the man could no longer handle the prisoners' quiet prayers and singing— *too bad*, she thought, *still, perhaps he now had a seed within his heart that God could work with.*

The jail in Lipu City held 60 of the mountain villagers since the late night raid almost two weeks ago. Ling's facial wounds were slowly healing. Her heart was healing more slowly. She still held the image of her doomed and injured husband Kwok being led off to face his destiny—a destiny without God. This terribly saddened her, although she clung to the slimmest hope that her loving example may have led him to God before he was executed for crimes against the state.

Chao Yongmin, Amoy's Falun Gong "Master", Brother Wang Ouyang, three other house church leaders and more than 300 followers and believers piled into six large old charter buses and headed out of Amoy for Lipu City. They got only five kilometers before they hit the first roadblock. One bus at a time, two soldiers boarded, then randomly inspected the papers of the occupants. Satisfied that there was nothing out of order with the travelers, the soldiers waved them on. Of course, it didn't hurt that the lieutenant in charge of the checkpoint was a Falun Gong practitioner.

The leaders had only a rough idea of what they were going to do when they got to Lipu where they knew some 60 Christians were being held in the local jail, collectively charged with subversion. From Brother Wang's understanding of the situation, the jailed villagers were quite popular in the region, being known for producing the county's best oranges and for their kindness and generosity. Wang shared his thoughts with Chao that this particular situation might be one that they could win—a small group of popular people jailed by a weak and minor Party official just far enough from the beaten path that the official would not have immediate recourse to excessive amounts of force. "Master" Chao agreed and the two of them arranged the trip. In the meantime the Christians viewed the adventure as a nice Sunday outing with the added advantage of having the opportunity to witness to their Falun Gong bus-mates. Likewise, the believers in Falun Gong listened politely and intently to the Christians (as would be expected since most Chinese like to hedge their religious bets, paying homage to a multitude of faiths—just in case).

Lee Bensui was growing increasingly worried. *True*, he had the 60 troublemakers behind bars. *True*, he had executed their ringleader and made a nice profit off his organs—although the thieving doctor charged far more for his services than Lee expected. No, his problems were more complex—he didn't know what to do next. On top of that, his beloved PAP company was torn from him only yesterday. They were needed for the war effort on Taiwan.

Lee furrowed his brow and resolved to handle his problem decisively—*After all, there was a war going on.* He drew up a letter for the Party headquarters in Amoy. In it, he stated his intent to execute every one of the 60 prisoners in custody as dangerous enemies of the state in a time of war. He sent off the letter via fax under his official seal just minutes before the three buses of religionists arrived from Amoy.

Lee's complex situation was about to assume another unexpected dimension.

*   *   *

Unit 23 of the ROC's Special Cross Straits Action Team was a closely guarded secret. Most of Unit 23's personnel were technically civilians; a few were intelligence officers. All were complete geeks. Unit 23 was really nothing more than an organized bunch of 145 hackers bound by two loves: Taiwan and computers.

Springing from Taiwan's national military intelligence directorate, Unit 23 was organized in 1991 out of a growing realization that computers were an indispensable part of modern conflict. Half of Unit 23 was dedicated to computer defense, the remainder were specialists in computer attack.

Min Bo-long belonged to an even more secret squad within the computer attack platoon. He was embarrassed by what he had to do for his job. Thankfully, both of his parents were dead and he had no nosy siblings to worry about. When you really got down to it, Min was a pornographer—at least he felt like one. While he didn't actually make pornographic movies or materials, he did run a couple of truly disgusting web sites: one in Macao and the other in Hong Kong. Both sites had as their target audience Communist Party officials in China. Min estimated his loyal Party viewership to be about 1,500 people and expanding (with another 5,000 or so businessmen and others on the Mainland hitting the site at least three times a week).

When the war started and the Chinese E-bombs knocked out much of Taiwan's computer capability, Unit 23 was hurriedly pressed into action to restore as much of the military's computer capability in Taipei as possible. Both the Macau and the Hong Kong web sites continued to operate autonomously, but without any new material on the free sites (free to those with certain prized web addresses—businessmen had to pay by credit card), the number of hits began to decline. A week later, both sites' traffic was half of what it was at the start of the war.

On Sunday, Min finally had time to turn his squad's attention back to the web sites. They all knew they had to work fast. Remotely communicating by SATCOM with the computer servers in Macao and Hong Kong, Min unleashed the porno sites' emergency files. He set the clock for 24 hours.

Immediately, a torrent of new material cued up on the sites. Those who did not visit either site within 12 hours would get a discrete e-mail notice about the posting of fresh photos and quick time videos. The data from Min's previous trials suggested that 85% the loyal viewers would return to the site twice within 24 hours, usually doing so from their computers at work (most Party officials did not have computer access at home). When they did, Min's crew would have a surprise waiting for them.

Feng Gou-Feng was a mid-level Party functionary in the Ministry of Agriculture. He was divorced. His ex-wife said she left him because of his "problem." He didn't think he had a problem— rather, it was she who had archaic attitudes about sex. In any event, his growing appetite for untraditional recreation doomed their relationship. Instead of fighting her divorce, Feng let his wife go (she threatened to tell his superiors about his habits if he didn't grant her her desire to be set free).

Since Feng was neither particularly handsome, young, rich or powerful, nor even very nice to be around, he had, without exception, been without female companionship since his divorce (prostitutes were too risky for the Party man). So, to fulfill his many sordid fantasies, he turned to the burgeoning Chinese Internet for relief.

Had the Party monitored its own Members' web use more judiciously, they would have eventually tracked down a disturbing trend within their ranks. Instead, Feng and hundreds of others, often enjoyed a few hours of Party-subsidized fun every day. Several users of smut were even praised by their unwitting supervisors for "working late" and "being dedicated."

Feng got into the office early on Monday morning, as was his tradition. Monday mornings before 6:00 AM were the best time to partake of his pastime without fear of discovery. He entered his favorite site's address onto his web browser (he didn't dare bookmark it, *that* could easily be traced). The site came up and proudly announced a wide new selection of delicacies to view. Feng greedily reviewed the choices and clicked onto a particularly promising page. He was so thoroughly engrossed in the material that he scarcely heard his computer's innards working harder than normal to process some commands in the background.

Feng heard someone in the hallway outside. He quickly logged off then erased the evidence of his visit from the browser's history log. He called up his e-mail program and attached a file he had prepared on Saturday outlining June's rice production numbers. (He had prepared the file early but not sent it, intending to use it later as cover for his early morning romp on the Internet.) He addressed the file to his superior and his deputy. After reviewing the file for errors, Feng knew they would forward it along to other key departmental heads, including representatives of most major ministries—after all, rice production was still one of the chief indicators of his nation's health (sadly, the numbers weren't as good as they should have been for June).

Feng's boss, the Assistant Minister of Agriculture for Rice, held a hard copy of Feng's report. It was 9:30 AM. He reviewed it, frowning at the modest production numbers. If the trend continued much longer, he knew his position would be at risk—*perhaps Feng himself was angling for my job*, he thought, noting the early morning time stamp on the document.

Seeing that all was in order, he ordered his secretary to attach the document to an e-mail and sent it out on his distribution list. The report would be considered an informal draft. The official report would be written up this afternoon and sent out on paper over his signature. China was learning to benefit from electronic data exchange, but old methods die hard and paper was still preferred for important official business (especially for classified communications).

Feng's boss' secretary moved to close her computer's e-mail window. Strange, she noticed, the screen was frozen. She rarely had a crash early in the morning when only a program or two had been opened. She heard the processor and the hard drive churning away—*very strange.*

When China planned its attack against Taiwan, a supporting element of that attack included a cyber assault on the American national security computer network comprising the White House, DoD, State Department and CIA. This computer attack was designed to clog critical e-mail and network arteries to increase confusion and delay the US response.

As it was, both sides overestimated their effectiveness—the Chinese at causing problems and the Americans at defending against them. The Chinese succeeded in penetrating a couple of firewalls protecting internal government networks from outside interference while their e-mail attack enjoyed a little more success, tying up routine message traffic for a few hours (doing things like delaying the White House's computerized automatic paging system designed to recall key National Security Council Staffers in an emergency). The Americans (everyone except for the computer experts) were shocked that any firewalls were breached at all.

China's modest effort at disrupting US computer systems (led by a small group of computer scientists and mathematicians, many of whom recently studied in the United States) had no defensive counterpart to speak of. Computers were only recently becoming important to Chinese government and business. While the authorities carefully monitored Internet communications, looking for any signs of unrest or subversion, it never really occurred to them to safeguard their systems. Most in government simply figured if the computers went down they'd simply shift to typewriters, fax machines, telephones and radios.

Against this backdrop, the desperate actions of Taiwan's Unit 23 produced effects far beyond the imagination of even the unit's most creative hacker. For the first hour after being downloaded from the Macao porn site, three special macro viruses attached themselves to any compatible document within the Chinese government network. These time-activated programs waited until noon Monday to activate. Once activated, they reworked the grammar of the documents in which they were embedded, changing affirmative statements to the negative, and vice versa. After two hours, the second time released phase of the viralpac kicked in. Based on the virulent "Melissa" virus coded by a lovelorn American hacker in 1999 and on the even more pernicious "LoveBug" virus coded in the Philippines in 2000, the Taiwanese variety (jokingly called "Merissa" by its inventor) worked by infecting a machine's e-mail system, causing it to send messages to every address in its address book. The messages thus sent also replicated themselves to every known address and so on.

By noon Monday, the Chinese telecommunications system was clogged with Internet traffic. The government had to switch to backup wireless voice systems to communicate. Lower priority messages simply didn't go through until Tuesday morning (all through Monday night, Chinese computer experts simply shut down computers, servers, and network switches in an attempt to quell the outbreak). In the end, the Chinese had to make a choice: working computers or a working national phone system—they chose the phones.

*   *   *

After a rainy night of meditation and prayer in the buses, 300 people from Amoy assembled themselves on a cloudy Monday morning. Foregoing food, they marched quietly into the just-awakening town market where they sat down in silence. In the center of the gathering, one wizened man held a neatly printed sign. It simply said, "Where are our friends the orange growers? Whom will the Party decide to jail next?"

At first, the local merchants and residents were annoyed at the crowd, then they were fearful, expecting the police to show up any minute and haul the protesters away. When no one came to arrest the group, one merchant began handing out oranges to the sitting mass just before noon, "They're not as good as old Chu's oranges," he apologized, "But you may have as many as you want." Someone tried to pay the fruit merchant and within seconds, vendors were plying the crowd with food and drink.

Seeing an opening, Brother Wang leaned over to "Master" Chao and whispered, "We must march on the jail now." Saying nothing further, he got up on legs that should have been stiff but felt remarkably strong. He began to walk out of the market. Almost as one, 300 people stood and began to follow. Several merchants and customers tagged along out of curiosity.

Lee Bensui could scarcely believe his eyes. In reply to his memo as to what to do with the Christian subversives, regional Party headquarters in Amoy sent him, via fax, a letter stating that they were to be released and not executed immediately. He was shocked. China was in the middle of a war and the Party was going soft. He weighed calling headquarters. He gave up after the fourth busy signal at Amoy Party headquarters, half glad he didn't get through to be heard second guessing his superiors. *Oh well, at least the memo didn't direct him to apologize to them too.* He gave the order for the prisoners' release. He considered whether to call in some trucks and buses to whisk them back to their village where they could cause little harm.

By 12:15 a swelling lunchtime crowd of more than 600 people descended on the Lipu County Party complex. Not wanting to project an overly threatening posture, Brother Wang sank to his knees, clasped his hands, and began praying silently. Everyone between Wang and the old man with the sign at the back of the crowd either went to their knees or sat quietly cross-legged. The locals simply stared at the crowd and at the Party headquarters, waiting for something to happen.

There was an urgent rap on Lee's door, "Comrade Lee, Comrade Lee!" It was his lackey, Ng.

"Come in and still yourself Ng! What is it?" Ng was given to overreaction, still, given the circumstances, Lee was a bit unnerved.

Lee's door flew open and Ng arrived wide-eyed and panting on his desk, "Oh, Comrade Lee, what do we do?"

"About what?"

"About the thousands of people outside protesting for the release of the prisoners from the village?"

"What?" A cold shiver went down Lee's spine—he had ordered the 60 immediately released only 15 minutes ago. He swiveled in his chair (Fu Mingjie's old chair, actually) and looked out his window on the small square below. His eyes focused on the sea of people below, then they panned out to the sign. He looked no further to see that the crowd was not as large as his deputy claimed, he saw enough to know that something bad was going to happen very soon. Lee reached into his desk and grabbed his pistol, "Call the warden immediately, tell him to delay the release. We cannot have those people released into this crowd!" Lee jumped up and ran for the door, yelling over his shoulder, "Then meet me outside!"

Lee raced down the flight of stairs, almost knocking over a couple of female clerks. He burst outside just as the clouds parted to reveal the midday sun. Lee blinked blindly, trying to gauge the situation and decide what to do next. He heard a commotion to his left as three jail guards led the 60 former prisoners out the front door of the local jail. Lee's legs went wobbly as he tried to shout and move towards the police. His legs and voice seemed to fail him as the crowd behind him rose up with a hearty shout. Scores of people pressed by him on their way to triumphantly mob the released prisoners. Lee just stood, hands at his side, his pistol hanging limp in his right hand.

Lee began to regain his senses. He tucked his pistol into his waistband and slowly pushed his way towards the center of the enlarging crowd. Someone recognized him and shouted, "There's Lee! Lee's the one that released the prisoners! God bless Lee!" Lee almost fainted.

A hush began to move over the crowd and a purposeful movement reached towards Lee. A half-minute later a small but unbroken woman stood before the dazed Party boss. It was Mrs. Chu. She bowed to Lee and he awkwardly returned the bow.

"God bless you Lee Bensui. You have done right in the sight of the Lord." She bowed again, hugged her husband's executioner and walked back into the crowd, which immediately burst out in cheers.

Lee was numb. He heard someone calling his name. His name. Lee slowly wheeled around. It was Ng.

"Comrade Lee, Comrade! Amoy Party headquarters called. It was a mistake! The directive was a mistake! The prisoners must be arres. . ." Ng stopped in mid-sentence and realized what he was saying in the midst of the growing mob. He skidded to a stop, suddenly looking very frightened.

Without his company of PAP goons, Lee was powerless to enforce the will of the "People" on the people. Tears streaming down his face, Lee began to climb the once-imposing steps of the Lipu Party headquarters and head for his office. He walked into his office, slamming the door on Ng's face. Lee sat down at his big desk—Fu's desk really—and winced absentmindedly at the stabbing in his back. He reached back and removed the painful lump—his pistol—Fu's old pistol actually. Lee stared at the pistol for several seconds. Acting on their own, his hands pulled the slide of the 9mm semiautomatic back and released. His ears registered a sharp, ringing *shlink*. As if he were an observer at his own execution, Lee raised the pistol to his temple. Before he pulled the trigger, he wondered if Ng or someone else would get the money for his kidneys. The joyful throng in the square now numbered more than 2,500—they heard nothing but the sound of their own freedom ringing out.

*   *   *

Brigadier General Mao did what he could to rally support to his cause. The garrison commander, General Wong, did what he could to dissuade Mao and anyone else Mao spoke with. The best Mao could hope for was delay.

In what seemed like only a few minutes, 1500 rolled around and they were all back in the meeting room. The mood was pensive. Mao knew his attempt to rally for delay was doomed. This was a defeated cadre simply waiting for the right moment to step out from under a white flag.

General Wong started to address the group from the front of the room. Deciding he had no career left to speak of anyway, Mao rose from amidst his colleagues, "Pardon me, sir." He turned to look at the remainder of the officers in the room. He held their rapt attention, "I know what you're all thinking. I know General Wong has convinced you all that we should give in; that it is inevitable that China become whole again. But, may I be permitted to remind all of you that Taiwan is a democracy. The people of Taiwan voted just a few months ago to ratify their separate status from China. Don't these people, our neighbors and relatives, deserve something more than to be ruled by the Butchers of Beijing? From here I know the struggle may appear to be hopeless, but, what if Chaing Kai-Shek and his men thought that in 1949? Would we have proven to ourselves and world that the Chinese people can govern themselves without dictator or emperor?"

The door to the meeting room opened and a note was passed into the room for General Wong. General Mao took a deep breath and pressed on, "Instead of waiting here to die or surrender let us instead attempt to win this war." Mao pounded his fist into his hand. About half the generals looked on as if he were crazy. "We have known for years that the Chinese people have become increasingly restive under the harsh and corrupt rule of the Communist Party. Have we forgotten how quickly and violently the government in Romania fell in 1989, then the rest of the Communist Empire in Europe, even the Soviet Union itself? Must China be Communist forever? The People's Liberation Army may outnumber us by ten to one, but have we all forgotten the words of

Sun Tzu?" Mao demanded. He noticed Wong had finished reading the note and was focusing on him. "What is the first of the five fundamental factors?" Mao jabbed the air with his finger.

Wong nodded thoughtfully and said, "Moral influence." His voice was hoarse. General Wong coughed then straightened himself before his men, "Moral influence," he said more strongly, "'...*that which causes the people to be in harmony with their leaders, so that they will accompany them in life and unto death without fear of mortal peril.*'"

Wong held up the note, "This message comes from a trusted source in Amoy." He pulled the note in front of his eyes to paraphrase from it, "It seems a computer virus attack initiated from Taiwan may have caused some confusion on the Mainland. There is concern among the Communist Party cadres that an uprising in Lipu County may spread and that there are insufficient resources on hand to deal with the situation." Wong smiled grimly and looked up, "Most of the troops and security police normally stationed opposite us are now rampaging about our homeland."

General Wong turned to the admiral, "Within an hour, I want to know how many small boats remain on the island, how many troops they can lift, and how many fishermen will help us cross over to Amoy."

Without missing a beat, the admiral replied, "More than 500 boats, 5,000 troops twice a night under cover of darkness, and a local captain for every boat, sir!"

Within a second, the underground bunker erupted in a deafening cheer. Mao just stood where he was. He wasn't sure if he just finished the hardest part or the easiest part of what he knew had to be done.

32
Rebellion

The three busloads of religionists from Amoy left Lipu City shortly after the prisoners of conscience were freed. Having no interest in staying around Lipu City, the 60 formerly jailed villagers quickly collected their 41 children from the state orphanage and returned to their orchards to resume their lives.

After Lee's suicide on Monday afternoon, Ng was in charge at Lipu County Party headquarters. Never more than an uninspired fool, Ng was more of a burden than a help to his comrades. By 4:05 PM, the crowd outside the Party's county headquarters grew to more than 5,000 people. Ng had no idea what to do next.

With scores to settle and little fear of immediate use of force, the situation in Lipu City rapidly deteriorated. The few regular police, more interested in the mundane issues of law, order, and petty bribery, were of little help to the Party.

At 4:12 PM, someone threw a rock at Party headquarters, breaking a window on the first floor. The mass of people shuttered, then waited, expecting gun shots. When there was no reply to the rock, they rushed the building.

Outwardly, the mob looked entirely unorganized, and while it was true that most in the riot were simply giving vent to decades of frustration and anger, there were many who had an agenda. Some went looking for Party officials to kill, others cut the phone lines, a few sought out the meticulous records of the Party and local security police, seeking the IDs of those who were actively collaborating with the authorities. By midnight, more than 150 Party members and informers were dead. By Tuesday morning, any vestige of Beijing's foreign and harsh rule in this southern land was wiped clean.

Remarkably, Lipu did not descend into complete chaos—the town's thriving business community had too much to lose to let that happen. The residents raged against the Party and little else. By nightfall, the town elected an informal council to handle civic affairs for the duration of the crisis.

*   *   *

Donna had never been so frightened in her life. The Chinese had bundled her and General Taylor into an appropriated limo and, with armored cars to the front and rear, they roared off to the front lines on the western edge of Taipei. Somehow, they had to cross the battle lines and make it to the Ambassador's residence to arrange for the surrender of the American soldiers there.

All along the route from CKS International Airport—she couldn't bring herself to think of it as "Deng Xiaoping International"—there were the uneven signs of war. Most neighborhoods close to the airport were unscathed. Sharp and alert-looking People's Armed Police paramilitaries stood on every corner in these areas. Wary-eyed residents peeked from their windows at the passing motorcade. Other areas, especially those closer to Taipei, simply featured smoking, charred ruins that only hinted at the residential, commercial, or industrial districts they used to be.

Just as Donna was growing anxious over trying to fathom the coordination and luck she'd need to cross alive from the Chinese side of the lines to the Taiwanese side, the motorcade slowed to a crawl in a brick, concrete, and glass-strewn street overlooking a large river. Donna noted an intact bridge over the river, and beyond, the city of Taipei. Dozen upon dozens of dark smoky columns rose up from the dying city to merge with the cloud deck. The thickening smoke burned Donna's eyes and made her throat a bit sore. She was shocked at the hellish scene. Donna stole a glance at General Taylor. He was intently observing everything he could with an impassive face.

Donna saw the lead armored car lurch forward. The vehicle now had a large white flag tied to a broomstick that was lashed to the AAA machine gun mount on its small turret. The four-wheeled armored car picked its way between piles of debris down to the bridge below. The driver of Donna's limo gunned the engine and made a mad dash for the far side of the bridge.

As soon as the car got to the other side of the bridge a roadblock forced them to turn to the left. There, out of sight from the far bank, a ROC checkpoint forced everyone out of the car for a close inspection. For a moment, Donna thought the war weary Taiwanese were going to beat the driver. Instead, they blindfolded him and put one of their own behind the wheel to drive the Americans to their Ambassador's residence. Donna could tell the Taiwanese held a mix of disgust and sorrow towards the betrayal she and General Taylor represented. But, the soldiers held their tongues.

It took two hours to travel less than five miles (it didn't help that the large car suffered a flat tire along the way). By 5:10 PM they rolled up in front of the Ambassador's residence. After the Marine guards carefully inspected the car, they were allowed to pass through the steel gates. Donna took a great quivering breath and exhaled. She made it alive to the Ambassador's residence—now she and General Taylor had to figure out how to persuade a group of American soldiers to surrender by 6:00 AM Tuesday morning or risk a torrent of threatened destruction on the Ambassador's residence and perhaps America itself.

Donna expected her and Taylor's arrival at the Ambassador's residence to be welcomed like a visit from the undertaker. As the two representatives from Washington were escorted into the Ambassador's ample living room, they were surprised to see a smiling Ambassador, a confident lieutenant colonel in torn and blackened camouflage fatigues, and a commando sergeant, heavily bandaged about the face, but otherwise erect and alert.

After a short round of introductions, there was an awkward silence as Taylor and Klein stood there, wondering how to break the news of the surrender demand. Donna spoke first, "Say, aren't you the National Guard colonel we saw on TV destroying several Chinese tanks?"

Alexander blushed and said, "Yes, I suppose that was me and my crew. We did some damage before we got ground down by the Chinese."

"Colonel," General Taylor began with a heavy voice, "We have some bad news for you and your men. The PRC is demanding your surrender by 0600 hours tomorrow morning. It seems you put a dent in their pride."

Alexander looked defiant, "And if we don't surrender?"

The Chinese have threatened to bombard the hell out of the Ambassador's residence and maybe even nuke Los Angeles."

"That's bullshit! Er, uh, pardon me general, but it is. The Chinese would never nuke LA, we have, what, 100 or 1,000 times as many nukes as they do!" Alexander protested.

Taylor sighed, "You folks must have been out of circulation for a while. Did you hear about the Chinese missile attack on the West Coast a week ago?"

Alexander's eyes went wide—*Judy! The children!* "Oh God! No! What hap. . .?"

Taylor cut in, "The Chinese fired a Long March space launch vehicle stuffed with propaganda leaflets at the West Coast's five major cities. Complete chaos erupted. LA was hit the worst. As of yesterday it's still burning."

Alexander pinched his forehead, then started to speak from behind his hand, slowly taking it away and looking up as began, "So, my government wants me and my men to surrender to appease the enemy and prevent any further attacks on American soil?"

Donna looked at Taylor. The general was caught between the competing obligations to duty and honor.

Ambassador Ross' smile had long since been erased, but now he saw fit to join the discussion, "Maybe it's the two of you who have been out of circulation for too long."

Taylor snapped his head towards the Ambassador.

Donna said, "What do you know to be happening?"

"Please, have a seat. I'll get you some coffee. I think we have some things to mull over together before we decide to do anything rash," the Ambassador suggested. "The ROCs came to us with some very interesting news about half an hour before you showed up." The room was quietly attentive. Artillery fire could be heard in the distance. "There is an uprising in the Chinese countryside of Fujian Province. We're seeking confirmation from national sources, thanks to Sergeant Heinzleman here who parachuted in last night with a load of communications gear and some other stuff he won't even let us look at."

Heinzleman looked at his boots.

"Rough landing?" Taylor asked, looking at the parachutist's bandaged face.

"You could say that, sir." Heinzleman said.

"I'm afraid my Marine guards got the jump on him," Ambassador Ross said, "They weren't expecting company on the roof last night."

Heinzleman looked at his boots again.

Taylor smiled gently, "Look, sergeant, everyone did his job. You landed on the roof, no doubt in incredibly adverse conditions, and the Marines butt-stroked you for your troubles. There's nothing to be ashamed of. You kicked ass just to get here, son."

Heinzleman's face brightened, "Thank you, sir."

Alexander, watching this exchange, decided he now had little to worry about in this general—*This man would do the right thing.* The young woman, however, was still an unknown.

Donna was deep in thought—*Word of an uprising. . . Could the Taiwanese be trusted to tell the truth right now? Were their sources reliable? What could be done to exploit the situation if it was true?* It was 5:30 PM. They had just a few hours to come to a decision if they were to act on the Chinese demands by six the next morning.

The Americans in Taipei received confirmation of the Chinese uprising in Lipu County by midnight. Outside, the sounds of war grew more intense and closer as the Chinese pressed their assault on the Taiwanese capital. The Ambassador, the Vice Chairman of the Joint Chiefs of Staff, the CIA analyst and the National Guardsman huddled and tried to come up with a plan.

"What exactly were the Chinese demands?" Alexander asked.

Donna removed a piece of paper from her briefcase, and read, "And I quote, 'First, all United States armed forces personnel unlawfully on the Chinese sovereign soil of the province of Taiwan will cease hostilities as of 1800 hours Monday. Second, said forces will surrender to representatives of the Peoples Liberation Army by 0600 hours Tuesday morning. Third, the United States of America will recognize Taiwan as a province of the People's Republic of China's by converting their illegal diplomatic presence into consulates of the United States of America to the People's Republic of China.'"

"Unlawfully on Chinese soil!" Alexander snorted, "Bastards forced us down and they say we're here unlawfully!" He paused, "Wait, read that first part again. . ."

Donna cocked her head, "Okay. 'First, all United States armed forces personnel unlawfully. . .'"

"That's it! The only United States armed forces personnel here are the embassy's Marines, General Taylor and Sergeant Heinzleman!"

Taylor narrowed his eyes, "How do you figure, colonel?"

"I'm a National Guardsman. My Commander-in-Chief is the governor of the state of California."

"But you're federalized, aren't you?"

"Yes, but we can be defederalized in a moment if the President releases us back to state service. At that point we'd no longer be 'United States armed forces personnel.'"

Donna looked at the two men, "Given the Chinese penchant for legalisms, it might work. However, I think that, right or wrong, there'll still be hell to pay if we don't come through under a white flag with a fair number of men." She shook her head.

"So, what do we do?" Taylor demanded.

"Why not blame the Taiwanese?" Ambassador Ross asked.

"We can say that they detained the American troops as bargaining chips."

"That might work!" Donna's face brightened, "The Chinese would try the same thing in a similar circumstance. Mr. Ambassador, can you arrange for a ROC 'road block' to be erected to prevent our troops from making it to the PLA lines?"

"Sure."

"Then we'll make sure the driver makes it back to the river to tell the Chinese about the Taiwanese treachery."

"Are we in or out of the car when it crosses back into enemy territory?" Taylor asked.

Donna exhaled, looking at the floor, "In." She looked at Taylor, "If there is a rebellion on the Mainland I want to be near Fu Zemin and his command center. I might be of use there."

"You mean, 'We. . . we might be of use there.'" Taylor said as if he wished it didn't have to be so.

"Right. Let's grab some shut-eye. Mr. Ambassador, can you arrange for enough cars and trucks to carry the Colonel's men to the 'road block' by around 4:00 AM?"

"No problem, get some sleep," the Ambassador replied.

*　　　*　　　*

Brigadier General Mao almost regretted his patriotism and his bold words. It was 0300 hours, only 11 hours since General Wong ordered the crossing to be made with a minimum of preparation. Some generals and the admiral argued for an additional night to prepare—that way, they'd have time to make two trips to the mainland in the fishing boats under cover of darkness. General Wong nixed the suggestion. As seasickness gripped Mao, he could still clearly hear General Wong's words, "We must cross tonight. We have fog. We have surprise. And we have the fires of an uprising on our side. In these circumstances, crossing with 10,000 soldiers instead of 5,000 will make little difference. We must make it to Amoy by tomorrow morning!"

Mao's brigade was on the smaller island only seven kilometers from Amoy. Because of his close proximity to the objective and because it was his idea to attack, the honors of leading the way fell to Mao.

He vomited again and weakly turned to his intelligence officer, trying to smile. Mao trusted his staff officer and was glad to hear his assessment that they'd probably make it across the bay undisturbed by ship or aircraft. Mao had queried him sharply on Chinese naval and air capabilities but the officer assured him that Quemoy's anti-ship and anti-air missile batteries had created a Chinese-free bubble around the islands—since China's objective was the capture of Taiwan itself, it made little sense to risk losing valuable aircraft or ships by challenging the defenses of two insignificant islands.

Only an hour later Mao and his lead battalions reached the shore. Downtown Amoy was only five kilometers away. Mao was shocked not to hear any gunfire. Either there were few Communist soldiers in this area or they were so poorly trained and led and overconfident that no one thought to keep a night watch.

Mao splashed ashore on wobbly legs. His stomach had been empty for half an hour now—that alone made him feel a little better. Visibility with the naked eye was about 20 meters. Mao picked up a starlight scope and looked right and left, north and south, along the deserted beach. The lack of fishing boats must have meant the military decided to clear the beach for fear the local fishermen might provide information to their brethren across the bay.

Mao shook his head and smiled to himself—*Unbelievable! The PLA is so occupied in devastating my homeland that they could not attend to defending their own.*

* * *

On the bus ride back to Amoy, Brother Wang Ouyang and "Master" Chao Yongmin discussed the events at Lipu City and openly wondered what to do next. Chao, flush with the possibilities of victory, wanted to immediately conduct a silent protest at Amoy Party headquarters where he would call for the release of the more than 150 recently jailed Falun Gong adherents. Wang wanted to confer with the other house church leaders first, then decide what to do after an organized day of fasting and prayer. When it became apparent that Chao was going to proceed with or without Wang and his Christians, Wang relented and pledged to do what he could to increase the size of the protest planned for Tuesday morning.

Brother Wang only snatched two hours of sleep; Chao didn't sleep at all. Assembling at an open-air market only three blocks from Party headquarters, about 500 Falun Gong believers and 50 Christians (Catholics and various Protestant denominations) listened intently to "Master" Chao's instructions. One scared looking young security officer saw the group, then scuttled off towards the Party building. Just before they were to march, Brother Wang offered a prayer for their safety and asked for God's blessing. All 550 people bowed their heads in respect to the elder Christian leader.

By 7:05 AM, the mass of protesters gathered in front of the Party offices. A squad of grim-faced guards stood on the imposing flight of steps leading into the building. They held their assault rifles waist high, pointing them warily in the direction of the protesters.

The protesters locked arms and sat down. A few trucks, whose expected morning route was now blocked, stopped, adding to the confusion. Another squad of soldiers showed up on the stairs.

About ten minutes passed. The protesters began to sing. Curious onlookers ringed the fringe of the sitting crowd, leaving a healthy distance between themselves and the protesters.

Just as a group of 20 soldiers moved into position on the street to the left of the Party's main entrance, a snaking column of hymn-singing Christians emerged from behind a produce truck to the front of the building. The column seemed to have no end—every two seconds another person appeared from behind the truck, winding around the sitting, signing mass until a bare patch of pavement was found upon which to sit.

A platoon of 40 soldiers marched in on the street to the right. There were now almost 100 armed representatives of the Party facing off against about 1,000 unarmed believers. "Master" Chao sat cross-legged, deep in meditation. Brother Wang, sitting nearby, looked about. He had seen a face-off like this before years ago. He knew he was about to become a martyr. He sighed and began praying for the souls of the soldiers and his fellow protesters.

Wang was deep in prayer. He was at peace, ready to die, if that was God's will. He heard shouts down the street behind him, then a shot. Before the protesters could react, Wang heard the familiar clatter of AKs on full automatic. The time had come. *Maybe others will draw inspiration from our example*, Wang thought as he felt, then heard, a bullet tear through the air above his head.

*   *   *

General Mao had shaken off the effects of the sea and was now

393

surging forward with his men, running on pure adrenaline. He couldn't believe he was in the middle of Amoy.

Mao was at the head of two companies totaling 220 men. Two blocks to his right and left were another company each, providing flank security for his main column. Their objective: Amoy Party headquarters.

Mao had assigned specific tasks to handpicked company commanders as well. One was to seize the radio station, another, the main telephone exchange, two more were to block the north and south roads into town—16 companies in all. Mao expected another brigade of 16 companies was about half an hour behind him from the larger Quemoy Island. The remaining force of about 1,000 men was conducting a diversionary landing on the coast to the northeast of Amoy in an attempt to seize the small fishing villages of Aotou, Lianhe and Shijing.

So far, Mao's force had only encountered eight shocked police officers, four of them simply stood in place, hands raised, and allowed themselves to be disarmed. Of the other four, three ran from the advancing Taiwanese, the last one, surprisingly, volunteered to lead Mao's battalion through the city to the Party complex.

The local police officer crouched down behind an idling truck. He pointed down the street, "The Party building is less than 100 meters away. A PAP company is assigned to guard it. They only have rifles and tear gas."

Mao acknowledged this bit of data and broke squelch on the small tactical radio his radioman carried, ordering his two flanking companies to move into position before they began the assault. Mao waited patiently, constantly sweeping his gaze back and forth and up and down, looking from street level to roof-top, some ten stories up. Civilians were curiously absent.

Just above the throaty idle of the diesel truck he was kneeling next to, Mao thought he heard the sound of singing from the direction of the Party headquarters. He frowned and ordered a soldier to switch off the ignition of the abandoned truck. The singing could now be clearly heard. *Could this be a sign of the rebellion we heard of?* A gunshot cut short Mao's thoughts on the matter. Instinctively, he waved his men into action.

Knowing their families and homeland had been pounded into submission by the Mainlanders, Mao's soldiers leapt into action, eagerly seeking their afflicters. General Mao raced down the street clogged with trucks, cars, and vendors' carts. He saw a line of enemy soldiers and crouched behind a car before realizing they were facing away from his men. Looking beyond the soldiers he saw why—they were firing at a mass of people sitting in the intersection at the foot of a large building that had to be the Party headquarters. Instantly filled with rage at the sight of butchery, Mao rose to his feet, his pistol spitting flame at the monstrous atrocity before him.

Moments later it was over. The enemy lay dead, injured or surrendered. The only sounds came from the crowd with the whimpering wounded or the wailing of those who just lost a loved one. Tears began to roll down Mao's face as he waded into the crowd, calling forth his medics to administer first aid.

Mao's mind registered the movement of his special shock platoon as it burst into Party HQ to clear the building. The muffled sound of an occasional shot from inside the building reminded him that there was still work to be done.

Mao stopped near the center of the rapidly quieting crowd (Mao and his men were finally recognized for what they were and the surprised mob hushed in expectation). General Mao cleared his throat, then boomed forth, "We are your brothers from Taiwan! We come to help you throw off the chains of your oppressor! Join us and we can be free together!" At this, Mao threw both hands into the air and slowly rotated to a roaring crowd.

This was not quite expected, Mao thought, *we must harness this momentum before the Mainlanders can recover.* As he completed this thought a dignified but bloodied man walked up to Mao and put his hand on Mao's shoulder, "You are an answer to prayer, sir. My name is Wang Ouyang. What can I do to help?"

*   *   *

By 8:00 AM Tuesday, the ROCs had a little more than 5,000 troops on Mainland soil. Most importantly, they had encountered little organized resistance. They even captured an entire artillery battalion, 18 guns, intact at Lianhe. Everywhere they went, enthusiastic crowds welcomed them as liberators. Soon, additional fishing boats from the Mainland were added to the effort and another 6,000 troops made it across the bay in the foggy morning hours.

General Wong was surprised at the success his landings enjoyed. His staff, knowing how extended and vulnerable they were, counseled caution. They recommended immediately fortifying the easily defensible Amoy and only sending out reconnaissance patrols to better understand the enemy's dispositions. Wong hesitated, then thought once again of General Mao's words and Sun Tzu, "No, we have no hope of victory if we stop now. Stopping will only give the Communists time to recover and bring sufficient force to bear to crush us no matter how strong our positions are. No. . ." he turned to his staff, "we are not fighting a war now, we're leading a rebellion!"

Wong stroked his chin, "In fact, the worst thing we can do right now is mass our forces. Instead, we must divide our forces! Divide them and plunge headlong into every city, town and village we can reach in the next day! Listen, our follow-on forces are disorganized right now. We didn't expect to land any more beyond the first 5,000. I want everyone here except for my deputy commander and the signal staff to fly over to the Mainland by 1000 hours. I want you 30 staff officers to choose objectives for today, tomorrow and the next day. Organize our forces on the beaches. Each of you should strive to reach towns and villages totaling no less than 10,000 people today, 20,000 people tomorrow and 50,000 the next day. Use civilian cars, buses and trucks. Fan out across the countryside. Recruit help from the populace, encourage them, organize them, seek out and destroy the Communist Party infrastructure! Speed! We must fan the flames before the storm from Beijing extinguishes them! Are there any questions?"

"Where will you be, sir?" someone asked.

Wong flashed a tea-stained grin back, "Fuzhou! Fuzhou is mine! I will be leading a column to liberate Fuzhou by Thursday morning. Who wants Shantou?"

Three fiery-eyed colonels stepped forward, hands raised.

"Now, I believe you understand my intent. Let's go!"

One of the colonels said, "Shantou, hell, what about Hong Kong?"

"Or Guangzhou?" said another.

General Wong strode strongly out of the underground briefing room then turned to say, "If one of you reaches Hong Kong or Guangzhou you will most assuredly go down in history as one of the greatest Chinese military leaders of all time. As for me, I'll settle for 'Hero of Fuzhou.'"

33
Last Card

Donna Klein and General Taylor were once again in the hotel near the airport. Fu Zemin had railed against them on Tuesday morning after they returned to PLA lines without the surrendered Americans. But once again, Fu was quickly occupied with more urgent matters and was forced to ignore the two Americans.

Taylor's cypto-pager kept up a continuous stream of messages (as long as he kept it near a window) about the rapidly changing situation on the Mainland. Donna noticed that traffic at the airport diminished to half its level on Tuesday, and half again on Wednesday. By Wednesday afternoon the airport was hosting only one in-bound and one out-bound flight every half hour—and every one of those was either a 747 or a large military transport. She wished she could call the office with the observation—but she no longer had her phone and Taylor's two-way pager no longer had enough of a charge to transmit.

Donna was in General Taylor's room when his pager went off again. He quickly snatched it off the windowsill as he always did and ran to the bathroom to read the display near the noise of running water. He whispered, "All seaborne resupply traffic out of Fuzhou and Shantou has come to a halt now. Add that to the message an hour ago that said every airport from Shantou to Fuzhou was apparently in rebel hands and I'd say our 'friends' here will run out of gas in a few days."

Donna was about to signal her agreement when the two heard a voice that made their blood run cold.

"Taylor? Klein? You in there? It's Lindley! We need to talk!"

*   *   *

When General Wong made it to Fuzhou, 299 kilometers north of Amoy on the coastal highway, he could barely believe his eyes. As he and his convoy of 300 ROC soldiers and 1,000 Mainland sympathizers crossed the Min Jiang River bridge into the suburb of Louzhou on Wednesday afternoon, one body limply swung in the breeze from every lamppost and power pole. And, judging by the cheering crowds who greeted him, the bodies were probably Party members and their hated PAP enforcers. Rather than being Fuzhou's victorious liberator, General Wong's arrival was simply a confirmation of the obvious—that China's affluent coastal southeast was rapidly casting off Beijing's bonds of oppression and corruption on its own accord.

The rebellion spread to Fuzhou ahead of General Wong's column due to a number of factors: Taiwan's exploitive use of captured radio and television facilities to spread the news, the rapid exchange of information over the Internet to the few (mostly influential) people who had access, the lack of sufficient paramilitaries and soldiers to suppress the rebellion, the building resentment of the corrupt and arbitrary Communist rule, and, the large increase in people believing in something larger than themselves or the State in a society where no one really took the Communist line seriously anymore.

Wong took out his Republic of China sunburst flag and waved it out of the sunroof of the Japanese import his men had requisitioned from a Party official in Amoy. The crowds now lining the street went wild. Wong smiled and waved at the people. Behind his smile he thought, *It is good they are enthusiastic because Beijing will soon seek to reassert its control here, then they will have to fight a determined foe.*

*   *   *

Colonel Chu knew the situation was serious—potentially without hope. Only two hours before he spoke with a junior staff officer replacement, fresh off the plane from Guangzhou, about the situation on the Mainland. The young officer was actually relieved to be in the war zone, "You wouldn't believe it," he said, "I was on the last transport out before a mob overran the airport—at least here we're winning and we know who our enemy is!" Shortly after a senior staff officer collected his new charge, Chu noticed the older man strongly warning the lieutenant about "defeatist talk" and "rumormongering."

Chu was once again seeing the raw side of Fu Zemin—the side that was on display shortly before the neutron bombs wiped out the Taiwanese counterattack a few days ago. Part of him felt pity for the Party man, another part, contempt.

Fu barked questions at General First Class Deng, "Why are we not taking the rest of Taipei? Why have we not yet pressed south of Taichung?"

The weary warrior could only stare glassy-eyed at the Party hack, wishing he could make the snake vanish.

Watching this exchange, Chu also wished things were not as

they were. Unlike General Deng, however, Chu began to formulate a plan to change the situation.

Fu turned to Chu and said, "I want you to be prepared to arrest the Americans. They might come in useful in the near future if I have to get off this island."

Fu's statement solidified Chu's nascent plans. "Sir, what about the American soldiers? What if we can force their surrender?"

"Eh? What do you mean Colonel? How could you possibly do what countless cycles of intimidation and negotiation failed to do?"

"Sir, I need to speak to you alone." Colonel Chu and Comrade Fu retreated to Fu's private office.

"Sir, Jia Battalion still has 120 effectees."

"So? The last time you tried to get into Taipei you were cut to ribbons, what makes you think you can succeed now with less than one-third your numbers?" Fu breathed exasperation.

Chu soothingly said, "Sir, Jia Battalion is air mobile qualified. My battalion was the first battalion trained in the use of the motorized hang gliders. Once we showed the army how easy they were to operate, they decided to equip two full divisions."

Fu's eyes were burning with the possibilities, "Yes, yes. Continue with your proposal."

"I propose we take 100 of Jia's best men in 100 of the 201st Air Mobile Division's aircraft and fly into Taipei at nightfall. Our target will be the American Ambassador's residence. Using surprise and superior numbers we will overcome the few American soldiers there, take as many as possible prisoner, then fly back to headquarters. If your television equipment still works you can broadcast your victory to China and the world as proof of your success. Such a propaganda victory might turn the tide back in our favor!"

Fu pounced on the idea, "Chu, you are brave and brilliant and I am a genius for recognizing that fact. How soon can you be ready?"

"Thursday night. You need to request the 201st's aircraft through General Deng as soon as possible. I also need you to request the return of Jia Battalion to my command. We need to rehearse the mission."

"I will order General Deng to make ready the preparations!"

"And remember, sir, complete secrecy—even Deng must not know the reason for our plans. The slightest leak of information and Jia would be destroyed and all would truly be lost."

34
A New China

Bob Lindley grilled General Taylor and Donna Klein for two hours on Wednesday afternoon, letting up only to drink water and take a painkiller for a "very bad headache." Lindley pressed and prodded for information about the American soldiers at the Ambassador's residence. "How many were there?" "What kind of shape were they in?" "How much equipment did they have?" "Had they improved their positions much?"

Taylor played dumb, "Gee, I'm just a fighter jock, what do I know about ground combat operations?"

Donna just shook her head and said she didn't recall anything, saying she only saw about ten soldiers and Marines.

Finally, Lindley got up to leave.

"Where are you going Bob?" Taylor asked.

Lindley began to answer, then coughed and walked out the door obviously flustered. Two Chinese soldiers immediately followed him down the darkened hall. Another soldier slammed the door shut.

"If that isn't proof that he's working for the other side, I don't know what is," Taylor said in disgust.

Donna held her hand, palm down, just in front of her throat with her fingers pointing inward. She made a short cutting motion in front of her neck signaling Taylor to shut-up. The general fell silent and looked at the floor.

"Oh hell. . ." he muttered.

"Right," Donna said, reaching out to grab Taylor's hand. She squeezed it tight and pulled Taylor close. "Tim, I don't like where this is leading. I think we've outlived our usefulness," she said quietly into his ear, her voice slightly trembling.

Taylor withdrew far enough from Donna to grab her shoulders. He moved his hands to her face, one hand cupping each side of her jaw. They stared into each other's eyes then embraced as if it was their last moment together.

Twenty minutes after Lindley left Taylor's room three Chinese soldiers beat on the door. The lead soldier demanded Taylor's pager in broken English. Taylor tried to act as if he didn't understand. The soldier shouted and threatened to shoot Taylor on the spot. Taylor angrily handed over his last lifeline to the outside world, disabling the little device as he did so.

As the door slammed in his face it was Taylor's turn to be comforted by Donna. She lightly put her hand on his back and said, "We'll do all right. They still think of us as bargaining chips, otherwise they would have simply killed us."

Taylor felt as helpless as he did the day his wife died of breast cancer. He drew strength from Donna's touch and turned to face her, "Donna, I know this is an extreme situation, but if we get out of this alive I would like it if we could see each other."

"I would like that too."

Taylor heaved a sigh of relief and pulled Donna into his chest, wishing he could protect her but knowing life was too fragile to be assured by his power alone.

The remainder of Wednesday passed slowly. It was well into Thursday afternoon when two very hungry Americans, a CIA analyst and an Air Force general, quietly discussed their situation.

"I'd say we march right out of here and demand a bowl of rice," Taylor grumbled.

Donna replied soothingly, "Tim, not being fed is a bad sign. Either things are going very badly for our hosts or they intend to kill us. In any event, I don't think we should draw attention to ourselves just right now."

"Damnit, I wish I knew what was happening."

"I just wish I could take a bath."

"So do I—wish you would take a bath, that is, you stink!" Taylor cracked a grin.

"You don't exactly smell like roses yourself." Donna said, tossing a wadded ball of paper at Taylor.

Taylor swatted it aside and said, "I can't smell anything. You're obviously not a very good analyst. . ."

Donna cut the banter off with a wave of her hand. "Do you hear that?"

"What?"

"It sounds like a chain saw or something." Donna sprang over to the heavily curtained window and parted it slightly to reveal a gray shaft of overcast afternoon light. "There, look at that!" she said triumphantly, excited to be seeing something different that she understood.

"What is it?" Taylor glanced out the window.

About five stories below them a motorized "V" winged hang

glider was climbing in a loose circle, arcing out away from the building then coming back. It passed right by their ten-story window with a loud drone. Its pilot wore goggles and the camouflage uniform of a PLA commando. "I wrote these things up in a report at headquarters. It's a poor man's solution to air assault. It doesn't surprise me to see it here."

"Why do. . ."

They heard footsteps pounding down the hallway outside. There was a shout at the door, "Away from the door!" Three seconds later the door splintered asunder and four masked soldiers burst into the room. Taylor instinctively stepped in front of Klein.

Two soldiers roughly grabbed Taylor, one man to an arm, and hustled him off. The other two painfully grabbed Donna and half carried her out the door into the dimly lit hall.

"Where are. . ." Taylor began to demand.

"Shut up!" a commando hissed in English.

Donna was surprised to find that when they hit the darkened stairwell, they went up, not down. Five frenzied flights later and Donna was on the roof, out of breath and blinking towards the ruddy western sunset.

The graveled roof of the hotel was packed with hang gliders, commandos, and a few Chinese officers. Donna saw Fu Zemin near the edge of the roof talking to a tall, well-muscled colonel. Donna heard another group of people pounding up the stairs. The soldiers pulled her forward and out of the way of the entrance to the stairwell. She saw Fu look in her direction and do a double take. He frowned and turned to Colonel Chu.

Donna looked over her shoulder just as Bob Lindley came into view, a commando on either arm. "What's going on here? I demand to speak to your commanding officer! This is an outrage!"

Before she could process this unexpected development she heard Fu Zemin and Colonel Chu walking towards her carrying on in Mandarin. ". . .I have no idea why the Americans are up here sir, I thought it was *your* idea," Chu said loudly enough that the small group of regular PLA officers heard it. Donna noticed Chu's right hand flash a signal behind Fu's back as the two walked in lockstep to where the three Americans stood with their six commando escorts.

A squad of commandos moved in amongst the knot of four officers.

Lindley raised his voice to Fu above the confusing din of

shouts and sputtering ultralight motors, "Mr. Fu, what is the meaning of this?"

Fu, a deeply troubled look on his face finally turned to Colonel Chu and said in Mandarin, "Yes, colonel, what is the meaning of this? You call me up to see you off on your raid. Only a few special staff officers even know about this mission, and the three Americans show up. . ." Fu turned to face the Americans, reaching with his right hand into his khaki jacket and stepping away from Chu. Fu took one fluid step away from Chu and turned toward the commando, gun in hand. "Now, what is going on Colonel *Chu*?" Fu spat the colonel's name out with contempt.

Chu stood his ground, "Comrade Fu, you have been under much stress recently. Please, I must be allowed to begin my mission. We are on a tight schedule."

Donna saw one of the officers tap a colleague on the shoulder and point in their direction. Chu took a gliding step forward, angling slightly towards Fu's gun hand.

Fu jumped back and screamed, "No! I know who you are now! I know why you looked so familiar. I won't let you kill me like your father killed my father! Get away from me! Guards! Guards!" Fu raised the gun, a black 9mm semi automatic. Chu lunged at the Party man, sidestepping the gun barrel and grabbing the older man's right arm and hand. The gun discharged, gouging out a dusty hole from the concrete housing of the stairwell just above Lindley's head. Chu spun into Fu, turning his back to Fu, then kicking his right foot out behind him and right into Fu's groin. Fu let loose a cry and crumpled as the pistol fired again, this time hitting the commando to Lindley's left in the forehead. The three Americans dove for cover while their commando guards scattered reflexively.

Donna had seen and heard enough to understand what was happening. She urgently yelled at Taylor, "The commando officer is mutinying. I think we may have a ticket out of here!"

Donna looked over to where the officers were standing just a moment before and saw the last one falling to the ground, grasping futilely at the strand of wire that was being tightened around his neck by a burly commando. She started to get up.

"You don't have a ticket anywhere!"

It was Lindley! Donna spun around.

Lindley was aiming an assault rifle past Donna at Colonel Chu.

"Lindley, you son of a bitch!" Taylor growled from a crouch then struck.

Lindley squeezed the trigger. The powerful weapon loosed a round that caught the general in the chest, knocking him back on his rear.

Chu hip shot Lindley three times in the chest. The weapon flew out of Lindley's arms as he staggered back, then fell forward, face down next to General Taylor.

Taylor struggled to one elbow and made a great effort to turn Lindley over. "Why?" he asked hoarsely, "Why the hell did you do it?"

Lindley stared up at the darkening pink clouds, "I. . . I thought they were unbeatable. That it would be better not to stop them. . . Destiny. . ." he coughed and lost consciousness.

"So did Benedict Arnold, ass hole." Taylor grimaced and sat up straight. Blood had soaked through his shirt down to his waist.

"Oh God, Tim!" Donna choked, kneeling at his side and helplessly trying to staunch the flow of blood.

Taylor didn't need to see Donna's horrified face to know he was badly wounded. "You gave me a chance to love again Donna," he coughed, a small dribble of blood ran down the side of his mouth.

Several ultralights whiz overhead. Colonel Chu barked orders and two commandos ran up, grabbed a still balled-up Fu, and dragged him to the nearest motorized hang glider. They began strapping him in to the back seat.

"Ms. Klein, Ms Klein!" Chu addressed Donna in Mandarin, "I believe you will want to fly with me." It wasn't a question.

Donna ignored the commando and stayed at Taylor's side.

Taylor looked up at the officer. He saw the look of urgent professionalism on the man's face. "Donna, you have to go. . . No time. Leave now!" He grabbed Donna's hand then let go, removing his Academy ring, then his wedding band. Both came easily off his blood-soaked fingers. "I want you to have these! Give the Academy ring to my son." He dropped the rings into Donna's fingers then shut her hand around them. "Keep the other ring. . ."

"Ms. Klein, we must go now!" Chu clamped his hand around Donna's wrist and wrenched her painfully away from Taylor's side.

"No!" She moaned, tears streaming from her face, "No! No! No!"

"Donna!" Taylor spat blood, "You have to go. I love you!"

Chu hustled Donna to his ultralight. She cried over her

shoulder, "I love you Tim!"

Taylor heard the stairwell begin reverberating with the sound of a hundred boots.

Donna looked back to General Taylor as Chu was strapping her into the ultralight. A commando was helping Taylor get to his feet when one of his colleagues rushed by and tossed two grenades down the stairwell. Two dull thuds echoed out but the sound of boots came on. Taylor yelled, "I'm not flight worthy. Tell your friend to have his men take me next to the door and leave me with a few grenades."

"I can't do. . ."

"Do it, Klein, that's an order!" Taylor coughed.

With fresh tears running down her face, Donna communicated the general's suggestion to Chu who instantly yelled orders to a squad of commandos. The men ran over to Taylor and set him up near the open door.

Donna forced herself to look away from Taylor. "Where are we going?" She asked the Chinese officer mechanically.

"The American ambassador's residence, of course. We are defecting."

"Defecting?"

"Look, no time to talk now!"

Donna didn't want to talk anyway.

One commando held each wing tip. Chu gunned the motor and the small craft leapt forward with surprising power. Only 30 feet before reaching the three-foot high wall at the edge of the building's roof, Chu pulled back on the stick and the collection of nylon, aluminum tubes, cable, and a large two-cycle motor scooter engine was airborne.

Donna looked back and saw General Taylor pulling the pin on a grenade and rolling down the stairwell. Her tears rolled straight back to her ears as the air rushed against her face.

Chu circled once around the hotel, picking up wingmen, organizing his formation. It was all precision and purpose.

Chu swooped down to about 100 feet off the ground and flew away from the sunset, towards the east and Taipei. He followed the darkened form of Tollway 1 below.

The road soon became almost impossible to see. Chu shifted to the softly glowing readout of a GPS receiver clamped to the metal frame in front of him. Chu pulled back on the stick and began climbing.

Donna's butt was beginning to grow numb from the hard metal

seat and its severe vibration from the motor mounted just to her back. She figured they must have been airborne at least an hour. She thought about Taylor the entire time, praying for him as she had never prayed for anyone or anything before.

Suddenly, Chu jinked the aircraft's wings back and forth, then climbed steeply. They circled tightly gaining altitude for at least three minutes. Then the engine died. Donna immediately panicked, "What's wrong?" she asked.

"I want to glide in. I assume your people are not expecting me?"

"Right."

"Then as we come in over the Ambassador's roof I want you to call out to the guards, 'Don't shoot! I'm an American!' Can you do that?"

"Yes." Donna suddenly wasn't so sure everything was as it seemed. "Why are you doing this? Why should I trust you?"

Chu began strapping on his night vision goggles. He remained silent, busy with his controls. Donna saw the big man's frame heave. He spoke just above the tugging wind, "I'm doing this for my nation. My father. My mother. Fu Zemin's father was a corrupt Party boss back in my home county. His father tried to squeeze every last drop of sweat and blood from my father, then he asked for more. My father confronted him one day. The authorities say my father was an assassin. I don't really care why he killed Fu Zemin's father, only that he did, and was in turn killed for his rebellion. My mother is now in jail. The Party says they may be lenient with her if I perform well in combat. They'll never let her go. She's a Christian, a true danger to them. She isn't afraid of the Party. Now I am no longer afraid as well. I finally realized that China could never be great with leaders such as these. I am only sorry that my father didn't live to hear me say that." Chu fell silent again.

Donna put her hand on Chu's shoulder.

"Look, we're 500 meters away and about 200 meters above the target. I'm going to line us up and bring us down. There may be antennas and wires on the roof, so hold on. When I say so, start yelling at the top of your lungs. If something were to happen to me, take the skyrocket out of my right cargo pouch and fire it, then ignite the flare that's in my left cargo pouch. Do you know how to use those?"

"No."

"Well, I guess I'll try to stay alive. My men need them to find us. I'd hate to have them drop in behind enemy lines right now, especially without a good explanation."

Donna chuckled, she was beginning to like this colonel.

"Now, start yelling!" Chu was madly sweeping his goggles back and forth, trying to make up for their lack of a wide-angle view. At the last instant he saw it, a large antenna probably supported by guy wires that extended right across their path.

Donna couldn't see a thing, "Don't shoot, don't shoot! This is Donna Klein! I'm an American. I'm an. . ."

The ultralight's left wing caught a guy wire, spinning the small craft violently around then flipping it upside down. Donna heard a snap and felt a wrenching pain in her shoulder. "Owwww! Help! Damn that hurts! Heeeeelp!"

Two seconds later Donna heard a gruff voice command, "Quiet! Shut-up!" She heard footsteps on the roof running towards her.

"Just hurry up Marine! I think my collarbone is broken! Get a medic up here quick!"

The Marine flashed a small red-lensed pen light in Donna's inverted face, "I recognize you, you were here a couple of days ago!"

"Right, now cut me out of here!"

"Who's your friend?"

"Colonel Chu, PLA commando. He's defecting."

"He's in bad shape."

"Look, he has flares in his pocket. We need to signal the rest of his men that we're all right and show them where to land."

The Marine cut Donna down with his K-bar. With only one arm working to break her fall she landed painfully on the roof.

"We can't do that. One guy I can handle. A flock of commandos at night at this place—you've got to be out of your mind, ma'am. Besides, we're expecting the extraction force to arrive any minute now."

"Extraction force?" Donna asked from behind a rush of pain as she stood up.

"Yes. Marines out of Okinawa. They'll be here in a few minutes to evacuate the Army troops."

"Day late and a dollar. . ." Donna was angry at an Administration that had obviously waited until the Chinese situation deteriorated to the point where they knew they could get away with snatching the potential hostages out from under China's nose.

Donna turned back towards the fabric-covered aircraft. She could barely see its form in the dark. Its ID strips glowed softly. She reached down to a softly groaning Chu and found the cool metal cylinder of the skyrocket in the pocket of one of his dangling legs. She remembered once from a movie how the devices worked. If this one worked the same way, she'd set it off. She tried to work the cap loose with her good hand, but couldn't.

The Marine called back to her, "Are you okay ma'am?"

"I think I need a stretcher."

Donna put the tube's cap between her knees and pulled hard. The cap came loose and clattered to the roof.

"Hey! What are you doing?" the Marine asked.

Donna found the cap and, cradling the tube between her knees, placed the cap on the other end of the tube. "Doing the right thing," she said as she firmly smacked the end cap and tube on her thigh. A blinding flash and loud pop announced the ascent of a green star cluster skyrocket. The rocket soared about 200 feet up then broke into five balls of green light. The roof of the ambassador's residence was momentarily illuminated by the flare. Donna could see a few other soldiers on the roof coming her way. She looked at Colonel Chu. He was stirring to life painfully.

The Marine ran at her and raised his rifle to butt stroke the insolent civilian when he heard the sound of far off helicopters.

Colonel Flint and newly promoted Lieutenant Colonel Ramirez were in the lead CH-53E Super Stallion only a mile off from the ambassador's residence when the pilot's voice came over the intercom, "I see a star cluster over the LZ. I don't remember a star cluster being part of our command and signal."

"It wasn't." Rez replied.

"What do you supposed is going on down there?" Flint asked.

"Well, I'd say someone's trying to signal someone else. Of course, there is a war going on down there. Maybe the flare was popped from somewhere nearby the target."

The copilot's voice came on the intercom, "I see a number of faint heat signatures above the target."

"Look's like we have company, Rez." Flint said.

Rez shook his head in admiration, "Hard to believe they'd use those things on a night like this."

The pilot, not privy to all the details of the previous 11 days' fighting said, "What? What? What things? What are you talking about?"

"Ultralights," Rez said.

"Come again?"

"Motorized hang gliders."

"Well, let's splash them!"

Flint broke in, "We don't have the time—they're a bitch to shoot down. I say we go in now and hope they're after some other target."

"And if they're not?" the pilot demanded.

"Then we'll hose them down," Flint said grimly.

Lieutenant Colonel Dan Alexander heard the commotion on the roof. He and his men were preparing for extraction out of Taipei. Everyone was in their place, had memorized their role, and knew exactly what order they would board what helicopter as they landed, one at a time, on the northern-most corner of the residence (away from the antenna).

Pistol in hand, Alexander ran up the stairwell leading to the roof of the large official manor. He burst out on the roof. A burning house up the hill behind the ambassador's residence lent a ruddy hue to the rooftop scene. Alexander saw the tangled wreckage of the ultralight and a Marine yelling at a woman in civilian clothes—*very strange, even for war.*

"Marine! You need some help?" Alexander called.

The young lance corporal replied, "Yes sir. This woman just crashed on the roof with a Chinese soldier. I think she's the CIA operative who was here a few days ago. She just popped a star cluster. We need to get her off the roof now!"

Walking up to the wreck, pistol still drawn, Alexander recognized Donna, "It's okay Marine. I know this woman. You're right, she's with the CIA."

"Colonel Alexander! I need your help," the CIA analyst looked as if she was ready to collapse.

"What can I do?"

"The officer in the plane is Colonel Chu. He's a PLA commando. He and his commando battalion are defecting. They have the chief Chinese political officer for the invasion with them. We have to get them safely down!"

"What do we have to do?"

"Colonel Chu has a flare in his cargo pocket. That flare was to be the signal for the commandos to land."

Colonel Chu groaned.

"I don't like it sir! It could be a trick!" the Marine protested, voice cracking.

"Can you trust this man?" Alexander asked.

"Colonel, I saw him kill someone who tried to stop us. I saw him order his chief political officer tied up and strapped to a hang glider. This is not a trick! This is the beginning of the end of the Chinese invasion force on Taiwan! You have to believe me!"

Alexander looked from Donna to the Marine, "Cover me while I retrieve the flare."

"Sir, you're not going to let them land are you?"

"Not on the roof anyway, there'd be too much traffic with the choppers due in in a couple of minutes." Alexander was already searching for the flare. He found it, ignited it, and tossed it off the roof and onto the street below. "I'm going to cut this man out of here and get him off the roof. I want you to take Ms. Klein here down below, ASAP!"

"Yes sir." The Marine, reluctant to leave his post, nevertheless moved swiftly to carry out the order.

"Tell my men to cover the street and watch for commandos landing in gliders. Tell them to shoot if the soldiers show hostile intent. Klein, make sure the Marine gets the story right with my men. If what you say is true we don't want to kill our guests, now do we? Also, tell Sergeant Heinzleman to call the inbound extraction force. I want you to tell them what you told me." Alexander returned to cutting Chu loose. The first helicopter's rotor wash was already tugging against Alexander's torn and dirty cammies.

"Sir! Someone just threw a flare off the roof of the roof!" Rez was bolt erect on his seat, looking out the left side of the helicopter. The door gunner held his machine gun at the ready next to Rez.

"I see inbounds. They're ultralights!" the copilot warned.

"How many?" Flint asked coolly.

"Five, ten. At least 20 that I can see."

Rez had heard and seen enough, "Sir, they're after the American Ambassador, or maybe the troops there. Remember how badly the Chinese wanted us to surrender? This is a snatch mission and we're rolling right into the middle of it!"

Flint responded immediately, "Put out a net call. Form an airborne fire line, one bird every 100 meters. Tell the door gunners to aim center mass at the pilots. Wing and engine shots won't do the trick. Then call the extractees and tell them they have company!"

Fu Zemin was beyond terror. He never knew how much he really hated heights. The sensation of flying in the little motorized glider as it tossed about in the air currents caused him to throw up so many times that he now had the dry heaves. His thoughts alternated between falling to his death and his probable future at the hands of the Taiwanese. He preferred the former: it was less painful and humiliating.

The commando-pilot of the little airplane suddenly nosed down. Fu's stomach stayed in the clouds for a brief moment, then struggled to catch up with Fu's writhing body. *So this was death's final act.* Fu shut his eyes and tried to think of his wife and only son.

The sound of machine gun fire rattled his eyes open. Fu wildly looked around. Flashes lit up the night sky to the left. A dragon's belly, glowing softly red, hung in the air beneath the biting sparks. Beautiful neon arcs extended in front of his eyes and flashed on by to the right. They came closer. *Crack-thud!* The pilot jerked sharply, then slumped over to the right. Fu's universe began to spin madly around. Fu squeezed his eyes shut again. The picture of his wife and son in his mind's eye was pushed aside by the angry red dragon. Fu briefly heard the sound of screeching metal before he lost consciousness.

"Cease fire, cease fire, ceasefire!" Colonel Flint had just received word of the defecting commandos from a female civilian attached to the embassy staff. He shook his head—*why can war never be clean and simple?* "How much loiter time do we have?"

"30 minutes," the copilot responded.

"I'm going down there. Tell the other birds to head north out over the ocean until I give them the all clear to come in. If you don't hear from me, scrub the mission."

Rez rolled his eyes—*Here we go again.*

The medic immobilized Donna's arm and administered a local painkiller. She could think clearly now, but the sound of grinding glass in her collarbone was disconcerting. Alexander was talking to one of his NCOs near the stairwell when an imposing presence of a Marine stomped by the NCO and planted his feet firmly in the middle of the dimly-lit hallway.

"Where's the commanding officer?" Flint said loudly.

Alexander straightened and barked, "Here sir! I'm Lieutenant Colonel Alexander, Task Force Grizzly!"

"I'm Colonel Flint. Damn glad to meet you!" Flint shook the hand of the citizen-warrior he heard so much about, "I have 25 minutes to pull you out of here or we have to try again some other night. Tell me what's going on outside."

"We have about 80 PLA commandos on the ground. My men are covering them. Some are hurt pretty badly. A few didn't make it. None of them drew weapons on us. Sir, I don't think we should pull out."

"Why?"

"Well, there aren't very many ROCs in this sector. They're all at the front. There aren't enough Marines on the staff here to guard them all either. I don't see how we can pull out of here right now. Besides, if these troops are defecting, doesn't that lessen the danger to us here?"

Lieutenant Colonel Ramirez walked up behind Flint, "He's half-right sir. Conventionally, the PLA is less dangerous. From a nuclear standpoint, though, I think they're more desperate than ever."

Flint thought about this for a moment and said, "If that's the case, they could just as easily nuke Okinawa as Taipei. Colonel Alexander, meet Colonel Ramirez—he's a hothead like you."

"Coming from a Marine, I'll take that as a compliment, sir."

*   *   *

Near Taiwan's CKS International Airport, General Deng considered suicide. He was faced with dwindling supplies and rapidly eroding morale. He had nowhere to retreat; no room for maneuver. The situation was hopeless. *No sense in prolonging the agony. Continued fighting would simply be a waste of brave men.*

Given what he represented and the suffering he had inflicted, Deng expected to be treated as a common criminal and killed. *Surrender to the Taiwanese would be almost impossible.* He looked at the pistol he had placed on the large desk in front of him.

His mind wandered through the events of the past two weeks. The images of his wounded soldiers stood out sharply from the chaos of war. Deng picked up his pistol—*suicide is for cowards, my men deserve better!* He holstered his pistol and walked quickly out of his office to the field hospital. He wanted to see the men who tried so hard to reunify their ancient nation; he needed their strength to bolster him for what he knew must be done.

Deng slowly walked through the brightly lit ward (an appropriated civilian hospital). Everywhere soldiers lay groaning, dying, or dead. The doctors ran out of pain deadening drugs yesterday. Deng comforted some, encouraging a soldier with a word or patting a young conscript on the foot as he made his rounds. He was about to exit the intensive care section when he saw two orderlies removing the body of a dead man. *It was one of the American negotiators!* In the bed next to where the dead man was lay a badly wounded man. He appeared unconscious, but was softly moaning. *One of the other Americans!*

Deng quickly called a doctor over. "Listen to me!" he lowered his voice, "If this man dies, we die with him. Understand?"

*   *   *

At midnight they heard it: a stillness blanketed the front. No explosions sounded, no pounding artillery, only barking dogs challenged the quiet air.

Colonel Flint and the Ambassador decided to send the wounded guardsmen back to Okinawa. Donna Klein joined them, her arm bound to her chest to immobilize her shoulder injury. Some of the wounded Chinese commandos were shipped out too.

Lieutenant Colonel Alexander remained with 25 of his men. A fresh contingent of 14 Marines from the rescue force stayed behind, bolstering morale significantly.

Alexander had collapsed on a couch in the ambassador's darkened living room when Flint and Ramirez came looking for him with their flashlights. "Alexander, wake-up!" Flint said, trying not to disturb the other resting soldiers.

Dan pried his eyes open, hoping that his nightmare was finally ending. "What?" Seeing the Marine officers he swung his feet around and sat erect on the couch, "Sir, what is it?"

Flint's smile was just visible in the dark, "The Chinese commander wants to surrender."

"That's great news sir! Thanks for telling me. Now maybe I

can get some sleep."

"I'm afraid not. He wants to surrender to us. He's afraid of reprisals. Besides, he claims to have a wounded high-ranking member of the American negotiating team with him. He says the man will die soon if we don't evacuate him. Two of my on-station Super Stallions have refueled and are coming in. They'll be here in less than ten minutes. I want you to join us in accepting the general's surrender—you earned the right as much as anyone around here."

Dan struggled to his feet. "Thanks sir! Let's go end this thing!"

*   *   *

Donna was walking off the effects of the ultralight crash, the helicopter ride and the restless night of sleep at Okinawa's main military hospital. Her shoulder ached dully through the painkillers. At first she wanted to find the USMC intelligence center and check in, but she soon felt a more pressing need to comfort the wounded. The dozen Chinese commandos were especially thankful to her for her language skills. As she visited with the men, her index finger caressed Taylor's two bloody rings on her left thumb. She thought about their brief time together—*if they stayed in D.C. would they have ever gotten together? If Tim lived, would they have ever stayed together on their return?*

A commotion at the end of the hall signaled an incoming batch of wounded. Concerned that the Chinese may have attacked the Ambassador's residence or decided to escalate the conflict some other way, she rushed to the end of the hall to get a better look.

She saw him there, strapped to a gurney and asking for a phone: Tim Taylor! Their eyes met. To the brief intensity of their first meeting six months ago was added a depth of understanding and tenderness.

Choking back a cry, Donna brushed past the orderlies and cupped her left hand on Tim's cheek. Tears streamed down her face. A few splashed on Taylor's shoulder.

Tim saw the rings on Donna's thumb. "I love you!"

Donna looked at Tim, holding his gaze deeply. Her brown eyes tried to see past their tense days together in Taiwan to gain insight into another part of his soul.

An orderly cleared his throat.

Taylor glanced briefly at the orderly, then refocused on Donna.

414

His crisp blue pilot's eyes suddenly seemed to relax. His lips turned upward, "I thought I'd be scared when I asked you this question, but I'm not; Donna Klein, will you marry me?"

Donna smiled back and carefully bent over Tim's face. Curly strands of red hair brushed against his forehead. She kissed him gently on the lips then pulled away just far enough to say, "Yes."

*　　*　　*

Beijing and every major coastal city from Shanghai to points south were gripped by massive demonstrations. The situation deteriorated faster than the Party could manage. With their ability to communicate degraded and the best PLA troops on Taiwan, the Party found itself unable to dampen the fires of revolt everywhere.

It seemed that every man, woman, and child had taken to the streets of Beijing in protest. Each had a grievance against the regime. There were parents still grieving over the loss of sons and daughters at Tiananmen. Others had suffered during the Cultural Revolution. Some were Christians. Still others were secret members of Falun Gong, seething under the continuing persecution of their sect. What united them was a common revulsion against the regime. They surrounded the leadership compound by the tens of thousands.

The Party leadership, fearing for their lives, made the decision to crush the demonstrators. They had just enough force to do so. The uprising took a week to quell and more than 125,000 people died. The Beijing revolt gave the provinces in the south the time they needed to organize and cast off the Communist Party machinery. More than 100,000 Party members were executed and twice that number were jailed pending trial.

*　　*　　*

The end came as it often did in China over the millennia, and as it last did at the end of the Manchu dynasty in 1911 when it was every Manchu general for himself—the regime simply collapsed upon itself in a chaotic, disorganized rebellion. Without armed force to maintain power, the Communist Party ceased to exist—often in a pool of blood.